NEW YORK REVIEW BOOKS
CLASSICS

THE NEW YORK STORIES
OF EDITH WHARTON

EDITH WHARTON (1862–1937) was born in New York City. Her father, George Jones, was a relative of the Joneses that fashionable people proverbially strive to keep up with; her mother, Lucretia Rhinelander, came from one of the city's oldest families. Raised in New York and in Europe, Edith Jones was twenty-three when she married Edward Robbins Wharton (known as Teddy). In 1902 they built themselves a forty-two-room house, The Mount, in Lenox, Massachusetts, but Teddy's mental instability and financial irregularities led to a divorce in 1913, after which Edith moved to France, where she lived for the rest of her life. During the First World War, Wharton threw herself into war relief, traveling to the front lines and founding a charity for refugees, in recognition of which she was made a Chevalier of the Legion of Honor in 1916. Wharton published her first book, a collection of poems, in her teens and in 1897 achieved popular success as co-author of *The Decoration of Houses*, a treatise on aesthetics and interior design. Her first volume of short stories, *The Greater Inclination*, came out in 1899. Among the most famous of her many novels are *The House of Mirth* (1905), *Ethan Frome* (1912), *The Custom of the Country* (1913), and *The Age of Innocence* (1920), for which she received the Pulitzer Prize in 1921, the first woman to do so.

ROXANA ROBINSON is the author of a biography of Georgia O'Keeffe and of six books of fiction, including the novel *Sweetwater* and the story collection *A Perfect Stranger*. She is a Guggenheim Fellow and lives in New York City.

THE NEW YORK STORIES
OF EDITH WHARTON

EDITH WHARTON

Selected and with an Introduction by

ROXANA ROBINSON

NEW YORK REVIEW BOOKS

New York

THIS IS A NEW YORK REVIEW BOOK
PUBLISHED BY THE NEW YORK REVIEW OF BOOKS
207 East 32nd Street, New York, NY 10016
www.nyrb.com

Library of Congress Cataloging-in-Publication Data

Wharton, Edith, 1862–1937.
  [Short stories. Selections]
  The New York stories of Edith Wharton / by Edith Wharton ; selected
and with an introduction by Roxana Robinson.
      p. cm. — (New York Review Books classics)
  ISBN-13: 978-1-59017-248-3 (alk. paper)
  ISBN-10: 1-59017-248-5 (alk. paper)
  1. New York (N.Y.)—Fiction. I. Robinson, Roxana. II. Title.
PS3545.H16A6 2007
813'.52—dc22

                                  2007019564

ISBN 978-1-59017-248-3
Available as an electronic book; ISBN 978-1-59017-436-4
Printed in the United States of America on acid-free paper.
10 9 8

CONTENTS

INTRODUCTION

THE WORLD into which Edith Wharton was born was a
dignified one, carefully structured, with a formal façade and an
elevated entrance. Based on a solid foundation of Puritan values,
it was framed by inherited wealth and insulated by the belief that
everything of worth was contained within. The unsettling winds
of ambition, need, and change rarely penetrated the thick walls
of tradition, pride, and entitlement. The interiors were polished,
gleaming, and perfectly composed. The windows were shrouded
with drapery, the floors were laid with a heavy carpet of decorum.
This was a place of silence, order, and restraint.

A writer's world both shelters and confines, and she must write
her way both into and out of it. She must form her own world,
but it will always be part of the one that formed her. It will always
be both beginning and end of her journey.

Edith Newbold Jones was born in 1862, in the family brownstone
on West 23rd Street. Her forebears were Dutch, English, and Hu-
guenot—a long line of successful merchants, bankers, and lawyers.
At the time of Edith's birth, her family had lived in New York for
nearly two hundred years.

The Joneses belonged to the small, privileged world of fashionable society. In these circles, family was more important than
wealth, and George Frederic Jones was well-off, but not rich. He
had an income from inherited real estate, and was mild, bookish,

and gentlemanly, an affectionate father and indulgent husband. His wife, Lucretia Stevens Rhinelander Jones, was not rich either, though she was from an old, grand family: she was one of the "poor Rhinelanders." Intellectually indolent, Lucretia was intensely absorbed by etiquette and appearances. As a mother she was cold and critical, as a wife she was possibly adulterous, and as a person she was mercilessly snobbish. From her father Edith learned a love of books and of France; from her mother she learned rigid self-discipline and sartorial perfectionism. From both parents she learned the rules of decorum.

Old New York was an insular, tribal society, with a rigid caste system and a strict code of behavior. In her memoir, *A Backward Glance*, published in 1933, Wharton wrote, "One was polite, considerate of others, careful of the accepted formula, because such were the principles of the well-bred . . . 'bad manners' were the worst offence." The code of manners governed all aspects of behavior, including trivial ones, such as the size of a calling card or the length of a widow's veil. At its core, however, was a stern Puritan ethos of moral rectitude, self-reliance, and stoic disregard of pain. Self-control was essential, and emotional display was utterly prohibited. To grow up in that society was to recognize the enormous social forces implicit in the command, delivered to a distraught person of any age, "*Don't make a scene.*"

Edith learned the rules of this formal, restrained world, but she felt the presence of another unacknowledged one that seethed around her like an invisible mist. This was the one of emotions and ideas. Wharton learned the power of this secret, forbidden realm and understood that the laws of decorum were set up to counteract it. The conflict between these worlds—the mannered, mandarin one, and the passionate, uncontrollable one—would provide the central dynamic of her work.

New York, however, was not Wharton's only point of reference: at an early age she had discovered Europe. The Civil War brought financial reverses to the Joneses, who rented out their American properties and moved to the Continent. There they lived cheaply for several years during Edith's childhood, returning because of her father's health when she was in her late teens. Edith developed an enduring affinity for European languages and culture. The great European capitals, with their wide boulevards, open plazas, and graceful architecture, offered captivating alternatives to New York's low, monotonous brown grid, just as European salons offered more lively and intellectual conversations than New York's bland dinner-party chatter. Europe became the vivid locus of Wharton's imagination, the place to which she was always longing to return.

Partly for financial reasons, Edith made her debut early, at the age of seventeen. She was neither rich nor beautiful, however, and she languished in the marriage market. Finally, at twenty-three, she married Edward Robbins Wharton. It was not a brilliant match: Teddy was twelve years her senior and of modest financial and intellectual means. A genial, aimless fellow, his chief interests were travel and sport, and at thirty-five he still lived with his mother. His father was in a mental institution, though doctors assured Lucretia that his condition was not hereditary. In 1885 Edith and Teddy were married.

At first the Whartons lived quietly in Newport and New York, traveling to Europe when they could afford it. When Edith came into an unexpected inheritance, their financial situation eased; later her royalties provided a substantial source of income. The couple built a grand house in Lenox, Massachusetts, and went more frequently to Europe.

Initially the marriage was affectionate, though probably companionate. Strains began to appear, however, due to intellectual disparity and Teddy's growing health problems, physical and mental. Edith's own health suffered as well, and in 1898 she spent several months in a rest cure. By 1902 Teddy was showing signs of his father's illness and, as his condition worsened, the marriage deteriorated. In 1907, Edith had a secret affair with an American journalist, Morton Fullerton. This was passionate, brief, and unhappy: Fullerton was a bisexual philanderer, cold, withholding, and duplicitous. Four years later, Teddy confessed to his own affair, as well as to the illicit appropriation of Edith's funds, over which he was trustee. Edith had spent twenty-eight years with an increasingly unstable husband, in an increasingly unhappy union. When Teddy humiliated her publicly and damaged her financially, she finally made the decision to end the marriage.

In 1913 Edith moved to France, where she sued for divorce. This choice was driven partly by discretion: unlike America, France did not require evidence of adultery to be made public in the courts. The move was part of a larger change, however: Wharton sold her house in Lenox and abandoned the world in which she had grown up. At the age of fifty-one she began a new life in a society that accepted her as the person she chose to be—an independent woman—instead of the person she was raised to be—a gentleman's wife. She spent the rest of her life in France, to which she became deeply devoted.

Wharton never gave up her American citizenship, however, and her deepest literary and emotional connections always remained to Old New York. Her first novel, a historical romance called *The Valley of Decision*, was set in Italy. When it was published in 1902, Henry James had famously advised her: "Use the American subject! Do New York! There it is round you." But New York was already Wharton's subject; she had been "doing" it in her stories for more than a decade, and would continue to throughout her career. New York was the center of her life, the place where she had struggled most ardently with conflicting claims of manners and passion, the place where her heart had beat most powerfully, where her soul had seemed most desperately constrained and her happiness most perilously at risk. New York received her most searching scrutiny, sternest criticism, and deepest understanding. It was her greatest subject.

The twenty stories collected here span the period of 1891 to 1934, nearly the entirety of Wharton's writing life, and represent more than two-thirds of her New York stories. Taken together—and more than any one of the novels—they reflect the evolution of her engagement with the city, and reveal the development of her imagination and her art. Her early stories show the awkwardness of apprenticeship, but from that apprenticeship come the magisterial reckonings of such late masterpieces as "After Holbein" and the peerless "Roman Fever." In the stories gathered here we find all of Wharton's great themes: stifled passion and the suffocating soul; the conflict between idealism and pragmatism; the charged erotic constellation of marriage, adultery, divorce, and betrayal.

The collection also reveals Wharton's swift growth as a writer. "Mrs. Manstey's View," of 1891, is the first story here as well as Wharton's first published one. In this lovely and beguiling work she lays claim to both her physical territory—the city of New York—and her metaphysical one—*les choses d'esprit*. Boldly, she chooses a protagonist and setting that are remote from her own experience.

Mrs. Manstey is poor, elderly, socially insignificant. She lives in a boardinghouse on "a street where the ash-barrels lingered late on the sidewalk." Her view is one of "broken barrels, the empty bottles and paths unswept." She is widowed and solitary, her neighbors are slatternly and philistine, and her environment grim. This New York seems soulless—but a secret landscape thrives within the slovenly urban one. Plants slip through the cracks in the pavement, invading the stone carapace, blooming and flourishing on their own. Untended and unauthorized, this natural world is powerful and alive.

"My powers of enjoyment have always been many-sided," Wharton wrote of herself, and Mrs. Manstey, too, finds pleasure in her world, despite her bleak surroundings:

> She had grown used to their disorder; the broken barrels, the empty bottles and paths unswept no longer annoyed her; hers was the happy faculty of dwelling on the pleasanter side of the prospect before her.

Nature performs its own triumphant annual pageant:

> ...did not a magnolia open its hard white flowers against the watery blue of April? And was there not...a fence foamed over every May by lilac waves of wistaria?

Mrs. Manstey's untended backyard view is filled with the glories of resurgent nature, and a church spire at sunset hints at that earthly paradise, Europe: Wharton declares that even a limited perspective can be sublime.

The story reveals Wharton's observant eye, her graceful style, and her sense of humor:

> "Of course I might move," said Mrs. Manstey aloud, and turning from the window she looked about her room. She might move, of course; so might she be flayed alive; but she was not likely to survive either operation.

Learning that her cherished view is threatened, Mrs. Manstey takes drastic measures. She can't win—a poor, elderly widow can't stop the juggernaut of commerce—but even in defeat Mrs. Manstey achieves a moral triumph, one that reflects the young Wharton's exuberant belief in the power of passion. The story is not only an impressive debut, it's a manifesto of Wharton's commitment to beauty and passion. Here she addresses the drama she'll continue to explore: the struggles of a woman's life. Wharton's women, whether born to privilege like herself or to poverty like Mrs. Manstey, will be threatened by the world. They may have scant power to combat the forces that threaten them, but they will be resourceful, determined, and high-spirited. They will astonish us.

"Never talk about money, and think about it as little as possible," was one of Lucretia Jones's imperious dictates. In that world it was the rule not to talk about money, but of course the Joneses thought about it like everyone else. Money was always an issue, and Wharton was always conscious of its power.

Neither her relatives nor her husband had jobs, but everyone had to have money. New York society demanded affluence; it disapproved, however, of striving. The bourgeois requirement for wealth, coupled with the Puritan demand for, in Wharton's words, "scrupulous probity, in business and private affairs," produced a complex and paradoxical dynamic. She explored this in a series of meditations on personal ethics—issues of morality and idealism, hypocrisy and nobility, greed and pragmatism.

Another early story, "A Cup of Cold Water," offers a startlingly realistic rendering of Wharton's own New York. She reveals its beautiful surfaces and grim undercurrents, its seductive appeal and ruthless mechanics.

Woburn is an impecunious young man in love with the rich Miss Talcott. Because they are both from good families they move in the same circles, but because Woburn is poor, Miss Talcott will never marry him. Wharton depicts the situation with fine irony.

> To the girls in Miss Talcott's set, the attentions of a clever man who had to work for his living had the zest of a forbidden pleasure; but to marry such a man would be as unpardonable as to have one's carriage seen at the door of a cheap dress-maker. Poverty might make a man fascinating; but a settled income was the best evidence of stability of character. If there were anything in heredity, how could a nice girl trust a man whose parents had been careless enough to leave him unprovided for?

Wealth has its own mesmerizing appeal, which Wharton both articulates and derides:

> Woburn was conscious that it was to the cheerful materialism of their parents that the girls he admired owed that fine distinction of outline in which their skillfully-rippled hair

and skillfully-hung draperies cooperated with the slimness and erectness that came of participating in the most expensive sports, eating the most expensive food and breathing the most expensive air.

Courting Miss Talbot has been expensive, and Woburn has borrowed heavily from his firm, drifting unintentionally into embezzlement. Facing ruin, he plans to flee to Canada. On his last night, before boarding the ship, he goes to a ball. There he stands apart like a revenant, observing the glittering scene:

> Was it possible that these were his friends? These mincing women, all paint and dye and whalebone, these apathetic men who looked as much alike as the figures that children cut out of a folded sheet of paper? Was it to live among such puppets that he had sold his soul? . . .
>
> It was a domino-party at which the guests were forbidden to unmask, though they all saw through each other's disguises.

Woburn, like many of Wharton's characters, is trapped within a moral cat's cradle: he yearns for acceptance by a society he does not respect. His ambivalence is that of Wharton, who remained a member of what she called "the young married set," even as she wrote about its flaws.

"Was not all morality based on a convention? What was the stanchest code of ethics but a trunk with a series of false bottoms? . . . There was no getting beyond the relative." Woburn scorns the hypocrisy of this world, and in trying to rise within it he has only lowered himself. He has now sunk below the level of those he scorns, and has abdicated his moral position. Still he cannot undertake the last act of cowardice and board the ship.

"Again there rose before him the repulsive vision of the dark cabin, with creaking noises overhead, and the cold wash of water against the pier." The darkness, the solitude, the cold all suggest that this is the voyage to hell. Woburn resists it, descending, as the night wears on, into increasing penury and a state of heightened awareness. He goes to a cheap hotel and takes a room for the remainder of the night. He follows the room clerk upstairs.

> At each landing Woburn glanced down the long passageway lit by a lowered gas-jet, with a double line of boots before the doors, waiting, like yesterday's deeds, to carry their owners so many miles farther on the morrow's destined road. On the third landing the man paused, and after examining the number on the key, turned to the left, and slouching past three or four doors, finally unlocked one and preceded Woburn into a room lit only by the upward gleam of the electric globes in the street below.
>
> The man felt in his pockets; then he turned to Woburn. "Got a match?" he asked.

Wharton's prose is strong and vivid. The contrast could not be more telling between this desolate, unlit bedroom and the ballroom earlier, with its graceful, beautiful girls, where "white skirts wavered across the floor like thistle-down on summer air; men rose from their seats and fresh couples filled the shining *parquet*." Woburn, in his dismal solitude, gazes out the window, "his elbows on the table ... till at length the contemplation of the abandoned sidewalks, above which the electric globes kept ... vigil, became intolerable to him, and he drew down the window-shade, and lit the gas-fixture beside the dressing-table."

Woburn has entered a new world, one without beauty or luxury. He had inhabited the old world under false pretenses: this, now, is his place, a kind of purgatory. By the end of the narrative Woburn has redeemed himself (through a somewhat unlikely act), but he must still suffer the consequences of his actions. A stern morality reigns here, as it does over much of Wharton's work.

———

In "A Journey," written around 1898, Wharton is in full command of her powers. The story is a masterpiece, powerful, concise, and startlingly modern. Morality plays no part in this hallucinatory narrative in which she weaves together the disturbing themes of isolation, incarceration, abandonment, and death.

The story opens abruptly at a high level of tension. It is set on a train, and takes place in the course of twenty-four unrelenting hours:

> As she lay in her berth, staring at the shadows overhead, the rush of the wheels was in her brain, driving her deeper and deeper into circles of wakeful lucidity. The sleeping-car had sunk into its night-silence. Through the wet window-pane she watched the sudden lights, the long stretches of hurrying blackness. Now and then she turned her head and looked through the opening in the hangings at her husband's curtains across the aisle . . .

At once we feel the desperation of a woman violated in her most intimate recesses—those of her mind. Wharton sets the scene with precision: here are darkness and distance, speed and dread. The anonymity of the wife makes her both remote and frighteningly familiar; the silence and concealment of the husband are ominous.

The husband, who had been sent west for his health, is now returning home. The wife understands that this means he will not recover, but for the moment he is merely ill, and they are on their way to the refuge of New York. It is the last lap of the terrible journey of her marriage: she has watched her husband's gradual metamorphosis from cheerful partner to deadly, inimical burden.

> She still loved him, of course; but he was gradually, undefinably ceasing to be himself. The man she had married had been strong, active, gently masterful . . . but now it was she who was the protector, he who must be shielded from importunities . . .

Sometimes he frightened her: his sunken expressionless face seemed that of a stranger...his thin-lipped smile a mere muscular contraction. Her hand avoided his damp soft skin...It frightened her to feel that this was the man she loved...

Part of the story's emotional power derives from the dreadful apparition of the failed marriage. There is an "imperceptible estrangement...Doubtless the fault was hers," the wife thinks bravely. This is the most fearsome aspect of her life, the fact that her marriage has so horribly changed, and that her husband has become a ghastly parody of his healthy self. The nameless woman is confined within his life, her own health and vitality suborned to the rigid demands of his illness.

When Wharton wrote this story, her own husband, Teddy, was sinking into chronic illness, becoming just such a monster of neediness and frailty. The horror of such a ghastly partnership and the fear of being buried alive within the role of caregiver echo throughout the narrative.

The wife's sense of loneliness and suffocation are powerfully conveyed by the hurrying rhythm of the wheels carrying her endlessly and forever into her suffocating life, by the claustrophobic confinement of the compartments, and by the odious other passengers—"the freckled child [who] hung about him like a fly," and the wheedling Christian Scientist who wants to convert her.

Wharton tightens the narrative hold as the wife discovers that her husband has died. She knows that the law requires the expulsion of a dead body from a train, and fears that she will be put out beside the tracks with the corpse. She now becomes a more passionate and terrified dissembler. Earlier she had pretended only that her husband was healthy and her marriage happy; now the stakes have been raised. Abandonment and banishment are risks, and the horror at her husband's death is enlarged by her fear of her own fate. The reader is drawn further and further into her consciousness, as into an unwanted dream.

One of the richest and most fertile themes in Wharton's work was that of the complicated connection between love and pain. Her own romantic history was not happy: her first engagement was broken off, not by her; a second romantic relationship, disappointingly, failed to produce an offer; her marriage was neither passionate nor fulfilling, and ended in misery; her brief erotic engagement with Morton Fullerton was wounding. These experiences are reflected in her fiction: rarely are her central male characters both sympathetic and effective. Those who are sympathetic are often passive or uncommitted; those who are powerful are often evasive and opaque, solipsistic or brutal. The presence of a subtle emotional sadism runs like a dark undercurrent through Wharton's fiction. This is very evident in the unsavory dynamics of her novel *The Reef*, of 1912. She acknowledged privately that the book related to Fullerton, but the same troubling theme is strikingly present in her story "The Dilettante," written in 1903, long before her affair.

Perhaps her most shocking story, it is a subtle disquisition on cruelty. Thursdale, an idle and worldly bachelor, maintains an *amitie amoureuse* with Mrs. Vervain, an elegant divorcée. Cold, cynical, and controlling, Thursdale considers their relationship and the "emotional training" he has given Mrs. Vervain.

> [I]n seeking to avoid the pitfalls of sentiment he had developed a science of evasion in which the woman of the moment became a mere implement of the game. He owed a great deal of delicate enjoyment to the cultivation of this art . . .
>
> He had taught a good many women not to betray their feelings, but he had never before had such fine material to work with. She had been surprisingly crude when he first knew her; capable of making the most awkward inferences . . . of recklessly undressing her emotions; but she had

acquired, under the discipline of his reticences and evasions, a skill almost equal to his own, and perhaps more remarkable in that it involved keeping time with any tune he played and reading at sight some uncommonly difficult passages.

As the narrative unfolds we learn of his decision to marry—though not, of course, the well-schooled Mrs. Vervain. Thursdale has found a fresh, untainted young woman. With sublime effrontery he asks Mrs. Vervain to lie about their relationship in order to support his marriage suit, and persuade his young fiancée of his worth.

In the character of Thursdale, who is subtle, ingenious, and pitiless, Wharton offers a remarkable glimpse into the mechanics of sadism. He takes a connoisseur's pleasure in causing pain, testing and savoring the limits of his partner's awful obedience, binding her with an excruciating knot of loyalty, dignity, and self-sacrifice. The lethal potency of the story arises partly from Mrs. Vervain's intelligence and vitality: she seems to have deliberately chosen this ghastly thralldom, this humiliating emotional martyrdom. In return for it she receives only a cruel intimacy. Love is what she wants, but it is not offered her, and she is too well-trained to make a scene.

The intolerable emotional bondage is chillingly portrayed. Mrs. Vervain's courage and integrity are revealed, ironically, through the nobility of her subservience. Placing loyalty above pride, she transcends the baseness of her tormentor's demands through the dignity of her response.

Divorce was the reason for Mrs. Vervain's vulnerability: it was a kind of social expunction. In Wharton's world, a lady's name was supposed to appear in the newspapers only three times: at birth, at marriage, and at death. Divorce, with its public disclosure of private betrayal, was scandalous by nature and a serious matter to "people who dreaded scandal more than disease," as Wharton wrote in *The Age of Innocence.* Divorce was a central and crucial subject in her work, and she explored its consequences throughout her writing life, with increasing intensity as her own marriage began to founder.

In "The Other Two," a small jewel published in 1904, Wharton considers a society in which divorce becomes common and accepted. The semi-comic narrative concerns the third husband of an oft-divorced woman. The husband's determination to ignore his wife's past is eroded by a cascade of small incidents, and he finds himself unwillingly immersed in her past lives. He begins, to his dismay, to perceive her in new and unsettling ways. The story is an exquisite meditation on possession, deception, and authenticity, as well as on marriage and divorce.

In Wharton's fiction divorce represents disgrace and failure: it is a great rending of the social fabric. The woman who has left her husband—as Wharton did—is often subject to shame, censure, and exile. In one of her great stories, "Autres Temps...," written in 1911, while her own marriage was in its final throes, Wharton delineates the subtle tortures of the social outcast's life. The title, part of the French phrase *autres temps, autres moeurs* (other times, other customs), refers to a worldly, tolerant attitude which accepts the inevitability of social change. The phrase is a verbal shrug of the shoulders, and the title is one of Wharton's sublime touches of irony.

Mrs. Lidcote is a New York matron who, years earlier, left her husband for another man, only to be deserted in her turn. Disgraced and alone, she fled New York. Since then she has lived a shadowy, humble existence in Florence, away from both the censorious glare of society and the comforting web of community.

> When she was alone, it was always the past that occupied her. She couldn't get away from it, and she didn't any longer care to...she had made her terms with it, had learned to accept the fact that it would always be there...

It was a great concrete fact in her path that she had to walk around every time she moved in any direction.

She is condemned to exile.

When Leila, her married daughter in New York, announces her own divorce and remarriage, Mrs. Lidcote boards a steamship for home, ready to offer comfort during Leila's ordeal. She dreads her arrival, expecting ostracism for them both, but on the ship she's told things have changed. It seems that divorce is no longer an ordeal, and Leila is not considered disreputable. Nor is Mrs. Lidcote anymore, according to her shy suitor, Franklin Ide. She has rejected Ide once, keeping herself free in case unhappily married Leila needs her. Ide modestly offers himself again, but Mrs. Lidcote thinks Leila still might need her. And she can't quite trust this new reading: Old New York is still the center of her world, regardless of eighteen years in Florence: "New York was the sphinx whose riddle she must read or perish."

Mrs. Lidcote arrives and moves from the uncertainty and displacement of the journey to the luxurious comfort of stability in her daughter's new country house. Her daughter, in sharp contrast to herself, has sacrificed nothing by her divorce. To the contrary, she is now cherished by her new husband, surrounded by devoted friends, and immensely rich. Shown to a luxurious room, Mrs. Lidcote meditates:

> [I]t was not the standard of affluence... that chiefly struck her... It was the look it shared with the rest of the house, and with the perspective of the gardens... of being part of an "establishment"—of something solid, avowed, founded on sacraments and precedents and principles. There was nothing about the place, or about Leila and Wilbour, that suggested either passion or peril: their relation seemed as comfortable as their furniture, and as respectable as their balance at the bank.

Mrs. Lidcote is assured that nowadays there are no rules, or at least that Old New York has loosened its petrified grasp of its denizens. She is welcome to return to the bright light of family and friends, to reenter the social world of interchange and affection. So she is told. But

> ...she continued to stand motionless in the middle of her soft spacious room. The fire...danced on the brightness of silver and mirrors...and the sofa toward which she had been urged...heaped up its cushions in inviting proximity to a table laden with new books...She could not recall having ever been more luxuriously housed, or having ever had so strange a sense of being out alone, under the night, in a wind-beaten plain.

This is one of the hallmarks of Wharton's fiction—the stunning juxtaposition of physical splendor and deep emotional need. Against a backdrop of luxury and ease Wharton presents a study of excruciating pain, as Mrs. Lidcote slowly learns her mistake. The world of Old New York has changed, but too late for her. The judgment on her is irreversible, her life has been sacrificed to the deadly demands of custom. Unwilling to inflict the basilisk glare of condemnation on her suitor, for the last time she rejects Ide, and returns forever to her solitary European exile.

In 1913, the year of her own divorce, Wharton published her novel *The Custom of the Country*. Written during the dissolution of her marriage, the book is filled with bitterness. Here Wharton explores the notion of divorce as a means of social advancement instead of as betrayal of a sacred trust. Here marriage is not gravely cherished but casually abandoned. This is a soulless world, driven by money. Though brilliantly conceived, the book lacks the depth and compassion of her great works. Filled with contempt for her shallow, venal, grasping characters, the novel resonates with Wharton's own deep-seated rage at herself. It is her own divorce, her own private failure, that drives her to heights of snobbish and judgmental disgust at Undine Spragg and her ilk—people who fail as human beings, who lack moral fiber, who utterly and callously fail their mates. Here Wharton sounds like her mother, Lucretia: snobbish, critical, and superficial. Lacking the deep resonance of tenderness, the book is like a great symphony played only on the brasses—cold, high, shrill.

Once installed in France, and a new world, Wharton became increasingly removed from her old one, which was rapidly changing. She would continue to write about America, taking on such subjects as the Jazz Age and the literary scene with characteristic energy but with varying success. Wharton's real engagement was with the New York of another time. The defining imaginative event of her later career was the realization, at the end of the First World War, that Old New York was entirely gone. With this reckoning came a change of heart, and she began to reconsider the mores she had once scorned. She wrote a friend, "I am steeping myself in the nineteenth century...such a blessed relief from the turmoil and mediocrity of today—like taking sanctuary in a mighty temple."

Reveries on her vanished world—emotions remembered in tranquillity—produced some of her greatest works, among them perhaps her finest novel, *The Age of Innocence*, and also the deeply moving story "After Holbein," written in 1928, just after the deaths of Teddy Wharton and of her closest friend, Walter Berry. The title of the story refers to a painting of a *danse macabre*, in which skeletons escort living figures toward the grave; here, the two protagonists totter toward death. It is an epitaph for a whole world, an elegant rendering of decline and fall, in which all the outward aspects of Wharton's society are flawlessly portrayed: the rites, the courtesy, the exquisite attention to form, the strict repression of inner life.

Anson Warley is a dapper old bachelor, polished, sleek, and debonair. He was once a man of parts, with intellectual aspirations, but slowly he has given way to the temptations of society. Now he is "a small poor creature, chattering with cold inside, in spite of his agreeable and even distinguished exterior." He has spent his life dining out, dressing perfectly for dinner.

On his last morning he has a small stroke, and his last day is spent in gathering confusion. That evening, unable to remember where he is to dine, he muses on his confusion:

> The doctors, poor fools, called it the stomach, or high blood-pressure; but it was only the dizzy plunge of the sands in the hour-glass, the everlasting plunge that emptied one of heart and bowels, like the drop of an elevator from the top floor of a sky-scraper.

On that ominous note, Warley sets out for the evening and dines, in befuddlement, at the house of Mrs. Jaspar, an ancient, rich, and famous hostess, now a senile octogenarian. The two attempt to perform the familiar ceremonies of the formal dinner: Warley admires the mineral water presented as wine, the bunched-up newspapers stuck like flowers into a porcelain bowl. He struggles for lucidity, but a mortal fog creeps into his brain. Wharton suggests that this ghastly parody echoes real long-ago dinners, when mindless responses and conventional murmurs were exchanged by people in full possession of their senses.

Like much of Wharton's work, the story is edged with satirical glitter, but to see this story as purely satirical—or Wharton as primarily a satirist—would be to miss its profound humanism. The great aim of Wharton's work, here and elsewhere, is not ridicule but compassion: her fiction is driven by tenderness. The emotional melody of this piece is carried by those who care for the ancient couple: their servants. Warley impatiently suffers the discreet solicitude of his valet; Mrs. Jaspar is tended by her elderly and arthritic maid, Lavinia. "Everything about [Lavinia] had dried, contracted, been volatized into nothingness, except her watchful gray eyes, in which intelligence and comprehension burned like two fixed stars." It is the servants to whom the fading life of the protagonists has been entrusted; their dedication and fidelity give the story its gravitas.

As was often the case, the story has parallels in Wharton's life: for years Teddy was cared for by his devoted valet, Alfred White, and Edith by a beloved maid/companion, Catherine Gross. At the time of the story, Gross had been with Wharton for more than forty years. Wharton was elderly, single, and wealthy, and in her private life she depended greatly on her maid for affection, companionship, and intimacy. Gross surely had some bearing on this depiction of an aged retainer, informed by such sympathy and love.

The story is poignant, not punishing; Wharton does not hold this society in contempt. She mocks its rituals but not their celebrants. The story records the end both of an era and of a particular kind of man—the social dandy. A measured and beautiful rendering of the final descent, it reminds us of our own connections to ceremony and society, our own vanities and shortcomings, our own inevitable plunge into darkness.

Wharton wrote brilliantly right up to the end of her life, and "Roman Fever," of 1934, just three years before her death, is one of her great stories. It is not a quiet rumination on mortality but the summoning up of rage, stifled passion, and sexuality: a remarkable work for a woman of seventy-two.

Though the story is set entirely on a rooftop terrace in contemporary Rome, Old New York is a looming presence and provides the background of "two American ladies of ripe but well-cared-for middle age." Friends since childhood, brownstone neighbors on East 73rd Street, now both widowed and the mothers of two marriageable daughters, the two sit decorously watching the sunset, "contemplating it in silence, with a sort of diffused serenity which might have been borrowed from the spring effulgence of the Roman skies." Mrs. Slade thinks slightingly that her friend's late husband "was—well, just the duplicate of his wife. Museum specimens of old New York. Good-looking, irreproachable, exemplary."

Slowly, through conversation and reminiscence, the two matrons recall their younger selves, inducting us into its secret sisterhood as they remember a common visit to Rome some twenty-five years earlier. If New York represents a moribund rigidity, Rome embodies a dark, charged vitality, worldly and unfathomable. The fever of the title refers to malaria, a fatal nineteenth-century disease and a real threat before the Roman marshes were drained. Fever was the ostensible reason for keeping young women inside during the evenings. The risk of illness was real, but so was the other, unspoken reason for sequestration—sexual adventure, with its terrifying consequences.

Seated overlooking a ravishing twilit view of Rome, with its "great accumulated wreckage of passion and splendor," the women are carried by the march of memory to the rising rhythm of animosity, through a landscape of jealousy and deception, illicit assignations, sexual thrall, and unwed pregnancy. It is a virtuoso's performance, and Wharton's greatest story of Old New York may be this one, set in Rome. Here she reverts to her most enduring theme, the power of passion—uncontrollable, inextinguishable, inexcusable. It is passion that has driven the lives of these two decorous matrons, and it is passion that reveals itself anew as they sit in the splendor of the Roman sunset.

Edith Wharton's lifetime spanned the Victorian era, the First World War, the Jazz Age, and the Depression. It was a period of enormous transitions, subject to the competing forces of conservatism and modernism. In her work, the great changes she witnessed are set against the abiding presence of Old New York, which was, for all its limitations, Wharton's touchstone, her social and moral measure, and the true north of her compass.

Her writing is hard to place, as her social and intellectual influences are so diverse. As a young woman, she schooled herself by reading nonfiction: history, philosophy, and scientific theory. This gave her a firm intellectual grounding and a rational, analytical approach to the world: she admired the novel of ideas, and the works of George Eliot and George Sand. One of her most powerful influences, however, was Nathaniel Hawthorne, whose dark Puritanism and punitive moral ethic was an important model for her. In his world, as in hers, passion is most often illicit, and renunciation and punishment are its consequences. Wharton's stern judgmental moralism is often blurred by her appreciation of and delight in the sensual world, but it is Hawthorne's bleak vision that offers the most direct antecedent to her own. Frequently, however, Wharton's work is linked with that of Henry James, her friend and mentor, because of the social circles about which they both write, as well as the elegance, intelligence, and nuanced quality of their styles. James is a very different sort of writer, however, and his vision is interior and more mysterious than hers. Wharton's work has more clarity and directness, more boldness and drama. It is also more modern. Wharton shares certain feminist concerns with her contemporary, Kate Chopin. Though no evidence shows that Wharton knew Chopin's work, the two authors explore many of the same themes, offering similarly disconcerting revelations about the inner lives of women.

Wharton wrote about the twentieth century, but her formal, ceremonial style and her belief in a moral order linked her inextricably to the nineteenth. The next generation—Hemingway, Faulkner, and Fitzgerald, among others—shared a sense of postwar disillusionment, and experimented with literary styles whose fractured rhythms echoed those of the twentieth century. Despite her decorous style, however, Wharton is anything but prim. Her work is informed by candor, clarity, and a deep understanding of the great subversive force of the emotions. Perhaps only one to whom the life of the emotions has been so explicitly forbidden can truly understand its potency.

Socially, Wharton was an Edwardian—worldly, informed,

confident. A member of a privileged and elitist society, she challenged its flaws and inequities, but also recognized its dignity and strengths. She was eloquent, proud, and perceptive, and as she witnessed the disruptions of modern life, she came to yearn for the order and ceremony she had once known. She was deeply committed to the concept of a moral order, though she recognized the complexities implied by its rule. She used the world into which she was born—the inner circles of Old New York—to create her own unique and individual landscape, as all great writers do. Wharton's characters are flawed and struggling, weak and noble, loving and heartless. Her New York is diverse, precise, and entirely her own. It is a place of beauty, complication, and authenticity.

Wharton's work was overlooked for many years because of its awkward placement, stranded between the nineteenth and twentieth centuries. Returned now to its rightful prominence in the history of American letters, it offers a profound and moving reflection on desire and its consequences, on freedom and its limits in American life.

The twenty stories collected here show Edith Wharton's world as she knew it. They show the crystalline brilliance of her literary style; they show the intellectual reach and complexity of her mind. They show the courage, depth, and compassion of her heart. They show her to be one of our greatest short-story writers.

—ROXANA ROBINSON

THE NEW YORK STORIES
OF EDITH WHARTON

MRS. MANSTEY'S VIEW

THE VIEW from Mrs. Manstey's window was not a striking one, but to her at least it was full of interest and beauty. Mrs. Manstey occupied the back room on the third floor of a New York boarding-house, in a street where the ash-barrels lingered late on the sidewalk and the gaps in the pavement would have staggered a Quintus Curtius. She was the widow of a clerk in a large wholesale house, and his death had left her alone, for her only daughter had married in California, and could not afford the long journey to New York to see her mother. Mrs. Manstey, perhaps, might have joined her daughter in the West, but they had now been so many years apart that they had ceased to feel any need of each other's society, and their intercourse had long been limited to the exchange of a few perfunctory letters, written with indifference by the daughter, and with difficulty by Mrs. Manstey, whose right hand was growing stiff with gout. Even had she felt a stronger desire for her daughter's companionship, Mrs. Manstey's increasing infirmity, which caused her to dread the three flights of stairs between her room and the street, would have given her pause on the eve of undertaking so long a journey; and without perhaps formulating these reasons she had long since accepted as a matter of course her solitary life in New York.

She was, indeed, not quite lonely, for a few friends still toiled up now and then to her room; but their visits grew rare as the years went by. Mrs. Manstey had never been a sociable woman, and during her husband's lifetime his companionship had been all-sufficient to her. For many years she had cherished a desire to live in the country, to have a hen-house and a garden; but this long-ing had faded with age, leaving only in the breast of the uncom-municative old woman a vague tenderness for plants and animals. It was, perhaps, this tenderness which made her cling so fervently to her view from her window, a view in which the most optimistic eye would at first have failed to discover anything admirable.

Mrs. Manstey, from her coign of vantage (a slightly project-ing bow-window where she nursed an ivy and a succession of unwholesome-looking bulbs), looked out first upon the yard of her own dwelling, of which, however, she could get but a restricted glimpse. Still, her gaze took in the topmost boughs of the ailan-thus below her window, and she knew how early each year the clump of dicentra strung its bending stalk with hearts of pink.

But of greater interest were the yards beyond. Being for the most part attached to boarding-houses they were in a state of chronic untidiness and fluttering, on certain days of the week, with miscellaneous garments and frayed table-cloths. In spite of this Mrs. Manstey found much to admire in the long vista which she commanded. Some of the yards were, indeed, but stony wastes, with grass in the cracks of the pavement and no shade in spring save that afforded by the intermittent leafage of the clothes-lines. These yards Mrs. Manstey disapproved of, but the others, the green ones, she loved. She had grown used to their disorder; the broken barrels, the empty bottles and paths unswept no longer annoyed her; hers was the happy faculty of dwelling on the pleas-anter side of the prospect before her.

In the very next enclosure did not a magnolia open its hard white flowers against the watery blue of April? And was there not, a little way down the line, a fence foamed over every May by lilac waves of wistaria? Farther still, a horse-chestnut lifted its cande-labra of buff and pink blossoms above broad fans of foliage; while in the opposite yard June was sweet with the breath of a neglected syringa, which persisted in growing in spite of the countless obsta-cles opposed to its welfare.

But if nature occupied the front rank in Mrs. Manstey's view, there was much of a more personal character to interest her in the aspect of the houses and their inmates. She deeply disapproved of the mustard-colored curtains which had lately been hung in the doctor's window opposite; but she glowed with pleasure when the house farther down had its old bricks washed with a coat of paint. The occupants of the houses did not often show themselves at the back windows, but the servants were always in sight. Noisy slatterns, Mrs. Manstey pronounced the greater number; she knew their ways and hated them. But to the quiet cook in the newly painted house, whose mistress bullied her, and who secretly fed the stray cats at nightfall, Mrs. Manstey's warmest sympathies were given. On one occasion her feelings were racked by the neglect of a house-maid, who for two days forgot to feed the parrot committed to her care. On the third day, Mrs. Manstey, in spite of her gouty hand, had just penned a letter, beginning: "Madam, it is now three days since your parrot has been fed," when the forgetful maid appeared at the window with a cup of seed in her hand.

But in Mrs. Manstey's more meditative moods it was the narrowing perspective of far-off yards which pleased her best. She loved, at twilight, when the distant brown-stone spire seemed melting in the fluid yellow of the west, to lose herself in vague memories of a trip to Europe, made years ago, and now reduced in her mind's eye to a pale phantasmagoria of indistinct steeples and dreamy skies. Perhaps at heart Mrs. Manstey was an artist; at all events she was sensible of many changes of color unnoticed by the average eye, and dear to her as the green of early spring was the black lattice of branches against a cold sulphur sky at the close of a snowy day. She enjoyed, also, the sunny thaws of March, when patches of earth showed through the snow, like ink-spots spreading on a sheet of white blotting-paper; and, better still, the haze of boughs, leafless but swollen, which replaced the clear-cut tracery of winter. She even watched with a certain interest the trail of smoke from a far-off factory chimney, and missed a detail in the landscape when the factory was closed and the smoke disappeared.

Mrs. Manstey, in the long hours which she spent at her window, was not idle. She read a little, and knitted numberless stockings; but the view surrounded and shaped her life as the sea does a lonely island. When her rare callers came it was difficult for her to detach herself from the contemplation of the opposite window-washing, or the scrutiny of certain green points in a neighboring flower-bed which might, or might not, turn into hyacinths, while she feigned an interest in her visitor's anecdotes about some unknown grandchild. Mrs. Manstey's real friends were the denizens of the yards, the hyacinths, the magnolia, the green parrot, the maid who fed the cats, the doctor who studied late behind his mustard-colored curtains; and the confidant of her tenderer musings was the church-spire floating in the sunset.

One April day, as she sat in her usual place, with knitting cast aside and eyes fixed on the blue sky mottled with round clouds, a knock at the door announced the entrance of her landlady. Mrs. Manstey did not care for her landlady, but she submitted to her visits with ladylike resignation. To-day, however, it seemed harder than usual to turn from the blue sky and the blossoming magnolia to Mrs. Sampson's unsuggestive face, and Mrs. Manstey was conscious of a distinct effort as she did so.

"The magnolia is out earlier than usual this year, Mrs. Sampson," she remarked, yielding to a rare impulse, for she seldom alluded to the absorbing interest of her life. In the first place it was a topic not likely to appeal to her visitors and, besides, she lacked the power of expression and could not have given utterance to her feelings had she wished to.

"The what, Mrs. Manstey?" inquired the landlady, glancing about the room as if to find there the explanation of Mrs. Manstey's statement.

"The magnolia in the next yard—in Mrs. Black's yard," Mrs. Manstey repeated.

"Is it, indeed? I didn't know there was a magnolia there," said Mrs. Sampson, carelessly. Mrs. Manstey looked at her; she did not know that there was a magnolia in the next yard!

"By the way," Mrs. Sampson continued, "speaking of Mrs. Black reminds me that the work on the extension is to begin next week."

"The what?" it was Mrs. Manstey's turn to ask.

"The extension," said Mrs. Sampson, nodding her head in the direction of the ignored magnolia. "You knew, of course, that Mrs. Black was going to build an extension to her house? Yes, ma'am. I hear it is to run right back to the end of the yard. How she can afford to build an extension in these hard times I don't see; but she always was crazy about building. She used to keep a boarding-house in Seventeenth Street, and she nearly ruined herself then by sticking out bow-windows and what not; I should have thought that would have cured her of building, but I guess it's a disease, like drink. Anyhow, the work is to begin on Monday."

Mrs. Manstey had grown pale. She always spoke slowly, so the landlady did not heed the long pause which followed. At last Mrs. Manstey said: "Do you know how high the extension will be?"

"That's the most absurd part of it. The extension is to be built right up to the roof of the main building; now, did you ever?"

Mrs. Manstey paused again. "Won't it be a great annoyance to you, Mrs. Sampson?" she asked.

"I should say it would. But there's no help for it; if people have got a mind to build extensions there's no law to prevent 'em, that I'm aware of." Mrs. Manstey, knowing this, was silent. "There is no help for it," Mrs. Sampson repeated, "but if I *am* a church member, I wouldn't be so sorry if it ruined Eliza Black. Well, good-day, Mrs. Manstey; I'm glad to find you so comfortable."

So comfortable—so comfortable! Left to herself the old woman turned once more to the window. How lovely the view was that day! The blue sky with its round clouds shed a brightness over everything; the ailanthus had put on a tinge of yellow-green, the hyacinths were budding, the magnolia flowers looked more than ever like rosettes carved in alabaster. Soon the wistaria would bloom, then the horse-chestnut; but not for her. Between her eyes and them a barrier of brick and mortar would swiftly rise; presently even the spire would disappear, and all her radiant world be blotted out. Mrs. Manstey sent away untouched the dinner-tray brought to her that evening. She lingered in the window until the windy sunset died in bat-colored dusk; then, going to bed, she lay sleepless all night.

Early the next day she was up and at the window. It was raining, but even through the slanting gray gauze the scene had its charm—and then the rain was so good for the trees. She had noticed the day before that the ailanthus was growing dusty.

"Of course I might move," said Mrs. Manstey aloud, and turning from the window she looked about her room. She might move, of course; so might she be flayed alive; but she was not likely to survive either operation. The room, though far less important to her happiness than the view, was as much a part of her existence. She had lived in it seventeen years. She knew every stain on the wall-paper, every rent in the carpet; the light fell in a certain way on her engravings, her books had grown shabby on their shelves, her bulbs and ivy were used to their window and knew which way to lean to the sun. "We are all too old to move," she said.

That afternoon it cleared. Wet and radiant the blue reappeared through torn rags of cloud; the ailanthus sparkled; the earth in the flower-borders looked rich and warm. It was Thursday, and on Monday the building of the extension was to begin.

On Sunday afternoon a card was brought to Mrs. Black, as she was engaged in gathering up the fragments of the boarders' dinner in the basement. The card, black-edged, bore Mrs. Manstey's name.

"One of Mrs. Sampson's boarders; wants to move, I suppose. Well, I can give her a room next year in the extension. Dinah," said Mrs. Black, "tell the lady I'll be upstairs in a minute."

Mrs. Black found Mrs. Manstey standing in the long parlor garnished with statuettes and antimacassars; in that house she could not sit down.

Stooping hurriedly to open the register, which let out a cloud of dust, Mrs. Black advanced to her visitor.

"I'm happy to meet you, Mrs. Manstey; take a seat, please," the landlady remarked in her prosperous voice, the voice of a woman who can afford to build extensions. There was no help for it; Mrs. Manstey sat down.

"Is there anything I can do for you, ma'am?" Mrs. Black continued. "My house is full at present, but I am going to build an extension, and—"

"It is about the extension that I wish to speak," said Mrs. Manstey, suddenly. "I am a poor woman, Mrs. Black, and I have never been a happy one. I shall have to talk about myself first to—to make you understand."

Mrs. Black, astonished but imperturbable, bowed at this parenthesis.

"I never had what I wanted," Mrs. Manstey continued. "It was always one disappointment after another. For years I wanted to live in the country. I dreamed and dreamed about it; but we never could manage it. There was no sunny window in our house, and so all my plants died. My daughter married years ago and went away—besides, she never cared for the same things. Then my husband died and I was left alone. That was seventeen years ago. I went to live at Mrs. Sampson's, and I have been there ever since. I have grown a little infirm, as you see, and I don't get out often; only on fine days, if I am feeling very well. So you can understand my sitting a great deal in my window—the back window on the third floor—"

"Well, Mrs. Manstey," said Mrs. Black, liberally, "I could give you a back room, I dare say; one of the new rooms in the ex—"

"But I don't want to move; I can't move," said Mrs. Manstey, almost with a scream. "And I came to tell you that if you build that extension I shall have no view from my window—no view! Do you understand?"

Mrs. Black thought herself face to face with a lunatic, and she had always heard that lunatics must be humored.

"Dear me, dear me," she remarked, pushing her chair back a little way, "that is too bad, isn't it? Why, I never thought of that.

To be sure, the extension *will* interfere with your view, Mrs. Manstey."

"You do understand?" Mrs. Manstey gasped.

"Of course I do. And I'm real sorry about it, too. But there, don't you worry, Mrs. Manstey. I guess we can fix that all right."

Mrs. Manstey rose from her seat, and Mrs. Black slipped toward the door.

"What do you mean by fixing it? Do you mean that I can induce you to change your mind about the extension? Oh, Mrs. Black, listen to me. I have two thousand dollars in the bank and I could manage, I know I could manage, to give you a thousand if—" Mrs. Manstey paused; the tears were rolling down her cheeks.

"There, there, Mrs. Manstey, don't you worry," repeated Mrs. Black, soothingly. "I am sure we can settle it. I am sorry that I can't stay and talk about it any longer, but this is such a busy time of day, with supper to get—"

Her hand was on the door-knob, but with sudden vigor Mrs. Manstey seized her wrist.

"You are not giving me a definite answer. Do you mean to say that you accept my proposition?"

"Why, I'll think it over, Mrs. Manstey, certainly I will. I wouldn't annoy you for the world—"

"But the work is to begin to-morrow, I am told," Mrs. Manstey persisted.

Mrs. Black hesitated. "It shan't begin, I promise you that; I'll send word to the builder this very night." Mrs. Manstey tightened her hold.

"You are not deceiving me, are you?" she said.

"No—no," stammered Mrs. Black. "How can you think such a thing of me, Mrs. Manstey?"

Slowly Mrs. Manstey's clutch relaxed, and she passed through the open door. "One thousand dollars," she repeated, pausing in the hall; then she let herself out of the house and hobbled down the steps, supporting herself on the cast-iron railing.

"My goodness," exclaimed Mrs. Black, shutting and bolting

the hall-door, "I never knew the old woman was crazy! And she looks so quiet and ladylike, too."

Mrs. Manstey slept well that night, but early the next morning she was awakened by a sound of hammering. She got to her window with what haste she might and, looking out, saw that Mrs. Black's yard was full of workmen. Some were carrying loads of brick from the kitchen to the yard, others beginning to demolish the old-fashioned wooden balcony which adorned each story of Mrs. Black's house. Mrs. Manstey saw that she had been deceived. At first she thought of confiding her trouble to Mrs. Sampson, but a settled discouragement soon took possession of her and she went back to bed, not caring to see what was going on.

Toward afternoon, however, feeling that she must know the worst, she rose and dressed herself. It was a laborious task, for her hands were stiffer than usual, and the hooks and buttons seemed to evade her.

When she seated herself in the window, she saw that the workmen had removed the upper part of the balcony, and that the bricks had multiplied since morning. One of the men, a coarse fellow with a bloated face, picked a magnolia blossom and, after smelling it, threw it to the ground; the next man, carrying a load of bricks, trod on the flower in passing.

"Look out, Jim," called one of the men to another who was smoking a pipe, "if you throw matches around near those barrels of paper you'll have the old tinder-box burning down before you know it." And Mrs. Manstey, leaning forward, perceived that there were several barrels of paper and rubbish under the wooden balcony.

At length the work ceased and twilight fell. The sunset was perfect and a roseate light, transfiguring the distant spire, lingered late in the west. When it grew dark Mrs. Manstey drew down the shades and proceeded, in her usual methodical manner, to light her lamp. She always filled and lit it with her own hands, keeping a kettle of kerosene on a zinc-covered shelf in a closet. As the lamp-light filled the room it assumed its usual peaceful aspect.

The books and pictures and plants seemed, like their mistress, to settle themselves down for another quiet evening, and Mrs. Manstey, as was her wont, drew up her armchair to the table and began to knit.

That night she could not sleep. The weather had changed and a wild wind was abroad, blotting the stars with close-driven clouds. Mrs. Manstey rose once or twice and looked out of the window; but of the view nothing was discernible save a tardy light or two in the opposite windows. These lights at last went out, and Mrs. Manstey, who had watched for their extinction, began to dress herself. She was in evident haste, for she merely flung a thin dressing-gown over her night-dress and wrapped her head in a scarf; then she opened her closet and cautiously took out the kettle of kerosene. Having slipped a bundle of wooden matches into her pocket she proceeded, with increasing precautions, to unlock her door, and a few moments later she was feeling her way down the dark staircase, led by a glimmer of gas from the lower hall. At length she reached the bottom of the stairs and began the more difficult descent into the utter darkness of the basement. Here, however, she could move more freely, as there was less danger of being overheard; and without much delay she contrived to unlock the iron door leading into the yard. A gust of cold wind smote her as she stepped out and groped shiveringly under the clothes-lines.

That morning at three o'clock an alarm of fire brought the engines to Mrs. Black's door, and also brought Mrs. Sampson's startled boarders to their windows. The wooden balcony at the back of Mrs. Black's house was ablaze, and among those who watched the progress of the flames was Mrs. Manstey, leaning in her thin dressing-gown from the open window.

The fire, however, was soon put out, and the frightened occupants of the house, who had fled in scant attire, reassembled at dawn to find that little mischief had been done beyond the cracking of window panes and smoking of ceilings. In fact, the chief sufferer by the fire was Mrs. Manstey, who was found in the morning gasping with pneumonia, a not unnatural result, as everyone remarked, of her having hung out of an open window at her age in a dressing-gown. It was easy to see that she was very ill, but no one had guessed how grave the doctor's verdict would be, and the faces gathered that evening about Mrs. Sampson's table were awe-struck and disturbed. Not that any of the boarders knew Mrs. Manstey well; she "kept to herself," as they said, and seemed to fancy herself too good for them; but then it is always disagreeable to have anyone dying in the house and, as one lady observed to another: "It might just as well have been you or me, my dear."

But it was only Mrs. Manstey; and she was dying, as she had lived, lonely if not alone. The doctor had sent a trained nurse, and Mrs. Sampson, with muffled step, came in from time to time; but both, to Mrs. Manstey, seemed remote and unsubstantial as the figures in a dream. All day she said nothing; but when she was asked for her daughter's address she shook her head. At times the nurse noticed that she seemed to be listening attentively for some sound which did not come; then again she dozed.

The next morning at daylight she was very low. The nurse called Mrs. Sampson and as the two bent over the old woman they saw her lips move.

"Lift me up—out of bed," she whispered.

They raised her in their arms, and with her stiff hand she pointed to the window.

"Oh, the window—she wants to sit in the window. She used to sit there all day," Mrs. Sampson explained. "It can do her no harm, I suppose?"

"Nothing matters now," said the nurse.

They carried Mrs. Manstey to the window and placed her in her chair. The dawn was abroad, a jubilant spring dawn; the spire had already caught a golden ray, though the magnolia and horse-chestnut still slumbered in shadow. In Mrs. Black's yard all was quiet. The charred timbers of the balcony lay where they had fallen. It was evident that since the fire the builders had not returned to their work. The magnolia had unfolded a few more sculptural flowers; the view was undisturbed.

It was hard for Mrs. Manstey to breathe; each moment it grew more difficult. She tried to make them open the window, but they would not understand. If she could have tasted the air, sweet with the penetrating ailanthus savor, it would have eased her; but the view at least was there—the spire was golden now, the heavens had warmed from pearl to blue, day was alight from east to west, even the magnolia had caught the sun.

Mrs. Manstey's head fell back and smiling she died.

That day the building of the extension was resumed.

THAT GOOD MAY COME

"OH, IT'S the same old story," said Birkton, impatiently. "They've all come home to roost, as usual."

He glanced at a heap of typewritten pages which lay on the shabby desk at his elbow; then, pushing back his chair, he began to stride up and down the length of the little bedroom in which he and Helfenridge sat.

"What magazines have you tried?"

"All the good ones—every one. Nobody wants poetry nowadays. One of the editors told me the other day that it 'was going out.'"

Helfenridge picked up the sheet which lay nearest him and began to read, half to himself, half aloud, with a warmth of undertoned emphasis which made the lines glow.

Neither of the men was far beyond twenty-five. Birkton, the younger of the two, had the musing, irresolute profile of the dreamer of dreams; while his friend, stouter, squarer, of more clayey make, was nevertheless too much like him to prove a useful counterpoise.

"I always liked 'The Old Odysseus,'" Helfenridge murmured. "There's something tremendously suggestive in that fancy of yours, that tradition has misrepresented the real feelings of all the great heroes and heroines; or rather, has only handed down to us the official statement of their sentiments, as an epitaph records the obligatory virtues which the defunct ought to have had, if he hadn't. That theory, now, that Odysseus never really forgot Circe; and that Esther was in love with Haman, and decoyed him to the banquet with Ahasuerus just for the sake of once having him near her and hearing him speak; and that Dante, perhaps, if he could have been brought to book, would have had to confess to caring a great deal more for the *pietosa donna* of the window than for the mummified memory of a long-dead Beatrice—well, you know, it tallies wonderfully with the inconsequences and surprises that one is always discovering under the superficial fitnesses of life."

"Ah," said Birkton, "I meant to get a cycle of poems out of that idea—but what's the use, when I can't even get the first one into print?"

"You've tried sending 'The Old Odysseus'?"

Birkton nodded.

"To *Scribner's* and *The Century*?"

"And all the rest."

"Queer!" protested Helfenridge. "If I were an editor—now this, for instance, is so fine:

"Circe, Circe, the sharp anguish of that last long speechless night
With the flame of tears unfallen scorches still mine aching sight;
Still I feel the thunderous blackness of the hot sky overhead,
While we two with close-locked fingers through thy pillared
    porches strayed,
And athwart the sullen darkness, from the shadow-muffled
    shore,
Heard aghast the savage summons of the sea's incoming roar,
Shouting like a voice from Ilium, wailing like a voice from
    home,
Shrieking through thy pillared porches, Up, Odysseus, wake
    and come!

"Devil take it, why isn't there an audience for that sort of thing? And this line too—

"Where Persephone remembers the Trinacrian buds and bees—

"what a light, allegretto movement it has, following on all that gloom and horror! Ah—and here's that delicious little nocturne from 'The New and the Old.'

> "*Before the yellow dawn is up,*
> *With pomp of shield and shaft,*
> *Drink we of night's fast ebbing cup*
> *One last delicious draught.*

> "*The shadowy wine of night is sweet,*
> *With subtle, slumberous fumes*
> *Pressed by the Hours' melodious feet*
> *From bloodless elder blooms.*

"There—isn't that just like a little bacchanalian scene on a Greek gem?"

"Oh, don't go on," said Birkton sharply, "I'm sick of them."

"Don't say that," Helfenridge rebuked him. "It's like disowning one's own children. But if they say that mythology and classicism and *plastik* are played out—if they want Manet in place of David, or Cazin instead of Claude—why don't they like 'Boulterby Ridge,' with its grim mystery intensified by a setting of such modern realism? What lines there are in that!

> "*It was dark on Boulterby Ridge, with an ultimate darkness*
>   *like death,*
> *And the weak wind flagged and gasped like a sick man strain-*
>   *ing for breath,*
> *And one star's ineffectual flicker shot pale through a gap in the*
>   *gloom,*
> *As faint as the taper that struggles with night in the sick man's*
>   *room.*

"There's something about that beginning that makes me feel quietly cold from head to foot. And how charming the description of the girl is:

"*She walked with a springing step, as if to some inner tune,*
And her cheeks had the lucent pink of maple wings in June.

"There's Millet and nature for you! And then when he meets her ghost on Boulterby Ridge—

"*White in the palpable black as a lily moored on a moat—*

"what a contrast, eh? And the deadly hopeless chill of the last line, too—

"*For the grave is deeper than grief, and longer than life is death.*

"By Jove, I don't see how that could be improved!"

"Neither do I," said Birkton, bitterly, "more's the pity."

"And what comes next? Ah, that strange sonnet on the Cinquecento. Did you ever carry out your scheme of writing a series of sonnets embodying all the great epochs of art?"

"No," said Birkton, indifferently.

"It seems a pity, after such a fine beginning. Now just listen to this—listen to it as if it had been written by somebody else:

"*Strange hour of art's august ascendency*
When Sin and Beauty, the old lovers, met
In a new paradise, still sword-beset
With monkish terrors, but wherein the tree
Of knowledge held its golden apples free
To lips unstayed by hell's familiar threat;
And men, grown mad upon the fruit they ate,
Dreamed a wild dream of lust and liberty;
Strange hour, when the dead gods arose in Rome
From altars where the mass was sacrificed,
When Phryne flaunted on the tiaraed tomb
Of him who dearly sold the grace unpriced.

And, twixt old shames and infamies to come,
Celline in his prison talked with Christ!

"There now, don't you call that a very happy definition of the most magical moment the world has ever known?"

"Don't," said Birkton, with an impatient gesture. "You're very good, old man, but don't go on."

Helfenridge, with a sigh, replaced the loose sheets on the desk.

"Well," he repeated, "I can't understand it. But the tide's got to turn, Maurice—it's got to. Don't forget that."

Birkton laughed drearily.

"Haven't you had a single opening—not one since I saw you?"

"Not one; at least nothing to speak of," said Birkton, reddening. "I've had one offer, but what do you suppose it was? Do you remember that idiotic squib that I wrote the other day about Mrs. Tolquitt's being seen alone with Dick Blason at Koster & Bial's? The thing I read that night in Bradley's rooms after supper?"

Helfenridge nodded.

"Well, I'm sorry I read it now. Somebody must have betrayed me (of course, though no names are mentioned, they all knew who was meant), for who should turn up yesterday but Baker Buley, the editor of the *Social Kite*, with an offer of a hundred and fifty dollars for my poem."

"You didn't, Maurice—?"

"Hang you, Helfenridge, what do you take me for? I told him to go to the devil."

There was a long pause, during which Helfenridge relit his pipe. Then he said, "But the book reviews in the *Symbolic* keep you going, don't they?"

"After a fashion," said Birkton, with a shrug. "Luckily my mother has had a tremendous lot of visiting lists to make up lately, and she has written the invitations for half the balls that have been given this winter, so that between us we manage to keep Annette and ourselves alive; but God knows what would happen if one of us fell ill."

"Something else will happen before that. You'll be offered a hundred and fifty dollars for one of *those*," said Helfenridge, pointing to the pile of verses.

"I wish you were an editor!" Birkton retorted.

Helfenridge rose, picking up his battered gray hat, and slipping his pipe into his pocket. "I'm not an editor and I'm no good at all," he said, mournfully.

"Don't say that, old man. It's been the saving of me to be believed in by somebody."

Their hands met closely, and with a quick nod and inarticulate grunt Helfenridge turned from the room.

Maurice, left alone, dropped the smile which he had assumed to speed his friend, and sank into the nearest chair. His eyes, the sensitive eyes of the seer whom Beauty has anointed with her mysterious unguent, traveled painfully about the little room. Not a detail of it but was stamped upon his mind with a morbid accuracy—the yellowish-brown paper which had peeled off here and there, revealing the discolored plaster beneath; the ink-stained desk at which all his poems had been written; the rickety washstand of ash, with a strip of marbled oilcloth nailed over it, and a cracked pitcher and basin; the gas stove in which a low flame glimmered, the blurred looking glass, and the bookcase which held his thirty or forty worn volumes; yet he never took note of his sordid surroundings without a fresh movement of disgust.

"And this is our best room," he muttered to himself.

His mother and sister slept in the next room, which opened on an air shaft in the center of the house, and beyond that was the kitchen, drawing its ventilation from the same shaft, and sending its smells with corresponding facility into the room occupied by the two women.

The apartment in which they lived, by courtesy called a flat, was in reality a thinly-disguised tenement in one of those ignoble quarters of New York where the shabby has lapsed into the degraded. They had moved there a year earlier, leaving reluctantly, under pressure of a diminished purse, the pleasant little flat uptown, with its three bedrooms and sunny parlor, which had been their former home. Maurice winced when he remembered that he had made the change imperative by resigning his clerkship in a wholesale warehouse in order to give more leisure to the writing of the literary criticisms with which he supplied the *Symbolic Weekly Review*. His mother had approved, had even urged, his course; but in the unsparing light of poverty it showed as less inevitable than he had imagined. And then, somehow, the great novel, which he had planned to write as soon as he should be released from his clerical task, was still in embryo. He had time and to spare, but his pen persisted in turning to sonnets, and only the opening chapters of the romance had been summarily blocked out. All this was not very satisfactory, and Maurice was glad to be called from the contemplation of facts so unamiable by the sound of his mother's voice in the adjoining room.

"Maurice, dear, has your friend gone?" Mrs. Birkton asked, advancing timidly across the threshold. She had the step and gesture of one who has spent her best energies in a vain endeavor to propitiate fate, and her small, pale face was like a palimpsest on which the record of suffering had been so deeply written that its orignal lines were concealed beyond recovery.

"If you are not writing, Maurice," she continued, "I might come and finish Mrs. Rushingham's list and save the gas for an hour longer. The light is so good at your window."

"Come," said Maurice, sweeping the poems into his desk and pushing a chair forward for his mother.

Mrs. Birkton, as she seated herself and opened her neat blankbook, glancing up almost furtively into her son's face.

"No news, dear?" she asked, in a low tone.

"None," said Maurice, briefly. "I tried the editor of the *Inter Oceanic* when I was out just now, and he likes 'The Old Odysseus' and 'Boulterby Ridge' very much, but they aren't exactly suited to his purpose. That's their formula, you know."

Mrs. Birkton dipped her fine steel pen into the inkstand, and began to write, in a delicate copperplate hand:

Mrs. Albert Lowbridge, 14 East Seventy-fifth Street.
Mrs. Charles M. McManus, 910 Fifth Avenue.
The Misses McManus, 910 Fifth Avenue.
Mr. & Mrs. Hugh Lovermore, 30 East Ninety-sixth Street.

She wrote on in silence, but Maurice, who had seated himself near her, saw a glimmer of tears on her thin lashes as her head moved mechanically to and fro with the motion of the pen.

"Well," he said, trying for a more cheerful note, "*your* literary productions are always in demand, at all events. Mrs. Stapleton's ball ought to bring you in a very tidy little sum. Someone told me the other day that she was going to send out two thousand invitations."

"Oh, Maurice—the Stapleton ball! Haven't you heard?"

"What about it?"

"Mr. Seymour Carbridge, Mrs. Stapleton's uncle, died yesterday, and the ball is given up."

Maurice rose from his seat with a movement of dismay.

"The stars in their courses fight against us!" he exclaimed. "I'm afraid this will make a great difference to you, won't it, mother?"

"It does make a difference," she assented, writing on uninterruptedly. "You see I was to have rewritten her whole visiting list, besides doing the invitations to the ball. And Lent comes so early this year."

Maurice was silent, and for some twenty minutes Mrs. Birkton's pen continued to move steadily forward over the ruled sheets of the visiting book. The short January afternoon was fast darkening into a snowy twilight, and Maurice presently stretched out his hand toward the matchbox which lay on the desk.

"Oh, Maurice, don't light the gas yet. I can see quite well, and you had better keep the stove going a little longer. It's so cold."

"Why not have both?"

"You extravagant boy! When it gets really dark I shall take my writing into the kitchen, but meanwhile it is so much pleasanter here; and I don't believe Annette has lit the kitchen stove yet. I haven't heard her come in."

"Where has she been this afternoon?"

"At her confirmation class. Father Thurifer holds a class every afternoon this week in the chantry. You know Annette is to be confirmed next Sunday."

"Is she? No—I had forgotten."

"But she must have come in by this time," Mrs. Birkton continued, with a glance at the darkening window. "Go and see, dear, will you?"

Maurice obediently stepped out into the narrow passageway which led from his bedroom to the kitchen. The kitchen door was shut, and as he opened it he came abruptly upon the figure of a young girl, seated in an attitude of tragic self-abandonment at the deal table in the middle of the room. She had evidently just come in, for her shabby hat and jacket and two or three devotional-looking little volumes lay on a chair at her side. Her arms were flung out across the table, with her face hidden between, so that the bluish glimmer of the gas jet overhead, vaguely outlining her figure, seemed to concentrate all its light upon the mass of her wheat-colored braids. At the sound of the opening door she sprang up suddenly, turning upon Maurice a small disordered face, with red lids and struggling mouth. She was evidently not more than fifteen years old and her undeveloped figure and little round face, in its setting of pale hair, presented that curious mixture of maturity and childishness often seen in girls of her age who have been carefully watched over at home, yet inevitably exposed to the grim diurnal spectacle of poverty and degradation.

"Annette!" Maurice said, catching the hand with which she tried to hide her face.

"Oh, Maurice, don't—don't please!" she entreated, "I wasn't crying—I wasn't! I was only a little tired; and it was so cold walking home from church."

"If you are cold, why haven't you lit the stove?" he asked, giving her time to regain her composure.

"I will—I was going to."

"Carry your things to your room, and I'll light it for you."

As he spoke his eye fell on the slim little volumes at her side, and he picked up one, which was emblazoned with a cross, surmounted by the title: *Passion Flowers.*

"And so you are going to be confirmed very soon, Annette?" he asked, his glance wandering over the wide-margined pages with their reiterated invocations in delicate italics:

> *O Jesu Christ! Eternal sweetness of them that love Thee,*
> *O Jesu, Paradise of delights and very glory of the Angels,*
> *O Jesu, mirror of everlasting love,*
> *O King most lovely, and Loving One most dear,*
> *impress I pray Thee, O Lord Jesus,*
> *all Thy wounds upon my heart!*

Annette's face was smoothed into instant serenity. "Next Sunday—just think, Maurice, only three days more to wait! It will be Sexagesima Sunday, you know."

"Will it? And are you glad to be confirmed?"

"Oh, Maurice! I have waited so long—some girls are confirmed at thirteen."

"Are they? And why did you have to wait?"

"Because Father Thurifer thought it best," she answered, humbly. "You see I am very young for my age, and very stupid in some ways. He was afraid that I might not understand all the holy mysteries."

"And do you now?"

"Oh, yes—as well as a girl can presume to. At least Father Thurifer says so."

"That is very nice," said Maurice. "Now run away and I'll light the fire. Mother will be coming soon to sit here."

He went back to his bedroom, where Mrs. Birkton's pen, in the thickening obscurity, still traveled unremittingly over the smooth pages.

"Mother, what's the matter with Annette? When I went into the kitchen I found her crying."

Mrs. Birkton pushed her work aside with a vexed exclamation.

"Poor child!" she said. "After all, Maurice, she is only a child; one can't be too hard on her."

"Hard on her? But why? What's the matter?"

"You see," continued Mrs. Birkton, who invariably put her apologies before her explanations, "she would never have allowed herself to think of it if we hadn't been so sure of the Stapleton ball."

"To think of what?"

"Her white dress, Maurice, her confirmation dress. At the Church of the Precious Blood all the girls are confirmed in white muslin dresses, with tulle veils and moire sashes. Father Thurifer makes a point of it."

"And you promised Annette such a dress?"

"I thought I might, dear, when Mrs. Stapleton decided to give her ball. You see there is a very large class of candidates for confirmation, and I knew it would be very trying for Annette to be the only one not dressed in white—and at such a solemn time, too. But now, of course, she will have to give it up."

"Yes," said Maurice, absently. He stood with his hands in his pockets, his unseeing eyes fixed upon the yellow gleam of the gas stove, which was now the only point of light in the room.

"And that is what Annette is crying about?" he asked at length.

"Poor child," murmured his mother, deprecatingly; "it is such a solemn moment, Maurice."

"Yes, yes—I know. That's just it. That's why I don't understand—Annette is a very religious girl, isn't she?"

"Father Thurifer tells me that he has never seen a more religious nature. He said that it was as natural to her to believe as to breathe. Isn't that a beautiful expression?"

"And yet—yet—at such a solemn moment, as you say, it is the color of her dress that is uppermost in her mind?"

"Oh, Maurice, don't you see that it is just because she has so much devotional feeling, poor child, that she suffers at the thought of not appearing worthily at such a time?"

"As if Mrs. Stapleton should ask me to lead the cotillion at her ball when my dress coat is in pawn?"

"Maurice!" said his mother.

"I beg your pardon, mother; I didn't mean that; forgive me. But it all seems so queer—I don't understand."

"I wish you went oftener to church, Maurice," said Mrs. Birkton, sadly.

"I wish I understood Annette better," he returned in a musing tone.

"Annette is a very good girl," said Mrs. Birkton, gathering up her pen and papers. "After the first shock is over she will bear her disappointment bravely; but don't tell her that I have spoken to you about it, for she would never forgive me."

"Poor little thing," Maurice sighed, as his mother groped her way to the door.

He sat still in the darkness after she had left, companioned by the dismal brood of his disappointments, until half an hour later Annette's knock told him that their slender supper was ready.

When he re-entered the kitchen his sister's face had grown as smooth and serene as that of some young seraph of Van Eyck's. She had tied a white apron over her dress and was busy carrying the hot toast and fried eggs from the stove to the table, which had meanwhile been covered with a white cloth and neatly set for the evening meal.

Maurice sat down between her and his mother, listening in silence to their talk, which fell like the trickle of a cool stream upon his aching nerves. They were speaking as usual of church matters, in which the daughter took an eager and precocious, the mother a somewhat ex-official interest; it seemed to Maurice as though Mrs. Birkton, who had resigned herself to getting on without so many things, had even surrendered her direct share in the scheme of redemption, or rather tacitly passed it on to her child. But what more especially struck him was the force of will displayed in Annette's demeanor. Her disappointment, which he felt to be very real, was impenetrably masked behind a mien of gay activity; and Maurice, knowing his own facile tendency to be swayed by the emotion of the moment, marveled at the child's self-control.

The next morning he went out earlier than usual. As he opened the hall door he turned back and called to his mother, who was washing the breakfast dishes in the kitchen:

"Mother, if Helfenridge comes you can say that you don't know when I shall be back. Say that I may not be in all day."

"Very well, dear," she replied, with some surprise; but her son's face forbade questioning, and she went on silently with her work.

Maurice, as it happened, returned in time for their one o'clock dinner. His mother thought that he looked pale and spiritless, and feared that he had endured another defeat at the hands of some unenlightened editor.

"Has Helfenridge been here?" he inquired.

"Yes," Mrs. Birkton answered. "He stopped on his way downtown just after you had gone out. He was very sorry not to find you, and said that he would come again tomorrow evening."

"Has Annette got back from school?" Maurice asked, irrelevantly.

"I think I hear her step now," Mrs. Birkton replied, and at the same moment the kitchen door opened, admitting the young girl, whose small face was touched with a frosty pink by the cold.

As she entered Maurice went up to her, extending something in his hand with an awkward gesture.

"Look here—will that buy you a white dress like the rest of the girls?" he said, abruptly.

Annette grew red and then pale; her lips parted, but she made no motion to take the roll of bills which he held out to her.

"Maurice!" his mother gasped. "Have they accepted something? What is it? What is it to appear in?"

Her small features, flattened into lifelong submission to failure, seemed almost convulsed by the unwonted expression of a less negative emotion.

Maurice made no answer; he was still looking at Annette.

"Why don't you take it, Annette?" he said, a tinge of impatience in his voice.

"Annette! Annette! why do you stand there? Can't you speak? Why don't you thank your brother?" Mrs. Birkton cried, in a storm of exultation.

Annette held out her hand, but as she took the bills her face again grew crimson.

"Maurice, how did you know about the dress? Mother, you promised not to tell him!" Then, glancing at the roll of money, "But what have you given me, Maurice? A hundred dollars—a hundred and fifty dollars? Mother, what does he mean?"

"Maurice!" Mrs. Birkton almost shrieked.

"Well," said Maurice with a laugh, "Isn't it enough to buy your dress?"

Annette stood, trembling, between sobs and laughter; but her mother's tears overflowed.

"Oh, my boy, my son, I'm so happy! I knew it would come. I knew it must—Mr. Helfenridge said so only this morning. But I didn't dream it would be so soon!" She lifted her poor, joy-distorted face to his averted kiss. "Oh, it's too beautiful, Maurice, it's too beautiful! But you haven't told us yet which poem it is."

Maurice turned sharply away, his hand on the door.

"Not yet—not now. I've forgotten something. I'm going out," he stammered.

"Why, Maurice! Without your dinner? You're not well, my son!"

"Nonsense, mother. I shall be back presently. Annette, keep some dinner for me."

"But, Maurice," the girl cried, springing forward, "you mustn't leave all this money with me."

"I've told you it's yours," he said, with a violence which made the women's startled eyes meet.

"Why, Maurice, you must be joking! A hundred and fifty dollars? I oughtn't to keep a penny of it, with all the things that you and mother need."

"Nonsense, keep it all. If it's too much for your dress, mother can take the rest for herself. I don't want it. But mind you spend it all on yourselves; don't use any of it for the household. And remember I won't touch a penny of it."

"But, Maurice," said Mrs. Birkton, "the dress won't cost twenty dollars."

"So much the worse," he retorted; and the door shut on him with a crash that was conclusive.

Helfenridge, whose work (he was a clerk in the same establishment which had been the scene of Maurice's brief commercial experience) often delayed him downtown long after his dinner hour, did not reach his friend's house until eight o'clock on the following evening. As he started on his long ascent of the steep tenement stairs someone ran against him on the first landing, and he drew back in surprise, recognizing Maurice in the flare of the gas jet against the whitewashed wall.

"Hullo, Maurice! Didn't Mrs. Birkton tell you that I was coming this evening?"

"I—yes—the fact is, I was just going out," Birkton said, confusedly.

Helfenridge glanced at him, marking his evasive eye.

"Oh, very well. If you're going out I'll try again."

"No—no. You'd better come up after all. I'd rather see you now. I've got something to say to you."

"Are you sure?" said Helfenridge. "I'd rather not be taken on sufferance."

"I want to see you," Birkton repeated, with sudden force; and the two men climbed the stairs together in silence.

"Come this way," said Maurice, leading Helfenridge into his bedroom.

He put a match to the gas burner, and another to the stove,

and pushed his only easy chair forward within the radius of the dry, yellow heat, while Helfenridge threw aside his hat and over-coat, which were fringed with frozen snow.

"You don't look well, Maurice," he said, taking the seat prof-fered by his friend.

"It's because I'm new at it, I suppose," the other returned, dryly.

"New at what? What do you mean?"

"Wait a minute," said Maurice; "I want to show you something first."

He opened the door as he spoke, and Helfenridge heard him walk along the narrow passageway to the kitchen; then came the opening of another door, which launched a confusion of soft, gay tones upon the intervening obscurity. "Oh, no, no," Helfenridge heard a young voice half laughingly protest; then an older tone in-terposed, gently urgent, mingled with an odd unfamiliar laugh from Maurice; lastly the door of the bedroom was suddenly thrown wide, and Maurice reappeared, pushing before him his sis-ter, clad from head to foot in white muslin, her flat, childish waist defined by a wide white sash, even her little feet shod in immacu-late ivory kid.

Above all this whiteness her flushed face emerged like a pink crocus from a snow drift; her lips were parted in tremulous, inar-ticulate apologies, but no explanatory word reached Helfenridge.

"Why, Miss Annette, how lovely!" he exclaimed at random, questioning Maurice with his eyes.

"There—doesn't she look nice?" the brother asked, retaining his grasp of her white shoulders. "That's her confirmation dress, if you please! She's going to be confirmed next Sunday at the Church of the Precious Blood, and you've got to be there to see it."

"Oh, Maurice," murmured Annette.

"Of course I shall be there," said Helfenridge, warmly. "But what a beautiful dress! Are all confirmation dresses as beautiful as that?"

"Oh, no, Mr. Helfenridge; but Maurice—"

"Father Thurifer likes all the girls in the class to be dressed like that," Maurice quickly interposed. "And now run off before your finery gets tumbled," he added, pushing her out of the room with a smile which softened the abruptness of the gesture.

He shut the door and the two men stood looking at each other.

"She's lovely," said Helfenridge, gently.

"Poor little girl," said Maurice. "Isn't it pretty fancy to dress them all in white?"

"Yes—I suppose it's a High Church idea?"

"I suppose so. I never knew anything about it until the other day—until two days ago, in fact. Then I found that Father Thurifer had requested all the girls who are to be confirmed to dress in white muslin; and we hadn't a penny between us to buy her a dress with."

"Yes?" said Helfenridge, tentatively.

"Annette's a very good little girl, you know—immensely religious. Father Thurifer says he never saw a more religious nature. And it nearly killed her not to have a white dress—not to appear worthy of the day. She regards it as the most solemn day of her life. Can you understand how she must have felt? I couldn't at first, but I think I do now. After all, she's only a child."

"I understand," said Helfenridge.

"Well, neither my mother nor I had a copper left. There was no way of getting the dress—and it seemed to me she had to have it."

"Yes?"

"I said the other day that I didn't know what would happen if one of us fell ill; but in a way it would have been simpler than this. Annette, now—if Annette had been ill we could have sent her to the hospital. My mother is too sensible to have any prejudice against hospitals. But this is different—there was no other way of getting the dress; and it had to be got somehow. I don't believe her wedding dress will seem half so important to her—there's so little perspective at fifteen."

"Well?" said Helfenridge after a pause.

"Well, so I—good God, Helfenridge, won't you understand?"

Both men were silent; Helfenridge sat with his hands clenched on the arms of his chair.

Suddenly he said, as if in a flash of remembrance: "You sent that thing to Baker Buley—the thing about Mrs. Tolquitt?"

"Yes," said Maurice.

A long pause followed, in which the thoughts of the two men cried aloud to each other.

At length Maurice exclaimed, "I wish you'd speak out—say what you think."

"I don't know," said Helfenridge, in a low tone.

"You don't know? You mean you don't know what to say?"

"What to think."

"What to think of a man who's sold his soul?"

"I'm not sure if you have. It seems to me that I'm not sure of anything," Helfenridge said.

"I am—I'm sure that Annette had to have her dress," said Maurice, with a defiant laugh.

"When does it come out?"

"It's out already—it came out this morning. It's all over town by this time."

"Do they know?" asked Helfenridge, suddenly.

"My mother and Annette? God forbid. Do you suppose they would have touched the money?"

"How did you account to them for having it?"

"I told them that was my secret—that they shouldn't know for the present. Of course the—the thing in the *Kite* is not signed; and later, if one of my poems ever finds its way into print, they'll think it's that—but they'll have to wait."

Helfenridge rose. "I must be going," he said.

"Why do you go? Because you're afraid to tell me what you think? You may say what you please—it can't make any difference. Annette had to have the dress. I've been trying to avoid you for two days because I was afraid to tell you, but now I'd rather talk about it —that is if you care to have anything more to do with me. Because, after all, I'm no better than a blackguard now, you know—there's no getting around that fact. You've a perfect right to cut me."

Helfenridge was mechanically pulling on his overcoat.

"At what time does the confirmation take place?" he asked. "Tell Miss Annette that I shall certainly be there."

On the ensuing Sunday morning, punctually at half-past ten o'clock, a closed carriage from the nearest livery stable drew up before the house occupied by the Birktons. It was snowing hard, and Annette's spotless draperies and flowing veil were concealed under an old cloak of her mother's as, sheltered by Maurice's umbrella, she stepped across the sidewalk, clasping her prayer book in one tremulous, white-gloved hand. Mrs. Birkton followed, her shabby bonnet refurbished with fresh velvet strings, and a glow of excitement on her small effaced features. She and her son placed themselves on the front seat, leaving Annette to expand her crisp robe over the width of the opposite cushions; and the carriage rolled off heavily through the deepening snow.

All three sat silent during their slow, noiseless drive. Maurice was looking out of the window, so that the women saw only his uncommunicative profile. Mrs. Birkton sat wiping away the tears from her flushed face. They were pleasant tears, and she let them roll gently down her cheeks before she dried them. As for Annette, her face was pale, with the candid pallor of an intense but scarce-comprehended emotion. She sat bolt upright, in a kind of Pre-Raphaelite rigidity which accorded with the primitive inexpressiveness of her rapt young features and the shadowless chalk-like mass of her dress and veil.

At length the carriage paused behind a train of others; and after some moments of delay, which seemed to lend a preparatory solemnity to their approach, Maurice, in the wake of his mother and sister, passed from the snowy crudeness of the outer world into the rich and complex atmosphere of the Church of the Precious Blood.

The raw, sunless daylight, mellowed by the jeweled opacity of stained-glass windows, fell with a caressing brilliance across the aisles, streaking the clustered shafts with heraldic emblazonments of gules and azure and leaving the intervening spaces swathed in a velvety dusk. On the altar, with its embroidered hanging, the candle flames hovered like yellow moths over the white lilies rigidly disposed in tall silver vases; while in their midst, relieved against the sculptured intricacies of the reredos of grayish stone, rose the outstretched arms of the great golden crucifix.

The church was already crowded; but a ribbon, latitudinally dividing the central aisle, indicated that the foremost rows of chairs (there were no pews in the Church of the Precious Blood) had been reserved for the candidates for confirmation and their relations. Thither Maurice followed his mother and Annette, passing through a dove-like subsidence of feathery white and a double row of innocent young faces to the seats assigned to them by the verger. Glancing about as he moved up the aisle he had caught a glimpse of Helfenridge seated far back, with his head against a pillar; and the sight lent him some momentary comfort.

Maurice cast down his eyes while Mrs. Birkton and Annette knelt to pray; and when he looked up the long white procession of choristers, preceded by the crucifer, was winding toward the chancel, while the first notes of the hymn

How bright these glorious spirits shine!
Whence all their white array?

leapt jubilantly out of the expectant hush.

Maurice, observing his sister, saw the gravity of her vague young profile intensified to awe as the procession swept past their seats, closed by the sumptuous grouping of the ample-sleeved bishop with his attendant clergy in their embroidered vestments, and seen through the mauve mist of drifting incense fumes. To him it was like fingering the leaves of a missal in some Umbrian sacristy, speculating idly, as he looked, upon the meaning of the delicate miniatures, wherein serene-visaged personages, saintly or seraphic, enacted their mysterious drama in a setting of fanciful white architecture or against a blue background tarred with gold.

But to Annette, he perceived, it was something real, as real as physical birth or death. Through the symbolic phantasmagoria, which she perhaps understood still less than he, ran a thread of actuality, linking her timid being to the occult significance of the whole splendid scene; and Maurice saw her tremble with the sense of that august alliance. Perhaps, after all, he reflected, it was the white dress which formed the actual point of contact. At least he was glad to think that it made her a part of the pageant, a conscious factor in the gorgeous sacrifice of praise and prayer.

As he mused thus his unquiet eyes again began to wander; and suddenly they fell upon a lady who sat near by with a little girl in white muslin at her side. The lady's face was very familiar to him, though he had never before seen it composed into its present expression of devotional repose. It was a pretty face, crowned by abrupt waves of reddish hair just dashed here and there with a streak of gray, and lit by an insinuating, agate-colored glance; but the sight of it burned Maurice's eyeballs like vitriol, for it was the face of Mrs. Tolquitt.

He had never seen her thus before, with sober lips and modestly meditative lids; nor had he ever seen the small, solemn replica of herself now seated beside her in billows of clean white muslin. The sight was an intolerable rebuke, and he would have given the world to hear her familiar laugh rattle derisively through the high quietude of the aisles. As he gazed she turned her head, fixing upon him an absent look which gradually melted into a subdued smile of recognition. Then she made a slight sideward motion of her eyes, which plainly said, "This is my little girl."

Maurice noticed that she showed no surprise at seeing him there; she seemed to consider his presence as much a matter of course as her own, and with a shudder he said to himself, "Good heavens, perhaps she thinks I have come to see her daughter confirmed!"

The service rolled on, with its bursts of music and interludes of prayer, its mystical moving of brilliant figures and flitting of lights about the altar; and at length Maurice was aware of a pause, followed by a stirring of the white dovecote in whose midst he sat. He saw Mrs. Birkton glance tearfully at Annette. The girl's lips and eyelids were trembling, and for a moment she seemed unable to move. At length she looked up, fixing her eyes on the golden crucifix above the altar; then, as if hypnotized by the sight, she rose and glided into the aisle, mingling with the fluctuant mass of white-veiled figures which had begun to move slowly toward the apse.

Presently they were all kneeling together on the chancel step, settling their dresses with the quick motions of a flock of birds; and above them, whitely hovering, Maurice saw the pontifical head and voluminous sleeves of the bishop. Annette knelt so that he could just see her between the intervening piers; but Mrs. Tolquitt's daughter was hidden from him, lost in the impersonal array of white veils and bowed heads.

The organ murmured a soft accompaniment, above which rose the monotonous cadence of the episcopal supplication, "Defend, O Lord, this thy child. . . . Defend, O Lord, this thy child. . . ." reiterated like an incantation, as the invoking hands passed slowly down the line of motionless young heads.

Maurice saw the hands sway above Annette's pale braids, which shone like winter sunshine through her veil; then they moved on, and his eyes turned involuntarily to Mrs. Tolquitt. But she did not see him now; she was crying, not daintily, for the gallery, but in genuine self-surrender, her shoulders shaking, her handkerchief pressed against her face.

There came over Maurice an uncontrollable longing to escape; the smoke of the incense and the strong fragrance of the lilies sickened him, and Mrs. Tolquitt's sobs seemed to be choking in his own throat.

At length the white line about the chancel swayed, broke, and dissolved itself; the choir burst into another victorious hymn, and the little veiled figures came fluttering back to their seats. In the ensuing disturbance, Maurice rose with a quick whisper to his mother—"Let me pass—I'm going out. I can't stand the incense"—and while Mrs. Birkton made way for him, startled and disappointed, his glance fell for a moment on Annette's illuminated face, as she moved toward her seat with fixed eyes and folded hands. Her whole gaze was bent upon the inner vision; she did not even see him as he brushed her dress in passing out.

It was like a new birth to get out into the snow again, and Maurice, after a sharp breath or two, stepped forth rapidly against the wind, courting the tingle of the barbed flakes upon his face.

He did not go home until late that evening, and when he entered the kitchen, he was met by the festal spectacle of the supper table adorned with a cluster of white lilies and a delicate array of fruit and angel cake. Annette, in her habitual dress of dark stuff, looked more familiar and less supernal than before, and though her face still shone, it now seemed to Maurice that he could discern the mingling of a gratified childish vanity with the mystical emotions of the morning.

"I'm so glad you have come, dear," Mrs. Birkton exclaimed, her countenance still dewy with a pleasant agitation. "Annette, is the chicken ready? We have a broiled chicken for you, Maurice, dear, and a little mayonnaise of tomatoes."

As she spoke her eye turned toward the supper table, dumbly challenging his praise.

"How nice it looks," he murmured, obediently.

"It is all owing to you, dear," his mother replied. "We asked Mr. Helfenridge to come to supper, too; we thought you would like to have him."

"Is he coming?" Maurice asked, abruptly.

"No, he couldn't, unfortunately. He said he had promised to go to his sister's."

They sat down, Annette mutely radiant at the head of the table, with her mother and Maurice at the sides; but to the dismay of the two women Maurice refused to partake of the delicacies which they had prepared. He had a headache, he said; but he sat watching them eat, in spite of his mother's entreaties that he should go and lie down in his own room.

When supper was over, however, he rose and bade them good

night; Annette's kiss was mingled with an inarticulate whisper of gratitude, but he pushed her gently aside, and the women heard him cross the passageway and shut himself into his own room.

In a few moments, however, he was aroused by a timorous knock, which he recognized as his mother's.

"Come in," he called, and Mrs. Birkton stepped apologetically across the threshold.

"Maurice, is your head very bad?"

"No, no—it's not bad at all. I only want to be quiet."

"I know, dear, and I'm very sorry to disturb you. But here is the rest of this money—I can't keep it, you know, Maurice. Annette's dress and shoes and veil, and the carriage and supper, and the new strings for my bonnet, only cost twenty-seven dollars and a half, and I can't possibly keep the rest unless you will let me use it for the household expenses, as usual."

Maurice sprang up, white to the lips.

"For God's sake mother, understand me. I don't want the money—I won't touch it. I can provide plenty for the household; I haven't let you starve yet. And this is Annette's, yours and hers. If you won't spend it for yourself let Annette put it in the savings bank; or let her throw it into the street; I don't care what becomes of it—but don't speak to me of it again. I'm sick to death of hearing about it!"

Mrs. Birkton shrank back, trembling at his unwonted tone. She was afraid that he was going to be really ill, and her one thought was to withdraw without increasing his agitation.

"Very well, dear—just as you please," she said, deprecatingly. "It was foolish of me to trouble you. Don't think of it again, but go to bed and try to sleep. I ought not to have disturbed you."

And she slipped back into the passageway, stealthily closing the door.

Maurice had no thought of going to bed. He sank into his armchair, which he had pushed close to the gas stove, and sat staring at the hard yellow brilliance of the polished radiator.

Helfenridge had gone to see Annette confirmed, but he had

not been willing to come to supper; and Maurice knew him too well not to penetrate the shallow excuse which had satisfied Mrs. Birkton. Well, Helfenridge was right; no man can handle pitch without being defiled. And once a man's hand is soiled, why should his friends care to touch it?

After all, no cheap condonation of Helfenridge's would have helped Maurice now; rather did he feel a tonic force in his friend's disapproval. It showed Helfenridge to be the better and stronger man; and there was a kind of dispassionate consolation in that. If one had to fail it was better that the other should hold fast than be dragged down with him; and Helfenridge had always been the firmer footed of the two.

So Maurice mused, letting the desolate hours travel on unregarded; till suddenly his vigil was disturbed by a knock, sharp and resolute this time, which made him start to his feet.

"Helfenridge!" he exclaimed, and there on the threshold stood his friend.

Maurice, on seeing him enter, had felt an involuntary thrill of relief, as though he were regaining his moral footing, but the illusion was transient and left him to sink back into profounder depths of self-accusal.

"I thought you weren't coming. You would have been quite right not to come," he said, without asking his friend to sit down.

"I didn't mean to come," Helfenridge answered, taking off his coat. "Your mother asked me to supper, but I refused. I couldn't see my way clear at first—even in church that little white seraph didn't seem to justify it for a moment; but I have been thinking hard all day—and now I've come."

He held out his hand, but Maurice made no motion to take it.

"It's no use," he said, heavily. "No amount of thinking will make it right. What's that in the Bible about doing evil that good may come? That's what I've done. I've done evil that good might come—but it hasn't come—it can't. The fellow in the Bible was right. You think Annette's dress was white? I tell you it was black—black as pitch."

"No, no," said Helfenridge taking the chair which Maurice had not offered him. "The whole business is horribly mixed up, like most human affairs, but there's a germ of right in it somewhere, and the best thing we can do now is to nurse that and get it to flower."

"To flower?—bah—a poison ivy—"

"Some poisons are valuable medicines," said Helfenridge.

"Oh, stop—drop that inane metaphor. I tell you there's no excuse for what I did, and what's worse there's no reparation. I'd give myself up, I'd go and proclaim the whole thing—but what good would that do? Smother everybody in mud—Annette, and my mother, and that poor woman! Helfenridge—"

"Well?"

"That woman—Mrs. Tolquitt—was in church with her little girl, who was confirmed. Think of it, will you! Her little girl was confirmed with Annette! And they sat next to us—only a few seats off. Helfenridge, I never knew she had a little girl."

"I don't suppose we any of us know much about anybody else," said Helfenridge.

"And there she sat crying—crying, I tell you. Just such tears as my mother's—glad and proud and sorry all at once!"

"Yes, I saw her."

"You saw her—and you're here now?"

"I'm here, Maurice, because I know what you're suffering."

They were both silent, Helfenridge seated with bowed head, Birkton stirring uneasily about the room with the thwarted movements of a caged animal.

At length he flung himself down in the chair in front of his desk and hid his face against his arms. Helfenridge heard his sobs.

It seemed a long time before either of them spoke; but finally Helfenridge rose and touched his friend's shoulder.

"My eyes are clearer than yours just now," he said, "and I shouldn't be here if I didn't see a way out of it."

"A way out of it?"

"Yes, only it's no empirical remedy: *geschehen ist geschehen.* But you spoke just now of the biblical axiom that good can't come out of evil; well, no generalization of that sort is final. It seems to me, on the contrary, that this good can come out of evil; that having done evil once it may become impossible to do it again. One ill act may become the strongest rampart one can build against further ill-doing. It divides things, it classifies them. It may be the means of lifting one forever out of the region of quibbles and compromises and moral subtleties, in which we who are curious in emotions are apt to loiter till we get a shaking up of some sort. It's horrible to make a steppingstone out of a poor woman's anguish and humiliation; but the anguish and humiliation can't be prevented now; and who knows? In the occult economy of things they may be of some use to her if they help somebody else."

Maurice flung off his hand with a passionate gesture. "Quibbles and compromises and moral subtleties! What else is your reasoning made up of, I should like to know? It's nothing but the basest Liguorianism. The plain fact is that I'm a dammed blackguard, not fit to look decent people in the face again."

His head sank once more upon his outstretched arms, and Helfenridge drew back.

"Shall I go then, Maurice?"

"Yes, go; it's worse when you're here."

Helfenridge for a few moments stood irresolute, as if waiting for his friend to recall him; but Maurice still sat without moving, bowed beneath the immensity of his shame.

"Well, I'm going," Helfenridge reluctantly declared.

Maurice made no reply; his shoulders still shook, although his grief had grown noiseless.

"Remember, Maurice," his friend conjured him, "that whatever you do your mother and sister mustn't find out about this business. That's your first duty now, to hide the whole thing from them."

Still there came no answer. Helfenridge turned to the door and slowly opened it, glancing back as he did so at Maurice's downcast head; then he stepped out into the passageway. But as the door

THE PORTRAIT

IT WAS at Mrs. Mellish's, one Sunday afternoon last spring. We were talking over George Lillo's portraits—a collection of them was being shown at Durand-Ruel's—and a pretty woman had emphatically declared:

"Nothing on earth would induce me to sit to him!"

There was a chorus of interrogations.

"Oh, because—he makes people look so horrid; the way one looks on board ship, or early in the morning, or when one's hair is out of curl and one knows it. I'd so much rather be done by Mr. Cumberton!"

Little Cumberton, the fashionable purveyor of rose-water pastels, stroked his mustache to hide a conscious smile.

"Lillo is a genius—that we must all admit," he said indulgently, as though condoning a friend's weakness; "but he has an unfortunate temperament. He has been denied the gift—so precious to an artist—of perceiving the ideal. He sees only the defects of his sitters; one might almost fancy that he takes a morbid pleasure in exaggerating their weak points, in painting them on their worst days; but I honestly believe he can't help himself. His peculiar limitations prevent his seeing anything but the most prosaic side of human nature—

> "*A primrose by the river's brim*
> *A yellow primrose is to him,*
> *And it is nothing more.*"

Cumberton looked round to surprise an order in the eye of the lady whose sentiments he had so deftly interpreted, but poetry always made her uncomfortable, and her nomadic attention had strayed to other topics. His glance was tripped up by Mrs. Mellish.

"Limitations? But, my dear man, it's because he hasn't any limitations, because he doesn't wear the portrait painter's conventional blinders, that we're all so afraid of being painted by him. It's not because he sees only one aspect of his sitters, it's because he selects the real, the typical one, as instinctively as a detective collars a pickpocket in a crowd. If there's nothing to paint—no real person—he paints nothing; look at the sumptuous emptiness of his portrait of Mrs. Guy Awdrey"—("Why," the pretty woman perplexedly interjected, "that's the only nice picture he ever did!") "If there's one positive trait in a negative whole he brings it out in spite of himself; if it isn't a nice trait, so much the worse for the sitter; it isn't Lillo's fault: he's no more to blame than a mirror. Your other painters do the surface—he does the depths; they paint the ripples on the pond, he drags the bottom. He makes flesh seem as fortuitous as clothes. When I look at his portraits of fine ladies in pearls and velvet I seem to see a little naked cowering wisp of a soul sitting beside the big splendid body, like a poor relation in the darkest corner of an opera box. But look at his pictures of really great people—how great *they* are! There's plenty of ideal there. Take his Professor Clyde; how clearly the man's history is written in those broad steady strokes of the brush: the hard work, the endless patience, the fearless imagination of the great savant! Or the picture of Mr. Domfrey—the man who has felt beauty without having the power to create it. The very brushwork expresses the difference between the two; the crowding of nervous tentative lines, the subtler gradations of color, somehow convey a suggestion of dilettantism. You feel what a delicate instrument the man is, how every sense has been tuned to the finest responsiveness." Mrs. Mellish paused, blushing a little at the echo of her own eloquence. "My advice is, don't let George Lillo paint you if you don't want to be found out—or to find yourself out. That's why I've never let him do *me*; I'm waiting for the day of judgment," she ended with a laugh.

Everyone but the pretty woman, whose eyes betrayed a quivering impatience to discuss clothes, had listened attentively to Mrs. Mellish. Lillo's presence in New York—he had come over from Paris for the first time in twelve years, to arrange the exhibition of his pictures—gave to the analysis of his methods as personal a flavor as though one had been furtively dissecting his domestic relations. The analogy, indeed, is not unapt; for in Lillo's curiously detached existence it is difficult to figure any closer tie than that which unites him to his pictures. In this light, Mrs. Mellish's flushed harangue seemed not unfitted to the trivialities of the tea hour, and some one almost at once carried on the argument by saying: "But according to your theory—that the significance of his work depends on the significance of the sitter—his portrait of Vard ought to be a masterpiece; and it's his biggest failure."

Alonzo Vard's suicide—he killed himself, strangely enough, the day that Lillo's pictures were first shown—had made his portrait the chief feature of the exhibition. It had been painted ten or twelve years earlier, when the terrible "Boss" was at the height of his power; and if ever man presented a type to stimulate such insight as Lillo's, that man was Vard; yet the portrait was a failure. It was magnificently composed; the technique was dazzling; but the face had been—well, expurgated. It was Vard as Cumberton might have painted him—a common man trying to look at ease in a good coat. The picture had never before been exhibited, and there was a general outcry of disappointment. It wasn't only the critics and the artists who grumbled. Even the big public, which had gaped and shuddered at Vard, reveling in his genial villainy, and enjoying in his death that succumbing to divine wrath which, as a spectacle, is next best to its successful defiance—even the public felt itself defrauded. What had the painter done with their hero? Where was the big sneering domineering face that figured so convincingly in political cartoons and patent medicine advertisements, on cigar boxes and electioneering posters? They had admired the man for looking his part so boldly; for showing the undisguised blackguard in every line of his coarse body and cruel face; the pseudo-gentleman of Lillo's picture was a poor thing compared to the real Vard. It had been vaguely expected that the great boss's portrait would have the zest of an incriminating document, the scandalous attraction of secret memoirs; and instead, it was as insipid as an obituary. It was as though the artist had been in league with his sitter, had pledged himself to oppose to the lust for post-mortem "revelations" an impassable blank wall of negation. The public was resentful, the critics were aggrieved. Even Mrs. Mellish had to lay down her arms.

"Yes, the portrait of Vard *is* a failure," she admitted, "and I've never known why. If he'd been an obscure elusive type of villain, one could understand Lillo's missing the mark for once; but with that face from the pit—!"

She turned at the announcement of a name which our discussion had drowned, and found herself shaking hands with Lillo.

The pretty woman started and put her hands to her curls; Cumberton dropped a condescending eyelid (he never classed himself by recognizing degrees in the profession), and Mrs. Mellish, cheerfully aware that she had been overheard, said, as she made room for Lillo—

"I wish you'd explain it."

Lillo smoothed his beard and waited for a cup of tea. Then, "Would there be any failures," he said, "if one could explain them?"

"Ah, in some cases I can imagine it's impossible to seize the type—or to say why one has missed it. Some people are like daguerreotypes; in certain lights one can't see them at all. But surely Vard was obvious enough. What I want to know is, what became of him? What did you do with him? How did you manage to shuffle him out of sight?"

"It was much easier than you think. I simply missed an opportunity—"

"That a sign painter would have seen!"

"Very likely. In fighting shy of the obvious one may miss the significant—"

"—And when I got back from Paris," the pretty woman was heard to wail, "I found all the women here were wearing the very models I'd brought home with me!"

Mrs. Mellish, as became a vigilant hostess, got up and shuffled her guests; and the question of Vard's portrait was dropped.

I left the house with Lillo; and on the way down Fifth Avenue, after one of his long silences, he suddenly asked:

"Is that what is generally said of my picture of Vard? I don't mean in the newspapers, but by the fellows who know?"

I said it was.

He drew a deep breath. "Well," he said, "it's good to know that when one tries to fail one can make such a complete success of it."

"Tries to fail?"

"Well, no; that's not quite it, either; I didn't want to make a failure of Vard's picture, but I did so deliberately, with my eyes open, all the same. It was what one might call a lucid failure."

"But why—?"

"The why of it is rather complicated. I'll tell you sometime—" He hesitated. "Come and dine with me at the club by and by, and I'll tell you afterwards. It's a nice morsel for a psychologist."

At dinner he said little; but I didn't mind that. I had known him for years, and had always found something soothing and companionable in his long abstentions from speech. His silence was never unsocial; it was bland as a natural hush; one felt one's self included in it, not left out. He stroked his beard and gazed absently at me; and when we had finished our coffee and liqueurs we strolled down to his studio.

At the studio—which was less draped, less posed, less consciously "artistic" than those of the smaller men—he handed me a cigar, and fell to smoking before the fire. When he began to talk it was of indifferent matters, and I had dismissed the hope of hearing more of Vard's portrait, when my eye lit on a photograph of the picture. I walked across the room to look at it, and Lillo presently followed with a light.

"It certainly is a complete disguise," he muttered over my shoulder; then he turned away and stooped to a big portfolio propped against the wall.

"Did you ever know Miss Vard?" he asked, with his head in the portfolio; and without waiting for my answer he handed me a crayon sketch of a girl's profile.

I had never seen a crayon of Lillo's, and I lost sight of the sitter's personality in the interest aroused by this new aspect of the master's complex genius. The few lines—faint, yet how decisive!—flowered out of the rough paper with the lightness of opening petals. It was a mere hint of a picture, but vivid as some word that wakens long reverberations in the memory.

I felt Lillo at my shoulder again.

"You knew her, I suppose?"

I had to stop and think. Why, of course I'd known her: a silent handsome girl, showy yet ineffective, whom I had seen without seeing the winter that society had capitulated to Vard. Still looking at the crayon, I tried to trace some connection between the Miss Vard I recalled and the grave young seraph of Lillo's sketch. Had the Vards bewitched him? By what masterstroke of suggestion had he been beguiled into drawing the terrible father as a barber's block, the commonplace daughter as this memorable creature?

"You don't remember much about her? No, I suppose not. She was a quiet girl and nobody noticed her much, even when"—he paused with a smile—"you were all asking Vard to dine."

I winced. Yes, it was true—we had all asked Vard to dine. It was some comfort to think that fate had made him expiate our weakness.

Lillo put the sketch on the mantelshelf and drew his armchair to the fire.

"It's cold tonight. Take another cigar, old man; and some whiskey? There ought to be a bottle and some glasses in that cupboard behind you. Help yourself."

II

About Vard's portrait? (He began.) Well, I'll tell you. It's a queer story, and most people wouldn't see anything in it. My enemies might say it was a roundabout way of explaining a failure; but you know better than that. Mrs. Mellish was right. Between me and Vard there could be no question of failure. The man was made for me—I felt that the first time I clapped eyes on him. I could hardly keep from asking him to sit to me on the spot; but somehow one couldn't ask favors of the fellow. I sat still and prayed he'd come to me, though; for I was looking for something big for the next Salon. It was twelve years ago—the last time I was out here—and I was ravenous for an opportunity. I had the feeling—do you writer fellows have it too?—that there was something tremendous in me if it could only be got out; and I felt Vard was the Moses to strike the rock. There were vulgar reasons, too, that made me hunger for a victim. I'd been grinding on obscurely for a good many years, without gold or glory, and the first thing of mine that had made a noise was my picture of Pepita, exhibited the year before. There'd been a lot of talk about that, orders were beginning to come in, and I wanted to follow it up with a rousing big thing at the next Salon. Then the critics had been insinuating that I could do only Spanish things—I suppose I *had* overdone the castanet business; it's a nursery disease we all go through—and I wanted to show that I had plenty more shot in my locker. Don't you get up every morning meaning to prove you're equal to Balzac or Thackeray? That's the way I felt then; *only give me a chance*, I wanted to shout out to them; and I saw at once that Vard was my chance.

I had come over from Paris in the autumn to paint Mrs. Clingsborough, and I met Vard and his daughter at one of the first dinners I went to. After that I could think of nothing but that man's head. What a type! I raked up all the details of his scandalous history; and there were enough to fill an encyclopedia. The papers were full of him just then; he was mud from head to foot; it was about the time of the big viaduct steal, and irreproachable citizens were forming ineffectual leagues to put him down. And all the time one kept meeting him at dinners—that was the beauty of it! Once I remember seeing him next to the Bishop's wife—I've got a little sketch of that duet somewhere—well, he was simply magnificent, a born ruler; what a splendid condottiere he would have made, in gold armor, with a griffin grinning on his casque! You remember those drawings of Leonardo's, where the knight's face and the outline of his helmet combine in one monstrous saurian profile? He always reminded me of that. . . .

But how was I to get at him? One day it occurred to me to try talking to Miss Vard. She was a monosyllabic person, who didn't seem to see an inch beyond the last remark one had made; but suddenly I found myself blurting out, "I wonder if you know how extraordinarily paintable your father is?" and you should have seen the change that came over her. Her eyes lit up and she looked—well, as I've tried to make her look there. (He glanced up at the sketch.) Yes, she said, *wasn't* her father splendid, and didn't I think him one of the handsomest men I'd ever seen?

That rather staggered me, I confess; I couldn't think her capable of joking on such a subject, yet it seemed impossible that she should be speaking seriously. But she was. I knew it by the way she looked at Vard, who was sitting opposite, his wolfish profile thrown back, the shaggy locks tossed off his narrow high white forehead. The girl worshipped him.

She went on to say how glad she was that I saw him as she did. So many artists admired only regular beauty, the stupid Greek type that was made to be done in marble; but she'd always fancied from what she'd seen of my work—she knew everything I'd done, it appeared—that I looked deeper, cared more for the way in which faces are modeled by temperament and circumstance; "and of course in that sense," she concluded, "my father's face *is* beautiful."

This was even more staggering; but one couldn't question her divine sincerity. I'm afraid my one thought was to take advantage of it; and I let her go on, perceiving that if I wanted to paint Vard all I had to do was to listen.

She poured out her heart. It was a glorious thing for a girl, she said, wasn't it, to be associated with such a life as that? She felt it so strongly, sometimes, that it oppressed her, made her shy and stupid. She was so afraid people would expect her to live up to *him*. But that was absurd, of course; brilliant men so seldom had clever children. Still—did I know?—she would have been happier, much happier, if he hadn't been in public life; if he and she could have hidden themselves away somewhere, with their books and music, and she could have had it all to herself: his cleverness, his learning, his immense unbounded goodness. For no one knew how good he was; no one but herself. Everybody recognized his cleverness, his brilliant abilities; even his enemies had to admit his extraordinary intellectual gifts, and hated him the worse, of course, for the admission; but no one, no one could guess what he was at home. She had heard of great men who were always giving gala performances in public, but whose wives and daughters saw only the empty theater, with the footlights out and the scenery stacked in the wings; but with him it was just the other way: wonderful as he was in public, in society, she sometimes felt he wasn't doing himself justice—he was so much more wonderful at home. It was like carrying a guilty secret about with her: his friends, his admirers, would never forgive her if they found out that he kept all his best things for *her*!

I don't quite know what I felt in listening to her. I was chiefly taken up with leading her on to the point I had in view; but even through my personal preoccupation I remember being struck by the fact that, though she talked foolishly, she didn't talk like a fool. She was not stupid; she was not obtuse; one felt that her impassive surface was alive with delicate points of perception; and this fact, coupled with her crystalline frankness, flung me back on a started revision of my impressions of her father. He came out of the test more monstrous than ever, as an ugly image reflected in clear water is made uglier by the purity of the medium. Even then I felt a pang at the use to which fate had put the mountain pool of Miss Vard's spirit, and an uneasy sense that my own reflection there was not one to linger over. It was odd that I should have scrupled to deceive, on one small point, a girl already so hugely cheated; perhaps it was the completeness of her delusion that gave it the sanctity of a religious belief. At any rate, a distinct sense of discomfort tempered at the satisfaction with which, a day or two later, I heard from her that her father had consented to give me a few sittings.

I'm afraid my scruples vanished when I got him before my easel. He was immense, and he was unexplored. From my point of view he'd never been done before—I was his Cortez. As he talked the wonder grew. His daughter came with him, and I began to think she was right in saying that he kept his best for her. It wasn't that she drew him out, or guided the conversation; but one had a sense of delicate vigilance, hardly more perceptible than one of those atmospheric influences that give the pulses a happier turn. She was a vivifying climate. I had meant to turn the talk to public affairs, but it slipped toward books and art, and I was faintly aware of its being kept there without undue pressure. Before long I saw the value of the diversion. It was easy enough to get at the political Vard: the other aspect was rarer and more instructive. His daughter had described him as a scholar. He wasn't that, of course, in any intrinsic sense: like most men of his type he had gulped his knowledge standing, as he had snatched his food from lunch counters; the wonder of it lay in his extraordinary power of assimilation. It was the strangest instance of a mind to which erudition had given force and fluency without culture; his learning had not educated his perceptions: it was an implement serving to slash others rather than to polish himself. I have said that at first sight he was immense; but as I studied him he began to lessen under my scrutiny. His depth was a false perspective painted on a wall.

It was there that my difficulty lay: I had prepared too big a canvas for him. Intellectually his scope was considerable, but it was like the digital reach of a mediocre pianist—it didn't make him a great musician. And morally he wasn't bad enough; his corruption wasn't sufficiently imaginative to be interesting. It was not so much a means to an end as a kind of virtuosity practiced for its own sake, like a highly-developed skill in cannoning billiard balls. After all, the point of view is what gives distinction to either vice or virtue: a morality with ground-glass windows is no duller than a narrow cynicism.

His daughter's presence—she always came with him—gave unintentional emphasis to these conclusions; for where she was richest he was naked. She had a deep-rooted delicacy that drew color and perfume from the very center of her being: his sentiments, good or bad, were as detachable as his cuffs. Thus her nearness, planned, as I guessed, with the tender intention of displaying, elucidating him, of making him accessible in detail to my dazzled perceptions—this pious design in fact defeated itself. She made him appear at his best, but she cheapened that best by her proximity. For the man was vulgar to the core; vulgar in spite of his force and magnitude; thin, hollow, spectacular; a lath-and-plaster bogey.

Did she suspect it? I think not—then. He was wrapped in her impervious faith. The papers? Oh, their charges were set down to political rivalry; and the only people she saw were his hangers-on, or the fashionable set who had taken him up for their amusement. Besides, she would never have found out in that way: at a direct accusation her resentment would have flamed up and smothered her judgment. If the truth came to her, it would come through knowing intimately some one—different; through—how shall I put it?—an imperceptible shifting of her center of gravity. My besetting fear was that I couldn't count on her obtuseness. She wasn't what is called clever; she left that to him; but she was exquisitely good; and now and then she had intuitive felicities that frightened me. Do I make you see her? We fellows can explain better with a brush; I don't know how to mix my words or lay them on. She wasn't clever; but her heart thought—that's all I can say.

If she'd been stupid it would have been easy enough: I could have painted him as he was. Could have? I did—brushed the face in one day from memory; it was the very man! I painted it out before she came: I couldn't bear to have her see it. I had the feeling that I held her faith in my hands, carrying it like a brittle object through a jostling mob; a hair's breadth swerve and it was in splinters.

When she wasn't there I tried to reason myself out of these subtleties. My business was to paint Vard as he was—if his daughter didn't mind his looks, why should I? The opportunity was magnificent—I knew that by the way his face had leapt out of the canvas at my first touch. It would have been a big thing. Before every sitting I swore to myself I'd do it; then she came, and sat near him, and I—didn't.

I knew that before long she'd notice I was shirking the face. Vard himself took little interest in the portrait, but she watched me closely, and one day when the sitting was over she stayed behind and asked me when I meant to begin what she called "the likeness." I guessed from her tone that the embarrassment was all on my side, or that if she felt any it was at having to touch a vulnerable point in my pride. Thus far the only doubt that troubled her was a distrust of my ability. Well, I put her off with any rot you please: told her she must trust me, must let me wait for the inspiration; that some day the face would come; I should see it suddenly—feel it under my brush. . . . The poor child believed me: you can make a woman believe almost anything she doesn't quite understand. She was abashed at her philistinism, and begged me not to tell her father—he would make such fun of her!

After that—well, the sittings went on. Not many, of course; Vard was too busy to give me much time. Still, I could have done him ten times over. Never had I found my formula with such ease, such assurance; there were no hesitations, no obstructions—the face was *there*, waiting for me; at times it almost shaped itself on the canvas. Unfortunately Miss Vard was there too. . . .

All this time the papers were busy with the viaduct scandal. The outcry was getting louder. You remember the circumstances? One of Vard's associates—Bardwell, wasn't it?—threatened disclosures. The rival machine got hold of him, the Independents took him to their bosom, and the press shrieked for an investigation. It was not the first storm Vard had weathered, and his face wore just the right shade of cool vigilance; he wasn't the man to fall into the mistake of appearing too easy. His demeanor would have been superb if it had been inspired by a sense of his own strength; but it struck me rather as based on contempt for his antagonists. Success is an inverted telescope through which one's enemies are apt to look too small and too remote. As for Miss Vard, her serenity was undiminished; but I half-detected a defiance in her unruffled sweetness, and during the last sittings I had the factitious vivacity of a hostess who hears her best china crashing.

One day it *did* crash: the headlines of the morning papers shouted the catastrophe at me—"The Monster forced to disgorge—Warrant out against Vard—Bardwell the Boss's Boomerang"—you know the kind of thing.

When I had read the papers I threw them down and went out. As it happened, Vard was to have given me a sitting that morning: but there would have been a certain irony in waiting for him. I wished I had finished the picture—I wished I'd never thought of painting it. I wanted to shake off the whole business, to put it out of my mind, if I could. I had the feeling—I don't know if I can describe it—that there was a kind of disloyalty to the poor girl in my even acknowledging to myself that I knew what all the papers were howling from the house-tops.

I had walked for an hour when it suddenly occurred to me that Miss Vard might, after all, come to the studio at the appointed hour. Why should she? I could conceive of no reason; but the mere thought of what, if she *did* come, my absence would imply to her, sent me bolting back to Twelfth Street. It was a presentiment, if you like, for she was there.

As she rose to meet me a newspaper slipped from her hand. I'd been fool enough, when I went out, to leave the damned things lying all over the place.

I muttered some apology for being late, and she said reassuringly: "But my father's not here yet."

"Your father—?" I could have kicked myself for the way I bungled it!

"He went out very early this morning, and left word that he would meet me here at the usual hour."

She faced me, with an eye full of bright courage, across the newspaper lying between us.

"He ought to be here in a moment now—he's always so punctual. But my watch is a little fast, I think."

She held it out to me almost gaily, and I was just pretending to compare it with mine, when there was a smart rap on the door and Vard stalked in. There was always a civic majesty in his gait, an air of having just stepped off his pedestal and of dissembling an oration in his umbrella; and that day he surpassed himself. Miss Vard had turned pale at the knock; but the mere sight of him replenished her veins, and if she now avoided my eye, it was in mere pity for my discomfiture.

I was in fact the only one of the three who didn't instantly "play up"; but such virtuosity was inspiring, and by the time Vard had thrown off his coat and dropped into a senatorial pose, I was ready to pitch into my work. I swore I'd do his face then and there; do it as she saw it; she sat close to him, and I had only to glance at her while I painted.

Vard himself was masterly: his talk rattled through my hesitations and embarrassments like a brisk northwester sweeping the dry leaves from its path. Even his daughter showed the sudden brilliance of a lamp from which the shade has been removed. We were all surprisingly vivid—it felt, somehow, as though we were being photographed by flashlight.

It was the best sitting we'd ever had—but unfortunately it didn't last more than ten minutes.

It was Vard's secretary who interrupted us—a slinking chap called Cornley, who burst in, as white as sweetbread, with the face of a depositor who hears his bank has stopped payment. Miss Vard started up as he entered, but caught herself together and dropped back into her chair. Vard, who had taken out a cigarette, held the tip tranquilly to his fusee.

"You're here, thank God!" Cornley cried. "There's no time to be lost, Mr. Vard. I've got a carriage waiting round the corner in Thirteenth Street—"

Vard looked at the tip of his cigarette.

"A carriage in Thirteenth Street? My good fellow, my own brougham is at the door."

"I know, I know—but *they're* there too, sir; or they will be, inside of a minute. For God's sake, Mr. Vard, don't trifle!—There's a way out by Thirteenth Street, I tell you!"

"Bardwell's myrmidons, eh?" said Vard. "Help me on with my overcoat, Cornley, will you?"

Cornley's teeth chattered.

"Mr. Vard, your best friends...Miss Vard, won't you speak to your father?" He turned to me haggardly, "We can get out by the back way?"

I nodded.

Vard stood towering—in some infernal way he seemed literally to rise to the situation—one hand in the bosom of his coat, in the attitude of patriotism in bronze. I glanced at his daughter: she hung on him with a drowning look. Suddenly she straightened herself; there was something of Vard in the way she faced her fears—a kind of primitive calm we drawing-room folk don't have. She stepped to him and laid her hand on his arm. The pause hadn't lasted ten seconds.

"Father—" she said.

Vard threw back his head and swept the studio with a sovereign eye.

"The back way, Mr. Vard, the back way," Cornley whimpered. "For God's sake, sir, don't lose a minute."

Vard transfixed his abject henchman.

"I have never yet taken the back way," he enunciated; and, with a gesture matching the words, he turned to me and bowed.

"I regret the disturbance—" and he walked to the door. His daughter was at his side, alert, transfigured.

"Stay here, my dear."

"Never!"

They measured each other an instant; then he drew her arm in his. She flung back one look at me—a paean of victory—and they passed out with Cornley at their heels.

I wish I'd finished the face then: I believe I could have caught something of the look she had tried to make me see in him. Unluckily I was too excited to work that day or the next, and within the week the whole business came out. If the indictment wasn't a put-up job—and on that I believe there were two opinions—all that followed was. You remember the farcical trial, the packed jury, the compliant judge, the triumphant acquittal? . . . It's a spectacle that always carries conviction to the voter: Vard was never more popular than after his "exoneration."

I didn't see Miss Vard for weeks. It was she who came to me at length; came to the studio alone, one afternoon at dusk. She had—what shall I say?—a veiled manner, as though she had dropped a fine gauze between us. I waited for her to speak.

She glanced about the room, admiring a hawthorn vase I had picked up at auction. Then, after a pause, she said:

"You haven't finished the picture?"

"Not quite," I said.

She asked to see it, and I wheeled out the easel and threw the drapery back.

"Oh," she murmured, "you haven't gone on with the face?"

I shook my head.

She looked down on her clasped hands and up at the picture; not once at me.

"You—you're going to finish it?"

"Of course," I cried, throwing the revived purpose into my voice. By God, I would finish it!

The merest tinge of relief stole over her face, faint as the first thin chirp before daylight.

"Is it so very difficult?" she asked tentatively.

"Not insuperably, I hope."

She sat silent, her eyes on the picture. At length, with an effort, she brought out: "Shall you want more sittings?"

For a second I blundered between two conflicting conjectures; then the truth came to me with a leap, and I cried out, "No, no more sittings!"

She looked up at me then for the first time; looked too soon, poor child; for in the spreading light of reassurance that made her eyes like a rainy dawn, I saw, with terrible distinctness, the rout of her disbanded hopes. I knew that she knew....

I finished the picture and sent it home within a week. I tried to make it—what you see. Too late, you say? Yes—for her; but not for me or for the public. If she could be made to feel, for a day longer, for an hour even, that her miserable secret *was* a secret—why, she'd made it seem worth-while to me to chuck my own ambitions for that....

Lillo rose, and taking down the sketch stood looking at it in silence.

After a while I ventured, "And Miss Vard—?"

He opened the portfolio and put the sketch back, tying the strings with deliberation. Then, turning to relight his cigar at the lamp, he said: "She died last year, thank God."

A CUP OF COLD WATER

IT WAS three o'clock in the morning, and the cotillion was at its height, when Woburn left the over-heated splendor of the Gildermere ball-room, and after a delay caused by the determination of the drowsy footman to give him a ready-made overcoat with an imitation astrachan collar in place of his own unimpeachable Poole garment, found himself breasting the icy solitude of the Fifth Avenue. He was still smiling, as he emerged from the awning, at his insistence in claiming his own overcoat: it illustrated, humorously enough, the invincible force of habit. As he faced the wind, however, he discerned a providence in his persistency, for his coat was fur-lined, and he had a cold voyage before him on the morrow.

It had rained hard during the earlier part of the night, and the carriages waiting in triple line before the Gildermeres' door were still domed by shining umbrellas, while the electric lamps extending down the avenue blinked Narcissus-like at their watery images in the hollows of the sidewalk. A dry blast had come out of the north, with pledge of frost before day-light, and to Woburn's shivering fancy the pools in the pavement seemed already stiffening into ice. He turned up his coat-collar and stepped out rapidly, his hands deep in his coat-pockets.

As he walked he glanced curiously up at the ladder-like doorsteps which may well suggest to the future archaeologist that all the streets of New York were once canals; at the spectral tracery of the trees about St. Luke's, the fretted mass of the Cathedral, and the mean vista of the long side-streets. The knowledge that he was perhaps looking at it all for the last time caused every detail to start out like a challenge to memory, and lit the brown-stone house-fronts with the glamor of sword-barred Edens.

It was an odd impulse that had led him that night to the Gildermere ball; but the same change in his condition which made him stare wonderingly at the houses in the Fifth Avenue gave the thrill of an exploit to the tame business of ball-going. Who would have imagined, Woburn mused, that such a situation as his would possess the priceless quality of sharpening the blunt edge of habit?

It was certainly curious to reflect, as he leaned against the doorway of Mrs. Gildermere's ball-room, enveloped in the warm atmosphere of the accustomed, that twenty-four hours later the people brushing by him with looks of friendly recognition would start at the thought of having seen him and slur over the recollection of having taken his hand!

And the girl he had gone there to see: what would she think of him? He knew well enough that her trenchant classifications of life admitted no overlapping of good and evil, made no allowance for that incalculable interplay of motives that justifies the subtlest casuistry of compassion. Miss Talcott was too young to distinguish the intermediate tints of the moral spectrum; and her judgments were further simplified by a peculiar concreteness of mind. Her bringing-up had fostered this tendency and she was surrounded by people who focused life in the same way. To the girls in Miss Talcott's set, the attentions of a clever man who had to work for his living had the zest of a forbidden pleasure; but to marry such a man would be as unpardonable as to have one's carriage seen at the door of a cheap dress-maker. Poverty might make a man fascinating; but a settled income was the best evidence of stability of character. If there were anything in heredity, how could a nice girl trust a man whose parents had been careless enough to leave him unprovided for?

Neither Miss Talcott nor any of her friends could be charged with formulating these views; but they were implicit in the slope of every white shoulder and in the ripple of every yard of imported tulle dappling the foreground of Mrs. Gildermere's ball-room. The advantages of line and color in veiling the crudities of a creed are obvious to emotional minds; and besides, Woburn was conscious that it was to the cheerful materialism of their parents that the young girls he admired owed that fine distinction of outline in which their skillfully-rippled hair and skillfully-hung draperies cooperated with the slimness and erectness that came of participating in the most expensive sports, eating the most expensive food and breathing the most expensive air. Since the process which had produced them was so costly, how could they help being costly themselves? Woburn was too logical to expect to give no more for a piece of old Sèvres than for a bit of kitchen crockery; he had no faith in wonderful bargains, and believed that one got in life just what one was willing to pay for. He had no mind to dispute the taste of those who preferred the rustic simplicity of the earthen crock; but his own fancy inclined to the piece of *pâte tendre* which must be kept in a glass case and handled as delicately as a flower.

It was not merely by the external grace of these drawing-room ornaments that Woburn's sensibilities were charmed. His imagination was touched by the curious exoticism of view resulting from such conditions. He had always enjoyed listening to Miss Talcott even more than looking at her. Her ideas had the brilliant bloom and audacious irrelevance of those tropical orchids which strike root in air. Miss Talcott's opinions had no connection with the actual; her very materialism had the grace of artificiality. Woburn had been enchanted once by seeing her helpless before a smoking lamp: she had been obliged to ring for a servant because she did not know how to put it out.

Her supreme charm was the simplicity that comes of taking it for granted that people are born with carriages and country-places: it never occurred to her that such congenital attributes could be matter for self-consciousness, and she had none of the *nouveau riche* prudery which classes poverty with the nude in art and is not sure how to behave in the presence of either.

The conditions of Woburn's own life had made him peculiarly

susceptible to those forms of elegance which are the flower of ease. His father had lost a comfortable property through sheer inability to go over his agent's accounts; and this disaster, coming at the outset of Woburn's school-days, had given a new bent to the family temperament. The father characteristically died when the effort of living might have made it possible to retrieve his fortunes; and Woburn's mother and sister, embittered by this final evasion, settled down to a vindictive war with circumstances. They were the kind of women who think that it lightens the burden of life to throw over the amenities, as a reduced housekeeper puts away her knick-knacks to make the dusting easier. They fought mean conditions meanly; but Woburn, in his resentment of their attitude, did not allow for the suffering which had brought it about: his own tendency was to overcome difficulties by conciliation rather than by conflict. Such surroundings threw into vivid relief the charming figure of Miss Talcott. Woburn instinctively associated poverty with bad food, ugly furniture, complaints and recriminations: it was natural that he should be drawn toward the luminous atmosphere where life was a series of peaceful and good-humored acts, unimpeded by petty obstacles. To spend one's time in such society gave one the illusion of unlimited credit; and also, unhappily, created the need for it.

It was here in fact that Woburn's difficulties began. To marry Miss Talcott it was necessary to be a rich man: even to dine out in her set involved certain minor extravagances. Woburn had determined to marry her sooner or later; and in the meanwhile to be with her as much as possible.

As he stood leaning in the doorway of the Gildermere ballroom, watching her pass him in the waltz, he tried to remember how it had begun. First there had been the tailor's bill; the fur-lined overcoat with cuffs and collar of Alaska sable had alone cost more than he had spent on his clothes for two or three years previously. Then there were theater-tickets; cab-fares; florist's bills; tips to servants at the country-houses where he went because he knew that she was invited; the *Omar Khayyám* bound by Sullivan that he sent her at Christmas; the contributions to her pet charities; the reckless purchases at fairs where she had a stall. His whole way of life had imperceptibly changed and his year's salary was gone before the second quarter was due.

He had invested the few thousand dollars which had been his portion of his father's shrunken estate: when his debts began to pile up, he took a flyer in stocks and after a few months of varying luck his little patrimony disappeared. Meanwhile his courtship was proceeding at an inverse ratio to his financial ventures. Miss Talcott was growing tender and he began to feel that the game was in his hands. The nearness of the goal exasperated him. She was not the girl to wait and he knew that it must be now or never. A friend lent him five thousand dollars on his personal note and he bought railway stocks on margin. They went up and he held them for a higher rise: they fluctuated, dragged, dropped below the level at which he had bought, and slowly continued their uninterrupted descent. His broker called for more margin; he could not respond and was sold out.

What followed came about quite naturally. For several years he had been cashier in a well-known banking-house. When the note he had given his friend became due it was obviously necessary to pay it and he used the firm's money for the purpose. To repay the money thus taken, he increased his debt to his employers and bought more stocks; and on these operations he made a profit of ten thousand dollars. Miss Talcott rode in the Park, and he bought a smart hack for seven hundred, paid off his tradesmen, and went on speculating with the remainder of his profits. He made a little more, but failed to take advantage of the market and lost all that he had staked, including the amount taken from the firm. He increased his over-draft by another ten thousand and lost that; he over-drew a farther sum and lost again. Suddenly he woke to the fact that he owed his employers fifty thousand dollars and that the partners were to make their semi-annual inspection in two days. He realized then that within forty-eight hours what he had called borrowing would become theft.

There was no time to be lost: he must clear out and start life over again somewhere else. The day that he reached this decision he was to have met Miss Talcott at dinner. He went to the dinner, but she did not appear: she had a headache, his hostess explained. Well, he was not to have a last look at her, after all; better so, perhaps. He took leave early and on his way home stopped at a florist's and sent her a bunch of violets. The next morning he got a little note from her: the violets had done her head so much good—she would tell him all about it that evening at the Gildermere ball. Woburn laughed and tossed the note into the fire. That evening he would be on board ship: the examination of the books was to take place the following morning at ten.

Woburn went down to the bank as usual; he did not want to do anything that might excite suspicion as to his plans, and from one or two questions which one of the partners had lately put to him he divined that he was being observed. At the bank the day passed uneventfully. He discharged his business with his accustomed care and went uptown at the usual hour.

In the first flush of his successful speculations he had set up bachelor lodgings, moved by the temptation to get away from the dismal atmosphere of home, from his mother's struggles with the cook and his sister's curiosity about his letters. He had been influenced also by the wish for surroundings more adapted to his tastes. He wanted to be able to give little teas, to which Miss Talcott might come with a married friend. She came once or twice and pronounced it all delightful: she thought it *so* nice to have only a few Whistler etchings on the walls and the simplest crushed levant for all one's books.

To these rooms Woburn returned on leaving the bank. His plans had taken definite shape. He had engaged passage on a steamer sailing for Halifax early the next morning; and there was nothing for him to do before going on board but to pack his clothes and tear up a few letters. He threw his clothes into a couple of portmanteaux, and when these had been called for by an expressman he emptied his pockets and counted up his ready money.

He found that he possessed just fifty dollars and seventy-five cents; but his passage to Halifax was paid, and once there he could pawn his watch and rings. This calculation completed, he unlocked his writing-table drawer and took out a handful of letters. They were notes from Miss Talcott. He read them over and threw them into the fire. On his table stood her photograph. He slipped it out of its frame and tossed it on top of the blazing letters. Having performed this rite, he got into his dress-clothes and went to a small French restaurant to dine.

He had meant to go on board the steamer immediately after dinner; but a sudden vision of introspective hours in a silent cabin made him call for the evening paper and run his eye over the list of theaters. It would be as easy to go on board at midnight as now.

He selected a new vaudeville and listened to it with surprising freshness of interest; but toward eleven o'clock he again began to dread the approaching necessity of going down to the steamer. There was something peculiarly unnerving in the idea of spending the rest of the night in a stifling cabin jammed against the side of a wharf.

He left the theater and strolled across to the Fifth Avenue. It was now nearly midnight and a stream of carriages poured up town from the opera and the theaters. As he stood on the corner watching the familiar spectacle it occurred to him that many of the people driving by him in smart broughams and C-spring landaus were on their way to the Gildermere ball. He remembered Miss Talcott's note of the morning and wondered if she were in one of the passing carriages; she had spoken so confidently of meeting him at the ball. What if he should go and take a last look at her? There was really nothing to prevent it. He was not likely to run across any member of the firm: in Miss Talcott's set his social standing was good for another ten hours at least. He smiled in anticipation of her surprise at seeing him, and then reflected with a start that she would not be surprised at all.

His meditations were cut short by a fall of sleety rain, and hailing a hansom he gave the driver Mrs. Gildermere's address.

As he drove up the avenue he looked about him like a traveler in a strange city. The buildings which had been so unobtrusively familiar stood out with sudden distinctness: he noticed a hundred details which had escaped his observation. The people on the side-walks looked like strangers: he wondered where they were going and tried to picture the lives they led; but his own relation to life had been so suddenly reversed that he found it impossible to re-cover his mental perspective.

At one corner he saw a shabby man lurking in the shadow of the side-street; as the hansom passed, a policeman ordered him to move on. Farther on, Woburn noticed a woman crouching on the door-step of a handsome house. She had drawn a shawl over her head and was sunk in the apathy of despair or drink. A well-dressed couple paused to look at her. The electric globe at the cor-ner lit up their faces, and Woburn saw the lady, who was young and pretty, turn away with a little grimace, drawing her compan-ion after her.

The desire to see Miss Talcott had driven Woburn to the Gil-dermere's; but once in the ball-room he made no effort to find her. The people about him seemed more like strangers than those he had passed in the street. He stood in the doorway, studying the petty maneuvers of the women and the resigned amenities of their partners. Was it possible that these were his friends? These mincing women, all paint and dye and whalebone, these apathetic men who looked as much alike as the figures that children cut out of a folded sheet of paper? Was it to live among such puppets that he had sold his soul? What had any of these people done that was no-ble, exceptional, distinguished? Who knew them by name even, except their tradesmen and the society reporters? Who were they, that they should sit in judgment on him?

The bald man with the globular stomach, who stood at Mrs. Gildermere's elbow surveying the dancers, was old Boylston, who had made his pile in wrecking railroads; the smooth chap with glazed eyes, at whom a pretty girl smiled up so confidingly, was Collerton, the political lawyer, who had been mixed up to his own advantage in an ugly lobbying transaction; near him stood Brice Lyndham, whose recent failure had ruined his friends and associates, but had not visibly affected the welfare of his large and expensive family. The slim fellow dancing with Miss Gildermere was Alec Vance, who lived on a salary of five thousand a year, but whose wife was such a good manager that they kept a brougham and victoria and always put in their season at Newport and their spring trip to Europe. The little ferret-faced youth in the corner was Regie Colby, who wrote the *Entre-Nous* paragraphs in the *Social Searchlight*: the women were charming to him and he got all the financial tips he wanted from their husbands and fathers.

And the women? Well, the women knew all about the men, and flattered them and married them and tried to catch them for their daughters. It was a domino-party at which the guests were forbidden to unmask, though they all saw through each other's disguises.

And these were the people who, within twenty-four hours, would be agreeing that they had always felt there was something wrong about Woburn! They would be extremely sorry for him, of course, poor devil; but there are certain standards, after all—what would society be without standards? His new friends, his future associates, were the suspicious-looking man whom the policeman had ordered to move on, and the drunken woman asleep on the door-step. To these he was linked by the freemasonry of failure.

Miss Talcott passed him on Collerton's arm: she was giving him one of the smiles of which Woburn had fancied himself sole owner. Collerton was a sharp fellow; he must have made a lot in that last deal; probably she would marry him. How much did she know about the transaction? She was a shrewd girl and her father was in Wall Street. If Woburn's luck had turned the other way she might have married him instead; and if he had confessed his sin to her one evening, as they drove home from the opera in their new brougham, she would have said that really it was of no use to tell her, for she never *could* understand about business, but that she did entreat him in future to be nicer to Regie Colby. Even now, if he made a big strike somewhere, and came back in ten years with a beard and a steam yacht, they would all deny that anything had been proved against him, and Mrs. Collerton might blush and remind him of their friendship. Well—why not? Was not all morality based on a convention? What was the stanchest code of ethics but a trunk with a series of false bottoms? Now and then one had the illusion of getting down to absolute right or wrong, but it was only a false bottom—a removable hypothesis—with another false bottom underneath. There was no getting beyond the relative.

The cotillion had begun. Miss Talcott sat nearly opposite him: she was dancing with young Boylston and giving him a Woburn-Collerton smile. So young Boylston was in the syndicate too!

Presently Woburn was aware that she had forgotten young Boylston and was glancing absently about the room. She was looking for some one, and meant the some one to know it: he knew that *Lost-Chord* look in her eyes.

A new figure was being formed. The partners circled about the room and Miss Talcott's flying tulle drifted close to him as she passed. Then the favors were distributed; white skirts wavered across the floor like thistle-down on summer air; men rose from their seats and fresh couples filled the shining *parquet*.

Miss Talcott, after taking from the basket a Legion of Honor in red enamel, surveyed the room for a moment; then she made her way through the dancers and held out the favor to Woburn. He fastened it in his coat, and emerging from the crowd of men about the doorway, slipped his arm about her. Their eyes met; hers were serious and a little sad. How fine and slender she was! He noticed the little tendrils of hair about the pink convolution of her ear. Her waist was firm and yet elastic; she breathed calmly and regularly, as though dancing were her natural motion. She did not look at him again and neither of them spoke.

When the music ceased they paused near her chair. Her partner was waiting for her and Woburn left her with a bow.

He made his way down-stairs and out of the house. He was glad that he had not spoken to Miss Talcott. There had been a healing power in their silence. All bitterness had gone from him and he thought of her now quite simply, as the girl he loved.

At Thirty-fifth Street he reflected that he had better jump into a car and go down to his steamer. Again there rose before him the repulsive vision of the dark cabin, with creaking noises overhead, and the cold wash of water against the pier: he thought he would stop in a café and take a drink. He turned into Broadway and entered a brightly-lit café; but when he had taken his whiskey and soda there seemed no reason for lingering. He had never been the kind of man who could escape difficulties in that way. Yet he was conscious that his will was weakening; that he did not mean to go down to the steamer just yet. What did he mean to do? He began to feel horribly tired and it occurred to him that a few hours' sleep in a decent bed would make a new man of him. Why not go on board the next morning at daylight?

He could not go back to his rooms, for on leaving the house he had taken the precaution of dropping his latch-key into his letter-box; but he was in a neighborhood of discreet hotels and he wandered on till he came to one which was known to offer a dispassionate hospitality to luggageless travelers in dress-clothes.

II

He pushed upon the swinging door and found himself in a long corridor with a tessellated floor, at the end of which, in a brightly-lit enclosure of plate-glass and mahogany, the night-clerk dozed over a copy of the *Police Gazette*. The air in the corridor was rich in reminiscences of yesterday's dinners, and a bronzed radiator poured a wave of dry heat into Woburn's face.

The night-clerk, roused by the swinging of the door, sat watching Woburn's approach with the unexpectant eye of one who has full confidence in his capacity for digesting surprises. Not that there was anything surprising in Woburn's appearance; but the night-clerk's callers were given to such imaginative flights in explaining their luggageless arrival in the small hours of the morning, that he fared habitually on fictions which would have staggered a less experienced stomach. The night-clerk, whose unwrinkled bloom showed that he throve on this high-seasoned diet, had a fancy for classifying his applicants before they could frame their explanations.

"This one's been locked out," he said to himself as he mustered Woburn.

Having exercised his powers of divination with his accustomed accuracy he listened without stirring an eye-lid to Woburn's statement; merely replying, when the latter asked the price of a room, "Two-fifty."

"Very well," said Woburn, pushing the money under the brass lattice, "I'll go up at once; and I want to be called at seven."

To this the night-clerk proffered no reply, but stretching out his hand to press an electric button, returned apathetically to the perusal of the *Police Gazette*. His summons was answered by the appearance of a man in shirt-sleeves, whose rumpled head indicated that he had recently risen from some kind of makeshift repose; to him the night-clerk tossed a key, with the brief comment, "Ninety-seven"; and the man, after a sleepy glance at Woburn, turned on his heel and lounged toward the staircase at the back of the corridor.

Woburn followed and they climbed three flights in silence. At each landing Woburn glanced down the long passage-way lit by a lowered gas-jet, with a double line of boots before the doors, waiting, like yesterday's deeds, to carry their owners so many miles farther on the morrow's destined road. On the third landing the man paused, and after examining the number on the key, turned to the left, and slouching past three or four doors, finally unlocked one and preceded Woburn into a room lit only by the upward gleam of the electric globes in the street below.

The man felt in his pockets; then he turned to Woburn. "Got a match?" he asked.

Woburn politely offered him one, and he applied it to the gas-fixture which extended its jointed arm above an ash dressing-table with a blurred mirror fixed between two standards. Having performed this office with an air of detachment designed to make Woburn recognize it as an act of supererogation, he turned without a word and vanished down the passage-way.

Woburn, after an indifferent glance about the room, which seemed to afford the amount of luxury generally obtainable for two dollars and a half in a fashionable quarter of New York, locked the door and sat down at the ink-stained writing-table in the window. Far below him lay the pallidly-lit depths of the forsaken thoroughfare. Now and then he heard the jingle of a horse-car and the ring of hoofs on the freezing pavement, or saw the lonely figure of a policeman eclipsing the illumination of the plate-glass windows on the opposite side of the street. He sat thus for a long time, his elbows on the table, his chin between his hands, till at length the contemplation of the abandoned sidewalks, above which the electric globes kept Stylites-like vigil, became intolerable to him, and he drew down the window-shade, and lit gas-fixture beside the dressing-table. Then he took a cigar from his case, and held it to the flame.

The passage from the stinging freshness of the night to the stale overheated atmosphere of the Haslemere Hotel had checked the preternaturally rapid working of his mind, and he was now scarcely conscious of thinking at all. His head was heavy, and he would have thrown himself on the bed had he not feared to oversleep the hour fixed for his departure. He thought it safest, instead, to seat himself once more by the table, in the most uncomfortable chair that he could find, and smoke one cigar after another till the first sign of dawn should give an excuse for action.

He had laid his watch on the table before him, and was gazing at the hour-hand, and trying to convince himself by so doing that he was still wide awake, when a noise in the adjoining room suddenly straightened him in his chair and banished all fear of sleep.

There was no mistaking the nature of the noise; it was that of a woman's sobs. The sobs were not loud, but the sound reached him distinctly through the frail door between the two rooms; it expressed an utter abandonment to grief; not the cloud-burst of some passing emotion, but the slow down-pour of a whole heaven of sorrow.

Woburn sat listening. There was nothing else to be done; and at least his listening was a mute tribute to the trouble he was powerless to relieve. It roused, too, the drugged pulses of his own grief: he was touched by the chance propinquity of two alien sorrows in a great city throbbing with multifarious passions. It would have been more in keeping with the irony of life had he found himself next to a mother singing her child to sleep: there seemed a mute commiseration in the hand that had led him to such neighborhood.

Gradually the sobs subsided, with pauses betokening an effort at self-control. At last they died off softly, like the intermittent drops that end a day of rain.

"Poor soul," Woburn mused, "she's got the better of it for the time. I wonder what it's all about?"

At the same moment he heard another sound that made him jump to his feet. It was a very low sound, but in that nocturnal silence which gives distinctness to the faintest noises, Woburn knew at once that he had heard the click of a pistol.

"What is she up to now?" he asked himself, with his eye on the door between the two rooms; and the brightly-lit keyhole seemed to reply with a glance of intelligence. He turned out the gas and crept to the door, pressing his eye to the illuminated circle.

After a moment or two of adjustment, during which he seemed to himself to be breathing like a steam-engine, he discerned a room like his own, with the same dressing-table flanked by gas-fixtures, and the same table in the window. This table was directly in his line of vision; and beside it stood a woman with a small revolver in her hands. The lights being behind her, Woburn could only infer her youth from her slender silhouette and the nimbus of fair hair defining her head. Her dress seemed dark and simple, and on a chair under one of the gas-jets lay a jacket edged with cheap fur and a small traveling-bag. He could not see the other end of the room, but something in her manner told him that she was alone. At length she put the revolver down and took up a letter that lay on the table. She drew the letter from its envelope and read it over two or three times; then she put it back, sealing the envelope, and placing it conspicuously against the mirror of the dressing-table.

There was so grave a significance in this dumb-show that Woburn felt sure that her next act would be to return to the table and take up the revolver; but he had not reckoned on the vanity of woman. After putting the letter in place she still lingered at the mirror, standing a little sideways, so that he could now see her face, which was distinctly pretty, but of a small and unelastic mold, inadequate to the expression of the larger emotions. For some moments she continued to study herself with the expression of a child looking at a playmate who has been scolded; then she turned to the table and lifted the revolver to her forehead.

A sudden crash made her arm drop, and sent her darting backward to the opposite side of the room. Woburn had broken down the door, and stood torn and breathless in the breach.

"Oh!" she gasped, pressing closer to the wall.

"Don't be frightened," he said; "I saw what you were going to do and I had to stop you."

She looked at him for a moment in silence, and he saw the terrified flutter of her breast; then she said, "No one can stop me for long. And besides, what right have you—"

"Every one has the right to prevent a crime," he returned, the sound of the last word sending the blood to his forehead.

"I deny it," she said passionately. "Every one who has tried to live and failed has the right to die."

"Failed in what?"

"In everything!" she replied. They stood looking at each other in silence.

At length he advanced a few steps.

"You've no right to say you've failed," he said, "while you have breath to try again." He drew the revolver from her hand.

"Try again—try again? I tell you I've tried seventy times seven!"

"What have you tried?"

She looked at him with a certain dignity.

"I don't know," she said, "that you've any right to question me —or to be in this room at all—" and suddenly she burst into tears.

The discrepancy between her words and action struck the chord which, in a man's heart, always responds to the touch of feminine unreason. She dropped into the nearest chair, hiding her face in her hands, while Woburn watched the course of her weeping.

At last she lifted her head, looking up between drenched lashes.

"Please go away," she said in childish entreaty.

"How can I?" he returned. "It's impossible that I should leave you in this state. Trust me—let me help you. Tell me what has gone wrong, and let's see if there's no other way out of it."

Woburn had a voice full of sensitive inflections, and it was now trembling with profoundest pity. Its note seemed to reassure the girl, for she said, with a beginning of confidence in her own tones, "But I don't even know who you are."

Woburn was silent: the words startled him. He moved nearer to her and went on in the same quieting tone.

"I am a man who has suffered enough to want to help others. I don't want to know any more about you than will enable me to do what I can for you. I've probably seen more of life than you have, and if you're willing to tell me your troubles perhaps together we may find a way out of them."

She dried her eyes and glanced at the revolver.

"That's the only way out," she said.

"How do you know? Are you sure you've tried every other?"

"Perfectly sure. I've written and written, and humbled myself like a slave before him, and she won't even let him answer my letters. Oh, but you don't understand"—she broke off with a renewal of weeping.

"I begin to understand—you're sorry for something you've done?"

"Oh, I've never denied that—I've never denied that I was wicked."

"And you want the forgiveness of some one you care about?"

"My husband," she whispered.

"You've done something to displease your husband?"

"To displease him? I ran away with another man!" There was a dismal exultation in her tone, as though she were paying Woburn off for having underrated her offense.

She had certainly surprised him; at worst he had expected a quarrel over a rival, with a possible complication of mother-in-law. He wondered how such helpless little feet could have taken so bold a step; then he remembered that there is no audacity like that of weakness.

He was wondering how to lead her to completer avowal when she added forlornly, "You see there's nothing else to do."

Woburn took a turn in the room. It was certainly a narrower strait than he had foreseen, and he hardly knew how to answer; but the first flow of confession had eased her, and she went on without farther persuasion.

"I don't know how I could ever have done it; I must have been downright crazy. I didn't care much for Joe when I married him—he wasn't exactly handsome, and girls think such a lot of that. But he just laid down and worshipped me, and I *was* getting fond of him in a way; only the life was so dull. I'd been used to a big city—I come from Detroit—and Hinksville is such a poky little place; that's where we lived; Joe is telegraph-operator on the railroad there. He'd have been in a much bigger place now, if he hadn't—well, after all, he behaved perfectly splendidly about *that*.

"I really was getting fond of him, and I believe I should have realized in time how good and noble and unselfish he was, if his mother hadn't been always sitting there and ever-lastingly telling me so. We learned in school about the Athenians hating some man who was always called just, and that's the way I felt about Joe. Whenever I did anything that wasn't quite right his mother would say how differently Joe would have done it. And she was forever telling me that Joe didn't approve of this and that and the other. When we were alone he approved of everything, but when his mother was round he'd sit quiet and let her say he didn't. I knew he'd let me have my way afterwards, but somehow that didn't prevent my getting mad at the time.

"And then the evenings were so long, with Joe away, and Mrs. Glenn (that's his mother) sitting there like an image knitting socks for the heathen. The only caller we ever had was the Baptist minister, and he never took any more notice of me than if I'd been a piece of furniture. I believe he was afraid to before Mrs. Glenn."

She paused breathlessly, and the tears in her eyes were now of anger.

"Well?" said Woburn gently.

"Well—then Arthur Hackett came along; he was traveling for a big publishing firm in Philadelphia. He was awfully handsome and as clever and sarcastic as anything. He used to lend me lots of novels and magazines, and tell me all about society life in New York. All the girls were after him, and Alice Sprague, whose father is the richest man in Hinksville, fell desperately in love with him and carried on like a fool; but he wouldn't take any notice of her. He never looked at anybody but me." Her face lit up with a reminiscent smile, and then clouded again. "I hate him now," she exclaimed, with a change of tone that startled Woburn. "I'd like to kill him—but he's killed me instead.

"Well, he bewitched me so I didn't know what I was doing; I was like somebody in a trance. When he wasn't there I didn't want to speak to anybody; I used to lie in bed half the day just to get away from folks; I hated Joe and Hinksville and everything else. When he came back the days went like a flash; we were together nearly all the time. I knew Joe's mother was spying on us, but I didn't care. And at last it seemed as if I couldn't let him go away again without me; so one evening he stopped at the back gate in a buggy, and we drove off together and caught the eastern express at River Bend. He promised to bring me to New York." She paused, and then added scornfully, "He didn't even do that!"

Woburn had returned to his seat and was watching her attentively. It was curious to note how her passion was spending itself in words; he saw that she would never kill herself while she had any one to talk to.

"That was five months ago," she continued, "and we traveled all through the southern states, and stayed a little while near Philadelphia, where his business is. He did things real stylishly at first. Then he was sent to Albany, and we stayed a week at the Delavan House. One afternoon I went out to do some shopping, and when I came back he was gone. He had taken his trunk with him, and hadn't left any address; but in my traveling-bag I found a fifty-dollar bill, with a slip of paper on which he had written, 'No use coming after me; I'm married.' We'd been together less than four months, and I never saw him again.

"At first I couldn't believe it. I stayed on, thinking it was a joke—or that he'd feel sorry for me and come back. But he never came and never wrote me a line. Then I began to hate him, and to see what a wicked fool I'd been to leave Joe. I was so lonesome—I thought I'd go crazy. And I kept thinking how good and patient Joe had been, and how badly I'd used him, and how lovely it would be to be back in the little parlor at Hinksville, even with Mrs. Glenn and the minister talking about free-will and predestination. So at last I wrote to Joe. I wrote him the humblest letters you ever read, one after another; but I never got any answer.

"Finally I found I'd spent all my money, so I sold my watch and my rings—Joe gave me a lovely turquoise ring when we were married—and came to New York. I felt ashamed to stay alone any longer in Albany; I was afraid that some of Arthur's friends, who had met me with him on the road, might come there and recognize me. After I got here I wrote to Susy Price, a great friend of mine who lives in Hinksville, and she answered at once, and told me just what I had expected—that Joe was ready to forgive me and crazy to have me back, but that his mother wouldn't let him stir a step or write me a line, and that she and the minister were at him all day long, telling him how bad I was and what a sin it would be to forgive me. I got Susy's letter two or three days ago, and after that I saw it was no use writing to Joe. He'll never dare go against his mother and she watches him like a cat. I suppose I deserve it—but he might have given me another chance! I know he would if he could only see me."

Her voice had dropped from anger to lamentation, and her tears again overflowed.

Woburn looked at her with the pity one feels for a child who is suddenly confronted with the result of some unpremeditated naughtiness.

"But why not go back to Hinksville," he suggested, "if your husband is ready to forgive you? You could go to your friend's house, and once your husband knows you are there you can easily persuade him to see you."

"Perhaps I could—Susy thinks I could. But I can't go back; I haven't got a cent left."

"But surely you can borrow money? Can't you ask your friend to forward you the amount of your fare?"

She shook her head.

"Susy ain't well off; she couldn't raise five dollars, and it costs twenty-five to get back to Hinksville. And besides, what would become of me while I waited for the money? They'll turn me out of here to-morrow; I haven't paid my last week's board, and I haven't got anything to give them; my bag's empty; I've pawned everything."

"And don't you know any one here who would lend you the money?"

"No; not a soul. At least I do know one gentleman; he's a friend of Arthur's, a Mr. Devine; he was staying at Rochester when we were there. I met him in the street the other day, and I didn't mean to speak to him, but he came up to me, and said he knew all about Arthur and how meanly he had behaved, and he wanted to know if he couldn't help me—I suppose he saw I was in trouble. He tried to persuade me to go and stay with his aunt, who has a lovely house right round here in Twenty-fourth Street; he must be very rich, for he offered to lend me as much money as I wanted."

"You didn't take it?"

"No," she returned; "I daresay he meant to be kind, but I didn't care to be beholden to any friend of Arthur's. He came here again yesterday, but I wouldn't see him, so he left a note giving me his aunt's address and saying she'd have a room ready for me at any time."

There was a long silence; she had dried her tears and sat looking at Woburn with eyes full of helpless reliance.

"Well," he said at length, "you did right not to take that man's money; but this isn't the only alternative," he added, pointing to the revolver.

"I don't know any other," she answered wearily. "I'm not smart enough to get employment; I can't make dresses or do type-writing, or any of the useful things they teach girls now; and besides, even if I could get work I couldn't stand the loneliness. I can never hold my head up again—I can't bear the disgrace. If I can't go back to Joe I'd rather be dead."

"And if you go back to Joe it will be all right?" Woburn suggested with a smile.

"Oh," she cried, her whole face alight, "if I could only go back to Joe!"

They were both silent again; Woburn sat with his hands in his pockets gazing at the floor. At length his silence seemed to rouse her to the unwontedness of the situation, and she rose from her seat, saying in a more constrained tone, "I don't know why I've told you all this."

"Because you believed that I would help you," Woburn answered, rising also; "and you were right; I'm going to send you home."

She colored vividly.

"You told me I was right not to take Mr. Devine's money," she faltered.

"Yes," he answered, "but did Mr. Devine want to send you home?"

"He wanted me to wait at his aunt's a little while first and then write to Joe again."

"I don't—I want you to start to-morrow morning; this morning, I mean. I'll take you to the station and buy your ticket, and your husband can send me back the money."

"Oh, I can't—I can't—you mustn't—" she stammered, reddening and paling. "Besides, they'll never let me leave here without paying."

"How much do you owe?"

"Fourteen dollars."

"Very well; I'll pay that for you; you can leave me your revolver as a pledge. But you must start by the first train; have you any idea at what time it leaves the Grand Central?"

"I think there's one at eight."

He glanced at his watch.

"In less than two hours, then; it's after six now."

She stood before him with fascinated eyes.

"You must have a very strong will," she said. "When you talk like that you make me feel as if I had to do everything you say."

"Well, you must," said Woburn lightly. "Man was made to be obeyed."

"Oh, you're not like other men," she returned; "I never heard a voice like yours; it's so strong and kind. You must be a very good man; you remind me of Joe; I'm sure you've got just such a nature; and Joe is the best man I've ever seen."

Woburn made no reply, and she rambled on, with little pauses and fresh bursts of confidence.

"Joe's a real hero, you know; he did the most splendid thing you ever heard of. I think I began to tell you about it, but I didn't finish. I'll tell you now. It happened just after we were married; I was mad with him at the time, I'm afraid, but now I see how splendid he was. He'd been telegraph-operator at Hinksville for four years and was hoping that he'd get promoted to a bigger place; but he was afraid to ask for a raise. Well, I was very sick with a bad attack of pneumonia and one night the doctor said he wasn't sure whether he could pull me through. When they sent word to Joe at the telegraph office he couldn't stand being away from me another minute. There was a poor consumptive boy always hanging round the station; Joe had taught him how to operate, just to help him along; so he left him in the office and tore home for half an hour, knowing he could get back before the eastern express came along.

"He hadn't been gone five minutes when a freight-train ran off the rails about a mile up the track. It was a very still night, and the boy heard the smash and shouting, and knew something had happened. He couldn't tell what it was, but the minute he heard it he sent a message over the wires like a flash, and caught the eastern express just as it was pulling out of the station above Hinksville. If he'd hesitated a second, or made any mistake, the express would have come on, and the loss of life would have been fearful. The next day the Hinksville papers were full of Operator Glenn's presence of mind; they all said he'd be promoted. That was early in November and Joe didn't hear anything from the company till the first of January. Meanwhile the boy had gone home to his father's farm out in the country, and before Christmas he was dead. Well, on New Year's day Joe got a notice from the company saying that his pay was to be raised, and that he was to be promoted to a big junction near Detroit, in recognition of his presence of mind in stopping the eastern express. It was just what we'd both been pining for and I was nearly wild with joy; but I noticed Joe didn't say much. He just telegraphed for leave, and the next day he went right up to Detroit and told the directors there what had really happened. When he came back he told us they'd suspended him; I cried every night for a week, and even his mother said he was a fool. After that we just lived on at Hinksville, and six months later the company took him back; but I don't suppose they'll ever promote him now."

Her voice again trembled with facile emotion.

"Wasn't it beautiful of him? Ain't he a real hero?" she said. "And I'm sure you'd behave just like him; you'd be just as gentle about little things, and you'd never move an inch about big ones. You'd never do a mean action, but you'd be sorry for people who did; I can see it in your face; that's why I trusted you right off."

Woburn's eyes were fixed on the window; he hardly seemed to hear her. At length he walked across the room and pulled up the shade. The electric lights were dissolving in the gray alembic of the dawn. A milk-cart rattled down the street and, like a witch returning late from the Sabbath, a stray cat whisked into an area. So rose the appointed day.

Woburn turned back, drawing from his pocket the roll of bills which he had thrust there with so different a purpose. He counted them out, and handed her fifteen dollars.

"That will pay for your board, including your breakfast this morning," he said. "We'll breakfast together presently if you like; and meanwhile suppose we sit down and watch the sunrise. I haven't seen it for years."

He pushed two chairs toward the window, and they sat down side by side. The light came gradually, with the icy reluctance of winter; at last a red disk pushed itself above the opposite house-tops and a long cold gleam slanted across their window. They did not talk much; there was a silencing awe in the spectacle.

Presently Woburn rose and looked again at his watch.

"I must go and cover up my dress-coat," he said, "and you had better put on your hat and jacket. We shall have to be starting in half an hour."

As he turned away she laid her hand on his arm.

"You haven't even told me your name," she said.

"No," he answered; "but if you get safely back to Joe you can call me Providence."

"But how am I to send you the money?"

"Oh—well, I'll write you a line in a day or two and give you my address; I don't know myself what it will be; I'm a wanderer on the face of the earth."

"But you must have my name if you mean to write to me."

"Well, what is your name?"

"Ruby Glenn. And I think—I almost think you might send the letter right to Joe's—send it to the Hinksville station."

"Very well."

"You promise?"

"Of course I promise."

He went back into his room, thinking how appropriate it was that she should have an absurd name like Ruby. As he re-entered the room, where the gas sickened in the daylight, it seemed to him that he was returning to some forgotten land; he had passed, with the last few hours, into a wholly new phase of consciousness. He put on his fur coat, turning up the collar and crossing the lapels to hide his white tie. Then he put his cigar-case in his pocket, turned out the gas, and, picking up his hat and stick, walked back through the open doorway.

Ruby Glenn had obediently prepared herself for departure and was standing before the mirror, patting her curls into place. Her eyes were still red, but she had the happy look of a child that has outslept its grief. On the floor he noticed the tattered fragments of the letter which, a few hours earlier, he had seen her place before the mirror.

"Shall we go down now?" he asked.

"Very well," she assented; then, with a quick movement, she stepped close to him, and putting her hands on his shoulders lifted her face to his.

"I believe you're the best man I ever knew," she said, "the very best—except Joe."

She drew back blushing deeply, and unlocked the door which led into the passage-way. Woburn picked up her bag, which she had forgotten, and followed her out of the room. They passed a frowzy chambermaid, who stared at them with a yawn. Before the doors the row of boots still waited; there was a faint new aroma of coffee mingling with the smell of vanished dinners, and a fresh blast of heat had begun to tingle through the radiators.

In the unventilated coffee-room they found a waiter who had the melancholy air of being the last survivor of an exterminated race, and who reluctantly brought them some tea made with water which had not boiled, and a supply of stale rolls and staler butter. On this meager diet they fared in silence, Woburn occasionally glancing at his watch; at length he rose, telling his companion to go and pay her bill while he called a hansom. After all, there was no use in economizing his remaining dollars.

In a few moments she joined him under the portico of the hotel. The hansom stood waiting and he sprang in after her, calling to the driver to take them to the Forty-second Street station.

When they reached the station he found a seat for her and went to buy her ticket. There were several people ahead of him at the window, and when he had bought the ticket he found that it was time to put her in the train. She rose in answer to his glance, and together they walked down the long platform in the murky chill of the roofed-in air. He followed her into the railway carriage, making sure that she had her bag, and that the ticket was safe inside it; then he held out his hand, in its pearl-colored evening glove: he felt that the people in the other seats were staring at them.

"Good-bye," he said.

"Good-bye," she answered, flushing gratefully. "I'll never forget—never. And you *will* write, won't you? Promise."

"Of course, of course," he said, hastening from the carriage.

He retraced his way along the platform, passed through the dismal waiting-room and stepped out into the early sunshine. On the sidewalk outside the station he hesitated awhile; then he strolled slowly down Forty-second Street and, skirting the melancholy flank of the Reservoir, walked across Bryant Park. Finally he sat down on one of the benches near the Sixth Avenue and lit a cigar.

The signs of life were multiplying around him; he watched the cars roll by with their increasing freight of dingy toilers, the shop-girls hurrying to their work, the children trudging schoolward, their small vague noses red with cold, their satchels clasped in woolen-gloved hands. There is nothing very imposing in the first stirring of a great city's activities; it is a slow reluctant process, like the waking of a heavy sleeper; but to Woburn's mood the sight of that obscure renewal of humble duties was more moving than the spectacle of an army with banners.

He sat for a long time, smoking the last cigar in his case, and murmuring to himself a line from Hamlet—the saddest, he thought, in the play—

For every man hath business and desire.

Suddenly an unpremeditated movement made him feel the pressure of Ruby Glenn's revolver in his pocket; it was like a devil's touch on his arm, and he sprang up hastily. In his other pocket there were just four dollars and fifty cents; but that didn't matter now. He had no thought of flight.

For a few minutes he loitered vaguely about the park; then the cold drove him on again, and with the rapidity born of a sudden resolve he began to walk down the Fifth Avenue towards his lodgings. He brushed past a maid-servant who was washing the vestibule and ran up stairs to his room. A fire was burning in the grate and his books and photographs greeted him cheerfully from the walls; the tranquil air of the whole room seemed to take it for granted that he meant to have his bath and breakfast and go down town as usual.

He threw off his coat and pulled the revolver out of his pocket; for some moments he held it curiously in his hand, bending over to examine it as Ruby Glenn had done; then he laid it in the top drawer of a small cabinet, and locking the drawer threw the key into the fire.

After that he went quietly about the usual business of his toilet. In taking off his dress-coat he noticed the Legion of Honor which Miss Talcott had given him at the ball. He pulled it out of his buttonhole and tossed it into the fire-place. When he had finished dressing he saw with surprise that it was nearly ten o'clock. Ruby Glenn was already two hours nearer home.

Woburn stood looking about the room of which he had

thought to take final leave the night before; among the ashes beneath the grate he caught sight of a little white heap which symbolized to his fancy the remains of his brief correspondence with Miss Talcott. He roused himself from this unseasonable musing and with a final glance at the familiar setting of his past, turned to face the future which the last hours had prepared for him.

He went down-stairs and stepped out of doors, hastening down the street towards Broadway as though he were late for an appointment. Every now and then he encountered an acquaintance, whom he greeted with a nod and smile; he carried his head high, and shunned no man's recognition.

At length he reached the doors of a tall granite building honeycombed with windows. He mounted the steps of the portico, and passing through the double doors of plate-glass, crossed a vestibule floored with mosaic to another glass door on which was emblazoned the name of the firm.

This door he also opened, entering a large room with wainscotted subdivisions, behind which appeared the stooping shoulders of a row of clerks.

As Woburn crossed the threshold a gray-haired man emerged from an inner office at the opposite end of the room.

At sight of Woburn he stopped short.

"Mr. Woburn!" he exclaimed; then he stepped nearer and added in a low tone: "I was requested to tell you when you came that the members of the firm are waiting; will you step into the private office?"

A JOURNEY

As SHE lay in her berth, staring at the shadows overhead, the rush of the wheels was in her brain, driving her deeper and deeper into circles of wakeful lucidity. The sleeping-car had sunk into its night-silence. Through the wet window-pane she watched the sudden lights, the long stretches of hurrying blackness. Now and then she turned her head and looked through the opening in the hangings at her husband's curtains across the aisle...

She wondered restlessly if he wanted anything and if she could hear him if he called. His voice had grown very weak within the last months and it irritated him when she did not hear. This irritability, this increasing childish petulance seemed to give expression to their imperceptible estrangement. Like two faces looking at one another through a sheet of glass they were close together, almost touching, but they could not hear or feel each other: the conductivity between them was broken. She, at least, had this sense of separation, and she fancied sometimes that she saw it reflected in the look with which he supplemented his failing words. Doubtless the fault was hers. She was too impenetrably healthy to be touched by the irrelevancies of disease. Her self-reproachful tenderness was tinged with the sense of his irrationality: she had a vague feeling that there was a purpose in his helpless tyrannies. The suddenness of the change had found her so unprepared. A year ago their pulses had beat to one robust measure; both had the same prodigal confidence in an exhaustless future. Now their energies no longer kept step: hers still bounded ahead of life, preempting unclaimed regions of hope and activity, while his lagged behind, vainly struggling to overtake her.

When they married, she had such arrears of living to make up: her days had been as bare as the white-washed school-room where she forced innutritious facts upon reluctant children. His coming had broken in on the slumber of circumstance, widening the present till it became the encloser of remotest chances. But imperceptibly the horizon narrowed. Life had a grudge against her: she was never to be allowed to spread her wings.

At first the doctors had said that six weeks of mild air would set him right; but when he came back this assurance was explained as having of course included a winter in a dry climate. They gave up their pretty house, storing the wedding presents and new furniture, and went to Colorado. She had hated it there from the first. Nobody knew her or cared about her; there was no one to wonder at the good match she had made, or to envy her the new dresses and the visiting-cards which were still a surprise to her. And he kept growing worse. She felt herself beset with difficulties too evasive to be fought by so direct a temperament. She still loved him, of course; but he was gradually, undefinably ceasing to be himself. The man she had married had been strong, active, gently masterful: the male whose pleasure it is to clear a way through the material obstructions of life; but now it was she who was the protector, he who must be shielded from importunities and given his drops or his beef-juice though the skies were falling. The routine of the sick-room bewildered her; this punctual administering of medicine seemed as idle as some uncomprehended religious mummery.

There were moments, indeed, when warm gushes of pity swept away her instinctive resentment of his condition, when she still found his old self in his eyes as they groped for each other through the dense medium of his weakness. But these moments had grown rare. Sometimes he frightened her: his sunken expressionless face seemed that of a stranger; his voice was weak and hoarse; his thin-lipped smile a mere muscular contraction. Her hand avoided his damp soft skin, which had lost the familiar roughness of health: she caught herself furtively watching him as she might have watched a strange animal. It frightened her to feel that this was the man she loved; there were hours when to tell him what she suffered seemed the one escape from her fears. But in general she judged herself more leniently, reflecting that she had perhaps been too long alone with him, and that she would feel differently when they were at home again, surrounded by her robust and buoyant family. How she had rejoiced when the doctors at last gave their consent to his going home! She knew, of course, what the decision meant; they both knew. It meant that he was to die; but they dressed the truth in hopeful euphuisms, and at times, in the joy of preparation, she really forgot the purpose of their journey, and slipped into an eager allusion to next year's plans.

At last the day of leaving came. She had a dreadful fear that they would never get away; that somehow at the last moment he would fail her; that the doctors held one of their accustomed treacheries in reserve; but nothing happened. They drove to the station, he was installed in a seat with a rug over his knees and a cushion at his back, and she hung out of the window waving unregretful farewells to the acquaintances she had really never liked till then.

The first twenty-four hours had passed off well. He revived a little and it amused him to look out of the window and to observe the humors of the car. The second day he began to grow weary and to chafe under the dispassionate stare of the freckled child with the lump of chewing-gum. She had to explain to the child's mother that her husband was too ill to be disturbed: a statement received by that lady with a resentment visibly supported by the maternal sentiment of the whole car. . . .

That night he slept badly and the next morning his temperature frightened her: she was sure he was growing worse. The day passed slowly, punctuated by the small irritations of travel. Watching his tired face, she traced in its contractions every rattle and jolt of the train, till her own body vibrated with sympathetic fatigue. She felt the others observing him too, and hovered restlessly between him and the line of interrogative eyes. The freckled child hung about him like a fly; offers of candy and picture-books failed to dislodge her: she twisted one leg around the other and watched him imperturbably. The porter, as he passed, lingered with vague proffers of help, probably inspired by philanthropic passengers swelling with the sense that "something ought to be done"; and one nervous man in a skull-cap was audibly concerned as to the possible effect on his wife's health.

The hours dragged on in a dreary inoccupation. Towards dusk she sat down beside him and he laid his hand on hers. The touch startled her. He seemed to be calling her from far off. She looked at him helplessly and his smile went through her like a physical pang.

"Are you very tired?" she asked.

"No, not very."

"We'll be there soon now."

"Yes, very soon."

"This time to-morrow—"

He nodded and they sat silent. When she had put him to bed and crawled into her own berth she tried to cheer herself with the thought that in less than twenty-four hours they would be in New York. Her people would all be at the station to meet her—she pictured their round unanxious faces pressing through the crowd. She only hoped they would not tell him too loudly that he was looking splendidly and would be all right in no time: the subtler sympathies developed by long contact with suffering were making her aware of a certain coarseness of texture in the family sensibilities.

Suddenly she thought she heard him call. She parted the curtains and listened. No, it was only a man snoring at the other end of the car. His snores had a greasy sound, as though they passed through tallow. She lay down and tried to sleep...Had she not heard him move? She started up trembling...The silence frightened her more than any sound. He might not be able to make her hear—he might be calling her now...What made her think of such things? It was merely the familiar tendency of an over-tired mind to fasten itself on the most intolerable chance within the range of its forebodings... Putting her head out, she listened; but she could not distinguish his breathing from that of the other pairs of lungs about her. She longed to get up and look at him, but she knew the impulse was a mere vent for her restlessness, and the fear of disturbing him restrained her.... The regular movement of his curtain reassured her, she knew not why; she remembered that he had wished her a cheerful good-night; and the sheer inability to endure her fears a moment longer made her put them from her with an effort of her whole sound tired body. She turned on her side and slept.

She sat up stiffly, staring out at the dawn. The train was rushing through a region of bare hillocks huddled against a lifeless sky. It looked like the first day of creation. The air of the car was close, and she pushed up her window to let in the keen wind. Then she looked at her watch: it was seven o'clock, and soon the people about her would be stirring. She slipped into her clothes, smoothed her disheveled hair and crept to the dressing-room. When she had washed her face and adjusted her dress she felt more hopeful. It was always a struggle for her not to be cheerful in the morning. Her cheeks burned deliciously under the coarse towel and the wet hair about her temples broke into strong upward tendrils. Every inch of her was full of life and elasticity. And in ten hours they would be at home!

She stepped to her husband's berth: it was time for him to take his early glass of milk. The window-shade was down, and in the dusk of the curtained enclosure she could just see that he lay sideways, with his face away from her. She leaned over him and drew up the shade. As she did so she touched one of his hands. It felt cold...

She bent closer, laying her hand on his arm and calling him by name. He did not move. She spoke again more loudly; she grasped his shoulder and gently shook it. He lay motionless. She caught hold of his hand again: it slipped from her limply, like a dead thing. A dead thing?... Her breath caught. She must see his face. She leaned forward, and hurriedly, shrinkingly, with a sick-ening reluctance of the flesh, laid her hands on his shoulders and turned him over. His head fell back; his face looked small and smooth; he gazed at her with steady eyes.

She remained motionless for a long time, holding him thus; and they looked at each other. Suddenly she shrank back: the longing to scream, to call out, to fly from him, had almost over-powered her. But a strong hand arrested her. Good God! If it were known that he was dead they would be put off the train at the next station—

In a terrifying flash of remembrance there arose before her a scene she had once witnessed in traveling, when a husband and wife, whose child had died in the train, had been thrust out at some chance station. She saw them standing on the platform with the child's body between them; she had never forgotten the dazed look with which they followed the receding train. And this was what would happen to her. Within the next hour she might find herself on the platform of some strange station, alone with her husband's body.... Anything but that! It was too horrible— She quivered like a creature at bay.

As she cowered there, she felt the train moving more slowly. It was coming then—they were approaching a station! She saw again the husband and wife standing on the lonely platform; and with a violent gesture she drew down the shade to hide her hus-band's face.

Feeling dizzy, she sank down on the edge of the berth, keeping away from his outstretched body, and pulling the curtains close, so that he and she were shut into a kind of sepulchral twilight. She tried to think. At all costs she must conceal the fact that he was dead. But how? Her mind refused to act: she could not plan, com-bine. She could think of no way but to sit there, clutching the cur-tains, all day long...

She heard the porter making up her bed; people were beginning to move about the car; the dressing-room door was being opened and shut. She tried to rouse herself. At length with a supreme effort she rose to her feet, stepping into the aisle of the car and drawing the curtains tight behind her. She noticed that they still parted slightly with the motion of the car, and finding a pin in her dress she fastened them together. Now she was safe. She looked round and saw the porter. She fancied he was watching her.

"Ain't he awake yet?" he inquired.

"No," she faltered.

"I got his milk all ready when he wants it. You know you told me to have it for him by seven."

She nodded silently and crept into her seat.

At half-past eight the train reached Buffalo. By this time the other passengers were dressed and the berths had been folded back for the day. The porter, moving to and fro under his burden of sheets and pillows, glanced at her as he passed. At length he said: "Ain't he going to get up? You know we're ordered to make up the berths as early as we can."

She turned cold with fear. They were just entering the station.

"Oh, not yet," she stammered. "Not till he's had his milk. Won't you get it, please?"

"All right. Soon as we start again."

When the train moved on he reappeared with the milk. She took it from him and sat vaguely looking at it: her brain moved slowly from one idea to another, as though they were stepping-stones set far apart across a whirling flood. At length she became aware that the porter still hovered expectantly.

"Will I give it to him?" he suggested.

"Oh, no," she cried, rising. "He—he's asleep yet, I think—"

She waited till the porter had passed on; then she unpinned the curtains and slipped behind them. In the semi-obscurity her husband's face stared up at her like a marble mask with agate eyes. The eyes were dreadful. She put out her hand and drew down the lids. Then she remembered the glass of milk in her other hand: what was she to do with it? She thought of raising the window and throwing it out; but to do so she would have to lean across his body and bring her face close to his. She decided to drink the milk.

She returned to her seat with the empty glass and after a while the porter came back to get it.

"When'll I fold up his bed?" he asked.

"Oh, not now—not yet; he's ill—he's very ill. Can't you let him stay as he is? The doctor wants him to lie down as much as possible."

He scratched his head. "Well, if he's *really* sick—"

He took the empty glass and walked away, explaining to the passengers that the party behind the curtains was too sick to get up just yet.

She found herself the center of sympathetic eyes. A motherly woman with an intimate smile sat down beside her.

"I'm real sorry to hear your husband's sick. I've had a remarkable amount of sickness in my family and maybe I could assist you. Can I take a look at him?"

"Oh, no—no, please! He mustn't be disturbed."

The lady accepted the rebuff indulgently.

"Well, it's just as you say, of course, but you don't look to me as if you'd had much experience in sickness and I'd have been glad to assist you. What do you generally do when your husband's taken this way?"

"I—I let him sleep."

"Too much sleep ain't any too healthful either. Don't you give him any medicine?"

"Y—yes."

"Don't you wake him to take it?"

"Yes."

"When does he take the next dose?"

"Not for—two hours—"

The lady looked disappointed. "Well, if I was you I'd try giving it oftener. That's what I do with my folks."

After that many faces seemed to press upon her. The passengers were on their way to the dining-car, and she was conscious that as they passed down the aisle they glanced curiously at the closed curtains. One lantern-jawed man with prominent eyes stood still and tried to shoot his projecting glance through the division be-tween the folds. The freckled child, returning from breakfast, waylaid the passers with a buttery clutch, saying in a loud whisper, "He's sick"; and once the conductor came by, asking for tickets. She shrank into her corner and looked out of the window at the flying trees and houses, meaningless hieroglyphs of an endlessly unrolled papyrus.

Now and then the train stopped, and the newcomers on enter-ing the car stared in turn at the closed curtains. More and more people seemed to pass—their faces began to blend fantastically with the images surging in her brain...

Later in the day a fat man detached himself from the mist of faces. He had a creased stomach and soft pale lips. As he pressed himself into the seat facing her she noticed that he was dressed in black broadcloth, with a soiled white tie.

"Husband's pretty bad this morning, is he?"

"Yes."

"Dear, dear! Now that's terribly distressing, ain't it?" An apos-tolic smile revealed his gold-filled teeth. "Of course you know there's no sech thing as sickness. Ain't that a lovely thought? Death itself is but a deloosion of our grosser senses. On'y lay yourself open to the influx of the sperrit, submit yourself passively to the action of the divine force, and disease and dissolution will cease to exist for you. If you could indooce your husband to read this little pamphlet—"

The faces about her again grew indistinct. She had a vague rec-ollection of hearing the motherly lady and the parent of the freck-led child ardently disputing the relative advantages of trying several medicines at once, or of taking each in turn; the motherly lady maintaining that the competitive system saved time; the other objecting that you couldn't tell which remedy had effected the cure; their voices went on and on, like bell-buoys droning through a fog... The porter came up now and then with ques-tions that she did not understand, but that somehow she must have answered since he went away again without repeating them;

every two hours the motherly lady reminded her that her husband ought to have his drops; people left the car and others replaced them...

Her head was spinning and she tried to steady herself by clutching at her thoughts as they swept by, but they slipped away from her like bushes on the side of a sheer precipice down which she seemed to be falling. Suddenly her mind grew clear again and she found herself vividly picturing what would happen when the train reached New York. She shuddered as it occurred to her that he would be quite cold and that some one might perceive he had been dead since morning.

She thought hurriedly:—"If they see I am not surprised they will suspect something. They will ask questions, and if I tell them the truth they won't believe me—no one would believe me! It will be terrible"—and she kept repeating to herself:—"I must pretend I don't know. I must pretend I don't know. When they open the curtains I must go up to him quite naturally—and then I must scream."... She had an idea that the scream would be very hard to do.

Gradually new thoughts crowded upon her, vivid and urgent: she tried to separate and restrain them, but they beset her clamorously, like her school-children at the end of a hot day, when she was too tired to silence them. Her head grew confused, and she felt a sick fear of forgetting her part, of betraying herself by some unguarded word or look.

"I must pretend I don't know," she went on murmuring. The words had lost their significance, but she repeated them mechanically, as though they had been a magic formula, until suddenly she heard herself saying: "I can't remember, I can't remember!"

Her voice sounded very loud, and she looked about her in terror; but no one seemed to notice that she had spoken.

As she glanced down the car her eye caught the curtains of her husband's berth, and she began to examine the monotonous arabesques woven through their heavy folds. The pattern was intricate and difficult to trace; she gazed fixedly at the curtains and as she did so the thick stuff grew transparent and through it she saw her husband's face—his dead face. She struggled to avert her look, but her eyes refused to move and her head seemed to be held in a vise. At last, with an effort that left her weak and shaking, she turned away; but it was of no use; close in front of her, small and smooth, was her husband's face. It seemed to be suspended in the air between her and the false braids of the woman who sat in front of her. With an uncontrollable gesture she stretched out her hand to push the face away, and suddenly she felt the touch of his smooth skin. She repressed a cry and half started from her seat. The woman with the false braids looked around, and feeling that she must justify her movement in some way she rose and lifted her traveling-bag from the opposite seat. She unlocked the bag and looked into it; but the first object her hand met was a small flask of her husband's, thrust there at the last moment, in the haste of departure. She locked the bag and closed her eyes . . . his face was there again, hanging between her eye-balls and lids like a waxen mask against a red curtain . . .

She roused herself with a shiver. Had she fainted or slept? Hours seemed to have elapsed; but it was still broad day, and the people about her were sitting in the same attitudes as before.

A sudden sense of hunger made her aware that she had eaten nothing since morning. The thought of food filled her with disgust, but she dreaded a return of faintness, and remembering that she had some biscuits in her bag she took one out and ate it. The dry crumbs choked her, and she hastily swallowed a little brandy from her husband's flask. The burning sensation in her throat acted as a counter-irritant, momentarily relieving the dull ache of her nerves. Then she felt a gently-stealing warmth, as though a soft air fanned her, and the swarming fears relaxed their clutch, receding through the stillness that enclosed her, a stillness soothing as the spacious quietude of a summer day. She slept.

Through her sleep she felt the impetuous rush of the train. It seemed to be life itself that was sweeping her on with head-long inexorable force—sweeping her into darkness and terror, and the awe of unknown days.—Now all at once everything was still—not a sound, not a pulsation... She was dead in her turn, and lay beside him with smooth upstaring face. How quiet it was!—and yet she heard feet coming, the feet of the men who were to carry them away... She could feel too—she felt a sudden prolonged vibration, a series of hard shocks, and then another plunge into darkness: the darkness of death this time—a black whirlwind on which they were both spinning like leaves, in wild uncoiling spirals, with millions and millions of the dead...

She sprang up in terror. Her sleep must have lasted a long time, for the winter day had paled and the lights had been lit. The car was in confusion, and as she regained her self-possession she saw that the passengers were gathering up their wraps and bags. The woman with the false braids had brought from the dressing-room a sickly ivy-plant in a bottle, and the Christian Scientist was reversing his cuffs. The porter passed down the aisle with his impartial brush. An impersonal figure with a gold-banded cap asked for her husband's ticket. A voice shouted "Baig-gage *ex*press!" and she heard the clicking of metal as the passengers handed over their checks.

Presently her window was blocked by an expanse of sooty wall, and the train passed into the Harlem tunnel. The journey was over; in a few minutes she would see her family pushing their joyous way through the throng at the station. Her heart dilated. The worst terror was past...

"We'd better get him up now, hadn't we?" asked the porter, touching her arm.

He had her husband's hat in his hand and was meditatively revolving it under his brush.

She looked at the hat and tried to speak; but suddenly the car grew dark. She flung up her arms, struggling to catch at something, and fell face downward, striking her head against the dead man's berth.

THE REMBRANDT

"YOU'RE *so* artistic," my cousin Eleanor Copt began.

Of all Eleanor's exordiums it is the one I most dread. When she tells me I'm so clever I know this is merely the preamble to inviting me to meet the last literary obscurity of the moment: a trial to be evaded or endured, as circumstances dictate; whereas her calling me artistic fatally connotes the request to visit, in her company, some distressed gentlewoman whose future hangs on my valuation of her old Saxe or of her grandfather's Marc Antonios. Time was when I attempted to resist these compulsions of Eleanor's; but I soon learned that, short of actual flight, there was no refuge from her beneficent despotism. It is not always easy for the curator of a museum to abandon his post on the plea of escaping a pretty cousin's importunities; and Eleanor, aware of my predicament, is none too magnanimous to take advantage of it. Magnanimity is, in fact, not in Eleanor's line. The virtues, she once explained to me, are like bonnets: the very ones that look best on other people may not happen to suit one's own particular style; and she added, with a slight deflection of metaphor, that none of the ready-made virtues ever *had* fitted her: they all pinched somewhere, and she'd given up trying to wear them.

Therefore when she said to me, "You're *so* artistic," emphasizing the conjunction with a tap of her dripping umbrella (Eleanor is out in all weathers: the elements are as powerless against her as man), I merely stipulated, "It's not old Saxe again?"

She shook her head reassuringly. "A picture—a Rembrandt!"

"Good Lord! Why not a Leonardo?"

"Well"—she smiled—"that, of course, depends on *you*."

"On me?"

"On your attribution. I dare say Mrs. Fontage would consent to the change—though she's very conservative."

A gleam of hope came to me and I pronounced: "One can't judge of a picture in this weather."

"Of course not. I'm coming for you to-morrow."

"I've an engagement to-morrow."

"I'll come before or after your engagement."

The afternoon paper lay at my elbow and I contrived a furtive consultation of the weather-report. It said "Rain to-morrow," and I answered briskly: "All right, then; come at ten"—rapidly calculating that the clouds on which I counted might lift by noon.

My ingenuity failed of its due reward; for the heavens, as if in league with my cousin, emptied themselves before morning, and punctually at ten Eleanor and the sun appeared together in my office.

I hardly listened, as we descended the Museum steps and got into Eleanor's hansom, to her vivid summing-up of the case. I guessed beforehand that the lady we were about to visit had lapsed by the most distressful degrees from opulence to a "hall-bedroom"; that her grandfather, if he had not been Minister to France, had signed the Declaration of Independence; that the Rembrandt was an heirloom, sole remnant of disbanded treasures; that for years its possessor had been unwilling to part with it, and that even now the question of its disposal must be approached with the most diplomatic obliquity.

Previous experience had taught me that all Eleanor's "cases" presented a harrowing similarity of detail. No circumstance tending to excite the spectator's sympathy and involve his action was omitted from the history of her beneficiaries; the lights and shades were indeed so skillfully adjusted that any impartial expression of opinion took on the hue of cruelty. I could have produced closetfuls of "heirlooms" in attestation of this fact; for it is one more mark of Eleanor's competence that her friends usually pay the interest on her philanthropy. My one hope was that in this case the object, being a picture, might reasonably be rated beyond my means; and as our cab drew up before a blistered brown-stone door-step I formed the self-defensive resolve to place an extreme valuation on Mrs. Fontage's Rembrandt. It is Eleanor's fault if she is sometimes fought with her own weapons.

The house stood in one of those shabby provisional-looking New York streets that seem resignedly awaiting demolition. It was the kind of house that, in its high days, must have had a bow-window with a bronze in it. The bow-window had been replaced by a plumber's *devanture*, and one might conceive the bronze to have gravitated to the limbo where Mexican onyx tables and bric-à-brac in buffalo-horn await the first signs of our next aesthetic reaction.

Eleanor swept me through a hall that smelled of poverty, up unlit stairs to a bare slit of a room. "And she must leave this in a month!" she whispered across her knock.

I had prepared myself for the limp widow's weed of a woman that one figures in such a setting; and confronted abruptly with Mrs. Fontage's white-haired erectness I had the disconcerting sense that I was somehow in her presence at my own solicitation. I instinctively charged Eleanor with this reversal of the situation; but a moment later I saw it must be ascribed to a something about Mrs. Fontage that precluded the possibility of her asking any one a favor. It was not that she was of forbidding, or even majestic, demeanor; but that one guessed, under her aquiline prettiness, a dignity nervously on guard against the petty betrayal of her surroundings. The room was unconcealably poor: the little faded "relics," the high-stocked ancestral silhouettes, the steel-engravings after Raphael and Correggio, grouped in a vain attempt to hide the most obvious stains on the wall-paper, served only to accentuate the contrast of a past evidently diversified by foreign travel and the enjoyment of the arts. Even Mrs. Fontage's dress had the air of being a last expedient, the ultimate outcome of a much-taxed ingenuity in darning and turning. One felt that all the poor lady's barriers were falling save that of her impregnable manner.

To this manner I found myself conveying my appreciation of being admitted to a view of the Rembrandt.

Mrs. Fontage's smile took my homage for granted. "It is always," she conceded, "a privilege to be in the presence of the great masters." Her slim wrinkled hand waved me to a dusky canvas near the window.

"It's *so* interesting, dear Mrs. Fontage," I heard Eleanor exclaiming, "and my cousin will be able to tell you exactly—" Eleanor, in my presence, always admits that she knows nothing about art; but she gives the impression that this is merely because she hasn't had time to look into the matter—and has had me to do it for her.

Mrs. Fontage seated herself without speaking, as though fearful that a breath might disturb my communion with the masterpiece. I felt that she thought Eleanor's reassuring ejaculations ill-timed; and in this I was of one mind with her; for the impossibility of telling her exactly what I thought of her Rembrandt had become clear to me at a glance.

My cousin's vivacities began to languish and the silence seemed to shape itself into a receptacle for my verdict. I stepped back, affecting a more distant scrutiny; and as I did so my eye caught Mrs. Fontage's profile. Her lids trembled slightly. I took refuge in the familiar expedient of asking the history of the picture, and she waved me brightly to a seat.

This was indeed a topic on which she could dilate. The Rembrandt, it appeared, had come into Mr. Fontage's possession many years ago, while the young couple were on their wedding-tour, and under circumstances so romantic that she made no excuse for relating them in all their parenthetic fullness. The picture belonged to an old Belgian Countess of redundant quarterings, whom the extravagances of an ungovernable nephew had compelled to part with her possessions (in the most private manner) about the time of the Fontages' arrival. By a really remarkable coincidence, it happened that their courier (an exceptionally intelligent and superior man) was an old servant of the Countess's, and had thus been able to put them in the way of securing the Rembrandt under the very nose of an English Duke, whose agent had been sent to Brussels to negotiate for its purchase. Mrs. Fontage could not recall the Duke's name, but he was a great collector and had a famous Highland castle, where somebody had been murdered, and which she herself had visited (by moonlight) when she had traveled in Scotland as a girl. The episode had in short been one of the most interesting "experiences" of a tour almost chromo-lithographic in vivacity of impression; and they had always meant to go back to Brussels for the sake of reliving so picturesque a moment. Circumstances (of which the narrator's surroundings declared the nature) had persistently interfered with the projected return to Europe, and the picture had grown doubly valuable as representing the high-water mark of their artistic emotions. Mrs. Fontage's moist eye caressed the canvas. "There is only," she added with a perceptible effort, "one slight drawback: the picture is not signed. But for that the Countess, of course, would have sold it to a museum. All the connoisseurs who have seen it pronounce it an undoubted Rembrandt, in the artist's best manner; but the museums"—she arched her brows in smiling recognition of a well-known weakness—"give the preference to signed examples—"

Mrs. Fontage's words evoked so touching a vision of the young tourists of fifty years ago, entrusting to an accomplished and versatile courier the direction of their helpless zeal for art, that I lost sight for a moment of the point at issue. The old Belgian Countess, the wealthy Duke with a feudal castle in Scotland, Mrs. Fontage's own maiden pilgrimage to Arthur's Seat and Holyrood, all the accessories of the naïf transaction, seemed a part of that vanished Europe to which our young race carried its indiscriminate ardors, its tender romantic credulity: the legendary castellated Europe of keep-sakes, brigands and old masters, that compensated, by one such "experience" as Mrs. Fontage's, for an after-life of aesthetic privation.

I was restored to the present by Eleanor's looking at her watch. The action mutely conveyed that something was expected of me. I risked the temporizing statement that the picture was very interesting; but Mrs. Fontage's polite assent revealed the poverty of the expedient. Eleanor's impatience overflowed.

"You would like my cousin to give you an idea of its value?" she suggested.

Mrs. Fontage grew more erect. "No one," she corrected with great gentleness, "can know its value quite as well as I, who live with it—"

We murmured our hasty concurrence.

"But it might be interesting to hear"—she addressed herself to me—"as a mere matter of curiosity—what estimate would be put on it from the purely commercial point of view—if such a term may be used in speaking of a work of art."

I sounded a note of deprecation.

"Oh, I understand, of course," she delicately anticipated me, "that that could never be *your* view, your personal view; but since occasions *may* arise—do arise—when it becomes necessary to—to put a price on the priceless, as it were—I have thought—Miss Copt has suggested—"

"Some day," Eleanor encouraged her, "you might feel that the picture ought to belong to some one who has more—more opportunity of showing it—letting it be seen by the public—for educational reasons—"

"I have tried," Mrs. Fontage admitted, "to see it in that light."

The crucial moment was upon me. To escape the challenge of Mrs. Fontage's brilliant composure I turned once more to the picture. If my courage needed reinforcement, the picture amply furnished it. Looking at that lamentable canvas seemed the surest way of gathering strength to denounce it; but behind me, all the while, I felt Mrs. Fontage's shuddering pride drawn up in a final effort of self-defense. I hated myself for my sentimental perversion of the situation. Reason argued that it was more cruel to deceive Mrs. Fontage than to tell her the truth; but that merely proved the inferiority of reason to instinct in situations involving any concession to the emotions. Along with her faith in the Rembrandt I must destroy not only the whole fabric of Mrs. Fontage's past, but even that life-long habit of acquiescence in untested formulas that makes the best part of the average feminine strength. I guessed the episode of the picture to be inextricably interwoven with the traditions and convictions which served to veil Mrs. Fontage's destitution not only from others but from herself. Viewed in that light the Rembrandt had perhaps been worth its purchase-money; and I regretted that works of art do not commonly sell on the merit of the moral support they may have rendered.

From this unavailing flight I was recalled by the sense that something must be done. To place a fictitious value on the picture was at best a provisional measure; while the brutal alternative of advising Mrs. Fontage to sell it for a hundred dollars at least afforded an opening to the charitably disposed purchaser. I intended, if other resources failed, to put myself forward in that light; but delicacy of course forbade my coupling my unflattering estimate of the Rembrandt with an immediate offer to buy it. All I could do was to inflict the wound: the healing unguent must be withheld for later application.

I turned to Mrs. Fontage, who sat motionless, her finely-lined cheeks touched with an expectant color, her eyes averted from the picture which was so evidently the one object they beheld.

"My dear madam—" I began. Her vivid smile was like a light held up to dazzle me. It shrouded every alternative in darkness and I had the flurried sense of having lost my way among the intricacies of my contention. Of a sudden I felt the hopelessness of finding a crack in her impenetrable conviction. My words slipped from me like broken weapons. "The picture," I faltered, "would of course be worth more if it were signed. As it is, I—I hardly think —on a conservative estimate—it can be valued at—at more— than—a thousand dollars, say—"

My deflected argument ran on somewhat aimlessly till it found itself plunging full tilt against the barrier of Mrs. Fontage's silence. She sat as impassive as though I had not spoken. Eleanor loosed a few fluttering words of congratulation and encouragement, but their flight was suddenly cut short. Mrs. Fontage had risen with a certain solemnity.

"I could never," she said gently—her gentleness was adamantine—"under any circumstances whatever, consider, for a moment even, the possibility of parting with the picture at such a price."

II

Within three weeks a tremulous note from Mrs. Fontage requested the favor of another visit. If the writing was tremulous, however, the writer's tone was firm. She named her own day and hour, without the conventional reference to her visitor's convenience.

My first impulse was to turn the note over to Eleanor. I had acquitted myself of my share in the ungrateful business of coming to Mrs. Fontage's aid, and if, as her letter denoted, she had now yielded to the closer pressure of need, the business of finding a purchaser for the Rembrandt might well be left to my cousin's ingenuity. But here conscience put in the uncomfortable reminder that it was I who, in putting a price on the picture, had raised the real obstacle in the way of Mrs. Fontage's rescue. No one would give a thousand dollars for the Rembrandt; but to tell Mrs. Fontage so had become as unthinkable as murder. I had, in fact, on returning from my first inspection of the picture, refrained from imparting to Eleanor my opinion of its value. Eleanor is porous, and I knew that sooner or later the unnecessary truth would exude through the loose texture of her dissimulation. Not infrequently she thus creates the misery she alleviates; and I have sometimes suspected her of paining people in order that she might be sorry for them. I had, at all events, cut off retreat in Eleanor's direction; and the remaining alternative carried me straight to Mrs. Fontage.

She received me with the same commanding sweetness. The room was even barer than before—I believe the carpet was gone —but her manner built up about her a palace to which I was welcomed with high state; and it was as a mere incident of the ceremony that I was presently made aware of her decision to sell the Rembrandt. My previous unsuccess in planning how to deal with Mrs. Fontage had warned me to leave my farther course to chance; and I listened to her explanation with complete detachment. She had resolved to travel for her health; her doctor advised it, and as her absence might be indefinitely prolonged she had reluctantly decided to part with the picture in order to avoid the expense of storage and insurance. Her voice drooped at the admission, and she hurried on, detailing the vague itinerary of a journey that was to combine long-promised visits to impatient friends with various "interesting opportunities" less definitely specified. The poor lady's skill in rearing a screen of verbiage about her enforced avowal had distracted me from my own share in the situation, and it was with dismay that I suddenly caught the drift of her assumptions. She expected me to buy the Rembrandt for the Museum; she had taken my previous valuation as a tentative bid, and when I came to my senses she was in the act of accepting my offer.

Had I had a thousand dollars of my own to dispose of, the bargain would have been concluded on the spot; but I was in the impossible position of being materially unable to buy the picture and morally unable to tell her that it was not worth acquiring for the Museum.

I dashed into the first evasion in sight. I had no authority, I explained, to purchase pictures for the Museum without the consent of the committee.

Mrs. Fontage coped for a moment in silence with the incredible fact that I had rejected her offer; then she ventured, with a kind of pale precipitation: "But I understood—Miss Copt tells me that you practically decide such matters for the committee." I could guess what the effort had cost her.

"My cousin is given to generalizations. My opinion may have some weight with the committee—"

"Well, then—" she timidly prompted.

"For that very reason I can't buy the picture."

She said, with a drooping note, "I don't understand."

"Yet you told me," I reminded her, "that you knew museums didn't buy unsigned pictures."

"Not for what they are worth! Every one knows that. But I—I understood—the price you named—" Her pride shuddered back from the abasement. "It's a misunderstanding then," she faltered.

To avoid looking at her, I glanced desperately at the Rembrandt. Could I—? But reason rejected the possibility. Even if the committee had been blind—and they all *were* but Crozier—I simply shouldn't have dared to do it. I stood up, feeling that to cut the matter short was the only alleviation within reach.

Mrs. Fontage had summoned her indomitable smile; but its brilliancy dropped, as I opened the door, like a candle blown out by a draft.

"If there's any one else—if you knew any one who would care to see the picture, I should be most happy—" She kept her eyes on me, and I saw that, in her case, it hurt less than to look at the Rembrandt. "I shall have to leave here, you know," she panted, "if nobody cares to have it—"

III

That evening at my club I had just succeeded in losing sight of Mrs. Fontage in the fumes of an excellent cigar, when a voice at my elbow evoked her harassing image.

"I want to talk to you," the speaker said, "about Mrs. Fontage's Rembrandt."

"There isn't any," I was about to growl; but looking up I recognized the confiding countenance of Mr. Jefferson Rose.

Mr. Rose was known to me chiefly as a young man suffused with a vague enthusiasm for Virtue and my cousin Eleanor.

One glance at his glossy exterior conveyed the assurance that his morals were as immaculate as his complexion and his linen. Goodness exuded from his moist eye, his liquid voice, the warm damp pressure of his trustful hand. He had always struck me as one of the most uncomplicated organisms I had ever met. His ideas were as simple and inconsecutive as the propositions in a primer, and he spoke slowly, with a kind of uniformity of emphasis that made his words stand out like the raised type for the blind. An obvious incapacity for abstract conceptions made him peculiarly susceptible to the magic of generalization, and one felt he would have been at the mercy of any Cause that spelled itself with a capital letter. It was hard to explain how, with such a superabundance of merit, he managed to be a good fellow: I can only say that he performed the astonishing feat as naturally as he supported an invalid mother and two sisters on the slender salary of a banker's clerk. He sat down beside me with an air of bright expectancy.

"It's a remarkable picture, isn't it?" he said.

"You've seen it?"

"I've been so fortunate. Miss Copt was kind enough to get Mrs. Fontage's permission; we went this afternoon."

I inwardly wished that Eleanor had selected another victim; unless indeed the visit were part of a plan whereby some third person, better equipped for the cultivation of delusions, was to be made to think the Rembrandt remarkable. Knowing the limitations of Mr. Rose's resources I began to wonder if he had any rich aunts.

"And her buying it in that way, too," he went on with his limpid smile, "from that old Countess in Brussels, makes it all the more interesting, doesn't it? Miss Copt tells me it's very seldom old pictures can be traced back for more than a generation. I suppose the fact of Mrs. Fontage's knowing its history must add a good deal to its value?"

Uncertain as to his drift, I said: "In her eyes it certainly appears to."

Implications are lost on Mr. Rose, who glowingly continued: "That's the reason why I wanted to talk to you about it—to consult you. Miss Copt tells me you value it at a thousand dollars."

There was no denying this, and I grunted a reluctant assent.

"Of course," he went on earnestly, "your valuation is based on the fact that the picture isn't signed—Mrs. Fontage explained that; and it *does* make a difference, certainly. But the thing is—if the picture's really good—ought one to take advantage—? I mean —one can see that Mrs. Fontage is in a tight place, and I wouldn't for the world—"

My astonished state arrested him.

"*You* wouldn't—?"

"I mean—you see, it's just this way"; he coughed and blushed: "I can't give more than a thousand dollars myself—it's as big a sum as I can manage to scrape together—but before I make the offer I want to be sure I'm not standing in the way of her getting more money."

My astonishment lapsed to dismay. "You're going to buy the picture for a thousand dollars?"

His blush deepened. "Why, yes. It sounds rather absurd, I suppose. It isn't much in my line, of course. I can see the picture's very beautiful, but I'm no judge—it isn't the kind of thing, naturally, that I could afford to go in for; but in this case I'm very glad to do what I can; the circumstances are so distressing; and knowing what you think of the picture I feel it's a pretty safe investment—"

"I don't think!" I blurted out.

"You—?"

"I don't think the picture's worth a thousand dollars; I don't think it's worth ten cents; I simply lied about it, that's all."

Mr. Rose looked as frightened as though I had charged him with the offense.

"Hang it, man, can't you see how it happened? I saw the poor woman's pride and happiness hung on her faith in that picture. I tried to make her understand that it was worthless—but she wouldn't; I tried to tell her so—but I couldn't. I behaved like a maudlin ass, but you shan't pay for my infernal bungling—you mustn't buy the picture!"

Mr. Rose sat silent, tapping one glossy boot-tip with another. Suddenly he turned on me a glance of stored intelligence. "But you know," he said good-humoredly, "I rather think I must."

"You haven't—already?"

"Oh, no; the offer's not made."

"Well, then—"

His look gathered a brighter significance.

"But if the picture's worth nothing, nobody will buy it—"

I groaned.

"Except," he continued, "some fellow like me, who doesn't know anything. *I* think it's lovely, you know; I mean to hang it in my mother's sitting-room." He rose and clasped my hand in his adhesive pressure. "I'm awfully obliged to you for telling me this; but perhaps you won't mind my asking you not to mention our talk to Miss Copt? It might bother her, you know, to think the picture isn't exactly up to the mark; and it won't make a rap of difference to me."

IV

Mr. Rose left me to a sleepless night. The next morning my resolve was formed, and it carried me straight to Mrs. Fontage's. She answered my knock by stepping out on the landing, and as she shut the door behind her I caught a glimpse of her devastated interior. She mentioned, with a careful avoidance of the note of pathos on which our last conversation had closed, that she was preparing to leave that afternoon; and the trunks obstructing the threshold showed that her preparations were nearly complete. They were, I felt certain, the same trunks that, strapped behind a rattling vettura, had accompanied the bride and groom on that memorable voyage of discovery of which the booty had till recently adorned her walls; and there was a dim consolation in the thought that those early "finds" in coral and Swiss wood-carving, in lava and alabaster, still lay behind the worn locks, in the security of worthlessness.

Mrs. Fontage, on the landing, among her strapped and corded treasures, maintained the same air of stability that made it impossible, even under such conditions, to regard her flight as anything less dignified than a departure. It was the moral support of what she tacitly assumed that enabled me to set forth with proper deliberation the object of my visit; and she received my announcement with an absence of surprise that struck me as the very flower of tact. Under cover of these mutual assumptions the transaction was rapidly concluded; and it was not till the canvas passed into my hands that, as though the physical contact had unnerved her, Mrs. Fontage suddenly faltered. "It's the giving it up—" she stammered, disguising herself to the last; and I hastened away from the collapse of her splendid effrontery.

I need hardly point out that I had acted impulsively, and that reaction from the most honorable impulses is sometimes attended by moral perturbation. My motives had indeed been mixed enough to justify some uneasiness, but this was allayed by the instinctive feeling that it is more venial to defraud an institution than a man. Since Mrs. Fontage had to be kept from starving by means not wholly defensible, it was better that the obligation should be borne by a rich institution than an impecunious youth. I doubt, in fact, if my scruples would have survived a night's sleep, had they not been complicated by some uncertainty as to my own future. It was true that, subject to the purely formal assent of the committee, I had full power to buy for the Museum, and that the one member of the committee likely to dispute my decision was opportunely traveling in Europe; but the picture once in place I must face the risk of any expert criticism to which chance might expose it. I dismissed this contingency for future study, stored the Rembrandt in the cellar of the Museum, and thanked heaven that Crozier was abroad.

Six months later he strolled into my office. I had just concluded, under conditions of exceptional difficulty, and on terms unexpectedly benign, the purchase of the great Bartley Reynolds; and this circumstance, by relegating the matter of the Rembrandt to a lower stratum of consciousness, enabled me to welcome Crozier with unmixed pleasure. My security was enhanced by his appearance. His smile was charged with amiable reminiscences, and I inferred that his trip had put him in the humor to approve of everything, or at least to ignore what fell short of his approval. I had therefore no uneasiness in accepting his invitation to dine that evening. It is always pleasant to dine with Crozier and never more so than when he is just back from Europe. His conversation gives even the food a flavor of the Café Anglais.

The repast was delightful, and it was not till we had finished a Camembert which he must have brought over with him, that my host said, in a tone of after-dinner perfunctoriness: "I see you've picked up a picture or two since I left."

I assented. "The Bartley Reynolds seemed too good an opportunity to miss, especially as the French government was after it. I think we got it cheap—"

"*Connu, connu*," said Crozier pleasantly. "I know all about the Reynolds. It was the biggest kind of a haul and I congratulate you. Best stroke of business we've done yet. But tell me about the other picture—the Rembrandt."

"I never said it was a Rembrandt." I could hardly have said why, but I felt distinctly annoyed with Crozier.

"Of course not. There's 'Rembrandt' on the frame, but I saw you'd modified it to 'Dutch School'; I apologize." He paused, but I offered no explanation. "What about it?" he went on. "Where did you pick it up?" As he leaned to the flame of the cigar-lighter his face seemed ruddy with enjoyment.

"I got it for a song," I said.

"A thousand, I think?"

"Have you seen it?" I asked abruptly.

"Went over the place this afternoon and found it in the cellar. Why hasn't it been hung, by the way?"

I paused a moment. "I'm waiting—"

"To—?"

"To have it varnished."

"Ah!" He leaned back and poured himself a second glass of Chartreuse. The smile he confided to its golden depths provoked me to challenge him with—

"What do you think of it?"

"The Rembrandt?" He lifted his eyes from the glass. "Just what you do."

"It isn't a Rembrandt."

"I apologize again. You call it, I believe, a picture of the same period?"

"I'm uncertain of the period."

"H'm." He glanced appreciatively along his cigar. "What are you certain of?"

"That it's a damned bad picture," I said savagely.

He nodded. "Just so. That's all we wanted to know."

"*We?*"

"We—I—the committee, in short. You see, my dear fellow, if you hadn't been certain it was a damned bad picture our position would have been a little awkward. As it is, my remaining duty—I ought to explain that in this matter I'm acting for the committee—is as simple as it's agreeable."

"I'll be hanged," I burst out, "if I understand one word you're saying!"

He fixed me with a kind of cruel joyousness. "You will—you will," he assured me; "at least you'll begin to, when you hear that I've seen Miss Copt."

"Miss Copt?"

"And that she has told me under what conditions the picture was bought."

"She doesn't know anything about the conditions! That is," I added, hastening to restrict the assertion, "she doesn't know my opinion of the picture." I thirsted for five minutes with Eleanor.

"Are you quite sure?" Crozier took me up. "Mr. Jefferson Rose does."

"Ah—I see."

"I thought you would," he reminded me. "As soon as I'd laid eyes on the Rembrandt—I beg your pardon!—I saw that it—well, required some explanation."

"You might have come to me."

"I meant to; but I happened to meet Miss Copt, whose encyclopedic information has often before been of service to me. I always go to Miss Copt when I want to look up anything; and I found she knew all about the Rembrandt."

"*All?*"

"Precisely. The knowledge was in fact causing her sleepless nights. Mr. Rose, who was suffering from the same form of insomnia, had taken her into his confidence, and she—ultimately—took me into hers."

"Of course!"

"I must ask you to do your cousin justice. She didn't speak till it became evident to her uncommonly quick perceptions that your buying the picture on its merits would have been infinitely worse for—for everybody—than your diverting a small portion of the Museum's funds to philanthropic uses. Then she told me the moving incident of Mr. Rose. Good fellow, Rose. And the old lady's case was desperate. Somebody had to buy that picture." I moved uneasily in my seat. "Wait a moment, will you? I haven't finished my cigar. There's a little head of Il Fiammingo's that you haven't seen, by the way; I picked it up the other day in Parma. We'll go in and have a look at it presently. But meanwhile what I want to say is that I've been charged—in the most informal way— to express to you the committee's appreciation of your admirable promptness and energy in capturing the Bartley Reynolds. We shouldn't have got it at all if you hadn't been uncommonly wide-awake, and to get it at such a price is a double triumph. We'd have thought nothing of a few more thousands—"

"I don't see," I impatiently interposed, "that, as far as I'm concerned, that alters the case."

"The case—?"

"Of Mrs. Fontage's Rembrandt. I bought the picture because, as you say, the situation was desperate, and I couldn't raise a thousand myself. What I did was of course indefensible; but the money shall be refunded to-morrow—"

Crozier raised a protesting hand. "Don't interrupt me when I'm talking ex cathedrâ. The money's been refunded already. The fact is, the Museum has sold the Rembrandt."

I stared at him wildly. "Sold it? To whom?"

"Why—to the committee.—Hold on a bit, please.—Won't you take another cigar? Then perhaps I can finish what I've got to say.—Why, my dear fellow, the committee's under an obligation to you—that's the way we look at it. I've investigated Mrs. Fontage's case, and—well, the picture had to be bought. She's eating meat now, I believe, for the first time in a year. And they'd have turned her out into the street that very day, your cousin tells me. Something had to be done at once, and you've simply given a number of well-to-do and self-indulgent gentlemen the opportunity of performing, at very small individual expense, a meritorious action in the nick of time. That's the first thing I've got to thank you for. And then—you'll remember, please, that I have the floor—that I'm still speaking for the committee—and secondly, as a slight recognition of your services in securing the Bartley Reynolds at a very much lower figure than we were prepared to pay, we beg you—the committee begs you—to accept the gift of Mrs. Fontage's Rembrandt. Now we'll go in and look at that little head. . . ."

THE OTHER TWO

WAYTHORN, on the drawing-room hearth, waited for his wife to come down to dinner.

It was their first night under his own roof, and he was surprised at his thrill of boyish agitation. He was not so old, to be sure—his glass gave him little more than the five-and-thirty years to which his wife confessed—but he had fancied himself already in the temperate zone; yet here he was listening for her step with a tender sense of all it symbolized, with some old trail of verse about the garlanded nuptial door-posts floating through his enjoyment of the pleasant room and the good dinner just beyond it.

They had been hastily recalled from their honeymoon by the illness of Lily Haskett, the child of Mrs. Waythorn's first marriage. The little girl, at Waythorn's desire, had been transferred to his house on the day of her mother's wedding, and the doctor, on their arrival, broke the news that she was ill with typhoid, but declared that all the symptoms were favorable. Lily could show twelve years of unblemished health, and the case promised to be a light one. The nurse spoke as reassuringly, and after a moment of alarm Mrs. Waythorn had adjusted herself to the situation. She was very fond of Lily—her affection for the child had perhaps been her decisive charm in Waythorn's eyes—but she had the perfectly balanced nerves which her little girl had inherited, and no woman ever wasted less tissue in unproductive worry. Waythorn was therefore quite prepared to see her come in presently, a little late because of a last look at Lily, but as serene and well-appointed as if her good-night kiss had been laid on the brow of health. Her composure was restful to him; it acted as ballast to his somewhat unstable sensibilities. As he pictured her bending over the child's bed he thought how soothing her presence must be in illness: her very step would prognosticate recovery.

His own life had been a gray one, from temperament rather than circumstance, and he had been drawn to her by the unperturbed gaiety which kept her fresh and elastic at an age when most women's activities are growing either slack or febrile. He knew what was said about her; for, popular as she was, there had always been a faint undercurrent of detraction. When she had appeared in New York, nine or ten years earlier, as the pretty Mrs. Haskett whom Gus Varick had unearthed somewhere—was it in Pittsburgh or Utica?—society, while promptly accepting her, had reserved the right to cast a doubt on its own indiscrimination. Inquiry, however, established her undoubted connection with a socially reigning family, and explained her recent divorce as the natural result of a runaway match at seventeen; and as nothing was known of Mr. Haskett it was easy to believe the worst of him.

Alice Haskett's remarriage with Gus Varick was a passport to the set whose recognition she coveted, and for a few years the Varicks were the most popular couple in town. Unfortunately the alliance was brief and stormy, and this time the husband had his champions. Still, even Varick's stanchest supporters admitted that he was not meant for matrimony, and Mrs. Varick's grievances were of a nature to bear the inspection of the New York courts. A New York divorce is in itself a diploma of virtue, and in the semi-widowhood of this second separation Mrs. Varick took on an air of sanctity, and was allowed to confide her wrongs to some of the most scrupulous ears in town. But when it was known that she was to marry Waythorn there was a momentary reaction. Her best friends would have preferred to see her remain in the role of the injured wife, which was as becoming to her as crape to a rosy complexion. True, a decent time had elapsed, and it was not even suggested that Waythorn had supplanted his predecessor. People shook their heads over him, however, and one grudging friend, to whom he affirmed that he took the step with his eyes open, replied oracularly: "Yes—and with your ears shut."

Waythorn could afford to smile at these innuendoes. In the Wall Street phrase, he had "discounted" them. He knew that society has not yet adapted itself to the consequences of divorce, and that till the adaptation takes place every woman who uses the freedom the law accords her must be her own social justification. Waythorn had an amused confidence in his wife's ability to justify herself. His expectations were fulfilled, and before the wedding took place Alice Varick's group had rallied openly to her support. She took it all imperturbably: she had a way of surmounting obstacles without seeming to be aware of them, and Waythorn looked back with wonder at the trivialities over which he had worn his nerves thin. He had the sense of having found refuge in a richer, warmer nature than his own, and his satisfaction, at the moment, was humorously summed up in the thought that his wife, when she had done all she could for Lily, would not be ashamed to come down and enjoy a good dinner.

The anticipation of such enjoyment was not, however, the sentiment expressed by Mrs. Waythorn's charming face when she presently joined him. Though she had put on her most engaging teagown she had neglected to assume the smile that went with it, and Waythorn thought he had never seen her look so nearly worried.

"What is it?" he asked. "Is anything wrong with Lily?"

"No; I've just been in and she's still sleeping." Mrs. Waythorn hesitated. "But something tiresome has happened."

He had taken her two hands, and now perceived that he was crushing a paper between them.

"This letter?"

"Yes—Mr. Haskett has written—I mean his lawyer has written."

Waythorn felt himself flush uncomfortably. He dropped his wife's hands.

"What about?"

"About seeing Lily. You know the courts—"

"Yes, yes," he interrupted nervously.

Nothing was known about Haskett in New York. He was vaguely supposed to have remained in the outer darkness from which his wife had been rescued, and Waythorn was one of the few who were aware that he had given up his business in Utica and followed her to New York in order to be near his little girl. In the days of his wooing, Waythorn had often met Lily on the door-step, rosy and smiling, on her way "to see papa."

"I am so sorry," Mrs. Waythorn murmured.

He roused himself. "What does he want?"

"He wants to see her. You know she goes to him once a week."

"Well—he doesn't expect her to go to him now, does he?"

"No—he has heard of her illness; but he expects to come here."

"*Here?*"

Mrs. Waythorn reddened under his gaze. They looked away from each other.

"I'm afraid he has the right.... You'll see...." She made a proffer of the letter.

Waythorn moved away with a gesture of refusal. He stood staring about the softly lighted room, which a moment before had seemed so full of bridal intimacy.

"I'm so sorry," she repeated. "If Lily could have been moved—"

"That's out of the question," he returned impatiently.

"I suppose so."

Her lip was beginning to tremble, and he felt himself a brute.

"He must come, of course," he said. "When is—his day?"

"I'm afraid—to-morrow."

"Very well. Send a note in the morning."

The butler entered to announce dinner.

Waythorn turned to his wife. "Come—you must be tired. It's beastly, but try to forget about it," he said, drawing her hand through his arm.

"You're so good, dear. I'll try," she whispered back.

Her face cleared at once, and as she looked at him across the flowers, between the rosy candle-shades, he saw her lips waver back into a smile.

"How pretty everything is!" she sighed luxuriously.

He turned to the butler. "The champagne at once, please. Mrs. Waythorn is tired."

In a moment or two their eyes met above the sparkling glasses. Her own were quite clear and untroubled: he saw that she had obeyed his injunction and forgotten.

II

Waythorn, the next morning, went down town earlier than usual. Haskett was not likely to come till the afternoon, but the instinct of flight drove him forth. He meant to stay away all day—he had thoughts of dining at his club. As his door closed behind him he reflected that before he opened it again it would have admitted another man who had as much right to enter it as himself, and the thought filled him with a physical repugnance.

He caught the "elevated" at the employees' hour, and found himself crushed between two layers of pendulous humanity. At Eighth Street the man facing him wriggled out, and another took his place. Waythorn glanced up and saw that it was Gus Varick. The men were so close together that it was impossible to ignore the smile of recognition on Varick's handsome overblown face. And after all—why not? They had always been on good terms, and Varick had been divorced before Waythorn's attentions to his wife began. The two exchanged a word on the perennial grievance of the congested trains, and when a seat at their side was miracu-lously left empty the instinct of self-preservation made Waythorn slip into it after Varick.

The latter drew the stout man's breath of relief. "Lord—I was beginning to feel like a pressed flower." He leaned back, looking unconcernedly at Waythorn. "Sorry to hear that Sellers is knocked out again."

"Sellers?" echoed Waythorn, starting at his partner's name.

Varick looked surprised. "You didn't know he was laid up with the gout?"

"No. I've been away—I only got back last night." Waythorn felt himself reddening in anticipation of the other's smile.

"Ah—yes; to be sure. And Sellers's attack came on two days ago. I'm afraid he's pretty bad. Very awkward for me, as it happens, because he was just putting through a rather important thing for me."

"Ah?" Waythorn wondered vaguely since when Varick had been dealing in "important things." Hitherto he had dabbled only in the shallow pools of speculation, with which Waythorn's office did not usually concern itself.

It occurred to him that Varick might be talking at random, to relieve the strain of their propinquity. That strain was becoming momentarily more apparent to Waythorn, and when, at Cortlandt Street, he caught sight of an acquaintance and had a sudden vision of the picture he and Varick must present to an initiated eye, he jumped up with a muttered excuse.

"I hope you'll find Sellers better," said Varick civilly, and he stammered back: "If I can be of any use to you—" and let the departing crowd sweep him to the platform.

At his office he heard that Sellers was in fact ill with the gout, and would probably not be able to leave the house for some weeks.

"I'm sorry it should have happened so, Mr. Waythorn," the senior clerk said with affable significance. "Mr. Sellers was very much upset at the idea of giving you such a lot of extra work just now."

"Oh, that's no matter," said Waythorn hastily. He secretly welcomed the pressure of additional business, and was glad to think that, when the day's work was over, he would have to call at his partner's on the way home.

He was late for luncheon, and turned in at the nearest restaurant instead of going to his club. The place was full, and the waiter hurried him to the back of the room to capture the only vacant table. In the cloud of cigar-smoke Waythorn did not at once distinguish his neighbors; but presently, looking about him, he saw Varick seated a few feet off. This time, luckily, they were too far apart for conversation, and Varick, who faced another way, had probably not even seen him; but there was an irony in their renewed nearness.

Varick was said to be fond of good living, and as Waythorn sat dispatching his hurried luncheon he looked across half enviously at the other's leisurely degustation of his meal. When Waythorn first saw him he had been helping himself with critical deliberation to a bit of Camembert at the ideal point of liquefaction, and now, the cheese removed, he was just pouring his *café double* from its little two-storied earthen pot. He poured slowly, his ruddy profile bent above the task, and one beringed white hand steadying the lid of the coffee-pot; then he stretched his other hand to the decanter of cognac at his elbow, filled a liqueur-glass, took a tentative sip, and poured the brandy into his coffee-cup.

Waythorn watched him in a kind of fascination. What was he thinking of—only of the flavor of the coffee and the liqueur? Had the morning's meeting left no more trace in his thoughts than on his face? Had his wife so completely passed out of his life that even this odd encounter with her present husband, within a week after her remarriage, was no more than an incident in his day? And as Waythorn mused, another idea struck him: had Haskett ever met Varick as Varick and he had just met? The recollection of Haskett perturbed him, and he rose and left the restaurant, taking a circuitous way out to escape the placid irony of Varick's nod.

It was after seven when Waythorn reached home. He thought the footman who opened the door looked at him oddly.

"How is Miss Lily?" he asked in haste.

"Doing very well, sir. A gentleman—"

"Tell Barlow to put off dinner for half an hour," Waythorn cut him off, hurrying upstairs.

He went straight to his room and dressed without seeing his wife. When he reached the drawing-room she was there, fresh and radiant. Lily's day had been good; the doctor was not coming back that evening.

At dinner Waythorn told her of Sellers's illness and of the

resulting complications. She listened sympathetically, adjuring him not to let himself be overworked, and asking vague feminine questions about the routine of the office. Then she gave him the chronicle of Lily's day; quoted the nurse and doctor, and told him who had called to inquire. He had never seen her more serene and unruffled. It struck him, with a curious pang, that she was very happy in being with him, so happy that she found a childish pleasure in rehearsing the trivial incidents of her day.

After dinner they went to the library, and the servant put the coffee and liqueurs on a low table before her and left the room. She looked singularly soft and girlish in her rosy pale dress, against the dark leather of one of his bachelor armchairs. A day earlier the contrast would have charmed him.

He turned away now, choosing a cigar with affected deliberation.

"Did Haskett come?" he asked, with his back to her.

"Oh, yes—he came."

"You didn't see him, of course?"

She hesitated a moment. "I let the nurse see him."

That was all. There was nothing more to ask. He swung round toward her, applying a match to his cigar. Well, the thing was over for a week, at any rate. He would try not to think of it. She looked up at him, a trifle rosier than usual, with a smile in her eyes.

"Ready for your coffee, dear?"

He leaned against the mantelpiece, watching her as she lifted the coffee-pot. The lamplight struck a gleam from her bracelets and tipped her soft hair with brightness. How light and slender she was, and how each gesture flowed into the next! She seemed a creature all compact of harmonies. As the thought of Haskett receded, Waythorn felt himself yielding again to the joy of possessorship. They were his, those white hands with their flitting motions, his the light haze of hair, the lips and eyes. . . .

She set down the coffee-pot, and reaching for the decanter of cognac, measured off a liqueur-glass and poured it into his cup.

Waythorn uttered a sudden exclamation.

"What is the matter?" she said, startled.

"Nothing; only—I don't take cognac in my coffee."

"Oh, how stupid of me," she cried.

Their eyes met, and she blushed a sudden agonized red.

III

Ten days later, Mr. Sellers, still house-bound, asked Waythorn to call on his way down town.

The senior partner, with his swaddled foot propped up by the fire, greeted his associate with an air of embarrassment.

"I'm sorry, my dear fellow; I've got to ask you to do an awkward thing for me."

Waythorn waited, and the other went on, after a pause apparently given to the arrangement of his phrases: "The fact is, when I was knocked out I had just gone into a rather complicated piece of business for—Gus Varick."

"Well?" said Waythorn, with an attempt to put him at his ease.

"Well—it's this way: Varick came to me the day before my attack. He had evidently had an inside tip from somebody, and had made about a hundred thousand. He came to me for advice, and I suggested his going in with Vanderlyn."

"Oh, the deuce!" Waythorn exclaimed. He saw in a flash what had happened. The investment was an alluring one, but required negotiation. He listened quietly while Sellers put the case before him, and, the statement ended, he said: "You think I ought to see Varick?"

"I'm afraid I can't as yet. The doctor is obdurate. And this thing can't wait. I hate to ask you, but no one else in the office knows the ins and outs of it."

Waythorn stood silent. He did not care a farthing for the success of Varick's venture, but the honor of the office was to be considered, and he could hardly refuse to oblige his partner.

"Very well," he said, "I'll do it."

That afternoon, apprised by telephone, Varick called at the office. Waythorn, waiting in his private room, wondered what the others thought of it. The newspapers, at the time of Mrs. Waythorn's marriage, had acquainted their readers with every detail of her previous matrimonial ventures, and Waythorn could fancy the clerks smiling behind Varick's back as he was ushered in.

Varick bore himself admirably. He was easy without being undignified, and Waythorn was conscious of cutting a much less impressive figure. Varick had no experience of business, and the talk prolonged itself for nearly an hour while Waythorn set forth with scrupulous precision the details of the proposed transaction.

"I'm awfully obliged to you," Varick said as he rose. "The fact is I'm not used to having much money to look after, and I don't want to make an ass of myself—" He smiled, and Waythorn could not help noticing that there was something pleasant about his smile. "It feels uncommonly queer to have enough cash to pay one's bills. I'd have sold my soul for it a few years ago!"

Waythorn winced at the allusion. He had heard it rumored that a lack of funds had been one of the determining causes of the Varick separation, but it did not occur to him that Varick's words were intentional. It seemed more likely that the desire to keep clear of embarrassing topics had fatally drawn him into one. Waythorn did not wish to be outdone in civility.

"We'll do the best we can for you," he said. "I think this is a good thing you're in."

"Oh, I'm sure it's immense. It's awfully good of you—" Varick broke off, embarrassed. "I suppose the thing's settled now—but if—"

"If anything happens before Sellers is about, I'll see you again," said Waythorn quietly. He was glad, in the end, to appear the more self-possessed of the two.

The course of Lily's illness ran smooth, and as the days passed Waythorn grew used to the idea of Haskett's weekly visit. The first time the day came round, he stayed out late, and questioned his wife as to the visit on his return. She replied at once that Haskett had merely seen the nurse down-stairs, as the doctor did not wish any one in the child's sick-room till after the crisis.

The following week Waythorn was again conscious of the recurrence of the day, but had forgotten it by the time he came home to dinner. The crisis of the disease came a few days later, with a rapid decline of fever, and the little girl was pronounced out of danger. In the rejoicing which ensued the thought of Haskett passed out of Waythorn's mind, and one afternoon, letting himself into the house with a latch-key, he went straight to his library without noticing a shabby hat and umbrella in the hall.

In the library he found a small effaced-looking man with a thinnish gray beard sitting on the edge of a chair. The stranger might have been a piano-tuner, or one of those mysteriously efficient persons who are summoned in emergencies to adjust some detail of the domestic machinery. He blinked at Waythorn through a pair of gold-rimmed spectacles and said mildly: "Mr. Waythorn, I presume? I am Lily's father."

Waythorn flushed. "Oh—" he stammered uncomfortably. He broke off, disliking to appear rude. Inwardly he was trying to adjust the actual Haskett to the image of him projected by his wife's reminiscences. Waythorn had been allowed to infer that Alice's first husband was a brute.

"I am sorry to intrude," said Haskett, with his over-the-counter politeness.

"Don't mention it," returned Waythorn, collecting himself. "I suppose the nurse has been told?"

"I presume so. I can wait," said Haskett. He had a resigned way of speaking, as though life had worn down his natural powers of resistance.

Waythorn stood on the threshold, nervously pulling off his gloves.

"I'm sorry you've been detained. I will send for the nurse," he said; and as he opened the door he added with an effort: "I'm glad we can give you a good report of Lily." He winced as the *we* slipped out, but Haskett seemed not to notice it.

"Thank you, Mr. Waythorn. It's been an anxious time for me."

"Ah, well, that's past. Soon she'll be able to go to you." Waythorn nodded and passed out.

In his own room he flung himself down with a groan. He hated the womanish sensibility which made him suffer so acutely from the grotesque chances of life. He had known when he married that his wife's former husbands were both living, and that amid the multiplied contacts of modern existence there were a thousand chances to one that he would run against one or the other, yet he found himself as much disturbed by his brief encounter with Haskett as though the law had not obligingly removed all difficulties in the way of their meeting.

Waythorn sprang up and began to pace the room nervously. He had not suffered half as much from his two meetings with Varick. It was Haskett's presence in his own house that made the situation so intolerable. He stood still, hearing steps in the passage.

"This way, please," he heard the nurse say. Haskett was being taken upstairs, then: not a corner of the house but was open to him. Waythorn dropped into another chair, staring vaguely ahead of him. On his dressing-table stood a photograph of Alice, taken when he had first known her. She was Alice Varick then—how fine and exquisite he had thought her! Those were Varick's pearls about her neck. At Waythorn's instance they had been returned before her marriage. Had Haskett ever given her any trinkets— and what had become of them, Waythorn wondered? He realized suddenly that he knew very little of Haskett's past or present situation; but from the man's appearance and manner of speech he could reconstruct with curious precision the surroundings of Alice's first marriage. And it startled him to think that she had, in the background of her life, a phase of existence so different from anything with which he had connected her. Varick, whatever his faults, was a gentleman, in the conventional, traditional sense of the term: the sense which at that moment seemed, oddly enough, to have most meaning to Waythorn. He and Varick had the same

social habits, spoke the same language, understood the same allusions. But this other man...it was grotesquely uppermost in
Waythorn's mind that Haskett had worn a made-up tie attached
with an elastic. Why should that ridiculous detail symbolize the
whole man? Waythorn was exasperated by his own paltriness, but
the fact of the tie expanded, forced itself on him, became as it
were the key to Alice's past. He could see her, as Mrs. Haskett, sitting in a "front parlor" furnished in plush, with a pianola, and a
copy of *Ben-Hur* on the center-table. He could see her going to
the theater with Haskett—or perhaps even to a "Church Sociable"
—she in a "picture hat" and Haskett in a black frock-coat, a little
creased, with the made-up tie on an elastic. On the way home
they would stop and look at the illuminated shop-windows, lingering over the photographs of New York actresses. On Sunday
afternoons Haskett would take her for a walk, pushing Lily ahead
of them in a white enameled perambulator, and Waythorn had a
vision of the people they would stop and talk to. He could fancy
how pretty Alice must have looked, in a dress adroitly constructed
from the hints of a New York fashion-paper, and how she must
have looked down on the other women, chafing at her life, and secretly feeling that she belonged in a bigger place.

For the moment his foremost thought was one of wonder at
the way in which she had shed the phase of existence which her
marriage with Haskett implied. It was as if her whole aspect, every
gesture, every inflection, every allusion, were a studied negation of
that period of her life. If she had denied being married to Haskett
she could hardly have stood more convicted of duplicity than in
this obliteration of the self which had been his wife.

Waythorn started up, checking himself in the analysis of her
motives. What right had he to create a fantastic effigy of her and
then pass judgment on it? She had spoken vaguely of her first
marriage as unhappy, had hinted, with becoming reticence, that
Haskett had wrought havoc among her young illusions....It was
a pity for Waythorn's peace of mind that Haskett's very inoffen-
siveness shed a new light on the nature of those illusions. A man

would rather think that his wife has been brutalized by her first husband than that the process has been reversed.

IV

"Mr. Waythorn, I don't like that French governess of Lily's."

Haskett, subdued and apologetic, stood before Waythorn in the library, revolving his shabby hat in his hand.

Waythorn, surprised in his armchair over the evening paper, stared back perplexedly at his visitor.

"You'll excuse my asking to see you," Haskett continued. "But this is my last visit, and I thought if I could have a word with you it would be a better way than writing to Mrs. Waythorn's lawyer."

Waythorn rose uneasily. He did not like the French governess either; but that was irrelevant.

"I am not so sure of that," he returned stiffly; "but since you wish it I will give your message to—my wife." He always hesitated over the possessive pronoun in addressing Haskett.

The latter sighed. "I don't know as that will help much. She didn't like it when I spoke to her."

Waythorn turned red. "When did you see her?" he asked.

"Not since the first day I came to see Lily—right after she was taken sick. I remarked to her then that I didn't like the governess."

Waythorn made no answer. He remembered distinctly that, after that first visit, he had asked his wife if she had seen Haskett. She had lied to him then, but she had respected his wishes since; and the incident cast a curious light on her character. He was sure she would not have seen Haskett that first day if she had divined that Waythorn would object, and the fact that she did not divine it was almost as disagreeable to the latter as the discovery that she had lied to him.

"I don't like the woman," Haskett was repeating with mild persistency. "She ain't straight, Mr. Waythorn—she'll teach the child to be underhand. I've noticed a change in Lily—she's too anxious to please—and she don't always tell the truth. She used to be the straightest child, Mr. Waythorn—" He broke off, his voice a little thick. "Not but what I want her to have a stylish education," he ended.

Waythorn was touched. "I'm sorry, Mr. Haskett; but frankly, I don't quite see what I can do."

Haskett hesitated. Then he laid his hat on the table, and advanced to the hearth-rug, on which Waythorn was standing. There was nothing aggressive in his manner, but he had the solemnity of a timid man resolved on a decisive measure.

"There's just one thing you can do, Mr. Waythorn," he said. "You can remind Mrs. Waythorn that, by the decree of the courts, I am entitled to have a voice in Lily's bringing up." He paused, and went on more deprecatingly: "I'm not the kind to talk about enforcing my rights, Mr. Waythorn. I don't know as I think a man is entitled to rights he hasn't known how to hold on to; but this business of the child is different. I've never let go there—and I never mean to."

The scene left Waythorn deeply shaken. Shamefacedly, in indirect ways, he had been finding out about Haskett; and all that he had learned was favorable. The little man, in order to be near his daughter, had sold out his share in a profitable business in Utica, and accepted a modest clerkship in a New York manufacturing house. He boarded in a shabby street and had few acquaintances. His passion for Lily filled his life. Waythorn felt that this exploration of Haskett was like groping about with a dark-lantern in his wife's past; but he saw now that there were recesses his lantern had not explored. He had never inquired into the exact circumstances of his wife's first matrimonial rupture. On the surface all had been fair. It was she who had obtained the divorce, and the court had given her the child. But Waythorn knew how many ambiguities such a verdict might cover. The mere fact that Haskett retained a right over his daughter implied an unsuspected compromise. Waythorn was an idealist. He always refused to recognize unpleasant contingencies till he found himself confronted with them, and then he saw them followed by a spectral train of consequences. His next days were thus haunted, and he determined to try to lay the ghosts by conjuring them up in his wife's presence.

When he repeated Haskett's request a flame of anger passed over her face; but she subdued it instantly and spoke with a slight quiver of outraged motherhood.

"It is very ungentlemanly of him," she said.

The word grated on Waythorn. "That is neither here nor there. It's a bare question of rights."

She murmured: "It's not as if he could ever be a help to Lily—"

Waythorn flushed. This was even less to his taste. "The question is," he repeated, "what authority has he over her?"

She looked downward, twisting herself a little in her seat. "I am willing to see him—I thought you objected," she faltered.

In a flash he understood that she knew the extent of Haskett's claims. Perhaps it was not the first time she had resisted them.

"My objecting has nothing to do with it," he said coldly; "if Haskett has a right to be consulted you must consult him."

She burst into tears, and he saw that she expected him to regard her as a victim.

Haskett did not abuse his rights. Waythorn had felt miserably sure that he would not. But the governess was dismissed, and from time to time the little man demanded an interview with Alice. After the first outburst she accepted the situation with her usual adaptability. Haskett had once reminded Waythorn of the piano-tuner, and Mrs. Waythorn, after a month or two, appeared to class him with that domestic familiar. Waythorn could not but respect the father's tenacity. At first he had tried to cultivate the suspicion that Haskett might be "up to" something, that he had an object in securing a foothold in the house. But in his heart Waythorn was sure of Haskett's single-mindedness; he even guessed in the latter a mild contempt for such advantages as his relation with the Waythorns might offer. Haskett's sincerity of purpose made him invulnerable, and his successor had to accept him as a lien on the property.

Mr. Sellers was sent to Europe to recover from his gout, and Varick's affairs hung on Waythorn's hands. The negotiations were prolonged and complicated; they necessitated frequent conferences between the two men, and the interests of the firm forbade Waythorn's suggesting that his client should transfer his business to another office.

Varick appeared well in the transaction. In moments of relaxation his coarse streak appeared, and Waythorn dreaded his geniality; but in the office he was concise and clear-headed, with a flattering deference to Waythorn's judgment. Their business relations being so affably established, it would have been absurd for the two men to ignore each other in society. The first time they met in a drawing-room, Varick took up their intercourse in the same easy key, and his hostess's grateful glance obliged Waythorn to respond to it. After that they ran across each other frequently, and one evening at a ball Waythorn, wandering through the remoter rooms, came upon Varick seated beside his wife. She colored a little, and faltered in what she was saying; but Varick nodded to Waythorn without rising, and the latter strolled on.

In the carriage, on the way home, he broke out nervously: "I didn't know you spoke to Varick."

Her voice trembled a little. "It's the first time—he happened to be standing near me; I didn't know what to do. It's so awkward, meeting everywhere—and he said you had been very kind about some business."

"That's different," said Waythorn.

She paused a moment. "I'll do just as you wish," she returned pliantly. "I thought it would be less awkward to speak to him when we meet."

Her pliancy was beginning to sicken him. Had she really no will of her own—no theory about her relationship to these men?

She had accepted Haskett—did she mean to accept Varick? It was "less awkward," as she had said, and her instinct was to evade difficulties or to circumvent them. With sudden vividness Waythorn saw how the instinct had developed. She was "as easy as an old shoe"—a shoe that too many feet had worn. Her elasticity was the result of tension in too many different directions. Alice Haskett—Alice Varick—Alice Waythorn—she had been each in turn, and had left hanging to each name a little of her privacy, a little of her personality, a little of the inmost self where the unknown god abides.

"Yes—it's better to speak to Varick," said Waythorn wearily.

V

The winter wore on, and society took advantage of the Waythorns' acceptance of Varick. Harassed hostesses were grateful to them for bridging over a social difficulty, and Mrs. Waythorn was held up as a miracle of good taste. Some experimental spirits could not resist the diversion of throwing Varick and his former wife together, and there were those who thought he found a zest in the propinquity. But Mrs. Waythorn's conduct remained irreproachable. She neither avoided Varick nor sought him out. Even Waythorn could not but admit that she had discovered the solution of the newest social problem.

He had married her without giving much thought to that problem. He had fancied that a woman can shed her past like a man. But now he saw that Alice was bound to hers both by the circumstances which forced her into continued relation with it, and by the traces it had left on her nature. With grim irony Waythorn compared himself to a member of a syndicate. He held so many shares in his wife's personality and his predecessors were his partners in the business. If there had been any element of passion in the transaction he would have felt less deteriorated by it. The fact that Alice took her change of husbands like a change of weather reduced the situation to mediocrity. He could have forgiven her for blunders, for excesses; for resisting Haskett, for yielding to Varick; for anything but her acquiescence and her tact. She reminded him of a juggler tossing knives; but the knives were blunt and she knew they would never cut her.

And then, gradually, habit formed a protecting surface for his sensibilities. If he paid for each day's comfort with the small change of his illusions, he grew daily to value the comfort more and set less store upon the coin. He had drifted into a dulling propinquity with Haskett and Varick and he took refuge in the cheap revenge of satirizing the situation. He even began to reckon up the advantages which accrued from it, to ask himself if it were not better to own a third of a wife who knew how to make a man happy than a whole one who had lacked opportunity to acquire the art. For it *was* an art, and made up, like all others, of concessions, eliminations and embellishments; of lights judiciously thrown and shadows skillfully softened. His wife knew exactly how to manage the lights, and he knew exactly to what training she owed her skill. He even tried to trace the source of his obligations, to discriminate between the influences which had combined to produce his domestic happiness: he perceived that Haskett's commonness had made Alice worship good breeding, while Varick's liberal construction of the marriage bond had taught her to value the conjugal virtues; so that he was directly indebted to his predecessors for the devotion which made his life easy if not inspiring.

From this phase he passed into that of complete acceptance. He ceased to satirize himself because time dulled the irony of the situation and the joke lost its humor with its sting. Even the sight of Haskett's hat on the hall table had ceased to touch the springs of epigram. The hat was often seen there now, for it had been decided that it was better for Lily's father to visit her than for the little girl to go to his boarding-house. Waythorn, having acquiesced in this arrangement, had been surprised to find how little difference it made. Haskett was never obtrusive, and the few visitors who met him on the stairs were unaware of his identity. Waythorn did not know how often he saw Alice, but with himself Haskett was seldom in contact.

One afternoon, however, he learned on entering that Lily's father was waiting to see him. In the library he found Haskett occupying a chair in his usual provisional way. Waythorn always felt grateful to him for not leaning back.

"I hope you'll excuse me, Mr. Waythorn," he said rising. "I wanted to see Mrs. Waythorn about Lily, and your man asked me to wait here till she came in."

"Of course," said Waythorn, remembering that a sudden leak had that morning given over the drawing-room to the plumbers.

He opened his cigar-case and held it out to his visitor, and Haskett's acceptance seemed to mark a fresh stage in their intercourse. The spring evening was chilly, and Waythorn invited his guest to draw up his chair to the fire. He meant to find an excuse to leave Haskett in a moment; but he was tired and cold, and after all the little man no longer jarred on him.

The two were enclosed in the intimacy of their blended cigar-smoke when the door opened and Varick walked into the room. Waythorn rose abruptly. It was the first time that Varick had come to the house, and the surprise of seeing him, combined with the singular inopportuneness of his arrival, gave a new edge to Waythorn's blunted sensibilities. He stared at his visitor without speaking.

Varick seemed too preoccupied to notice his host's embarrassment.

"My dear fellow," he exclaimed in his most expansive tone, "I must apologize for tumbling in on you in this way, but I was too late to catch you down town, and so I thought—"

He stopped short, catching sight of Haskett, and his sanguine color deepened to a flush which spread vividly under his scant blond hair. But in a moment he recovered himself and nodded slightly. Haskett returned the bow in silence, and Waythorn was still groping for speech when the footman came in carrying a tea-table.

The intrusion offered a welcome vent to Waythorn's nerves. "What the deuce are you bringing this here for?" he said sharply.

"I beg your pardon, sir, but the plumbers are still in the drawing-room, and Mrs. Waythorn said she would have tea in the library." The footman's perfectly respectful tone implied a reflection on Waythorn's reasonableness.

"Oh, very well," said the latter resignedly, and the footman proceeded to open the folding tea-table and set out its complicated appointments. While this interminable process continued the three men stood motionless, watching it with a fascinated stare, till Waythorn, to break the silence, said to Varick: "Won't you have a cigar?"

He held out the case he had just tendered to Haskett, and Varick helped himself with a smile. Waythorn looked about for a match, and finding none, proffered a light from his own cigar. Haskett, in the background, held his ground mildly, examining his cigar-tip now and then, and stepping forward at the right moment to knock its ashes into the fire.

The footman at last withdrew, and Varick immediately began: "If I could just say half a word to you about this business—"

"Certainly," stammered Waythorn; "in the dining-room—"

But as he placed his hand on the door it opened from without, and his wife appeared on the threshold.

She came in fresh and smiling, in her street dress and hat, shedding a fragrance from the boa which she loosened in advancing.

"Shall we have tea in here, dear?" she began; and then she caught sight of Varick. Her smile deepened, veiling a slight tremor of surprise.

"Why, how do you do?" she said with a distinct note of pleasure.

As she shook hands with Varick she saw Haskett standing behind him. Her smile faded for a moment, but she recalled it quickly, with a scarcely perceptible side-glance at Waythorn.

"How do you do, Mr. Haskett?" she said, and shook hands with him a shade less cordially.

The three men stood awkwardly before her, till Varick, always the most self-possessed, dashed into an explanatory phrase.

"We—I had to see Waythorn a moment on business," he stammered, brick-red from chin to nape.

Haskett stepped forward with his air of mild obstinacy. "I am sorry to intrude; but you appointed five o'clock—" he directed his resigned glance to the time-piece on the mantel.

She swept aside their embarrassment with a charming gesture of hospitality.

"I'm so sorry—I'm always late; but the afternoon was so lovely." She stood drawing off her gloves, propitiatory and graceful, diffusing about her a sense of ease and familiarity in which the situation lost its grotesqueness. "But before talking business," she added brightly, "I'm sure every one wants a cup of tea."

She dropped into her low chair by the tea-table, and the two visitors, as if drawn by her smile, advanced to receive the cups she held out.

She glanced about for Waythorn, and he took the third cup with a laugh.

THE QUICKSAND

As MRS. Quentin's victoria, driving homeward, turned from the Park into Fifth Avenue, she divined her son's tall figure walking ahead of her in the twilight. His long stride covered the ground more rapidly than usual, and she had a premonition that, if he were going home at that hour, it was because he wanted to see her.

Mrs. Quentin, though not a fanciful woman, was sometimes aware of a sixth sense enabling her to detect the faintest vibrations of her son's impulses. She was too shrewd to fancy herself the one mother in possession of this faculty, but she permitted herself to think that few could exercise it more discreetly. If she could not help overhearing Alan's thoughts, she had the courage to keep her discoveries to herself, the tact to take for granted nothing that lay below the surface of their spoken intercourse: she knew that most people would rather have their letters read than their thoughts. For this superfeminine discretion Alan repaid her by—being Alan. There could have been no completer reward. He was the key to the meaning of life, the justification of what must have seemed as incomprehensible as it was odious, had it not all-sufficingly ended in himself. He was a perfect son, and Mrs. Quentin had always hungered for perfection.

Her house, in a minor way, bore witness to the craving. One felt it to be the result of a series of eliminations: there was nothing fortuitous in its blending of line and color. The almost morbid finish of every material detail of her life suggested the possibility that a diversity of energies had, by some pressure of circumstance, been forced into the channel of a narrow dilettantism. Mrs. Quentin's fastidiousness had, indeed, the flaw of being too one-sided. Her friends were not always worthy of the chairs they sat in, and she overlooked in her associates defects she would not have tolerated in her bric-à-brac. Her house was, in fact, never so distinguished as when it was empty; and it was at its best in the warm fire-lit silence that now received her.

Her son, who had overtaken her on the door-step, followed her into the drawing-room, and threw himself into an armchair near the fire, while she laid off her furs and busied herself about the tea-table. For a while neither spoke; but glancing at him across the kettle, his mother noticed that he sat staring at the embers with a look she had never seen on his face, though its arrogant young outline was as familiar to her as her own thoughts. The look extended itself to his negligent attitude, to the droop of his long fine hands, the dejected tilt of his head against the cushions. It was like the moral equivalent of physical fatigue: he looked, as he himself would have phrased it, dead-beat, played out. Such an air was so foreign to his usual bright indomitableness that Mrs. Quentin had the sense of an unfamiliar presence, in which she must observe herself, must raise hurried barriers against an alien approach. It was one of the drawbacks of their excessive intimacy that any break in it seemed a chasm.

She was accustomed to let his thoughts circle about her before they settled into speech, and she now sat in motionless expectancy, as though a sound might frighten them away.

At length, without turning his eyes from the fire, he said: "I'm so glad you're a nice old-fashioned intuitive woman. It's painful to see them think."

Her apprehension had already preceded him. "Hope Fenno—?" she faltered.

He nodded. "She's been thinking—hard. It was very painful—to me at least; and I don't believe she enjoyed it: she said she didn't." He stretched his feet to the fire. "The result of her cogitations is that she won't have me. She arrived at this by pure ratiocination

—it's not a question of feeling, you understand. I'm the only man she's ever loved—but she won't have me. What novels did you read when you were young, dear? I'm convinced it all turns on that. If she'd been brought up on Trollope and Whyte-Melville, instead of Tolstoy and Mrs. Ward, we should have now been vulgarly sitting on a sofa, trying on the engagement ring."

Mrs. Quentin at first was kept silent by the mother's instinctive anger that the girl she has not wanted for her son should have dared to refuse him. Then she said: "Tell me, dear."

"My good woman, she has scruples."

"Scruples?"

"Against the paper. She objects to me in my official capacity as owner of the *Radiator*."

His mother did not echo his laugh.

"She had found a solution, of course—she overflows with expedients. I was to chuck the paper, and we were to live happily ever afterward on canned food and virtue. She even had an alternative ready—women are so full of resources! I was to turn the *Radiator* into an independent organ, and run it at a loss to show the public what a model newspaper ought to be. On the whole, I think she fancied this plan more than the other—it commended itself to her as being more uncomfortable and aggressive. It's not the fashion nowadays to be good by stealth."

Mrs. Quentin said to herself: "I don't know how much he cared!" Aloud she murmured: "You must give her time."

"Time?"

"To move out the old prejudices and make room for new ones."

"My dear mother, those she has are brand-new; that's the trouble with them. She's tremendously up to date. She takes in all the moral fashion papers, and wears the newest thing in ethics."

Her resentment lost its way in the intricacies of his metaphor. "Is she so very religious?"

"You dear archaic woman! She's hopelessly irreligious; that's the difficulty. You can make a religious woman believe almost anything: there's the habit of credulity to work on. But when a girl's faith in the Deluge has been shaken, it's very hard to inspire her with confidence. She makes you feel that, before believing in you, it's her duty as a conscientious agnostic to find out whether you're not obsolete, or whether the text isn't corrupt, or somebody hasn't proved conclusively that you ever existed, anyhow."

Mrs. Quentin was again silent. The two moved in that atmosphere of implications and assumptions where the lightest word may shake down the dust of countless stored impressions; and speech was sometimes more difficult between them than had their union been less close.

Presently she ventured, "It's impossible?"

"Impossible?"

She seemed to use her words cautiously, like weapons that might slip and inflict a cut. "What she suggests."

Her son, raising himself, turned to look at her for the first time. Their glance met in a shock of comprehension. He was with her against the girl, then! Her satisfaction overflowed in a murmur of tenderness.

"Of course not, dear. One can't change—change one's life. . . ."

"One's self," he amended. "That's what I tell her. What's the use of my giving up the paper if I keep my point of view?"

The psychological distinction attracted her. "Which is it she minds most?"

"Oh, the paper—for the present. She undertakes to modify the point of view afterward. All she asks is that I shall renounce my heresy: the gift of grace will come later."

Mrs. Quentin sat gazing into her untouched cup. Her son's first words had produced in her the hallucinated sense of struggling in the thick of a crowd that he could not see. It was horrible to feel herself hemmed in by influences imperceptible to him; yet if anything could have increased her misery it would have been the discovery that her ghosts had become visible.

As though to divert his attention, she precipitately asked: "Are you—?"

His answer carried the shock of an evocation. "I merely asked her what she thought of *you.*"

"Of me?"

"She admires you immensely, you know."

For a moment Mrs. Quentin's cheek showed the lingering light of girlhood: praise transmitted by her son acquired something of the transmitter's merit. "Well—?" she smiled.

"Well—you didn't make my father give up the *Radiator*, did you?"

His mother, stiffening, made a circuitous return: "She never comes here. How can she know me?"

"She's so poor! She goes out so little." He rose and leaned against the mantelpiece, dislodging with impatient fingers a slender bronze wrestler poised on a porphyry base, between two warm-toned Spanish ivories. "And then her mother—" he added, as if involuntarily.

"Her mother has never visited me," Mrs. Quentin finished for him.

He shrugged his shoulders. "Mrs. Fenno has the scope of a wax doll. Her rule of conduct is taken from her grandmother's sampler."

"But the daughter is so modern—and yet—"

"The result is the same? Not exactly. *She* admires you—oh, immensely!" He replaced the bronze and turned to his mother with a smile. "Aren't you on some hospital committee together? What especially strikes her is your way of doing good. She says philanthropy is not a line of conduct but a state of mind—and it appears that you are one of the elect."

As, in the vague diffusion of physical pain, relief seems to come with the acuter pang of a single nerve, Mrs. Quentin felt herself suddenly eased by a rush of anger against the girl. "If she loved you—" she began.

His gesture checked her. "I'm not asking you to get her to do that."

The two were again silent, facing each other in the disarray of a common catastrophe—as though their thoughts, at the summons of danger, had rushed naked into action. Mrs. Quentin, at this revealing moment, saw for the first time how many elements of her son's character had seemed comprehensible simply because they were familiar: as, in reading a foreign language, we take the meaning of certain words for granted till the context corrects us. Often as, in a given case, her maternal musings had figured his conduct, she now found herself at a loss to forecast it; and with this failure of intuition came a sense of the subserviency which had hitherto made her counsels but the anticipation of his wish. Her despair escaped in the moan, "What *is* it you ask me?"

"To talk to her."

"Talk to her?"

"Show her—tell her—make her understand that the paper has always been a thing outside your life—that hasn't touched you—that needn't touch *her*. Only, let her hear you—watch you—be with you—she'll see . . . she can't help seeing. . . ."

His mother faltered. "But if she's given you her reasons?"

"Let her give them to you! If she can—when she sees you. . . ." His impatient hand again displaced the wrestler. "I care abominably," he confessed.

II

On the Fenno threshold a sudden sense of the futility of the attempt had almost driven Mrs. Quentin back to her carriage; but the door was already opening, and a parlor-maid who believed that Miss Fenno was in led the way to the depressing drawing-room. It was the kind of room in which no member of the family is likely to be found except after dinner or after death. The chairs and tables looked like poor relations who had repaid their keep by a long career of grudging usefulness: they seemed banded together against intruders in a sullen conspiracy of discomfort. Mrs. Quentin, keenly susceptible to such influences, read failure in every angle of the upholstery. She was incapable of the vulgar error of thinking that Hope Fenno might be induced to marry Alan for his money; but between this assumption and the inference that the girl's imagination might be touched by the finer possibilities of wealth, good taste admitted a distinction. The Fenno furniture, however, presented to such reasoning the obtuseness of its black walnut chamferings; and something in its attitude suggested that its owners would be as uncompromising. The room showed none of the modern attempts at palliation, no apologetic draping of facts; and Mrs. Quentin, provisionally perched on a green reps Gothic sofa with which it was clearly impossible to establish any closer relation, concluded that, had Mrs. Fenno needed another seat of the same size, she would have set out placidly to match the one on which her visitor now languished.

To Mrs. Quentin's fancy, Hope Fenno's opinions, presently imparted in a clear young voice from the opposite angle of the Gothic sofa, partook of the character of their surroundings. The girl's mind was like a large light empty place, scantily furnished with a few massive prejudices, not designed to add to anyone's comfort but too ponderous to be easily moved. Mrs. Quentin's own intelligence, in which its owner, in an artistically shaded half-light, had so long moved amid a delicate complexity of sensations, seemed in comparison suddenly close and crowded; and in taking refuge there from the glare of the young girl's candor, the older woman found herself stumbling in an unwonted obscurity. Her uneasiness resolved itself into a sense of irritation against her listener. Mrs. Quentin knew that the momentary value of any argument lies in the capacity of the mind to which it is addressed; and as her shafts of persuasion spent themselves against Miss Fenno's obduracy, she said to herself that, since conduct is governed by emotions rather than ideas, the really strong people are those who mistake their sensations for opinions. Viewed in this light, Miss Fenno was certainly very strong: there was an unmistakable ring of finality in the tone with which she declared:

"It's impossible."

Mrs. Quentin's answer veiled the least shade of feminine resentment. "I told Alan that where he had failed there was no chance of my making an impression."

Hope Fenno laid on her visitor's an almost reverential hand. "Dear Mrs. Quentin, it's the impression you make that confirms the impossibility."

Mrs. Quentin waited a moment: she was perfectly aware that, where her feelings were concerned, her sense of humor was not to be relied on. "Do I make such an odious impression?" she asked at length, with a smile that seemed to give the girl her choice of two meanings.

"You make such a beautiful one! It's too beautiful—it obscures my judgment."

Mrs. Quentin looked at her thoughtfully. "Would it be permissible, I wonder, for an older woman to suggest that, at your age, it isn't always a misfortune to have what one calls one's judgment temporarily obscured?"

Miss Fenno flushed. "I try not to judge others—"

"You judge Alan."

"Ah, *he* is not others," she murmured with an accent that touched the older woman.

"You judge his mother."

"I don't; I don't!"

Mrs. Quentin pressed her point. "You judge yourself, then, as you would be in my position—and your verdict condemns me."

"How can you think it? It's because I appreciate the difference in our point of view that I find it so difficult to defend myself—"

"Against what?"

"The temptation to imagine that I might be as *you* are—feeling as I do."

Mrs. Quentin rose with a sigh. "My child, in my day love was less subtle." She added, after a moment: "Alan is a perfect son."

"Ah, that again—that makes it worse!"

"Worse?"

"Just as your goodness does, your sweetness, your immense indulgence in letting me discuss things with you in a way that must seem almost an impertinence."

Mrs. Quentin's smile was not without irony. "You must remember that I do it for Alan."

"That's what I love you for!" the girl instantly returned; and again her tone touched her listener.

"And yet you're sacrificing him—and to an idea!"

"Isn't it to ideas that all the sacrifices that were worth-while have been made?"

"One may sacrifice one's self."

Miss Fenno's color rose. "That's what I'm doing," she said gently.

Mrs. Quentin took her hand. "I believe you are," she answered. "And it isn't true that I speak only for Alan. Perhaps I did when I began; but now I want to plead for you too—against yourself." She paused, and then went on with a deeper note: "I have let you, as you say, speak your mind to me in terms that some women might have resented, because I wanted to show you how little, as the years go on, theories, ideas, abstract conceptions of life, weigh against the actual, against the particular way in which life presents itself to us—to women especially. To decide beforehand exactly how one ought to behave in given circumstances is like deciding that one will follow a certain direction in crossing an unexplored country. Afterward we find that we must turn out for the obstacles —cross the rivers where they're shallowest—take the tracks that others have beaten—make all sorts of unexpected concessions. Life is made up of compromises: that is what youth refuses to understand. I've lived long enough to doubt whether any real good ever came of sacrificing beautiful facts to even more beautiful theories. Do I seem casuistical? I don't know—there may be losses either way... but the love of the man one loves... of the child one loves... that makes up for everything...."

She had spoken with a thrill which seemed to communicate itself to the hand her listener had left in hers. Her eyes filled suddenly, but through their dimness she saw the girl's lips shape a last desperate denial: "Don't you see it's because I feel all this that I mustn't—that I can't?"

III

Mrs. Quentin, in the late spring afternoon, had turned in at the doors of the Metropolitan Museum. She had been walking in the Park, in a solitude oppressed by the ever-present sense of her son's trouble, and had suddenly remembered that someone had added a Beltraffio to the collection. It was an old habit of Mrs. Quentin's to seek in the enjoyment of the beautiful the distraction that most of her acquaintances appeared to find in each other's company. She had few friends, and their society was welcome to her only in her more superficial moods; but she could drug anxiety with a picture as some women can soothe it with a bonnet.

During the six months which had elapsed since her visit to Miss Fenno she had been conscious of a pain of which she had supposed herself no longer capable: as a man will continue to feel the ache of an amputated arm. She had fancied that all her centers of feeling had been transferred to Alan; but she now found herself subject to a kind of dual suffering, in which her individual pang was the keener in that it divided her from her son's. Alan had surprised her: she had not foreseen that he would take a sentimental rebuff so hard. His disappointment took the uncommunicative form of a sterner application to work. He threw himself into the concerns of the *Radiator* with an aggressiveness which almost betrayed itself in the paper. Mrs. Quentin never read the *Radiator*, but from the glimpses of it reflected in the other journals she gathered that it was at least not being subjected to the moral reconstruction which had been one of Miss Fenno's alternatives.

Mrs. Quentin never spoke to her son of what had happened. She was superior to the cheap satisfaction of avenging his injury by deprecating its cause. She knew that in sentimental sorrows such consolations are as salt in the wound. The avoidance of a subject so vividly present to both could not but affect the closeness of their relation. An invisible presence hampered their liberty of speech and thought. The girl was always between them; and to hide the sense of her intrusion they began to be less frequently together. It was then that Mrs. Quentin measured the extent of her isolation. Had she ever dared to forecast such a situation, she would have proceeded on the conventional theory that her son's suffering must draw her nearer to him; and this was precisely the relief that was denied her. Alan's uncommunicativeness extended below the level of speech, and his mother, reduced to the helplessness of dead reckoning, had not even the solace of adapting her sympathy to his needs. She did not know what he felt: his course was incalculable to her. She sometimes wondered if she had become as incomprehensible to him; and it was to find a moment's refuge from the dogging misery of such conjectures that she had now turned in at the Museum.

The long line of mellow canvases seemed to receive her into the rich calm of an autumn twilight. She might have been walking in an enchanted wood where the footfall of care never sounded. So deep was the sense of seclusion that, as she turned from her prolonged communion with the new Beltraffio, it was a surprise to find that she was not alone.

A young lady who had risen from the central ottoman stood in suspended flight as Mrs. Quentin faced her. The older woman was the first to regain her self-possession.

"Miss Fenno!" she said.

The girl advanced with a blush. As it faded, Mrs. Quentin noticed a change in her. There had always been something bright and banner-like in her aspect, but now her look drooped, and she hung at half-mast, as it were. Mrs. Quentin, in the embarrassment of surprising a secret that its possessor was doubtless unconscious of betraying, reverted hurriedly to the Beltraffio.

"I came to see this," she said. "It's very beautiful."

Miss Fenno's eye traveled incuriously over the mystic blue

reaches of the landscape. "I suppose so," she assented; adding, after another tentative pause: "You come here often, don't you?"

"Very often," Mrs. Quentin answered. "I find pictures a great help."

"A help?"

"A rest, I mean . . . if one is tired or out of sorts."

"Ah," Miss Fenno murmured, looking down.

"This Beltraffio is new, you know," Mrs. Quentin continued. "What a wonderful background, isn't it? Is he a painter who interests you?"

The girl glanced again at the dusky canvas, as though in a final endeavor to extract from it a clue to the consolations of art. "I don't know," she said at length; "I'm afraid I don't understand pictures." She moved nearer to Mrs. Quentin and held out her hand.

"You're going?"

"Yes."

Mrs. Quentin looked at her. "Let me drive you home," she said, impulsively. She was feeling, with a shock of surprise, that it gave her, after all, no pleasure to see how much the girl had suffered.

Miss Fenno stiffened perceptibly. "Thank you; I shall like the walk."

Mrs. Quentin dropped her hand with a corresponding movement of withdrawal, and a momentary wave of antagonism seemed to sweep the two women apart. Then, as Mrs. Quentin, bowing slightly, again addressed herself to the picture, she felt a sudden touch on her arm.

"Mrs. Quentin," the girl faltered, "I really came here because I saw your carriage." Her eyes sank, and then fluttered back to her hearer's face. "I've been horribly unhappy!" she exclaimed.

Mrs. Quentin was silent. If Hope Fenno had expected an immediate response to her appeal, she was disappointed. The older woman's face was like a veil dropped before her thoughts.

"I've thought so often," the girl went on precipitately, "of what you said that day you came to see me last autumn. I think I understand now what you meant—what you tried to make me see. . . . Oh, Mrs. Quentin," she broke out, "I didn't mean to tell you this—I never dreamed of it till this moment—but you *do* remember what you said, don't you? You must remember it! And now that I've met you in this way, I can't help telling you that I believe—I begin to believe—that you were quite right, after all."

Mrs. Quentin had listened without moving; but now she raised her eyes with a slight smile. "Do you wish me to say this to Alan?" she asked.

The girl flushed, but her glance braved the smile. "Would he still care to hear it?" she said fearlessly.

Mrs. Quentin took momentary refuge in a renewed inspection of the Beltraffio; then, turning, she said, with a kind of reluctance: "He would still care."

"Ah!" broke from the girl.

During this exchange of words the two speakers had drifted unconsciously toward one of the benches. Mrs. Quentin glanced about her: a custodian who had been hovering in the doorway sauntered into the adjoining gallery, and they remained alone among the silvery Van Dykes and flushed bituminous Halses. Mrs. Quentin sank down on the bench and reached a hand to the girl.

"Sit by me," she said.

Miss Fenno dropped beside her. In both women the stress of emotion was too strong for speech. The girl was still trembling, and Mrs. Quentin was the first to regain her composure.

"You say you've suffered," she began at last. "Do you suppose *I* haven't?"

"I knew you had. That made it so much worse for me—that I should have been the cause of your suffering for Alan!"

Mrs. Quentin drew a deep breath. "Not for Alan only," she said. Miss Fenno turned on her a wondering glance. "Not for Alan only. *That* pain every woman expects—and knows how to bear. We all know our children must have such disappointments, and to suffer with them is not the deepest pain. It's the suffering apart—in ways they don't understand." She breathed deeply. "I want you to know what I mean. You were right—that day—and I was wrong."

"Oh," the girl faltered.

Mrs. Quentin went on in a voice of passionate lucidity. "I knew it then—I knew it even while I was trying to argue with you—I've always known it! I didn't want my son to marry you till I heard your reasons for refusing him; and then—then I longed to see you his wife!"

"Oh, Mrs. Quentin!"

"I longed for it; but I knew it mustn't be."

"Mustn't be?"

Mrs. Quentin shook her head sadly, and the girl, gaining courage from this mute negation, cried with an uncontrollable escape of feeling:

"It's because you thought me hard, obstinate, narrow-minded? Oh, I understand that so well! My self-righteousness must have seemed so petty! A girl who could sacrifice a man's future to her own moral vanity—for it *was* a form of vanity; you showed me that plainly enough—how you must have despised me! But I am not that girl now—indeed I'm not. I'm not impulsive—I think things out. I've thought this out. I know Alan loves me—I know *how* he loves me—and I believe I can help him—oh, not in the ways I had fancied before—but just merely by loving him." She paused, but Mrs. Quentin made no sign. "I see it all so differently now. I see what an influence love itself may be—how my believing in him, loving him, accepting him just as he is, might help him more than any theories, any arguments. I might have seen this long ago in looking at *you*—as he often told me—in seeing how you'd kept yourself apart from—from—Mr. Quentin's work and his—been always the beautiful side of life to them—kept their faith alive in spite of themselves—not by interfering, preaching, reforming, but by—just loving them and being there—" She looked at Mrs. Quentin with a simple nobleness. "It isn't as if I cared for the money, you know; if I cared for that, I should be afraid—"

"You will care for it in time," Mrs. Quentin said suddenly.

Miss Fenno drew back, releasing her hand. "In time?"

"Yes; when there's nothing else left." She stared a moment at the pictures. "My poor child," she broke out, "I've heard all you say so often before!"

"You've heard it?"

"Yes—from myself. I felt as you do, I argued as you do, I acted as I mean to prevent your doing, when I married Alan's father."

The long empty gallery seemed to reverberate with the girl's startled exclamation—"Oh, Mrs. Quentin—"

"Hush; let me speak. Do you suppose I'd do this if you were the kind of pink and white idiot he ought to have married? It's because I see you're alive, as I was, tingling with beliefs, ambitions, energies, as I was—that I can't see you walled up alive, as I was, without stretching out a hand to save you!" She sat gazing rigidly forward, her eyes on the pictures, speaking in the low precipitate tone of one who tries to press the meaning of a lifetime into a few breathless sentences.

"When I met Alan's father," she went on, "I knew nothing of his—his work. We met abroad, where I had been living with my mother. That was twenty-six years ago, when the *Radiator* was less—less notorious than it is now. I knew my husband owned a newspaper—a great newspaper—and nothing more. I had never seen a copy of the *Radiator*; I had no notion what it stood for, in politics—or in other ways. We were married in Europe, and a few months afterward we came to live here. People were already beginning to talk about the *Radiator*. My husband, on leaving college, had bought it with some money an old uncle had left him, and the public at first was merely curious to see what an ambitious, stirring young man without any experience of journalism was going to make out of his experiment. They found first of all that he was going to make a great deal of money out of it. I found that out too. I was so happy in other ways that it didn't make much difference at first; though it was pleasant to be able to help my mother, to be generous and charitable, to live in a nice house, and wear the handsome gowns he liked to see me in. But still it didn't really count—it counted so little that when, one day, I learned what the *Radiator* was, I would have gone out into the streets barefooted rather than live another hour on the money it brought in." Her voice sank, and she paused to steady it. The girl at her side did not speak or move. "I shall never forget that day," she began again. "The paper had stripped bare some family scandal— some miserable bleeding secret that a dozen unhappy people had been struggling to keep out of print—that *would* have been kept out if my husband had not—Oh, you must guess the rest! I can't go on!"

She felt a hand on hers. "You mustn't go on," the girl whispered.

"Yes, I must—I must! You must be made to understand." She drew a deep breath. "My husband was not like Alan. When he found out how I felt about it he was surprised at first—but gradually he began to see—or at least I fancied he saw—the hatefulness of it. At any rate he saw how I suffered, and he offered to give up the whole thing—to sell the paper. It couldn't be done all of a sudden, of course—he made me see that—for he had put all his money in it, and he had no special aptitude for any other kind of work. He was a born journalist—like Alan. It was a great sacrifice for him to give up the paper, but he promised to do it—in time— when a good opportunity offered. Meanwhile, of course, he wanted to build it up, to increase the circulation—and to do that he had to keep on in the same way—he made that clear to me. I saw that we were in a vicious circle. The paper, to sell well, had to be made more and more detestable and disgraceful. At first I rebelled—but somehow—I can't tell you how it was—after that first concession the ground seemed to give under me: with every struggle I sank deeper. And then—then Alan was born. He was such a delicate baby that there was very little hope of saving him. But money did it—the money from the paper. I took him abroad to see the best physicians—I took him to a warm climate every winter. In hot weather the doctors recommended sea air, and we had a yacht and cruised every summer. I owed his life to the *Radiator*. And when he began to grow stronger the habit was formed—the habit of luxury. He could not get on without the things he had always been used to. He pined in bad air; he drooped under monotony and discomfort; he throve on variety, amusement, travel, every kind of novelty and excitement. And all I wanted for him his inexhaustible foster mother was there to give!

"My husband said nothing, but he must have seen how things were going. There was no more talk of giving up the *Radiator*. He never reproached me with my inconsistency, but I thought he must despise me, and the thought made me reckless. I determined to ignore the paper altogether—to take what it gave as though I didn't know where it came from. And to excuse this I invented the theory that one may, so to speak, purify money by putting it to good uses. I gave away a great deal in charity—I indulged myself very little at first. All the money that was not spent on Alan I tried to do good with. But gradually, as my boy grew up, the problem became more complicated. How was I to protect Alan from the contamination I had let him live in? I couldn't preach by example—couldn't hold up his father as a warning, or denounce the money we were living on. All I could do was to disguise the inner ugliness of life by making it beautiful outside—to build a wall of beauty between him and the facts of life, turn his tastes and interests another way, hide the *Radiator* from him as a smiling woman at a ball may hide a cancer in her breast! Just as Alan was entering college his father died. Then I saw my way clear. I had loved my husband—and yet I drew my first free breath in years. For the *Radiator* had been left to Alan outright—there was nothing on earth to prevent his selling it when he came of age. And there was no excuse for his not selling it. I had brought him up to depend on money, but the paper had given us enough money to gratify all his tastes. At last we could turn on the monster that had nourished us. I felt a savage joy in the thought—I could hardly bear to wait till Alan came of age. But I had never spoken to him of the paper, and I didn't dare speak of it now. Some false shame kept me back, some vague belief in his ignorance. I would wait till he was twenty-one, and then we should be free.

"I waited—the day came, and I spoke. You can guess his answer, I suppose. He had no idea of selling the *Radiator*. It wasn't the money he cared for—it was the career that tempted him. He was a born journalist, and his ambition, ever since he could remember, had been to carry on his father's work, to develop, to surpass it. There was nothing in the world as interesting as modern journalism. He couldn't imagine any other kind of life that wouldn't bore him to death. A newspaper like the *Radiator* might be made one of the biggest powers on earth, and he loved power, and meant to have all he could get. I listened to him in a kind of trance. I couldn't find a word to say. His father had had scruples—he had none. I seemed to realize at once that argument would be useless. I don't know that I even tried to plead with him—he was so bright and hard and inaccessible! Then I saw that he was, after all, what I had made him—the creature of my concessions, my connivances, my evasions. That was the price I had paid for him—I had kept him at that cost!

"Well—I *had* kept him, at any rate. That was the feeling that survived. He was my boy, my son, my very own—till some other woman took him. Meanwhile the old life must go on as it could. I gave up the struggle. If at that point he was inaccessible, at others he was close to me. He has always been a perfect son. Our tastes grew together—we enjoyed the same books, the same pictures, the same people. All I had to do was to look at him in profile to see the side of him that was really mine. At first I kept thinking of the dreadful other side—but gradually the impression faded, and I kept my mind turned from it, as one does from a deformity in a face one loves. I thought I had made my last compromise with life—had hit on a *modus vivendi* that would last my time.

"And then he met you. I had always been prepared for his marrying, but not a girl like you. I thought he would choose a sweet thing who would never pry into his closets—he hated women with ideas! But as soon as I saw you I knew the struggle would have to begin again. He is so much stronger than his father—he is full of the most monstrous convictions. And he has the courage of them, too—you saw last year that his love for you never made him waver. He believes in his work: he adores it—it is a kind of hideous idol to which he would make human sacrifices! He loves you still—I've been honest with you—but his love wouldn't change him. It is you who would have to change—to die gradually, as I have died, till there is only one live point left in me. Ah, if one died completely—that's simple enough! But something persists—remember that—a single point, an aching nerve of truth. Now and then you may drug it—but a touch wakes it again, as your face has waked it in me. There's always enough of one's old self left to suffer with...."

She stood up and faced the girl abruptly. "What shall I tell Alan?" she said.

Miss Fenno sat motionless, her eyes on the ground. Twilight was falling on the gallery—a twilight which seemed to emanate not so much from the glass dome overhead as from the crepuscular depths into which the faces of the pictures were receding. The custodian's step sounded warningly down the corridor. When the girl looked up she was alone.

THE DILETTANTE

IT WAS on an impulse hardly needing the arguments he found himself advancing in its favor, that Thursdale, on his way to the club, turned as usual into Mrs. Vervain's street.

The "as usual" was his own qualification of the act; a convenient way of bridging the interval—in days and other sequences—that lay between this visit and the last. It was characteristic of him that he instinctively excluded his call two days earlier, with Ruth Gaynor, from the list of his visits to Mrs. Vervain: the special conditions attending it had made it no more like a visit to Mrs. Vervain than an engraved dinner invitation is like a personal letter. Yet it was to talk over his call with Miss Gaynor that he was now returning to the scene of that episode; and it was because Mrs. Vervain could be trusted to handle the talking over as skillfully as the interview itself that, at her corner, he had felt the dilettante's irresistible craving to take a last look at a work of art that was passing out of his possession.

On the whole, he knew no one better fitted to deal with the unexpected than Mrs. Vervain. She excelled in the rare art of taking things for granted, and Thursdale felt a pardonable pride in the thought that she owed her excellence to his training. Early in his career Thursdale had made the mistake, at the outset of his acquaintance with a lady, of telling her that he loved her, and exacting the same avowal in return. The latter part of that episode had been like the long walk back from a picnic, when one has to carry all the crockery one has finished using: it was the last time Thursdale ever allowed himself to be encumbered with the debris of a feast. He thus incidentally learned that the privilege of loving her is one of the least favors that a charming woman can accord; and in seeking to avoid the pitfalls of sentiment he had developed a science of evasion in which the woman of the moment became a mere implement of the game. He owed a great deal of delicate enjoyment to the cultivation of this art. The perils from which it had been his refuge became naïvely harmless: was it possible that he who now took his easy way along the levels had once preferred to gasp on the raw heights of emotion? Youth is a high-colored season; but he had the satisfaction of feeling that he had entered earlier than most into that chiaroscuro of sensation where every half-tone has its value.

As a promoter of this pleasure no one he had known was comparable to Mrs. Vervain. He had taught a good many women not to betray their feelings, but he had never before had such fine material to work with. She had been surprisingly crude when he first knew her; capable of making the most awkward inferences, of plunging through thin ice, of recklessly undressing her emotions; but she had acquired, under the discipline of his reticences and evasions, a skill almost equal to his own, and perhaps more remarkable in that it involved keeping time with any tune he played and reading at sight some uncommonly difficult passages.

It had taken Thursdale seven years to form this fine talent; but the result justified the effort. At the crucial moment she had been perfect: her way of greeting Miss Gaynor had made him regret that he had announced his engagement by letter. It was an evasion that confessed a difficulty; a deviation implying an obstacle, where, by common consent, it was agreed to see none; it betrayed, in short, a lack of confidence in the completeness of his method. It had been his pride never to put himself in a position which had to be quitted, as it were, by the back door; but here, as he perceived, the main portals would have opened for him of their own accord. All this, and much more, he read in the finished naturalness with which Mrs. Vervain had met Miss Gaynor. He had never seen a better piece of work: there was no overeagerness, no suspicious warmth, above all (and this gave her art the grace of a natural quality) there were none of those damnable implications whereby a woman, in welcoming her friend's betrothed, may keep him on pins and needles while she laps the lady in complacency. So masterly a performance, indeed, hardly needed the offset of Miss Gaynor's door-step words—"To be so kind to me, how she must have liked you!"—though he caught himself wishing it lay within the bounds of fitness to transmit them, as a final tribute, to the one woman he knew who was unfailingly certain to enjoy a good thing. It was perhaps the one drawback to his new situation that it might develop good things which it would be impossible to hand on to Margaret Vervain.

The fact that he had made the mistake of underrating his friend's powers, the consciousness that his writing must have betrayed his distrust of her efficiency, seemed an added reason for turning down her street instead of going on to the club. He would show her that he knew how to value her; he would ask her to achieve with him a feat infinitely rarer and more delicate than the one he had appeared to avoid. Incidentially, he would also dispose of the interval of time before dinner: ever since he had seen Miss Gaynor off, an hour earlier, on her return journey to Buffalo, he had been wondering how he should put in the rest of the afternoon. It was absurd, how he missed the girl.... Yes, that was it: the desire to talk about her was, after all, at the bottom of his impulse to call on Mrs. Vervain! It was absurd, if you like—but it was delightfully rejuvenating. He could recall the time when he had been afraid of being obvious: now he felt that this return to the primitive emotions might be as restorative as a holiday in the Canadian woods. And it was precisely by the girl's candor, her directness, her lack of complications, that he was taken. The sense that she might say something rash at any moment was positively exhilarating: if she had thrown her arms about him at the station he would not have given a thought to his crumpled dignity. It surprised Thursdale to find what freshness of heart he brought to the adventure; and though his sense of irony prevented his ascribing his intactness to any conscious purpose, he could but rejoice in the fact that his sentimental economies had left him such a large surplus to draw upon.

Mrs. Vervain was at home—as usual. When one visits the cemetery one expects to find the angel on the tombstone, and it struck Thursdale as another proof of his friend's good taste that she had been in no undue haste to change her habits. The whole house appeared to count on his coming; the footman took his hat and overcoat as naturally as though there had been no lapse in his visits; and the drawing-room at once enveloped him in that atmosphere of tacit intelligence which Mrs. Vervain imparted to her very furniture.

It was a surprise that, in this general harmony of circumstances, Mrs. Vervain should herself sound the first false note.

"You?" she exclaimed; and the book she held slipped from her hand.

It was crude, certainly; unless it were a touch of the finest art. The difficulty of classifying it disturbed Thursdale's balance.

"Why not?" he said, restoring the book. "Isn't it my hour?" And as she made no answer, he added gently, "Unless it's someone else's?"

She laid the book aside and sank back into her chair. "Mine, merely," she said.

"I hope that doesn't mean that you're unwilling to share it?"

"With you? By no means. You're welcome to my last crust."

He looked at her reproachfully. "Do you call this the last?"

She smiled as he dropped into the seat across the hearth. "It's a way of giving it more flavor!"

He returned the smile. "A visit to you doesn't need such condiments."

She took this with just the right measure of retrospective amusement.

"Ah, but I want to put into this one a very special taste," she confessed.

Her smile was so confident, so reassuring, that it lulled him into the imprudence of saying: "Why should you want it to be different from what was always so perfectly right?"

She hesitated. "Doesn't the fact that it's the last constitute a difference?"

"The last—my last visit to you?"

"Oh, metaphorically, I mean—there's a break in the continuity."

Decidedly, she was pressing too hard: unlearning his arts already!

"I don't recognize it," he said. "Unless you make me—" he added, with a note that slightly stirred her attitude of languid attention.

She turned to him with grave eyes. "You recognize no difference whatever?"

"None—except an added link in the chain."

"An added link?"

"In having one more thing to like you for—your letting Miss Gaynor see why I had already so many." He flattered himself that this turn had taken the least hint of fatuity from the phrase.

Mrs. Vervain sank into her former easy pose. "Was it that you came for?" she asked, almost gaily.

"If it is necessary to have a reason—that was one."

"To talk to me about Miss Gaynor?"

"To tell you how she talks about you."

"That will be very interesting—especially if you have seen her since her second visit to me."

"Her second visit?" Thursdale pushed his chair back with a start and moved to another. "She came to see you again?"

"This morning, yes—by appointment."

He continued to look at her blankly. "You sent for her?"

"I didn't have to—she wrote and asked me last night. But no doubt you have seen her since."

Thursdale sat silent. He was trying to separate his words from his thoughts, but they still clung together inextricably. "I saw her off just now at the station."

"And she didn't tell you that she had been here again?"

"There was hardly time, I suppose—there were people about—" he floundered.

"Ah, she'll write, then."

He regained his composure. "Of course she'll write: very often, I hope. You know I'm absurdly in love," he cried audaciously.

She tilted her head back, looking up at him as he leaned against the chimney piece. He had leaned there so often that the attitude touched a pulse which set up a throbbing in her throat. "Oh, my poor Thursdale!" she murmured.

"I suppose it's rather ridiculous," he owned; and as she remained silent, he added, with a sudden break—"Or have you another reason for pitying me?"

Her answer was another question. "Have you been back to your rooms since you left her?"

"Since I left her at the station? I came straight here."

"Ah, yes—you *could*: there was no reason—" Her words passed into a silent musing.

Thursdale moved nervously nearer. "You said you had something to tell me?"

"Perhaps I had better let her do so. There may be a letter at your rooms."

"A letter? What do you mean? A letter from *her*? What has happened?"

His paleness shook her, and she raised a hand of reassurance. "Nothing has happened—perhaps that is just the worst of it. You always *hated*, you know," she added incoherently, "to have things happen: you never would let them."

"And now—"

"Well, that was what she came here for: I supposed you had guessed. To know if anything had happened."

"Had happened?" He gazed at her slowly. "Between you and me?" he said with a rush of light.

The words were so much cruder than any that had ever passed between them, that the color rose to her face; but she held his startled gaze.

"You know girls are not quite as unsophisticated as they used to be. Are you surprised that such an idea should occur to her?"

His own color answered hers: it was the only reply that came to him.

Mrs. Vervain went on smoothly: "I supposed it might have struck you that there were times when we presented that appearance."

He made an impatient gesture. "A man's past is his own!"

"Perhaps—it certainly never belongs to the woman who has shared it. But one learns such truths only by experience; and Miss Gaynor is naturally inexperienced."

"Of course—but—supposing her act a natural one—" he floundered lamentably among his innuendoes "—I still don't see—how there was anything—"

"Anything to take hold of? There wasn't—"

"Well, then—?" escaped him, in undisguised satisfaction; but as she did not complete the sentence he went on with a faltering laugh: "She can hardly object to the existence of a mere friendship between us!"

"But she does," said Mrs. Vervain.

Thursdale stood perplexed. He had seen, on the previous day, no trace of jealousy or resentment in his betrothed: he could still hear the candid ring of the girl's praise of Mrs. Vervain. If she were such an abyss of insincerity as to dissemble distrust under such frankness, she must at least be more subtle than to bring her doubts to her rival for solution. The situation seemed one through which one could no longer move in a penumbra, and he let in a burst of light with the direct query: "Won't you explain what you mean?"

Mrs. Vervain sat silent, not provokingly, as though to prolong his distress, but as if, in the attenuated phraseology he had taught her, it was difficult to find words robust enough to meet his challenge. It was the first time he had ever asked her to explain anything: and she had lived so long in dread of offering elucidations which were not wanted, that she seemed unable to produce one on the spot.

At last she said slowly: "She came to find out if you were really free."

Thursdale colored again. "Free?" he stammered, with a sense of physical disgust at contact with such crassness.

"Yes—if I had quite done with you." She smiled in recovered security. "It seems she likes clear outlines; she has a passion for definitions."

"Yes—well?" he said, wincing at the echo of his own subtlety.

"Well—and when I told her that you had never belonged to me, she wanted me to define *my* status—to know exactly where I had stood all along."

Thursdale sat gazing at her intently; his hand was not yet on the clue. "And even when you had told her that—"

"Even when I had told her that I had had no status—that I had never stood anywhere, in any sense she meant," said Mrs. Vervain, slowly, "even then she wasn't satisfied, it seems."

He uttered an uneasy exclamation. "She didn't believe you, you mean?"

"I mean that she *did* believe me: too thoroughly."

"Well, then—in God's name, what did she want?"

"Something more—those were the words she used."

"Something more? Between—between you and me? Is it a conundrum?" He laughed awkwardly.

"Girls are not what they were in my day; they are no longer forbidden to contemplate the relation of the sexes."

"So it seems!" he commented. "But since, in this case, there wasn't any—" he broke off, catching the dawn of a revelation in her gaze.

"That's just it. The unpardonable offense has been—in our not offending."

He flung himself down despairingly. "I give up! What did you tell her?" he burst out with sudden crudeness.

"The exact truth. If I had only known," she broke off with a beseeching tenderness, "won't you believe that I would still have lied for you?"

"Lied for me? Why on earth should you have lied for either of us?"

"To save you—to hide you from her to the last! As I've hidden you from myself all these years!" She stood up with a sudden tragic import in her movement. "You believe me capable of that, don't you? If I had only guessed—but I have never known a girl like her; she had the truth out of me with a spring."

"The truth that you and I had never—"

"Had never—never in all these years! Oh, she knew why—she measured us both in a flash. She didn't suspect me of having haggled with you—her words pelted me like hail. 'He just took what he wanted—sifted and sorted you to suit his taste. Burnt out the gold and left a heap of cinders. And you let him—you let yourself be cut in bits'—she mixed her metaphors a little—'be cut in bits, and used or discarded, while all the while every drop of blood in you belonged to him! But he's Shylock—he's Shylock—and you have bled to death of the pound of flesh he has cut off you.' But she despises me the most, you know—far, far the most—" Mrs. Vervain ended.

The words fell strangely on the scented stillness of the room: they seemed out of harmony with its setting of afternoon intimacy, the kind of intimacy on which, at any moment, a visitor might intrude without perceptibly lowering the atmosphere. It was as though a grand opera singer had strained the acoustics of a private music room.

Thursdale stood up, facing his hostess. Half the room was between them, but they seemed to stare close at each other now that the veils of reticence and ambiguity had fallen.

His first words were characteristic: "She *does* despise me, then?" he exclaimed.

"She thinks the pound of flesh you took was a little too near the heart."

He was excessively pale. "Please tell me exactly what she said of me."

"She did not speak much of you: she is proud. But I gather that while she understands love or indifference, her eyes have never been opened to the many intermediate shades of feeling. At any rate, she expressed an unwillingness to be taken with reservations—she thinks you would have loved her better if you had loved someone else first. The point of view is original—she insists on a man with a past!"

"Oh, a past—if she's serious—I could rake up a past!" he said with a laugh.

"So I suggested: but she has her eyes on this particular portion of it. She insists on making it a test case. She wanted to know what you had done to me; and before I could guess her drift I blundered into telling her."

Thursdale drew a difficult breath. "I never supposed—your revenge is complete," he said slowly.

He heard a little gasp in her throat. "My revenge? When I sent for you to warn you—to save you from being surprised as *I* was surprised?"

"You're very good—but it's rather late to talk of saving me." He held out his hand in the mechanical gesture of leave-taking.

"How you must care!—for I never saw you so dull," was her answer. "Don't you see that it's not too late for me to help you?" And as he continued to stare, she brought out sublimely: "Take the rest—in imagination! Let it at least be of that much use to you. Tell her I lied to her—she's too ready to believe it! And so, after all, in a sense, I shan't have been wasted."

His stare hung on her, widening to a kind of wonder. She gave the look back brightly, unblushingly, as though the expedient were too simple to need oblique approaches. It was extraordinary how a few words had swept them from an atmosphere of the most complex dissimulations to this contact of naked souls.

It was not in Thursdale to expand with the pressure of fate; but something in him cracked with it, and the rift let in new light. He went up to his friend and took her hand.

"You would do it—you would do it!"

She looked at him, smiling, but her hand shook.

"Good-bye," he said, kissing it.

"Good-bye? You are going—?"

"To get my letter."

"Your letter? The letter won't matter, if you will only do what I ask."

He returned her gaze. "I might, I suppose, without being out of character. Only, don't you see that if your plan helped me it could only harm her?"

"Harm *her?*"

"To sacrifice you wouldn't make me different. I shall go on being what I have always been—sifting and sorting, as she calls it. Do you want my punishment to fall on *her?*"

She looked at him long and deeply. "Ah, if I had to choose between you—!"

"You would let her take her chance? But I can't, you see. I must take my punishment alone."

She drew her hand away, sighing. "Oh, there will be no punishment for either of you."

"For either of us? There will be the reading of her letter for me."

She shook her head with a slight laugh. "There will be no letter."

Thursdale faced about from the threshold with fresh life in his look. "No letter? You don't mean—"

"I mean that she's been with you since I saw her—she's seen you and heard your voice. If there *is* a letter, she has recalled it—from the first station, by telegraph."

He turned back to the door, forcing an answer to her smile. "But in the meanwhile I shall have read it," he said.

The door closed on him, and she hid her eyes from the dreadful emptiness of the room.

THE RECKONING

"THE MARRIAGE law of the new dispensation will be: *Thou shalt not be unfaithful—to thyself.*"

A discreet murmur of approval filled the studio, and through the haze of cigarette smoke Mrs. Clement Westall, as her husband descended from his improvised platform, saw him merged in a congratulatory group of ladies. Westall's informal talks on "The New Ethics" had drawn about him an eager following of the mentally unemployed—those who, as he had once phrased it, liked to have their brain-food cut up for them. The talks had begun by accident. Westall's ideas were known to be "advanced," but hitherto their advance had not been in the direction of publicity. He had been, in his wife's opinion, almost pusillanimously careful not to let his personal views endanger his professional standing. Of late, however, he had shown a puzzling tendency to dogmatize, to throw down the gauntlet, to flaunt his private code in the face of society; and the relation of the sexes being a topic always sure of an audience, a few admiring friends had persuaded him to give his after-dinner opinions a larger circulation by summing them up in a series of talks at the Van Sideren studio.

The Herbert Van Siderens were a couple who subsisted, socially, on the fact that they had a studio. Van Sideren's pictures were chiefly valuable as accessories to the *mise en scène* which differentiated his wife's "afternoons" from the blighting functions held in long New York drawing-rooms, and permitted her to offer their friends whiskey-and-soda instead of tea. Mrs. Van Sideren, for her part, was skilled in making the most of the kind of atmosphere which a lay-figure and an easel create; and if at times she found the illusion hard to maintain, and lost courage to the extent of almost wishing that Herbert could paint, she promptly overcame such moments of weakness by calling in some fresh talent, some extraneous re-enforcement of the "artistic" impression. It was in quest of such aid that she had seized on Westall, coaxing him, somewhat to his wife's surprise, into a flattered participation in her fraud. It was vaguely felt, in the Van Sideren circle, that all the audacities were artistic, and that a teacher who pronounced marriage immoral was somehow as distinguished as a painter who depicted purple grass and a green sky. The Van Sideren set were tired of the conventional color-scheme in art and conduct.

Julia Westall had long had her own views on the immorality of marriage; she might indeed have claimed her husband as a disciple. In the early days of their union she had secretly resented his disinclination to proclaim himself a follower of the new creed; had been inclined to tax him with moral cowardice, with a failure to live up to the convictions for which their marriage was supposed to stand. That was in the first burst of propagandism, when, womanlike, she wanted to turn her disobedience into a law. Now she felt differently. She could hardly account for the change, yet being a woman who never allowed her impulses to remain unaccounted for, she tried to do so by saying that she did not care to have the articles of her faith misinterpreted by the vulgar. In this connection, she was beginning to think that almost every one was vulgar; certainly there were few to whom she would have cared to entrust the defense of so esoteric a doctrine. And it was precisely at this point that Westall, discarding his unspoken principles, had chosen to descend from the heights of privacy, and stand hawking his convictions at the street-corner!

It was Una Van Sideren who, on this occasion, unconsciously focused upon herself Mrs. Westall's wandering resentment. In the first place, the girl had no business to be there. It was "horrid"— Mrs. Westall found herself slipping back into the old feminine vocabulary—simply "horrid" to think of a young girl's being allowed to listen to such talk. The fact that Una smoked cigarettes and sipped an occasional cocktail did not in the least tarnish a certain radiant innocency which made her appear the victim, rather than the accomplice, of her parents' vulgarities. Julia Westall felt in a hot helpless way that something ought to be done—that some one ought to speak to the girl's mother. And just then Una glided up.

"Oh, Mrs. Westall, how beautiful it was!" Una fixed her with large limpid eyes. "You believe it all, I suppose?" she asked with seraphic gravity.

"All—what, my dear child?"

The girl shone on her. "About the higher life—the freer expansion of the individual—the law of fidelity to one's self," she glibly recited.

Mrs. Westall, to her own wonder, blushed a deep and burning blush.

"My dear Una," she said, "you don't in the least understand what it's all about!"

Miss Van Sideren stared, with a slowly answering blush. "Don't *you*, then?" she murmured.

Mrs. Westall laughed. "Not always—or altogether! But I should like some tea, please."

Una led her to the corner where innocent beverages were dispensed. As Julia received her cup she scrutinized the girl more carefully. It was not such a girlish face, after all—definite lines were forming under the rosy haze of youth. She reflected that Una must be six-and-twenty, and wondered why she had not married. A nice stock of ideas she would have as her dower! If *they* were to be a part of the modern girl's trousseau—

Mrs. Westall caught herself up with a start. It was as though some one else had been speaking—a stranger who had borrowed her own voice: she felt herself the dupe of some fantastic mental ventriloquism. Concluding suddenly that the room was stifling and Una's tea too sweet, she set down her cup and looked about for Westall: to meet his eyes had long been her refuge from every uncertainty. She met them now, but only, as she felt, in transit;

they included her parenthetically in a larger flight. She followed the flight, and it carried her to a corner to which Una had withdrawn—one of the palmy nooks to which Mrs. Van Sideren attributed the success of her Saturdays. Westall, a moment later, had overtaken his look, and found a place at the girl's side. She bent forward, speaking eagerly; he leaned back, listening, with the depreciatory smile which acted as a filter to flattery, enabling him to swallow the strongest doses without apparent grossness of appetite. Julia winced at her own definition of the smile.

On the way home, in the deserted winter dusk, Westall surprised his wife by a sudden boyish pressure of her arm. "Did I open their eyes a bit? Did I tell them what you wanted me to?" he asked gaily.

Almost unconsciously, she let her arm slip from his. "What *I* wanted—?"

"Why, haven't you—all this time?" She caught the honest wonder of his tone. "I somehow fancied you'd rather blamed me for not talking more openly—before—. You almost made me feel, at times, that I was sacrificing principles to expediency."

She paused a moment over her reply; then she asked quietly: "What made you decide not to—any longer?"

She felt again the vibration of a faint surprise. "Why—the wish to please you!" he answered, almost too simply.

"I wish you would not go on, then," she said abruptly.

He stopped in his quick walk, and she felt his stare through the darkness.

"Not go on—?"

"Call a hansom, please. I'm tired," broke from her with a sudden rush of physical weariness.

Instantly his solicitude enveloped her. The room had been infernally hot—and then that confounded cigarette smoke—he had noticed once or twice that she looked pale—she mustn't come to another Saturday. She felt herself yielding, as she always did, to the warm influence of his concern for her, the feminine in her leaning on the man in him with a conscious intensity of abandonment.

He put her in the hansom, and her hand stole into his in the darkness. A tear or two rose, and she let them fall. It was so delicious to cry over imaginary troubles!

That evening, after dinner, he surprised her by reverting to the subject of his talk. He combined a man's dislike of uncomfortable questions with an almost feminine skill in eluding them; and she knew that if he returned to the subject he must have some special reason for doing so.

"You seem not to have cared for what I said this afternoon. Did I put the case badly?"

"No—you put it very well."

"Then what did you mean by saying that you would rather not have me go on with it?"

She glanced at him nervously, her ignorance of his intention deepening her sense of helplessness.

"I don't think I care to hear such things discussed in public."

"I don't understand you," he exclaimed. Again the feeling that his surprise was genuine gave an air of obliquity to her own attitude. She was not sure that she understood herself.

"Won't you explain?" he said with a tinge of impatience.

Her eyes wandered about the familiar drawing-room which had been the scene of so many of their evening confidences. The shaded lamps, the quiet-colored walls hung with mezzotints, the pale spring flowers scattered here and there in Venice glasses and bowls of old Sèvres, recalled, she hardly knew why, the apartment in which the evenings of her first marriage had been passed—a wilderness of rosewood and upholstery, with a picture of a Roman peasant above the mantelpiece, and a Greek slave in "statuary marble" between the folding-doors of the back drawing-room. It was a room with which she had never been able to establish any closer relation than that between a traveler and a railway station; and now, as she looked about at the surroundings which stood for her deepest affinities—the room for which she had left that other room—she was startled by the same sense of strangeness and unfamiliarity. The prints, the flowers, the subdued tones of the old porcelains, seemed to typify a superficial refinement which had no relation to the deeper significances of life.

Suddenly she heard her husband repeating his question.

"I don't know that I can explain," she faltered.

He drew his armchair forward so that he faced her across the hearth. The light of a reading-lamp fell on his finely drawn face, which had a kind of surface-sensitiveness akin to the surface-refinement of its setting.

"Is it that you no longer believe in our ideas?" he asked.

"In our ideas—?"

"The ideas I am trying to teach. The ideas you and I are supposed to stand for." He paused a moment. "The ideas on which our marriage was founded."

The blood rushed to her face. He had his reasons, then—she was sure now that he had his reasons! In the ten years of their marriage, how often had either of them stopped to consider the ideas on which it was founded? How often does a man dig about the basement of his house to examine its foundation? The foundation is there, of course—the house rests on it—but one lives above-stairs and not in the cellar. It was she, indeed, who in the beginning had insisted on reviewing the situation now and then, on recapitulating the reasons which justified her course, on proclaiming, from time to time, her adherence to the religion of personal independence; but she had long ceased to feel the want of any such ideal standards, and had accepted her marriage as frankly and naturally as though it had been based on the primitive needs of the heart, and required no special sanction to explain or justify it.

"Of course I still believe in our ideas!" she exclaimed.

"Then I repeat that I don't understand. It was a part of your theory that the greatest possible publicity should be given to our view of marriage. Have you changed your mind in that respect?"

She hesitated. "It depends on circumstances—on the public one is addressing. The set of people that the Van Siderens get about them don't care for the truth or falseness of a doctrine. They are attracted simply by its novelty."

"And yet it was in just such a set of people that you and I met, and learned the truth from each other."

"That was different."

"In what way?"

"I was not a young girl, to begin with. It is perfectly unfitting that young girls should be present at—at such times—should hear such things discussed—"

"I thought you considered it one of the deepest social wrongs that such things never *are* discussed before young girls; but that is beside the point, for I don't remember seeing any young girl in my audience to-day—"

"Except Una Van Sideren!"

He turned slightly and pushed back the lamp at his elbow.

"Oh, Miss Van Sideren—naturally—"

"Why naturally?"

"The daughter of the house—would you have had her sent out with her governess?"

"If I had a daughter I should not allow such things to go on in my house!"

Westall, stroking his mustache, leaned back with a faint smile. "I fancy Miss Van Sideren is quite capable of taking care of herself."

"No girl knows how to take care of herself—till it's too late."

"And yet you would deliberately deny her the surest means of self-defense?"

"What do you call the surest means of self-defense?"

"Some preliminary knowledge of human nature in its relation to the marriage tie."

She made an impatient gesture. "How should you like to marry that kind of a girl?"

"Immensely—if she were my kind of girl in other respects."

She took up the argument at another point.

"You are quite mistaken if you think such talk does not affect young girls. Una was in a state of the most absurd exaltation—"
She broke off, wondering why she had spoken.

Westall reopened a magazine which he had laid aside at the beginning of their discussion. "What you tell me is immensely flattering to my oratorical talent—but I fear you overrate its effect. I can assure you that Miss Van Sideren doesn't have to have her thinking done for her. She's quite capable of doing it herself."

"You seem very familiar with her mental processes!" flashed unguardedly from his wife.

He looked up quietly from the pages he was cutting.

"I should like to be," he answered. "She interests me."

II

If there be a distinction in being misunderstood, it was one denied to Julia Westall when she left her first husband. Every one was ready to excuse and even to defend her. The world she adorned agreed that John Arment was "impossible," and hostesses gave a sigh of relief at the thought that it would no longer be necessary to ask him to dine.

There had been no scandal connected with the divorce: neither side had accused the other of the offense euphemistically described as "statutory." The Arments had indeed been obliged to transfer their allegiance to a State which recognized desertion as a cause for divorce, and construed the term so liberally that the seeds of desertion were shown to exist in every union. Even Mrs. Arment's second marriage did not make traditional morality stir in its sleep. It was known that she had not met her second husband till after she had parted from the first, and she had, moreover, replaced a rich man by a poor one. Though Clement Westall was acknowledged to be a rising lawyer, it was generally felt that his fortunes would not rise as rapidly as his reputation. The Westalls would probably always have to live quietly and go out to dinner in cabs. Could there be better evidence of Mrs. Arment's complete disinterestedness?

If the reasoning by which her friends justified her course was somewhat cruder and less complex than her own elucidation of the matter, both explanations led to the same conclusion: John Arment was impossible. The only difference was that, to his wife, his impossibility was something deeper than a social disqualification. She had once said, in ironical defense of her marriage, that it had at least preserved her from the necessity of sitting next to him at dinner; but she had not then realized at what cost the immunity was purchased. John Arment was impossible; but the sting of his impossibility lay in the fact that he made it impossible for those about him to be other than himself. By an unconscious process of elimination he had excluded from the world everything of which he did not feel a personal need: had become, as it were, a climate in which only his own requirements survived. This might seem to imply a deliberate selfishness; but there was nothing deliberate about Arment. He was as instinctive as an animal or a child. It was this childish element in his nature which sometimes for a moment unsettled his wife's estimate of him. Was it possible that he was simply undeveloped, that he had delayed, somewhat longer than is usual, the laborious process of growing up? He had the kind of sporadic shrewdness which causes it to be said of a dull man that he is "no fool"; and it was this quality that his wife found most trying. Even to the naturalist it is annoying to have his deductions disturbed by some unforeseen aberrancy of form or function; and how much more so to the wife whose estimate of herself is inevitably bound up with her judgment of her husband!

Arment's shrewdness did not, indeed, imply any latent intellectual power; it suggested, rather, potentialities of feeling, of suffering, perhaps, in a blind rudimentary way, on which Julia's sensibilities naturally declined to linger. She so fully understood her own reasons for leaving him that she disliked to think they were not as comprehensible to her husband. She was haunted, in her analytic moments, by the look of perplexity, too inarticulate for words, with which he had acquiesced in her explanations.

These moments were rare with her, however. Her marriage had been too concrete a misery to be surveyed philosophically. If she had been unhappy for complex reasons, the unhappiness was as real as though it had been uncomplicated. Soul is more bruisable than flesh, and Julia was wounded in every fiber of her spirit. Her husband's personality seemed to be closing gradually in on her, obscuring the sky and cutting off the air, till she felt herself shut up among the decaying bodies of her starved hopes. A sense of having been decoyed by some world-old conspiracy into this bondage of body and soul filled her with despair. If marriage was the slow life-long acquittal of a debt contracted in ignorance, then marriage was a crime against human nature. She, for one, would have no share in maintaining the pretense of which she had been a victim: the pretense that a man and a woman, forced into the narrowest of personal relations, must remain there till the end, though they may have outgrown the span of each other's natures as the mature tree outgrows the iron brace about the sapling.

It was in the first heat of her moral indignation that she had met Clement Westall. She had seen at once that he was "interested," and had fought off the discovery, dreading any influence that should draw her back into the bondage of conventional relations. To ward off the peril she had, with an almost crude precipitancy, revealed her opinions to him. To her surprise, she found that he shared them. She was attracted by the frankness of a suitor who, while pressing his suit, admitted that he did not believe in marriage. Her worst audacities did not seem to surprise him: he had thought out all that she had felt, and they had reached the same conclusion. People grew at varying rates, and the yoke that was an easy fit for the one might soon become galling to the other. That was what divorce was for: the readjustment of personal relations. As soon as their necessarily transitive nature was recognized they would gain in dignity as well as in harmony. There would be no farther need of the ignoble concessions and connivances, the perpetual sacrifice of personal delicacy and moral pride, by means of which imperfect marriages were now held together. Each partner to the contract would be on his mettle, forced to live up to the highest standard of self-development, on pain of losing the other's respect and affection. The low nature could no longer drag the

She took the nerve tonic diligently, but it failed to act as a sedative to her fears. She did not know what she feared; but that made her anxiety the more pervasive. Her husband had not reverted to the subject of his Saturday talks. He was unusually kind and considerate, with a softening of his quick manner, a touch of shyness in his consideration, that sickened her with new fears. She told herself that it was because she looked badly—because he knew about the doctor and the nerve tonic—that he showed this deference to her wishes, this eagerness to screen her from moral drafts; but the explanation simply cleared the way for fresh inferences.

The week passed slowly, vacantly, like a prolonged Sunday. On Saturday the morning post brought a note from Mrs. Van Sideren. Would dear Julia ask Mr. Westall to come half an hour earlier than usual, as there was to be some music after his "talk"? Westall was just leaving for his office when his wife read the note. She opened the drawing-room door and called him back to deliver the message.

He glanced at the note and tossed it aside. "What a bore! I shall have to cut my game of racquets. Well, I suppose it can't be helped. Will you write and say it's all right?"

Julia hesitated a moment, her hand stiffening on the chair-back against which she leaned.

"You mean to go on with these talks?" she asked.

"I—why not?" he returned; and this time it struck her that his surprise was not quite unfeigned. The perception helped her to find words.

"You said you had started them with the idea of pleasing me—"

"Well?"

"I told you last week that they didn't please me."

"Last week?—Oh—" He seemed to make an effort of memory. "I thought you were nervous then; you sent for the doctor the next day."

"It was not the doctor I needed; it was your assurance—"

"My assurance?"

Suddenly she felt the floor fail under her. She sank into the chair with a choking throat, her words, her reasons slipping away from her like straws down a whirling flood.

"Clement," she cried, "isn't it enough for you to know that I hate it?"

He turned to close the door behind them; then he walked toward her and sat down. "What is it that you hate?" he asked gently.

She had made a desperate effort to rally her routed argument.

"I can't bear to have you speak as if—as if—our marriage—were like the other kind—the wrong kind. When I heard you there, the other afternoon, before all those inquisitive gossiping people, proclaiming that husbands and wives had a right to leave each other whenever they were tired—or had seen some one else—"

Westall sat motionless, his eyes fixed on a pattern of the carpet.

"You *have* ceased to take this view, then?" he said as she broke off. "You no longer believe that husbands and wives *are* justified in separating—under such conditions?"

"Under such conditions?" she stammered. "Yes—I still believe that—but how can we judge for others? What can we know of the circumstances—?"

He interrupted her. "I thought it was a fundamental article of our creed that the special circumstances produced by marriage were not to interfere with the full assertion of individual liberty." He paused a moment. "I thought that was your reason for leaving Arment."

She flushed to the forehead. It was not like him to give a personal turn to the argument.

"It was my reason," she said simply.

"Well, then—why do you refuse to recognize its validity now?"

"I don't—I don't—I only say that one can't judge for others."

He made an impatient movement. "This is mere hair-splitting. What you mean is that, the doctrine having served your purpose when you needed it, you now repudiate it."

"Well," she exclaimed, flushing again, "what if I do? What does it matter to us?"

Westall rose from his chair. He was excessively pale, and stood before his wife with something of the formality of a stranger.

"It matters to me," he said in a low voice, "because I do *not* repudiate it."

"Well—?"

"And because I had intended to invoke it as"—

He paused and drew his breath deeply. She sat silent, almost deafened by her heart-beats.

—"as a complete justification of the course I am about to take."

Julia remained motionless. "What course is that?" she asked.

He cleared his throat. "I mean to claim the fulfillment of your promise."

For an instant the room wavered and darkened; then she recovered a torturing acuteness of vision. Every detail of her surroundings pressed upon her: the tick of the clock, the slant of sunlight on the wall, the hardness of the chair-arms that she grasped, were a separate wound to each sense.

"My promise—" she faltered.

"Your part of our mutual agreement to set each other free if one or the other should wish to be released."

She was silent again. He waited a moment, shifting his position nervously; then he said, with a touch of irritability: "You acknowledge the agreement?"

The question went through her like a shock. She lifted her head to it proudly. "I acknowledge the agreement," she said.

"And—you don't mean to repudiate it?"

A log on the hearth fell forward, and mechanically he advanced and pushed it back.

"No," she answered slowly, "I don't mean to repudiate it."

There was a pause. He remained near the hearth, his elbow resting on the mantelshelf. Close to his hand stood a little cup of jade that he had given her on one of their wedding anniversaries. She wondered vaguely if he noticed it.

"You intend to leave me, then?" she said at length.

His gesture seemed to deprecate the crudeness of the allusion.

"To marry some one else?"

Again his eye and hand protested. She rose and stood before him.

"Why should you be afraid to tell me? Is it Una Van Sideren?"

He was silent.

"I wish you good luck," she said.

III

She looked up, finding herself alone. She did not remember when or how he had left the room, or how long afterward she had sat there. The fire still smoldered on the hearth, but the slant of sunlight had left the wall.

Her first conscious thought was that she had not broken her word, that she had fulfilled the very letter of their bargain. There had been no crying out, no vain appeal to the past, no attempt at temporizing or evasion. She had marched straight up to the guns.

Now that it was over, she sickened to find herself alive. She looked about her, trying to recover her hold on reality. Her identity seemed to be slipping from her, as it disappears in a physical swoon. "This is my room—this is my house," she heard herself saying. Her room? Her house? She could almost hear the walls laugh back at her.

She stood up, weariness in every bone. The silence of the room frightened her. She remembered, now, having heard the front door close a long time ago: the sound suddenly re-echoed through her brain. Her husband must have left the house, then—her *husband*? She no longer knew in what terms to think: the simplest phrases had a poisoned edge. She sank back into her chair, overcome by a strange weakness. The clock struck ten—it was only ten o'clock! Suddenly she remembered that she had not ordered dinner...or were they dining out that evening? *Dinner—dining out*—the old meaningless phraseology pursued her! She must try to think of herself as she would think of some one else, a some one dissociated from all the familiar routine of the past, whose wants and habits must gradually be learned, as one might spy out the ways of a strange animal. . . .

The clock struck another hour—eleven. She stood up again and walked to the door: she thought she would go up stairs to her room. *Her* room? Again the word derided her. She opened the door, crossed the narrow hall, and walked up the stairs. As she passed, she noticed Westall's sticks and umbrellas: a pair of his gloves lay on the hall table. The same stair-carpet mounted between the same walls; the same old French print, in its narrow black frame, faced her on the landing. This visual continuity was intolerable. Within, a gaping chasm; without, the same untroubled and familiar surface. She must get away from it before she could attempt to think. But, once in her room, she sat down on the lounge, a stupor creeping over her. . . .

Gradually her vision cleared. A great deal had happened in the interval—a wild marching and countermarching of emotions, arguments, ideas—a fury of insurgent impulses that fell back spent upon themselves. She had tried, at first, to rally, to organize these chaotic forces. There must be help somewhere, if only she could master the inner tumult. Life could not be broken off short like this, for a whim, a fancy; the law itself would side with her, would defend her. The law? What claim had she upon it? She was the prisoner of her own choice: she had been her own legislator, and she was the predestined victim of the code she had devised. But this was grotesque, intolerable—a mad mistake, for which she could not be held accountable! The law she had despised was still there, might still be invoked . . . invoked, but to what end? Could she ask it to chain Westall to her side? *She* had been allowed to go free when she claimed her freedom—should she show less magnanimity than she had exacted? Magnanimity? The word lashed her with its irony—one does not strike an attitude when one is fighting for life! She would threaten, grovel, cajole . . . she would yield anything to keep her hold on happiness. Ah, but the difficulty lay deeper! The law could not help her—her own apostasy could not help her. She was the victim of the theories she renounced. It was as though some giant machine of her own making had caught her up in its wheels and was grinding her to atoms....

It was afternoon when she found herself out-of-doors. She walked with an aimless haste, fearing to meet familiar faces. The day was radiant, metallic: one of those searching American days so calculated to reveal the shortcomings of our street-cleaning and the excesses of our architecture. The streets looked bare and hideous; everything stared and glittered. She called a passing hansom, and gave Mrs. Van Sideren's address. She did not know what had led up to the act; but she found herself suddenly resolved to speak, to cry out a warning. It was too late to save herself—but the girl might still be told. The hansom rattled up Fifth Avenue; she sat with her eyes fixed, avoiding recognition. At the Van Siderens' door she sprang out and rang the bell. Action had cleared her brain, and she felt calm and self-possessed. She knew now exactly what she meant to say.

The ladies were both out . . . the parlor-maid stood waiting for a card. Julia, with a vague murmur, turned away from the door and lingered a moment on the sidewalk. Then she remembered that she had not paid the cab-driver. She drew a dollar from her purse and handed it to him. He touched his hat and drove off, leaving her alone in the long empty street. She wandered away westward, toward strange thoroughfares, where she was not likely to meet acquaintances. The feeling of aimlessness had returned. Once she found herself in the afternoon torrent of Broadway, swept past tawdry shops and flaming theatrical posters, with a succession of meaningless faces gliding by in the opposite direction....

A feeling of faintness reminded her that she had not eaten since morning. She turned into a side-street of shabby houses, with rows of ash-barrels behind bent area-railings. In a basement window she saw the sign *Ladies' Restaurant*: a pie and a dish of doughnuts lay against the dusty pane like petrified food in an ethnological museum. She entered, and a young woman with a weak mouth and a brazen eye cleared a table for her near the window. The table was covered with a red and white cotton cloth and adorned with a bunch of celery in a thick tumbler and a salt-cellar full of grayish lumpy salt. Julia ordered tea, and sat a long time waiting for it. She was glad to be away from the noise and confusion of the streets. The low-ceilinged room was empty, and two or three waitresses with thin pert faces lounged in the background staring at her and whispering together. At last the tea was brought in a discolored metal teapot. Julia poured a cup and drank it hastily. It was black and bitter, but it flowed through her veins like an elixir. She was almost dizzy with exhilaration. Oh, how tired, how unutterably tired she had been!

She drank a second cup, blacker and bitterer, and now her mind was once more working clearly. She felt as vigorous, as decisive, as when she had stood on the Van Siderens' door-step —but the wish to return there had subsided. She saw now the futility of such an attempt—the humiliation to which it might have exposed her.... The pity of it was that she did not know what to do next. The short winter day was fading, and she realized that she could not remain much longer in the restaurant without attracting notice. She paid for her tea and went out into the street. The lamps were alight, and here and there a basement shop cast an oblong of gas-light across the fissured pavement. In the dusk there was something sinister about the aspect of the street, and she hastened back toward Fifth Avenue. She was not used to being out alone at that hour.

At the corner of Fifth Avenue she paused and stood watching the stream of carriages. At last a policeman caught sight of her and signed to her that he would take her across. She had not meant to cross the street, but she obeyed automatically, and presently found herself on the farther corner. There she paused again for a moment; but she fancied the policeman was watching her, and this sent her hastening down the nearest side-street.... After that she walked a long time, vaguely.... Night had fallen, and now and then, through the windows of a passing carriage, she caught the expanse of an evening waistcoat or the shimmer of an opera cloak. . . .

Suddenly she found herself in a familiar street. She stood still a moment, breathing quickly. She had turned the corner without noticing whither it led; but now, a few yards ahead of her, she saw the house in which she had once lived—her first husband's house. The blinds were drawn, and only a faint translucence marked the windows and the transom above the door. As she stood there she heard a step behind her, and a man walked by in the direction of the house. He walked slowly, with a heavy middle-aged gait, his head sunk a little between the shoulders, the red crease of his neck visible above the fur collar of his overcoat. He crossed the street, went up the steps of the house, drew forth a latch-key, and let himself in. . . .

There was no one else in sight. Julia leaned for a long time against the area-rail at the corner, her eyes fixed on the front of the house. The feeling of physical weariness had returned, but the strong tea still throbbed in her veins and lit her brain with an unnatural clearness. Presently she heard another step draw near, and moving quickly away, she too crossed the street and mounted the steps of the house. The impulse which had carried her there prolonged itself in a quick pressure of the electric bell—then she felt suddenly weak and tremulous, and grasped the balustrade for support. The door opened and a young footman with a fresh inexperienced face stood on the threshold. Julia knew in an instant that he would admit her.

"I saw Mr. Arment going in just now," she said. "Will you ask him to see me for a moment?"

The footman hesitated. "I think Mr. Arment has gone up to dress for dinner, madam."

Julia advanced into the hall. "I am sure he will see me—I will not detain him long," she said. She spoke quietly, authoritatively, in the tone which a good servant does not mistake. The footman had his hand on the drawing-room door.

"I will tell him, madam. What name, please?"

Julia trembled: she had not thought of that. "Merely say a lady," she returned carelessly.

The footman wavered and she fancied herself lost; but at that instant the door opened from within and John Arment stepped into the hall. He drew back sharply as he saw her, his florid face turning sallow with the shock; then the blood poured back to it, swelling the veins on his temples and reddening the lobes of his thick ears.

It was long since Julia had seen him, and she was startled at the change in his appearance. He had thickened, coarsened, settled down into the enclosing flesh. But she noted this insensibly: her one conscious thought was that, now she was face to face with him, she must not let him escape till he had heard her. Every pulse in her body throbbed with the urgency of her message.

She went up to him as he drew back. "I must speak to you," she said.

Arment hesitated, red and stammering. Julia glanced at the footman, and her look acted as a warning. The instinctive shrinking from a "scene" predominated over every other impulse, and Arment said slowly: "Will you come this way?"

He followed her into the drawing-room and closed the door. Julia, as she advanced, was vaguely aware that the room at least was unchanged: time had not mitigated its horrors. The contadina still lurched from the chimney-breast, and the Greek slave obstructed the threshold of the inner room. The place was alive with memories: they started out from every fold of the yellow satin curtains and glided between the angles of the rosewood furniture. But while some subordinate agency was carrying these impressions to her brain, her whole conscious effort was centered in the act of dominating Arment's will. The fear that he would refuse to hear her mounted like fever to her brain. She felt her purpose melt before it, words and arguments running into each other in the heat of her longing. For a moment her voice failed her, and she imagined herself thrust out before she could speak; but as she was struggling for a word Arment pushed a chair forward, and said quietly: "You are not well."

The sound of his voice steadied her. It was neither kind nor unkind—a voice that suspended judgment, rather, awaiting unforeseen developments. She supported herself against the back of the chair and drew a deep breath.

"Shall I send for something?" he continued, with a cold embarrassed politeness.

Julia raised an entreating hand. "No—no—thank you. I am quite well."

He paused midway toward the bell, and turned on her. "Then may I ask—?"

"Yes," she interrupted him. "I came here because I wanted to see you. There is something I must tell you."

Arment continued to scrutinize her. "I am surprised at that," he said. "I should have supposed that any communication you may wish to make could have been made through our lawyers."

"Our lawyers!" She burst into a little laugh. "I don't think they could help me—this time."

Arment's face took on a barricaded look. "If there is any question of help—of course—"

It struck her, whimsically, that she had seen that look when some shabby devil called with a subscription-book. Perhaps he thought she wanted him to put his name down for so much in sympathy—or even in money. . . . The thought made her laugh again. She saw his look change slowly to perplexity. All his facial changes were slow, and she remembered, suddenly, how it had once diverted her to shift that lumbering scenery with a word. For the first time it struck her that she had been cruel. "There *is* a question of help," she said in a softer key; "you can help me; but only by listening. . . . I want to tell you something. . . ."

Arment's resistance was not yielding. "Would it not be easier to—write?" he suggested.

She shook her head. "There is no time to write . . . and it won't take long." She raised her head and their eyes met. "My husband has left me," she said.

"Westall—?" he stammered, reddening again.

"Yes. This morning. Just as I left you. Because he was tired of me."

The words, uttered scarcely above a whisper, seemed to dilate to the limit of the room. Arment looked toward the door; then his embarrassed glance returned to Julia.

"I am very sorry," he said awkwardly.

"Thank you," she murmured.

"But I don't see—"

"No—but you will—in a moment. Won't you listen to me? Please!" Instinctively she had shifted her position, putting herself between him and the door. "It happened this morning," she went on in short breathless phrases. "I never suspected anything—I thought we were—perfectly happy.... Suddenly he told me he was tired of me... there is a girl he likes better.... He has gone to her...." As she spoke, the lurking anguish rose upon her, possessing her once more to the exclusion of every other emotion. Her eyes ached, her throat swelled with it, and two painful tears ran down her face.

Arment's constraint was increasing visibly. "This—this is very unfortunate," he began. "But I should say the law—"

"The law?" she echoed ironically. "When he asks for his freedom?"

"You are not obliged to give it."

"You were not obliged to give me mine—but you did."

He made a protesting gesture.

"You saw that the law couldn't help you—didn't you?" she went on. "That is what I see now. The law represents material rights—it can't go beyond. If we don't recognize an inner law... the obligation that love creates... being loved as well as loving... there is nothing to prevent our spreading ruin unhindered... is there?" She raised her head plaintively, with the look of a bewildered child. "That is what I see now... what I wanted to tell you. He leaves me because he's tired . . . but *I* was not tired; and I don't understand why he is. That's the dreadful part of it—the not understanding: I hadn't realized what it meant. But I've been thinking of it all day, and things have come back to me—things I hadn't noticed . . . when you and I . . ." She moved closer to him, and fixed her eyes on his with the gaze which tries to reach beyond words. "I see now that *you* didn't understand—did you?"

Their eyes met in a sudden shock of comprehension: a veil seemed to be lifted between them. Arment's lip trembled.

"No," he said, "I didn't understand."

She gave a little cry, almost of triumph. "I knew it! I knew it! You wondered—you tried to tell me—but no words came. . . . You saw your life falling in ruins . . . the world slipping from you . . . and you couldn't speak or move!"

She sank down on the chair against which she had been leaning. "Now I know—now I know," she repeated.

"I am very sorry for you," she heard Arment stammer.

She looked up quickly. "That's not what I came for. I don't want you to be sorry. I came to ask you to forgive me . . . for not understanding that *you* didn't understand. . . . That's all I wanted to say." She rose with a vague sense that the end had come, and put out a groping hand toward the door.

Arment stood motionless. She turned to him with a faint smile. "You forgive me?"

"There is nothing to forgive—"

"Then you will shake hands for good-bye?" She felt his hand in hers: it was nerveless, reluctant.

"Good-bye," she repeated. "I understand now."

She opened the door and passed out into the hall. As she did so, Arment took an impulsive step forward; but just then the footman, who was evidently alive to his obligations, advanced from the background to let her out. She heard Arment fall back. The footman threw open the door, and she found herself outside in the darkness.

EXPIATION

"I CAN NEVER," said Mrs. Fetherel, "hear the bell ring without a shudder."

Her unruffled aspect—she was the kind of woman whose emotions never communicate themselves to her clothes—and the conventional background of the New York drawing-room, with its pervading implication of an imminent tea-tray and of an atmosphere in which the social functions have become purely reflex, lent to her declaration a relief not lost on her cousin Mrs. Clinch, who, from the other side of the fireplace, agreed, with a glance at the clock, that it *was* the hour for bores.

"Bores!" cried Mrs. Fetherel impatiently. "If I shuddered at *them*, I should have a chronic ague!"

She leaned forward and laid a sparkling finger on her cousin's shabby black knee. "I mean the newspaper clippings," she whispered.

Mrs. Clinch returned a glance of intelligence. "They've begun already?"

"Not yet; but they're sure to now, at any minute, my publisher tells me."

Mrs. Fetherel's look of apprehension sat oddly on her small features, which had an air of neat symmetry somehow suggestive of being set in order every morning by the housemaid. Someone (there was rumors that it was her cousin) had once said that Paula Fetherel would have been very pretty if she hadn't looked so like a moral axiom in a copy-book hand.

Mrs. Clinch received her confidence with a smile. "Well," she said, "I suppose you were prepared for the consequences of authorship?"

Mrs. Fetherel blushed brightly. "It isn't their coming," she owned—"it's their coming *now*."

"Now?"

"The Bishop's in town."

Mrs. Clinch leaned back and shaped her lips to a whistle which deflected in a laugh. "Well!" she said.

"You see!" Mrs. Fetherel triumphed.

"Well—weren't you prepared for the Bishop?"

"Not now—at least, I hadn't thought of his seeing the clippings."

"And why should he see them?"

"Bella—*won't* you understand? It's John."

"John?"

"Who has taken the most unexpected tone—one might almost say out of perversity."

"Oh, perversity—" Mrs. Clinch murmured, observing her cousin between lids wrinkled by amusement. "What tone has John taken?"

Mrs. Fetherel threw out her answer with the desperate gesture of a woman who lays bare the traces of a marital fist. "The tone of being proud of my book."

The measure of Mrs. Clinch's enjoyment overflowed in laughter.

"Oh, you may laugh," Mrs. Fetherel insisted, "but it's no joke to me. In the first place, John's liking the book is so—so—such a false note—it puts me in such a ridiculous position; and then it has set him watching for the reviews—who would ever have suspected John of knowing that books were *reviewed*? Why, he's actually found out about the Clipping Bureau, and whenever the postman rings I hear John rush out of the library to see if there are any yellow envelopes. Of course, when they *do* come he'll bring them into the drawing-room and read them aloud to everybody who happens to be here—and the Bishop is sure to happen to be here!"

Mrs. Clinch repressed her amusement. "The picture you draw is a lurid one," she conceded, "but your modesty strikes me as abnormal, especially in an author. The chances are that some of the clippings will be rather pleasant reading. The critics are not all union men."

Mrs. Fetherel stared. "Union men?"

"Well, I mean they don't all belong to the well-known Society-for-the-Persecution-of-Rising-Authors. Some of them have even been known to defy its regulations and say a good word for a new writer."

"Oh, I dare say," said Mrs. Fetherel, with the laugh her cousin's epigram exacted. "But you don't quite see my point. I'm not at all nervous about the success of my book—my publisher tells me I have no need to be—but I *am* afraid of its being a *succès de scandale*."

"Mercy!" said Mrs. Clinch, sitting up.

The butler and footman at this moment appeared with the tea-tray, and when they had withdrawn, Mrs. Fetherel, bending her brightly rippled head above the kettle, continued in a murmur of avowal, "The title, even, is a kind of challenge."

"*Fast and Loose*," Mrs. Clinch mused. "Yes, it ought to take."

"I didn't choose it for that reason!" the author protested. "I should have preferred something quieter—less pronounced; but I was determined not to shirk the responsibility of what I had written. I want people to know beforehand exactly what kind of book they are buying."

"Well," said Mrs. Clinch, "that's a degree of conscientiousness that I've never met with before. So few books fulfill the promise of their titles that experienced readers never expect the fare to come up to the menu."

"*Fast and Loose*, will be no disappointment on that score," her cousin significantly returned. "I've handled the subject without gloves. I've called a spade a spade."

"You simply make my mouth water! And to think I haven't been able to read it yet because every spare minute of my time has been given to correcting the proofs of *How the Birds Keep Christmas*! There's an instance of the hardships of an author's life!"

Mrs. Fetherel's eye clouded. "Don't joke, Bella, please. I suppose to experienced authors there's always something absurd in the nervousness of a new writer, but in my case so much is at stake; I've put so much of myself into this book and I'm so afraid of being misunderstood . . . of being, as it were, in advance of my time . . . like poor Flaubert. . . . I *know* you'll think me ridiculous . . . and if only my own reputation were at stake, I should never give it a thought . . . but the idea of dragging John's name through the mire . . ."

Mrs. Clinch, who had risen and gathered her cloak about her, stood surveying from her genial height her cousin's agitated countenance.

"Why did you use John's name, then?"

"That's another of my difficulties! I *had* to. There would have been no merit in publishing such a book under an assumed name; it would have been an act of moral cowardice. *Fast and Loose* is not an ordinary novel. A writer who dares to show up the hollowness of social conventions must have the courage of her convictions and be willing to accept the consequences of defying society. Can you imagine Ibsen or Tolstoy writing under a false name?" Mrs. Fetherel lifted a tragic eye to her cousin. "You don't know, Bella, how often I've envied you since I began to write. I used to wonder sometimes—you won't mind my saying so?— why, with all your cleverness, you hadn't taken up some more exciting subject than natural history; but I see now how wise you were. Whatever happens, you will never be denounced by the press!"

"Is that what you're afraid of?" asked Mrs. Clinch, as she grasped the bulging umbrella which rested against her chair. "My dear, if I had ever had the good luck to be denounced by the press, my brougham would be waiting at the door for me at this very moment, and I shouldn't have had to ruin this umbrella by using it in the rain. Why, you innocent, if I'd ever felt the slightest aptitude for showing up social conventions, do you suppose I should waste my time writing *Nests Ajar* and *How to Smell the*

Flowers? There's a fairly steady demand for pseudo-science and colloquial ornithology, but it's nothing, simply nothing, to the ravenous call for attacks on social institutions—especially by those inside the institutions!"

There was often, to her cousin, a lack of taste in Mrs. Clinch's pleasantries, and on this occasion they seemed more than usually irrelevant.

"*Fast and Loose* was not written with the idea of a large sale."

Mrs. Clinch was unperturbed. "Perhaps that's just as well," she returned, with a philosophic shrug. "The surprise will be all the pleasanter, I mean. For of course it's going to sell tremendously; especially if you can get the press to denounce it."

"Bella, how *can* you? I sometimes think you say such things expressly to tease me; and yet I should think you of all women would understand my purpose in writing such a book. It has always seemed to me that the message I had to deliver was not for myself alone, but for all the other women in the world who have felt the hollowness of our social shams, the ignominy of bowing down to the idols of the market, but have lacked either the courage or the power to proclaim their independence; and I have fancied, Bella dear, that, however severely society might punish me for revealing its weaknesses, I could count on the sympathy of those who, like you"—Mrs. Fetherel's voice sank—"have passed through the deep waters."

Mrs. Clinch gave herself a kind of canine shake, as though to free her ample shoulders from any drop of the element she was supposed to have traversed.

"Oh, call them muddy rather than deep," she returned; "and you'll find, my dear, that women who've had any wading to do are rather shy of stirring up mud. It sticks—especially on white clothes."

Mrs. Fetherel lifted an undaunted brow. "I'm not afraid," she proclaimed; and at the same instant she dropped her teaspoon with a clatter and shrank back into her seat. "There's the bell," she exclaimed, "and I know it's the Bishop!"

It was in fact the Bishop of Ossining, who, impressively announced by Mrs. Fetherel's butler, now made an entry that may best be described as not inadequate to the expectations the announcement raised. The Bishop always entered a room well; but, when unannounced, or preceded by a Low Church butler who gave him his surname, his appearance lacked the impressiveness conferred on it by the due specification of his diocesan dignity. The Bishop was very fond of his niece Mrs. Fetherel, and one of the traits he most valued in her was the possession of a butler who knew how to announce a bishop.

Mrs. Clinch was also his niece; but, aside from the fact that she possessed no butler at all, she had laid herself open to her uncle's criticism by writing insignificant little books which had a way of going into five or ten editions, while the fruits of his own episcopal leisure—*The Wail of Jonah* (twenty cantos in blank verse), and *Through a Glass Brightly; or, How to Raise Funds for a Memorial Window*—inexplicably languished on the back shelves of a publisher noted for his dexterity in pushing "devotional goods." Even this indiscretion the Bishop might, however, have condoned, had his niece thought fit to turn to him for support and advice at the painful juncture of her history when, in her own words, it became necessary for her to invite Mr. Clinch to look out for another situation. Mr. Clinch's misconduct was of the kind especially designed by Providence to test the fortitude of a Christian wife and mother, and the Bishop was absolutely distended with seasonable advice and edification; so that when Bella met his tentative exhortations with the curt remark that she preferred to do her own housecleaning unassisted, her uncle's grief at her ingratitude was not untempered with sympathy for Mr. Clinch.

It is not surprising, therefore, that the Bishop's warmest greetings were always reserved for Mrs. Fetherel; and on this occasion Mrs. Clinch thought she detected, in the salutation which fell to her share, a pronounced suggestion that her own presence was superfluous—a hint which she took with her usual imperturbable good humor.

II

Left alone with the Bishop, Mrs. Fetherel sought the nearest refuge from conversation by offering him a cup of tea. The Bishop accepted with the preoccupied air of a man to whom, for the moment, tea is but a subordinate incident. Mrs. Fetherel's nervousness increased; and knowing that the surest way of distracting attention from one's own affairs is to affect an interest in those of one's companion, she hastily asked if her uncle had come to town on business.

"On business—yes—" said the Bishop in an impressive tone. "I had to see my publisher, who has been behaving rather unsatisfactorily in regard to my last book."

"Ah—your last book?" faltered Mrs. Fetherel, with a sickening sense of her inability to recall the name or nature of the work in question, and a mental vow never again to be caught in such ignorance of a colleague's productions.

"*Through a Glass Brightly,*" the Bishop explained, with an emphasis which revealed his detection of her predicament. "You may remember that I sent you a copy last Christmas?"

"Of course I do!" Mrs. Fetherel brightened. "It was that delightful story of the poor consumptive girl who had no money, and two little brothers to support—"

"Sisters—idiot sisters—" the Bishop gloomily corrected.

"I mean sisters; and who managed to collect money enough to put up a beautiful memorial window to her—her grandfather, whom she had never seen—"

"But whose sermons had been her chief consolation and support during her long struggle with poverty and disease." The Bishop gave the satisfied sigh of the workman who reviews his completed task. "A touching subject, surely; and I believe I did it justice; at least so my friends assured me."

"Why, yes—I remember there was a splendid review of it in the *Reredos!*" cried Mrs. Fetherel, moved by the incipient instinct of reciprocity.

"Yes—by my dear friend Mrs. Gollinger, whose husband, the

late Dean Gollinger, was under very particular obligations to me. Mrs. Gollinger is a woman of rare literary acumen, and her praise of my book was unqualified; but the public wants more highly seasoned fare, and the approval of a thoughtful church-woman carries less weight than the sensational comments of an illiterate journalist." The Bishop bent a meditative eye on his spotless gaiters. "At the risk of horrifying you, my dear," he added, with a slight laugh, "I will confide to you that my best chance of a popular success would be to have my book denounced by the press."

"Denounced?" gasped Mrs. Fetherel. "On what ground?"

"On the ground of immorality." The Bishop evaded her startled gaze. "Such a thing is inconceivable to you, of course; but I am only repeating what my publisher tells me. If, for instance, a critic could be induced—I mean, if a critic were to be found, who called in question the morality of my heroine in sacrificing her own health and that of her idiot sisters in order to put up a memorial window to her grandfather, it would probably raise a general controversy in the newspapers, and I might count on a sale of ten or fifteen thousand within the next year. If he described her as morbid or decadent, it might even run to twenty thousand; but that is more than I permit myself to hope. In fact I should be satisfied with any general charge of immorality." The Bishop sighed again. "I need hardly tell you that I am actuated by no mere literary ambition. Those whose opinion I most value have assured me that the book is not without merit; but, though it does not become me to dispute their verdict, I can truly say that my vanity as an author is not at stake. I have, however, a special reason for wishing to increase the circulation of *Through a Glass Brightly*; it was written for a purpose—a purpose I have greatly at heart—"

"I know," cried his niece sympathetically. "The chantry window—?"

"Is still empty, alas! and I had great hopes that, under Providence, my little book might be the means of filling it. All our wealthy parishioners have given lavishly to the cathedral, and it was for this reason that, in writing *Through a Glass*, I addressed

ignoble compromises one may be driven in such cases!..." He paused, as though to give her the opportunity of confirming this conjecture, but she preserved an apprehensive silence, and he went on, as though taking up the second point in his sermon— "Or, again, the name may have taken your fancy without your realizing all that it implies to minds more alive than yours to offensive innuendoes. It is—ahem—excessively suggestive, and I hope I am not too late to warn you of the false impression it is likely to produce on the very readers whose approbation you would most value. My friend Mrs. Gollinger, for instance—"

Mrs. Fetherel, as the publication of her novel testified, was in theory a woman of independent views; and if in practice she sometimes failed to live up to her standard, it was rather from an irresistible tendency to adapt herself to her environment than from any conscious lack of moral courage. The Bishop's exordium had excited in her that sense of opposition which such admonitions are apt to provoke; but as he went on she felt herself gradually enclosed in an atmosphere in which her theories vainly gasped for breath. The Bishop had the immense dialectical advantage of invalidating any conclusions at variance with his own by always assuming that his premises were among the necessary laws of thought. This method, combined with the habit of ignoring any classifications but his own, created an element in which the first condition of existence was the immediate adoption of his standpoint; so that his niece, as she listened, seemed to feel Mrs. Gollinger's Mechlin cap spreading its conventual shadow over her rebellious brow and the *Revue de Paris* at her elbow turning into a copy of the *Reredos*. She had meant to assure her uncle that she was quite aware of the significance of the title she had chosen, that it had been deliberately selected as indicating the subject of her novel, and that the book itself had been written in direct defiance of the class of readers for whose susceptibilities he was alarmed. The words were almost on her lips when the irresistible suggestion conveyed by the Bishop's tone and language deflected them into the apologetic murmur, "Oh, uncle, you mustn't think—I never meant—" How much farther this current of reaction might have carried her the historian is unable to compute, for at this point the door opened and her husband entered the room.

"The first review of your book!" he cried, flourishing a yellow envelope. "My dear Bishop, how lucky you're here!"

Though the trials of married life have been classified and catalogued with exhaustive accuracy, there is one form of conjugal misery which has perhaps received inadequate attention; and that is the suffering of the versatile woman whose husband is not equally adapted to all her moods. Every woman feels for the sister who is compelled to wear a bonnet which does not "go" with her gown; but how much sympathy is given to her whose husband refuses to harmonize with the pose of the moment? Scant justice has, for instance, been done to the misunderstood wife whose husband persists in understanding her; to the submissive helpmate whose task-master shuns every opportunity of browbeating her, and to the generous and impulsive being whose bills are paid with philosophic calm. Mrs. Fetherel, as wives go, had been fairly exempt from trials of this nature, for her husband, if undistinguished by pronounced brutality or indifference, had at least the negative merit of being her intellectual inferior. Landscape-gardeners, who are aware of the usefulness of a valley in emphasizing the height of a hill, can form an idea of the account to which an accomplished woman may turn such deficiencies; and it need scarcely be said that Mrs. Fetherel had made the most of her opportunities. It was agreeably obvious to every one, Fetherel included, that he was not the man to appreciate such a woman; but there are no limits to man's perversity, and he did his best to invalidate this advantage by admiring her without pretending to understand her. What she most suffered from was this fatuous approval: the maddening sense that, however she conducted herself, he would always admire her. Had he belonged to the class whose conversational supplies are drawn from the domestic circle, his wife's name would never have been off his lips; and to Mrs. Fetherel's sensitive perceptions his frequent silences were indicative of the fact that she was his one topic.

It was, in part, the attempt to escape this persistent approbation that had driven Mrs. Fetherel to authorship. She had fancied that even the most infatuated husband might be counted on to resent, at least negatively, an attack on the sanctity of the hearth; and her anticipations were heightened by a sense of the unpardonableness of her act. Mrs. Fetherel's relations with her husband were in fact complicated by an irrepressible tendency to be fond of him; and there was a certain pleasure in the prospect of a situation that justified the most explicit expiation.

These hopes Fetherel's attitude had already defeated. He read the book with enthusiasm, he pressed it on his friends, he sent a copy to his mother; and his very soul now hung on the verdict of the reviewers. It was perhaps this proof of his general inaptitude that made his wife doubly alive to his special defects; so that his inopportune entrance was aggravated by the very sound of his voice and the hopeless aberration of his smile. Nothing, to the observant, is more indicative of a man's character and circumstances than his way of entering a room. The Bishop of Ossining, for instance, brought with him not only an atmosphere of episcopal authority, but an implied opinion on the verbal inspiration of the Scriptures and on the attitude of the Church toward divorce; while the appearance of Mrs. Fetherel's husband produced an immediate impression of domestic felicity. His mere aspect implied that there was a well-filled nursery up stairs; that his wife, if she did not sew on his buttons, at least superintended the performance of that task; that they both went to church regularly, and that they dined with his mother every Sunday evening punctually at seven o'clock.

All this and more was expressed in the affectionate gesture with which he now raised the yellow envelope above Mrs. Fetherel's clutch; and knowing the uselessness of begging him not to be silly, she said, with a dry despair, "You're boring the Bishop horribly."

Fetherel turned a radiant eye on that dignitary. "She bores us all horribly, doesn't she, sir?" he exulted.

"Have you read it?" said his wife, uncontrollably.

"Read it? Of course not—it's just this minute come. I say, Bishop, you're not going—?"

"Not till I've heard this," said the Bishop, settling himself in his chair with an indulgent smile.

His niece glanced at him despairingly. "Don't let John's nonsense detain you," she entreated.

"Detain him? That's good," guffawed Fetherel. "It isn't as long as one of his sermons—won't take me five minutes to read. Here, listen to this, ladies and gentlemen: 'In this age of festering pessimism and decadent depravity, it is no surprise to the nauseated reviewer to open one more volume saturated with the fetid emanations of the sewer—'"

Fetherel, who was not in the habit of reading aloud, paused with a gasp, and the Bishop glanced sharply at his niece, who kept her gaze fixed on the tea-cup she had not yet succeeded in transferring to his hand.

"'Of the sewer,'" her husband resumed; "'but his wonder is proportionately great when he lights on a novel as sweetly inoffensive as Paula Fetherel's *Fast and Loose*. Mrs. Fetherel is, we believe, a new hand at fiction, and her work reveals frequent traces of inexperience; but these are more than atoned for by her pure fresh view of life and her altogether unfashionable regard for the reader's moral susceptibilities. Let no one be induced by its distinctly misleading title to forego the enjoyment of this pleasant picture of domestic life, which, in spite of a total lack of force in character-drawing and of consecutiveness in incident, may be described as a distinctly pretty story.'"

III

It was several weeks later that Mrs. Clinch once more brought the plebeian aroma of heated tram-cars and muddy street-crossings into the violet-scented atmosphere of her cousin's drawing-room.

"Well," she said, tossing a damp bundle of proof into the

corner of a silk-cushioned bergère, "I've read it at last and I'm not so awfully shocked!"

Mrs. Fetherel, who sat near the fire with her head propped on a languid hand, looked up without speaking.

"Mercy, Paula," said her visitor, "you're ill."

Mrs. Fetherel shook her head. "I was never better," she said, mournfully.

"Then may I help myself to tea? Thanks."

Mrs. Clinch carefully removed her mended glove before taking a buttered tea-cake; then she glanced again at her cousin.

"It's not what I said just now—?" she ventured.

"Just now?"

"About *Fast and Loose*? I came to talk it over."

Mrs. Fetherel sprang to her feet. "I never," she cried dramatically, "want to hear it mentioned again!"

"Paula!" exclaimed Mrs. Clinch, setting down her cup.

Mrs. Fetherel slowly turned on her an eye brimming with the incommunicable; then, dropping into her seat again, she added, with a tragic laugh: "There's nothing left to say."

"Nothing—?" faltered Mrs. Clinch, longing for another tea-cake, but feeling the inappropriateness of the impulse in an atmosphere so charged with the portentous. "Do you mean that everything *has* been said?" She looked tentatively at her cousin. "Haven't they been nice?"

"They've been odious—odious—" Mrs. Fetherel burst out, with an ineffectual clutch at her handkerchief. "It's been perfectly intolerable!"

Mrs. Clinch, philosophically resigning herself to the propriety of taking no more tea, crossed over to her cousin and laid a sympathizing hand on that lady's agitated shoulder.

"It *is* a bore at first," she conceded; "but you'll be surprised to see how soon one gets used to it."

"I shall—never—get—used to it—" Mrs. Fetherel brokenly declared.

"Have they been so very nasty—all of them?"

"Every one of them!" the novelist sobbed.

"I'm so sorry, dear; it *does* hurt, I know—but hadn't you rather expected it?"

"Expected it?" cried Mrs. Fetherel, sitting up.

Mrs. Clinch felt her way warily. "I only mean, dear, that I fancied from what you said before the book came out—that you rather expected—that you'd rather discounted—"

"Their recommending it to everybody as a perfectly harmless story?"

"Good gracious! Is *that* what they've done?"

Mrs. Fetherel speechlessly nodded.

"Every one of them?"

"Every one."

"Whew!" said Mrs. Clinch, with an incipient whistle.

"Why, you've just said it yourself!" her cousin suddenly reproached her.

"Said what?"

"That you weren't so *awfully* shocked—"

"I? Oh, well—you see, you'd keyed me up to such a pitch that it wasn't quite as bad as I expected—"

Mrs. Fetherel lifted a smile steeled for the worst. "Why not say at once," she suggested, "that it's a distinctly pretty story?"

"They haven't said *that*?"

"They've all said it."

"My poor Paula!"

"Even the Bishop—"

"The Bishop called it a pretty story?"

"He wrote me—I've his letter somewhere. The title rather scared him—he wanted me to change it; but when he'd read the book he wrote that it was all right and that he'd sent several copies to his friends."

"The old hypocrite!" cried Mrs. Clinch. "That was nothing but professional jealousy."

"Do you think so?" cried her cousin, brightening.

"Sure of it, my dear. His own books don't sell, and he knew the quickest way to kill yours was to distribute it through the diocese with his blessing."

"Then you don't really think it's a pretty story?"

"Dear me, no! Not nearly as bad as that—"

"You're so good, Bella—but the reviewers?"

"Oh, the reviewers," Mrs. Clinch jeered. She gazed meditatively at the cold remains of her tea-cake. "Let me see," she said, suddenly; "do you happen to remember if the first review came out in an important paper?"

"Yes—the *Radiator*."

"That's it! I thought so. Then the others simply followed suit: they often do if a big paper sets the pace. Saves a lot of trouble. Now if you could only have got the *Radiator* to denounce you—"

"That's what the Bishop said!" cried Mrs. Fetherel.

"He did?"

"He said his only chance of selling *Through a Glass Brightly* was to have it denounced on the ground of immorality."

"H'm," said Mrs. Clinch, "I thought he knew a trick or two." She turned an illuminated eye on her cousin. "You ought to get *him* to denounce *Fast and Loose*!" she cried.

Mrs. Fetherel looked at her suspiciously. "I suppose every book must stand or fall on its own merits," she said in an unconvinced tone.

"Bosh! That view is as extinct as the post-chaise and the packet-ship—it belongs to the time when people read books. Nobody does that now; the reviewer was the first to set the example, and the public were only too thankful to follow it. At first they read the reviews; now they read only the publishers' extracts from them. Even these are rapidly being replaced by paragraphs borrowed from the vocabulary of commerce. I often have to look twice before I am sure if I am reading a department-store advertisement or the announcement of a new batch of literature. The publishers will soon be having their 'fall and spring openings' and their 'special importations for Horse-Show Week.' But the Bishop is right, of course—nothing helps a book like a rousing attack on its morals;

and as the publishers can't exactly proclaim the impropriety of their own wares, the task has to be left to the press or the pulpit."

"The pulpit—?" Mrs. Fetherel mused.

"Why, yes—look at those two novels in England last year—"

Mrs. Fetherel shook her head hopelessly. "There is so much more interest in literature in England than here."

"Well, we've got to make the supply create the demand. The Bishop could run your novel up into the hundred thousands in no time."

"But if he can't make his own sell—"

"My dear, a man can't very well preach against his own writings!"

Mrs. Clinch rose and picked up her proofs.

"I'm awfully sorry for you, Paula dear," she concluded, "but I can't help being thankful that there's no demand for pessimism in the field of natural history. Fancy having to write *The Fall of a Sparrow*, or *How the Plants Misbehave!*"

IV

Mrs. Fetherel, driving up to the Grand Central Station one morning about five months later, caught sight of the distinguished novelist, Archer Hynes, hurrying into the waiting-room ahead of her. Hynes, on his side, recognizing her brougham, turned back to greet her as the footman opened the carriage door.

"My dear colleague! Is it possible that we are traveling together?"

Mrs. Fetherel blushed with pleasure. Hynes had given her two columns of praise in the *Sunday Meteor*, and she had not yet learned to disguise her gratitude.

"I am going to Ossining," she said smilingly.

"So am I. Why, this is almost as good as an elopement."

"And it will end where elopements ought to—in church."

"In church? You're not going to Ossining to go to church?"

"Why not? There's a special ceremony in the cathedral—the chantry window is to be unveiled."

"The chantry window? How picturesque! What *is* a chantry?

And why do you want to see it unveiled? Are you after copy—doing something in the Huysmans manner? *La Cathédrale*, eh?"

"Oh, no." Mrs. Fetherel hesitated. "I'm going simply to please my uncle," she said, at last.

"Your uncle?"

"The Bishop, you know." She smiled.

"The Bishop—the Bishop of Ossining? Why, wasn't he the chap who made that ridiculous attack on your book? Is that pre-historic ass your uncle? Upon my soul, I think you're mighty forgiving to travel all the way to Ossining for one of his stained-glass sociables!"

Mrs. Fetherel's smiles flowed into a gentle laugh. "Oh, I've never allowed that to interfere with our friendship. My uncle felt dreadfully about having to speak publicly against my book—it was a great deal harder for him than for me—but he thought it his duty to do so. He has the very highest sense of duty."

"Well," said Hynes, with a shrug, "I don't know that he didn't do you a good turn. Look at that!"

They were standing near the book-stall and he pointed to a placard surmounting the counter and emblazoned with the con-spicuous announcement: "*Fast and Loose*. New Edition with Author's Portrait. Hundred and Fiftieth Thousand."

Mrs. Fetherel frowned impatiently. "How absurd! They've no right to use my picture as a poster!"

"There's our train," said Hynes; and they began to push their way through the crowd surging toward one of the inner doors.

As they stood wedged between circumferent shoulders, Mrs. Fetherel became conscious of the fixed stare of a pretty girl who whispered eagerly to her companion: "Look, Myrtle! That's Paula Fetherel right behind us—I knew her in a minute!"

"Gracious—where?" cried the other girl, giving her head a twist which swept her Gainsborough plumes across Mrs. Fetherel's face.

The first speaker's words had carried beyond her companion's ear, and a lemon-colored woman in spectacles, who clutched a copy of the *Journal of Psychology* in one drab-cotton-gloved hand, stretched her disengaged hand across the intervening barrier of humanity.

"Have I the privilege of addressing the distinguished author of *Fast and Loose*? If so, let me thank you in the name of the Woman's Psychological League of Peoria for your magnificent courage in raising the standard of revolt against—"

"You can tell us the rest in the car," said a fat man, pressing his good-humored bulk against the speaker's arm.

Mrs. Fetherel, blushing, embarrassed and happy, slipped into the space produced by this displacement, and a few moments later had taken her seat in the train.

She was a little late, and the other chairs were already filled by a company of elderly ladies and clergymen who seemed to belong to the same party, and were still busy exchanging greetings and settling themselves in their places.

One of the ladies, at Mrs. Fetherel's approach, uttered an exclamation of pleasure and advanced with outstretched hand. "My dear Mrs. Fetherel! I am so delighted to see you here. May I hope you are going to the unveiling of the chantry window? The dear Bishop so hoped that you would do so! But perhaps I ought to introduce myself. I am Mrs. Gollinger"—she lowered her voice expressively—"one of your uncle's oldest friends, one who has stood close to him through all this sad business, and who knows what he suffered when he felt obliged to sacrifice family affection to the call of duty."

Mrs. Fetherel, who had smiled and colored slightly at the beginning of this speech, received its close with a deprecating gesture.

"Oh, pray don't mention it," she murmured. "I quite understood how my uncle was placed—I bore him no ill will for feeling obliged to preach against my book."

"He understood that, and was so touched by it! He has often

told me that it was the hardest task he was ever called upon to perform—and, do you know, he quite feels that this unexpected gift of the chantry window is in some way a return for his courage in preaching that sermon."

Mrs. Fetherel smiled faintly. "Does he feel that?"

"Yes; he really does. When the funds for the window were so mysteriously placed at his disposal, just as he had begun to despair of raising them, he assured me that he could not help connecting the fact with his denunciation of your book."

"Dear uncle!" sighed Mrs. Fetherel. "Did he say that?"

"And now," continued Mrs. Gollinger, with cumulative rapture—"now that you are about to show, by appearing at the ceremony to-day, that there has been no break in your friendly relations, the dear Bishop's happiness will be complete. He was so longing to have you come to the unveiling!"

"He might have counted on me," said Mrs. Fetherel, still smiling.

"Ah, that is so beautifully forgiving of you!" cried Mrs. Gollinger enthusiastically. "But then, the Bishop has always assured me that your real nature was very different from that which—if you will pardon my saying so—seems to be revealed by your brilliant but—er—rather subversive book. 'If you only knew my niece, dear Mrs. Gollinger,' he always said, 'you would see that her novel was written in all innocence of heart'; and to tell you the truth, when I first read the book I didn't think it so very, *very* shocking. It wasn't till the dear Bishop had explained to me—but, dear me, I mustn't take up your time in this way when so many others are anxious to have a word with you."

Mrs. Fetherel glanced at her in surprise, and Mrs. Gollinger continued with a playful smile: "You forget that your face is familiar to thousands whom you have never seen. We all recognized you the moment you entered the train, and my friends here are so eager to make your acquaintance—even those"—her smile deepened—"who thought the dear Bishop not *quite unjustified* in his attack on your remarkable novel."

V

A religious light filled the chantry of Ossining Cathedral, filtering through the linen curtain which veiled the central window and mingling with the blaze of tapers on the richly adorned altar.

In this devout atmosphere, agreeably laden with the incense-like aroma of Easter lilies and forced lilacs, Mrs. Fetherel knelt with a sense of luxurious satisfaction. Beside her sat Archer Hynes, who had remembered that there was to be a church scene in his next novel and that his impressions of the devotional environment needed refreshing. Mrs. Fetherel was very happy. She was conscious that her entrance had sent a thrill through the female devotees who packed the chantry, and she had humor enough to enjoy the thought that, but for the good Bishop's denunciation of her book, the heads of his flock would not have been turned so eagerly in her direction. Moreover, as she entered she had caught sight of a society reporter, and she knew that her presence, and the fact that she was accompanied by Hynes, would be conspicuously proclaimed in the morning papers. All these evidences of the success of her handiwork might have turned a calmer head than Mrs. Fetherel's; and though she had now learned to dissemble her gratification, it still filled her inwardly with a delightful glow.

The Bishop was somewhat late in appearing, and she employed the interval in meditating on the plot of her next novel, which was already partly sketched out, but for which she had been unable to find a satisfactory denouement. By a not uncommon process of ratiocination, Mrs. Fetherel's success had convinced her of her vocation. She was sure now that it was her duty to lay bare the secret plague-spots of society, and she was resolved that there should be no doubt as to the purpose of her new book. Experience had shown her that where she had fancied she was calling a spade a spade she had in fact been alluding in guarded terms to the drawing-room shovel. She was determined not to repeat the same mistake, and she flattered herself that her coming novel would not need an episcopal denunciation to insure its sale, however likely it was to receive this crowning evidence of success.

She had reached this point in her meditations when the choir burst into song and the ceremony of the unveiling began. The Bishop, almost always felicitous in his addresses to the fair sex, was never more so than when he was celebrating the triumph of one of his cherished purposes. There was a peculiar mixture of Christian humility and episcopal exultation in the manner with which he called attention to the Creator's promptness in responding to his demand for funds, and he had never been more happily inspired than in eulogizing the mysterious gift of the chantry window.

Though no hint of the donor's identity had been allowed to escape him, it was generally understood that the Bishop knew who had given the window, and the congregation awaited in a flutter of suspense the possible announcement of a name. None came, however, though the Bishop deliciously titillated the curiosity of his flock by circling ever closer about the interesting secret. He would not disguise from them, he said, that the heart which had divined his inmost wish had been a woman's—is it not to woman's intuitions that more than half the happiness of earth is owing? What man is obliged to learn by the laborious process of experience, woman's wondrous instinct tells her at a glance; and so it had been with this cherished scheme, this unhoped-for completion of their beautiful chantry. So much, at least, he was allowed to reveal; and indeed, had he not done so, the window itself would have spoken for him, since the first glance at its touching subject and exquisite design would show it to have originated in a woman's heart. This tribute to the sex was received with an audible sigh of contentment, and the Bishop, always stimulated by such evidence of his sway over his hearers, took up his theme with gathering eloquence.

Yes—a woman's heart had planned the gift, a woman's hand had executed it, and, might he add, without too far withdrawing the veil in which Christian beneficence ever loved to drape its acts—might he add that, under Providence, a book, a simple book, a mere tale, in fact, had had its share in the good work for which they were assembled to give thanks?

At this unexpected announcement, a ripple of excitement ran through the assemblage, and more than one head was abruptly turned in the direction of Mrs. Fetherel, who sat listening in an agony of wonder and confusion. It did not escape the observant novelist at her side that she drew down her veil to conceal an uncontrollable blush, and this evidence of dismay caused him to fix an attentive gaze on her, while from her seat across the aisle Mrs. Gollinger sent a smile of unctuous approval.

"A book—a simple book—" the Bishop's voice went on above this flutter of mingled emotions. "What is a book? Only a few pages and a little ink—and yet one of the mightiest instruments which Providence has devised for shaping the destinies of man... one of the most powerful influences for good or evil which the Creator has placed in the hands of his creatures...."

The air seemed intolerably close to Mrs. Fetherel, and she drew out her scent-bottle, and then thrust it hurriedly away, conscious that she was still the center of an unenviable attention. And all the while the Bishop's voice droned on...

"And of all forms of literature, fiction is doubtless that which has exercised the greatest sway, for good or ill, over the passions and imagination of the masses. Yes, my friends, I am the first to acknowledge it—no sermon, however eloquent, no theological treatise, however learned and convincing, has ever inflamed the heart and imagination like a novel—a simple novel. Incalculable is the power exercised over humanity by the great magicians of the pen—a power ever enlarging its boundaries and increasing its responsibilities as popular education multiplies the number of readers... Yes, it is the novelist's hand which can pour balm on countless human sufferings, or inoculate mankind with the festering poison of a corrupt imagination...."

Mrs. Fetherel had turned white, and her eyes were fixed with a blind stare of anger on the large-sleeved figure in the center of the chancel.

"And too often, alas, it is the poison and not the balm which the unscrupulous hand of genius proffers to its unsuspecting readers. But, my friends, why should I continue? None know better than an assemblage of Christian women, such as I am now addressing, the beneficent or baleful influences of modern fiction; and so, when I say that this beautiful chantry window of ours owes its existence in part to the romancer's pen"—the Bishop paused, and bending forward, seemed to seek a certain face among the countenances eagerly addressed to his—"when I say that this pen, which for personal reasons it does not become me to celebrate unduly—"

Mrs. Fetherel at this point half rose, pushing back her chair, which scraped loudly over the marble floor; but Hynes involuntarily laid a warning hand on her arm, and she sank down with a confused murmur about the heat.

"When I confess that this pen, which for once at least has proved itself so much mightier than the sword, is that which was inspired to trace the simple narrative of *Through a Glass Brightly*"—Mrs. Fetherel looked up with a gasp of mingled relief and anger—"when I tell you, my dear friends, that it was your Bishop's own work which first roused the mind of one of his flock to the crying need of a chantry window, I think you will admit that I am justified in celebrating the triumphs of the pen, even though it be the modest instrument which your own Bishop wields."

The Bishop paused impressively, and a faint gasp of surprise and disappointment was audible throughout the chantry. Something very different from this conclusion had been expected, and even Mrs. Gollinger's lips curled with a slightly ironic smile. But Archer Hynes's attention was chiefly reserved for Mrs. Fetherel, whose face had changed with astonishing rapidity from surprise to annoyance, from annoyance to relief, and then back again to something very like indignation.

The address concluded, the actual ceremony of the unveiling was about to take place, and the attention of the congregation soon reverted to the chancel, where the choir had grouped themselves beneath the veiled window, prepared to burst into a chant of praise as the Bishop drew back the hanging. The moment was an impressive one, and every eye was fixed on the curtain. Even Hynes's gaze strayed to it for a moment, but soon returned to his neighbor's face; and then he perceived that Mrs. Fetherel, alone of all the persons present, was not looking at the window. Her eyes were fixed in an indignant stare on the Bishop; a flush of anger burned becomingly under her veil, and her hands nervously crumpled the beautifully printed program of the ceremony.

Hynes broke into a smile of comprehension. He glanced at the Bishop, and back at the Bishop's niece; then, as the episcopal hand was solemnly raised to draw back the curtain, he bent and whispered in Mrs. Fetherel's ear:

"Why, you gave it yourself! You wonderful woman, of course you gave it yourself!"

Mrs. Fetherel raised her eyes to his with a start. Her blush deepened and her lips shaped a hasty "No"; but the denial was deflected into the indignant murmur—"It wasn't *his* silly book that did it, anyhow!"

THE POT-BOILER

THE STUDIO faced north, looking out over a dismal reach of roofs and chimneys, and fire-escapes hung with heterogeneous garments. A crust of dirty snow covered the level surfaces, and a December sky with more snow in it lowered above them.

The room was bare and gaunt, with blotched walls and a stained uneven floor. On a divan lay a pile of "properties"—limp draperies, an Algerian scarf, a moth-eaten fan of peacock feathers. The janitor had forgotten to fill the coal-scuttle overnight, and the cast-iron stove projected its cold flanks into the room like a black iceberg. Ned Stanwell, who had just added his hat and great-coat to the heap on the divan, turned from the empty stove with a shiver.

"By Jove, this is a little too much like the last act of *Bohème*," he said, slipping into his coat again after a vain glance at the coal-scuttle. Much solitude, and a lively habit of mind, had bred in him the habit of audible soliloquy, and having flung a shout for the janitor down the six flights dividing the studio from the basement, he turned back, picking up the thread of his monologue. "Exactly like *Bohème*, really—that crack in the wall is much more like a stage-crack than a real one—just the sort of crack Mungold would paint if he were doing a Humble Interior."

Mungold, the fashionable portrait-painter of the hour, was the favorite object of the younger men's irony.

"It only needs Kate Arran to be borne in dying," Stanwell continued with a laugh. "Much more likely to be poor little Caspar, though," he concluded.

His neighbor across the landing—the little sculptor Caspar Arran, humourously called "Gasper" on account of his bronchial asthma—had lately been joined by a sister, Kate Arran, a strapping girl, fresh from the country, who had installed herself in the little room off her brother's studio, keeping house for him with a chafing-dish and a coffee-machine, to the mirth and envy of the other young men in the building.

Poor little Gasper had been very bad all the autumn, and it was surmised that his sister's presence, which he spoke of growlingly, as a troublesome necessity imposed on him by the death of an aunt, was really a sign of his failing ability to take care of himself. Kate Arran took his complaints with unfailing good humor, darned his socks, brushed his clothes, fed him with steaming broths and foaming milk-punches, and listened with reverential assent to his interminable disquisitions on art. Every one in the house was sorry for little Gasper, and the other fellows liked him all the more because it was so impossible to like his sculpture; but his talk was a bore, and when his colleagues ran in to see him they were apt to keep a hand on the door-knob and to plead a pressing engagement. At least they had been till Kate came; but now they began to show a disposition to enter and sit down. Caspar, who was no fool, perceived the change, and perhaps detected its cause; at any rate he showed no special gratification at the increased cordiality of his friends, and Kate, who followed him in everything, took this as a sign that guests were to be discouraged.

There was one exception, however: Ned Stanwell, who was deplorably good-natured, had always lent a patient ear to Caspar, and he now reaped his reward by being taken into Kate's favor. Before she had been a month in the building they were on confidential terms as to Caspar's health, and lately Stanwell had penetrated farther, even to the inmost recesses of her anxiety about her brother's career. Caspar had recently had a bad blow in the refusal of his *magnum opus*—a vast allegorical group—by the Commissioners of the Minneapolis Exhibition. He took the rejection with Promethean irony, proclaimed it as the clinching proof of his genius, and abounded in reasons why, even in an age of such crass artistic ignorance, a refusal so egregious must react to the advantage of its object. But his sister's indignation, if as glowing, was a shade less hopeful. Of course Caspar was going to succeed—she knew it was only a question of time—but she paled at the word and turned imploring eyes on Stanwell. *Was there time enough?* It was the one element in the combination that she could not count on; and Stanwell, reddening under her look, and cursing his own glaring robustness, would affirm that of course, of course, of course, by everything that was holy there was time enough—with the mental reservation that there wouldn't be, even if poor Caspar lived to be a hundred.

"Vos dat you yelling for the shanitor, Mr. Sdanwell?" inquired an affable voice through the doorway; and Stanwell, turning with a laugh, confronted the squat figure of a middle-aged man in an expensive fur coat, who looked as if his face secreted the oil which he used on his hair.

"Hullo, Shepson—I should say I *was* yelling. Did you ever feel such cold? That fool has forgotten to light the stove. Come in, but for heaven's sake don't take off your coat."

Mr. Shepson glanced about the studio with a look which seemed to say that, where so much else was lacking, the absence of a fire hardly added to the general sense of destitution.

"Vell, you ain't as vell fixed as Mr. Mungold—ever been to his studio, Mr. Sdanwell? De most ex*qui*site blush hangings, and a gas-fire, shoost as natural—"

"Oh, hang it, Shepson, do you call *that* a studio? It's like a manicure's parlor—or a beauty-doctor's. By George," broke off Stanwell, "and that's just what he is!"

"A peauty-doctor?"

"Yes—oh, well, you wouldn't see," murmured Stanwell, mentally storing his epigram for more appreciative ears. "But you didn't come just to make me envious of Mungold's studio, did you?" And he pushed forward a chair for his visitor.

The latter, however, declined it with a friendly motion. "Of gourse not, of gourse not—but Mr. Mungold is a sensible man. He makes a lot of money, you know."

"Is that what you came to tell me?" said Stanwell, still humorously.

"My gootness, no—I was down stairs looking at Holbrook's sdained class, and I shoost thought I'd sdep up a minute and take a beep at your vork."

"Much obliged, I'm sure—especially as I assume that you don't want any of it." Try as he would, Stanwell could not keep a note of eagerness from his voice. Mr. Shepson caught the note, and eyed him shrewdly through gold-rimmed glasses.

"Vell, vell, vell—I'm not prepared to commit myself. Shoost let me take a look round, vill you?"

"With the greatest pleasure—and I'll give another shout for the coal."

Stanwell went out on the landing, and Mr. Shepson, left to himself, began a meditative progress about the room. On an easel facing the improvised dais stood a canvas on which a young woman's head had been blocked in. It was just in that state of semi-evocation when a picture seems to detach itself from the grossness of its medium and live a wondrous moment in the actual; and the quality of the head—a vigorous dusky youthfulness, a kind of virgin majesty—lent itself to this illusion of life. Stanwell, who had re-entered the studio, could not help drawing a sharp breath as he saw the picture-dealer pausing with tilted head before this portrait: it seemed, at one moment, so impossible that he should not be struck with it, at the next so incredible that he should be.

Shepson cocked his parrot-eye at the canvas with a desultory "Vat's dat?" which sent a twinge through the young man.

"That? Oh—a sketch of a young lady," stammered Stanwell, flushing at the imbecility of his reply. "It's Miss Arran, you know," he added, "the sister of my neighbor here, the sculptor."

"Sgulpture? There's no market for modern sgulpture except dombstones," said Shepson disparagingly, passing on as if he included the sister's portrait in his condemnation of her brother's trade.

Stanwell smiled, but more at himself than Shepson. How could he have supposed that the gross fool would see anything in his sketch of Kate Arran? He stood aside, straining after detachment, while the dealer continued his round of exploration, waddling up to the canvases on the walls, prodding with his stick at those stacked in corners, prying and peering sideways like a great bird rummaging for seed. He seemed to find little nutriment in the course of his search, for the sounds he emitted expressed a weary distaste for misdirected effort, and he completed his round without having thought it worth-while to draw a single canvas from its obscurity.

As his visits always had the same result, Stanwell was reduced to wondering why he had come again; but Shepson was not the man to indulge in vague roamings through the field of art, and it was safe to conclude that his purpose would in due course reveal itself. His tour brought him at length face to face with the painter, where he paused, clasping his plump gloved hands behind him, and shaking an admonitory head.

"Gleffer—very gleffer, of course—I suppose you'll let me know when you want to sell anything?"

"Let you know?" gasped Stanwell, to whom the room grew so suddenly hot that he thought for a moment the janitor must have made up the fire.

Shepson gave a dry laugh. "Vell, it doesn't sdrike me that you want to now—doing this kind of thing, you know!" And he swept a disparaging hand about the studio.

"Ah," said Stanwell, who could not keep a note of flatness out of his laugh.

"See here, Mr. Sdanwell, vot you do it for? If you do it for yourself and the other fellows, vell and good—only don't ask me round. I sell pictures, I don't theorize about them. Ven you vant to sell, gome to me with what my gustomers vant. You can do it—you're smart enough. You can do most anything. Vere's dat bortrait of

Gladys Glyde dat you showed at the Fake Club last autumn?
Dat little thing in de Romney style? Dat vas a little shem, now,"
exclaimed Mr. Shepson, whose pronunciation grew increasingly
Semitic in moments of excitement.

Stanwell stared. Called on a few months previously to con-
tribute to an exhibition of skits on well-known artists, he had used
the photograph of a favorite music-hall "star" as the basis of a picture in the pseudo-historical style affected by the fashionable por-
trait-painters of the day.

"That thing?" he said contemptuously. "How on earth did you
happen to see it?"

"I see everything," returned the dealer with an oracular smile.
"If you've got it here let me look at it, please."

It cost Stanwell a few minutes' search to unearth his skit—a
clever blending of dash and sentimentality, in just the right pro-
portion to create the impression of a powerful brush subdued to
mildness by the charms of the sitter. Stanwell had thrown it off in
a burst of imitative frenzy, beginning for the mere joy of the satire,
but gradually fascinated by the problem of producing the requisite
mingling of attributes. He was surprised now to see how well he
had mixed the brew, and Shepson's face reflected his approval.

"By George! Dat's something like," the dealer ejaculated.

"Like what? Like Mungold?"

"Like business! Like a big order for a bortrait, Mr. Sdanwell —
dat's what it's like!" cried Shepson, swinging round on him.

Stanwell's stare widened. "An order for me?"

"Vy not? Accidents *vill* happen," said Shepson jocosely. "De
fact is, Mrs. Archer Millington wants to be bainted—you know
her sdyle? Well, she prides herself on her likeness to little Gladys.
And so ven she saw dat bicture of yours at de Fake Show she made
a note of your name, and de udder day she sent for me and she
says: 'Mr. Shepson, I'm tired of Mungold—all my friends are
done by Mungold. I vant to break away and be orishinal—I vant
to be done by the bainter that did Gladys Glyde.'"

Shepson waited to observe the result of this overwhelming

announcement, and Stanwell, after a momentary halt of surprise, brought out laughingly: "But this *is* a Mungold. Is that what she calls being original?"

"Shoost exactly," said Shepson with unexpected acuteness. "That's vat dey all want—something different from vat all deir friends have got, but shoost like it all de same. Dat's de public all over! Mrs. Millington don't want a Mungold, because everybody's got a Mungold, but she wants a picture that's in the same sdyle, because dat's de sdyle, and she's afraid of any oder!"

Stanwell was listening with real enjoyment. "Ah, you know your public," he murmured.

"Vell, you do too, or you couldn't have painted dat," the dealer retorted. "And I don't say dey're wrong—mind dat. I like a bretty picture myself. And I understand the way dey feel. Dey're villing to let Sargent take liberties vid them, because it's like being punched in de ribs by a King; but if anybody else baints them, they vant to look as sweet as an obituary." He turned earnestly to Stanwell. "The thing is to attract their notice. Vonce you got it they von't gif you dime to sleep. And dat's why I'm here to-day—you've attracted Mrs. Millington's notice, and vonce you're hung in dat new ball-room—dat's vere she vants you, in a big gold panel—vonce you're dere, vy, you'll be like the Pianola—no home gompleat without you. And I ain't going to charge you any commission on the first job!"

He stood before the painter, exuding a mixture of deference and patronage in which either element might prevail as events developed; but Stanwell could see in the incident only the stuff for a good story.

"My dear Shepson," he said, "what are you talking about? This is no picture of mine. Why don't you ask me to do you a Corot? I hear there's a great demand for them still in the West. Or an Arthur Schracker—I can do Schracker as well as Mungold," he added, turning around a small canvas at which a paint-pot seemed to have been hurled with violence from a considerable distance.

Shepson ignored the allusion to Corot, but screwed his eyes at the picture. "Ah, Schracker—vell, the Schracker sdyle would take first rate if you were a foreigner—but for goodness sake don't try it on Mrs. Millington!"

Stanwell pushed the two skits aside. "Oh, you can trust me," he cried humorously. "The pearls and the eyes very large—the hands and feet very small. Isn't that about the size of it?"

"Dat's it—dat's it. And the check as big as you vant to make it! Mrs. Millington vants the picture finished in time for her first barty in the new ball-room, and if you rush the job she won't sdickle at an extra thousand. Vill you come along with me now and arrange for your first zitting?"

He stood before the young man, urgent, paternal, and so im-bued with the importance of his mission that his face stretched to a ludicrous length of dismay when Stanwell, giving him a good-humored push, cried gaily: "My dear fellow, it will make my price rise still higher when the lady hears I'm too busy to take any or-ders at present—and that I'm actually obliged to turn you out now because I'm expecting a sitter!"

It was part of Shepson's business to have a quick ear for the note of finality, and he offered no resistance to Stanwell's push; but on the threshold he paused to murmur, with a regretful glance at the denuded studio: "You could half done it, Mr. Sdanwell—you could haf done it!"

II

Kate Arran was Stanwell's sitter; but the janitor had hardly filled the stove when she came in to say she could not sit. Caspar had had a bad night; he was depressed and feverish, and in spite of his protests she had resolved to fetch the doctor. Care sat on her usu-ally tranquil features, and Stanwell, as he offered to go for the doc-tor, wished he could have caught in his picture the wide gloom of her brow. There was always a kind of biblical breadth in the ex-pression of her emotions, and to-day she suggested a text from Isaiah.

"But you're not busy?" she hesitated, in the full voice which seemed tuned to a solemn rhetoric.

"I meant to be—with you. But since that's off I'm quite unemployed."

She smiled interrogatively. "I thought perhaps you had an order. I met Mr. Shepson rubbing his hands on the landing."

"Was he rubbing his hands? Well, it was not over me. He says that from the style of my pictures he doesn't suppose I want to sell."

She looked at him superbly. "Well, do you?"

He embraced his bleak walls in a circular gesture. "Judge for yourself!"

"Ah, but it's splendidly furnished!"

"With rejected pictures, you mean?"

"With ideals!" she exclaimed, in a tone caught from her brother, and which would have been irritating to Stanwell if it had not been moving.

He gave a slight shrug and took up his hat; but she interposed to say that if it didn't make any difference she would prefer to have him go and sit with poor Caspar, while she ran for the doctor and did some household errands by the way. Stanwell divined in her request the need of a brief respite from Caspar, and though he shivered at the thought of her facing the cold in the scant jacket which had been her only wear since he had known her, he let her go without protest, and betook himself to Arran's studio.

He found the little sculptor dressed and roaming fretfully about the melancholy room in which he and his plastic offspring lodged. In one corner, where Kate's chair and work-table stood, a scrupulous order prevailed; but the rest of the apartment had the dreary untidiness, the damp gray look, which the worker in clay usually creates about him. In the center of this desert stood the shrouded image of Caspar's disappointment: the colossal rejected group as to which his friends could seldom remember whether it represented Jove hurling a Titan from Olympus or Science Subjugating Religion. Caspar was the sworn foe of religion, which he appeared to regard as indirectly connected with his inability to sell his statues.

The sculptor was too ill to work, and Stanwell's appearance loosed the pent-up springs of his talk.

"Hallo! What are you doing here? I thought Kate had gone over to sit to you. She wanted a little fresh air? I should say enough of it came in through these windows. How like a woman, when she's agreed to do a certain thing, to make up her mind at once that she's got to do another! They don't call it caprice—it's always duty; that's the humor of it. I'll be bound Kate alleged a pressing engagement. Sorry she should waste your time so, my dear fellow. Here am I with plenty of it to burn—look at my hand shake; I can't do a thing! Well, luckily nobody wants me to—posterity may suffer, but the present generation isn't worrying. The present generation wants to be carved in sugar-candy, or painted in maple syrup. It doesn't want to be told the truth about itself or about anything in the universe. The prophets have always lived in a garret, my dear fellow—only the ravens don't always find out their address! Speaking of ravens, though, Kate told me she saw old Shepson coming out of your place—I say, old man, you're not meditating an apostasy? You're not doing the kind of thing that Shepson would look at?"

Stanwell laughed. "He looked at them—but only to confirm his reasons for rejecting them."

"Ha! ha! That's right—he wanted to refresh his memory with their badness. But how on earth did he happen to have any doubts on the subject? I should as soon have thought of his coming in here!"

Stanwell winced at the comparison, but replied in Caspar's key: "Oh, he's not as sure of any of us as he is of you!"

The sculptor received this tribute with a joyous expletive. "By God, no, he's sure of me, as you say! He and his tribe know that I'll starve in my tracks sooner than make a concession—a single concession. A fellow came after me once to do an angel on a tombstone—an angel leaning against a broken column, and looking as if it was waiting for the elevator and wondering why in hell it didn't come. He said he wanted me to show that the deceased was pining to get to heaven. As she was his wife I didn't dispute the proposition, but when I asked him what he understood by *heaven* he grabbed his hat and walked out of the studio. *He* didn't wait for the elevator."

Stanwell listened with a practiced smile. The story of the man who had come to order the angel was so familiar to Arran's friends that its only interest consisted in waiting to see what variation he would give to the retort which had put the mourner to flight. It was generally supposed that this visit represented the sculptor's nearest approach to an order, and one of his fellow-craftsmen had been heard to remark that if Caspar *had* made the tombstone, the lady under it would have tried harder than ever to get to heaven. To Stanwell's present mood, however, there was something more than usually irritating in the gratuitous assumption that Arran had only to descend from his altitude to have a press of purchasers at his door.

"Well—what did you gain by kicking your widower out?" he objected. "Why can't a man do two kinds of work—one to please himself and the other to boil the pot?"

Caspar stopped in his jerky walk—the stride of a tall man attempted with short legs (it sometimes appeared to Stanwell to symbolize his artistic endeavor).

"Why can't a man—why can't he? You ask me that, Stanwell?" he blazed out.

"Yes; and what's more, I'll answer you: it isn't everybody who can adapt his art as he wants to!"

Caspar stood before him, gasping with incredulous scorn. "Adapt his art? As he wants to? Unhappy wretch, what lingo are you talking? If you mean that it isn't every honest man who can be a renegade—"

"That's just what I do mean: he can't unless he's clever enough to see the other side."

The deep groan with which Caspar met this casuistry was cut

short by a knock at the studio door, which thereupon opened to admit a small dapperly-dressed man with a silky mustache and mildly-bulging eyes.

"Ah, Mungold," exclaimed Stanwell, to cover the gloomy silence with which Arran received the newcomer; whereat the latter, with the air of a man who does not easily believe himself unwelcome, bestowed a sympathetic pressure on the sculptor's hand.

"My dear chap, I've just met Miss Arran, and she told me you were laid up with a bad cold, so I thought I'd pop in and cheer you up."

He looked about him with a smile evidently intended as the first act in his beneficent program.

Mr. Mungold, freshly soaped and scented, with a neat glaze of gentility extending from his varnished boot-tips to his glossy hat, looked like the "flattered" portrait of a common man—just such an idealized presentment as his own brush might have produced. As a rule, however, he devoted himself to the portrayal of the other sex, painting ladies in syrup, as Arran said, with marsh-mallow children against their knees. He was as quick as a dressmaker at catching new ideas, and the style of his pictures changed as rapidly as that of the fashion-plates. One year all his sitters were done on oval canvases, with gauzy draperies and a back-ground of clouds; the next they were seated under an immemorial elm, caressing enormous dogs obviously constructed out of door-mats. Whatever their occupation they always looked straight out of the canvas, giving the impression that their eyes were fixed on an invisible camera. This gave rise to the rumor that Mungold "did" his portraits from photographs; it was even said that he had invented a way of transferring an enlarged photograph to the canvas, so that all that remained was to fill in the colors. If he heard of this charge he took it calmly, but probably it had not reached the high spheres in which he moved, and in which he was esteemed for painting pearls better, and making unsuggestive children look lovelier, than any of his fellow-craftsmen. Mr. Mungold, in fact, deemed it a part of his professional duty to study his sitters in their home-life;

and as this life was chiefly led in the homes of others, he was too busy dining out and going to the opera to mingle much with his colleagues. But as no one is wholly consistent, Mr. Mungold had lately belied his ambitions by falling in love with Kate Arran; and with that gentle persistency which made him so wonderful in managing obstreperous infantile sitters, he had contrived to establish a footing in her brother's studio.

Part of his success was due to the fact that he could not easily think himself the object of a rebuff. If it seemed to hit him he regarded it as deflected from its aim, and brushed it aside with a discreet gesture. A touch of comedy was lent to the situation by the fact that, till Kate Arran's coming, Mungold had always served as her brother's Awful Example. It was a mark of Arran's lack of humor that he persisted in regarding the little man as a conscious apostate, instead of perceiving that he painted as he could, in a world which really looked to him like a vast confectioner's window. Stanwell had never quite divined how Mungold had won over the sister, to whom her brother's prejudices were a religion; but he suspected the painter of having united a deep belief in Caspar's genius with the occasional offer of opportune delicacies—the port-wine or game which Kate had no other means of procuring for the patient.

Stanwell, persuaded that Mungold would stick to his post till Miss Arran's return, felt himself freed from his promise to the latter and left the incongruous pair to themselves. There had been a time when it amused him to see Caspar submerge the painter in a torrent of denunciatory eloquence, and to watch poor Mungold sputtering under its rush, yet emitting little bland phrases of assent, like a gentleman drowning correctly, in gloves and eyeglasses. But Stanwell was beginning to find less food for gaiety than for envy in the contemplation of his colleague. After all, Mungold held his ground, he did not go under. Spite of his manifest absurdity he had succeeded in propitiating the sister, in making himself tolerated by the brother; and the fact that his success was due to the ability to purchase port-wine and game was not in this case a mitigating circumstance. Stanwell knew that the Arrans really preferred him to Mungold, but the knowledge only sharpened his envy of the latter, whose friendship could command visible tokens of expression, while poor Stanwell's remained gloomily inarticulate. As he returned to his overpopulated studio and surveyed anew the pictures of which Shepson had not offered to relieve him, he found himself wishing, not for Mungold's lack of scruples, for he believed him to be the most scrupulous of men, but for that happy mean of talent which so completely satisfied the artistic requirements of the inartistic. Mungold was not to be despised as an apostate—he was to be congratulated as a man whose aptitudes were exactly in line with the taste of the persons he liked to dine with.

At this point in his meditations, Stanwell's eye fell on the portrait of Miss Gladys Glyde. It was really, as Shepson said, as good as a Mungold; yet it could never be made to serve the same purpose, because it was the work of a man who knew it was bad art. That at least would have been Caspar Arran's contention—poor Caspar, who produced as bad art in the service of the loftiest convictions! The distinction began to look like mere casuistry to Stanwell. He had never been very proud of his own adaptability. It had seemed to him to indicate the lack of an individual standpoint, and he had tried to counteract it by the cultivation of an aggressively personal style. But the cursed knack was in his fingers—he was always at the mercy of some other man's sensations, and there were moments when he blushed to remember that his grandfather had spent a laborious life-time in Rome, copying the Old Masters for a generation which lacked the resource of the camera. Now, however, it struck him that the ancestral versatility might be a useful inheritance. In art, after all, the greatest of them did what they could; and if a man could do several things instead of one, why should he not profit by his multiplicity of gifts? If one had two talents why not serve two masters?

III

Stanwell, while seeing Caspar through the attack which had been the cause of his sister's arrival, had struck up a friendship with the young doctor who climbed the patient's six flights with unremitting fidelity. The two, since then, had continued to exchange confidences regarding the sculptor's health, and Stanwell, anxious to waylay the doctor after his visit, left the studio door ajar, and went out when he heard a sound of leave-taking across the landing. But it appeared that the doctor had just come, and that it was Mungold who was making his adieux.

The latter at once assumed that Stanwell had been on the alert for him, and met the supposed advance by inviting himself into the studio.

"May I come and take a look around, my dear fellow? I've been meaning to drop in for an age—" Mungold always spoke with a girlish emphasis and effusiveness— "but I have been so busy getting up Mrs. Van Orley's tableaux—English eighteenth century portraits, you know—that really, what with that and my sittings, I've hardly had time to think. And then you know you owe me about a dozen visits! But you're a savage—you don't pay visits. You stay here and *piocher*—which is wiser, as the results prove. Ah, you're strong—immensely strong!" He paused in the middle of the studio, glancing about a little apprehensively, as though he thought the stored energy of the pictures might result in an explosion. "Very original—very striking—ah, Miss Arran! A powerful head; but—excuse the suggestion—isn't there just the least little lack of sweetness? You don't think she has the sweet type? Perhaps not—but could she be so lovely if she were not intensely feminine? Just at present, though, she's not looking her best—she is horribly tired. I'm afraid there is very little money left—and poor dear Caspar is so impossible: he won't hear of a loan. Otherwise I should be most happy—. But I came just now to propose a piece of work—in fact to give an order. Mrs. Archer Millington has built a new ball-room, as I daresay you may have seen in the papers, and she's been kind enough to ask me for some hints—oh, merely as a friend: I don't presume to do more than advise. But her decorator wants to do something with Cupids—something light and playful. And so I ventured to say that I knew a very clever sculptor—well, I *do* believe Caspar has talent—latent talent, you know—and at any rate a job of that sort would be a big lift for him. At least I thought he would regard it so; but you should have heard him when I showed him the decorator's sketch. He asked me what the Cupids were to be done in—lard? And if I thought he had had his training at a confectioner's? And I don't know what more besides—but he worked himself up to such a degree that he brought on a frightful fit of coughing, and Miss Arran, I'm afraid, was rather annoyed with me when she came in, though I'm sure an order from Mrs. Archer Millington is not a thing that would annoy most people!"

Mr. Mungold paused, breathless with the rehearsal of his wrongs, and Stanwell said with a smile: "You know poor Caspar's terribly stiff on the purity of the artist's aim."

"The artist's aim?" Mr. Mungold stared. "What is the artist's aim but to please—isn't that the purpose of all true art? But his theories are so extravagant. I really don't know what I shall say to Mrs. Millington—she's not used to being refused. I suppose I'd better put it on the ground of ill-health." The artist glanced at his handsome repeater. "Dear me, I promised to be at Mrs. Van Orley's before twelve. We're to settle about the curtain before luncheon. My dear fellow, it's been a privilege to see your work. By the way, *you* have never done any modeling, I suppose? You're so extraordinarily versatile—I didn't know whether you might care to undertake the Cupids yourself."

Stanwell had to wait a long time for the doctor; and when the latter came out he looked grave. Worse? No, he couldn't say that Caspar was worse—but then he wasn't better. There was nothing mortal the matter, but the question was how long he could hold out. It was the kind of case where there is no use in drugs—he had merely scribbled a prescription to quiet Miss Arran.

"It's the cold, I suppose," Stanwell groaned. "He ought to be shipped off to Florida."

The doctor made a negative gesture. "Florida be hanged! What he wants is to sell his group. That would set him up quicker than sitting on the equator."

"Sell his group?" Stanwell echoed. "But he's so indifferent to recognition—he believes in himself so thoroughly. I thought at first he would be hard hit when the Exhibition Committee refused it, but he seems to regard that as another proof of its superiority."

His visitor turned on him the keen eye of the confessor. "Indifferent to recognition? He's eating his heart out for it. Can't you see that all that talk is just so much whistling to keep his courage up? The name of his disease is failure—and I can't write the prescription that will cure that. But if somebody would come along and take a fancy to those two naked parties who are breaking each other's heads we'd have Mr. Caspar putting on a pound a day."

The truth of this diagnosis became suddenly vivid to Stanwell. How dull of him not to have seen before that it was not cold or privation which was killing Caspar—not anxiety for his sister's future, nor the ache of watching her daily struggle—but simply the cankering thought that he might die before he had made himself known! It was his vanity that was starving to death, and all Mungold's hampers could not appease that hunger. Stanwell was not shocked by the discovery—he was only the more sorry for the little man, who was, after all, denied that solace of self-sufficiency which his talk so noisily proclaimed. His lot seemed hard enough when Stanwell had pictured him as buoyed up by the scorn of public opinion—it became tragic if he was denied that support. The artist wondered if Kate had guessed her brother's secret, or if she were still the dupe of his stoicism. Stanwell was sure that the sculptor would take no one into his confidence, and least of all his sister, whose faith in his artistic independence was the chief prop of that tottering pose. Kate's penetration was not great, and Stanwell recalled the incredulous smile with which she had heard him defend poor Mungold's "sincerity" against Caspar's assaults; but she had the insight of the heart, and where her brother's happiness was concerned she might have seen deeper than any of them. It was this last consideration which took the strongest hold on Stanwell—he felt Caspar's sufferings chiefly through the thought of his sister's possible disillusionment.

IV

Within three months two events had set the studio building talking. Stanwell had painted a full-length portrait of Mrs. Archer Millington, and Caspar Arran had received an order to execute his group in marble.

The name of the sculptor's patron had not been divulged. The order came through Shepson, who explained that an American customer living abroad, having seen a photograph of the group in one of the papers, had at once cabled home to secure it. He intended to bestow it on a public building in America, and not wishing to advertise his munificence, had preferred that even the sculptor should remain ignorant of his name. The group bought by an enlightened compatriot for the adornment of a civic building in his native land! There could hardly be a more complete vindication of unappreciated genius, and Caspar made the most of the argument. He was not exultant, he was sublimely magnanimous. He had always said that he could afford to await the Verdict of Posterity, and his unknown patron's act clearly shadowed forth that impressive decision. Happily it also found expression in a check which it would have taken more philosophy to await. The group was paid for in advance, and Kate's joy in her brother's recognition was deliciously mingled with the thrill of ordering him some new clothes, and coaxing him out to dine succulently at a neighboring restaurant. Caspar flourished insufferably on this régime: he began to strike the attitude of the Great Master, who gives advice and encouragement to the struggling neophyte. He held himself up as an example of the reward of disinterestedness, of the triumph of the artist who clings doggedly to his ideals.

"A man must believe in his star—look at Napoleon! It's the trust in one's convictions that tells—it always ends by forcing the public into line. Only be sure you make no concessions—don't give in to any of their humbug! An artist who listens to the critics is ruined—they never have any use for the poor devils who do what they're told. Run after fame and she'll keep you running, but stay in your own corner and do your own work, and by George sir, she'll come crawling up on her hands and knees and ask to have her likeness done!"

These exhortations were chiefly directed to Stanwell, partly because the inmates of the other studios were apt to elude them, partly also because the rumors concerning Stanwell's portrait of Mrs. Millington had begun to disquiet the sculptor. At first he had taken a condescending interest in the fact of his friend's receiving an order, and had admonished him not to lose the chance of "showing up" his sitter and her environment. It was a splendid opportunity for a fellow with a "message" to be introduced into the tents of the Philistine, and Stanwell was charged to drive a long sharp nail into the enemy's skull. But presently Arran began to suspect that the portrait was not as comminatory as he could have wished. Mungold, the most kindly of rivals, let drop a word of injudicious praise: the picture, he said, promised to be delightfully "in keeping" with the decorations of the ball-room, and the lady's gown harmonized exquisitely with the window-curtains. Stanwell, called to account by his monitor, reminded the latter that he himself had been selected by Mungold to do the Cupids for Mrs. Millington's ball-room, and that the friendly artist's praise could, therefore, not be taken as positive evidence of incapacity.

"Ah, but I didn't do them—I kicked him out!" Caspar rejoined; and Stanwell could only plead that, even in the cause of art, one could hardly kick a lady.

"Ah, that's the worst of it. If the women get at you you're lost. You're young, you're impressionable, you won't mind my saying that you're not built for a Stoic, and hang it, they'll coddle you, they'll enervate you, they'll sentimentalize you, they'll make a Mungold of you!"

"Poor Mungold," Stanwell laughed. "If he lived the life of an anchorite he couldn't help painting pictures that would please Mrs. Millington."

"Whereas you could," Kate interjected, raising her head from the ironing-board where, Sphinx-like, magnificent, she swung a splendid arm above her brother's shirts.

"Oh, well, perhaps I shan't please her; perhaps I shall elevate her taste."

Caspar directed a groan to his sister. "That's what they all think at first—Childe Roland to the Dark Tower came. But inside the Dark Tower there's the Venusberg. Oh, I don't mean that you'll be taken with truffles and plush footmen, like Mungold. But praise, my poor Ned—praise is a deadly drug! It's the absinthe of the artist—and they'll stupefy you with it. You'll wallow in the mire of success."

Stanwell raised a protesting hand. "Really, for one order you're a little lurid!"

"One? Haven't you already had a dozen others?"

"Only one other, so far—and I'm not sure I shall do that."

"Not sure—wavering already! That's the way the mischief begins. If the women get a fad for you they'll work you like a galley-slave. You'll have to do your round of 'copy' every morning. What becomes of inspiration then? How are you going to loaf and invite the soul? Don't barter your birthright for a mess of pottage! Oh, I understand the temptation—I know the taste of money and success. But look at me, Stanwell. You know how long I had to wait for recognition. Well, now it's come to me I don't mean to let it knock me off my feet. I don't mean to let myself be overworked; I've already made it known that I will not be bullied into taking more orders than I can do full justice to. And my sister is with me,

God bless her; Kate would rather go on ironing my shirts in a garret than see me prostitute my art!"

Kate's radiant glance confirmed this declaration of independence,
and Stanwell, with his evasive laugh, asked her if, meanwhile, she
should object to his investing a part of his ill-gotten gains in theater
tickets for the party that evening.

It appeared that Stanwell had also been paid in advance, and
well paid; for he began to permit himself various mild distrac-
tions, in which he generally contrived to have the Arrans share. It
seemed perfectly natural to Kate that Caspar's friends should
spend their money for his recreation, and by one of the most
touching sophistries of her sex she thus reconciled herself to taking a little pleasure on her own account. Mungold was less often
in the way, for she had never been able to forgive him for propos-
ing that Caspar should do Mrs. Millington's Cupids; and for a few
happy weeks Stanwell had the undisputed enjoyment of her pride
in her brother's achievement.

Stanwell had "rushed" through Mrs. Millington's portrait in
time for the opening of her new ball-room; and it was perhaps in
return for this favor that she consented to let the picture be exhibited at a big Portrait Show which was held in April for the benefit
of a fashionable charity.

In Mrs. Millington's ball-room the picture had been seen and
approved only by the distinguished few who had access to that social sanctuary; but on the walls of the exhibition it became a center of comment and discussion. One of the immediate results of
this publicity was a visit from Shepson, with two or three orders in
his pocket, as he put it. He surveyed the studio with fresh disgust,
asked Stanwell why he did not move, and was impressed rather
than downcast on learning that the painter had not decided whether he would take any more orders that spring.

"You might haf a studio at Newport," he suggested. "It would
be rather new to do your sitters out-of-doors, with the sea behind
them—showing they had a blace on the gliffs!"

The picture produced a different and less flattering effect on the critics. They gave it, indeed, more space than they had ever before accorded to the artist's efforts, but their estimate seemed to confirm Caspar Arran's forebodings, and Stanwell had perhaps never despised them so little as when he read their comments on his work. On the whole, however, neither praise nor blame disquieted him. He was engrossed in the contemplation of Kate Arran's happiness, and basking in the refracted warmth it shed about her. The doctor's prognostications had come true. Caspar was putting on a pound a week, and had plunged into a fresh "creation" more symbolic and encumbering than the monument of which he had been so opportunely relieved. If there was any cloud on Stanwell's enjoyment of life, it was caused by the discovery that success had quadrupled Caspar's artistic energies. Meanwhile it was delightful to see Kate's joy in her brother's recovered capacity for work, and to listen to the axioms which, for Stanwell's guidance, she deduced from the example of Caspar's heroic devotion to the ideal. There was nothing repellent in Kate's borrowed didacticism. If it sometimes bored Stanwell to hear her quote her brother, he was sure it would never bore him to be quoted by her himself; and there were moments when he felt he had nearly achieved that distinction.

Caspar was not addicted to the visiting of art exhibitions. He took little interest in any productions save his own, and was disposed to believe that good pictures, like clever criminals, are apt to go unhung. Stanwell therefore thought it unlikely that his portrait of Mrs. Millington would be seen by Kate, who was not given to independent explorations in the field of art; but one day, on entering the exhibition—which he had hitherto rather nervously shunned—he saw the Arrans at the end of the gallery in which the portrait hung. They were not looking at it, they were moving away from it, and to Stanwell's quickened perceptions their movement was almost that of flight. For a moment he thought of flying too; then a desperate resolve nerved him to meet them, and stemming the crowd he made a circuit which brought him face to face with their retreat.

The room in which they met was nearly empty, and there was nothing to intervene between the shock of their interchanged glances. Caspar was flushed and bristling: his little body quivered like a machine from which the steam has just been turned off. Kate lifted a stricken glance. Stanwell read in it the reflection of her brother's tirade, but she held out her hand in silence.

For a moment Caspar was silent too; then, with a terrible smile: "My dear fellow, I congratulate you: Mungold will have to look to his laurels," he said.

The shot delivered, he stalked away with his seven-league stride, and Kate followed sadly in his wake.

V

Shepson took up his hat with a despairing gesture. "Vell, I gif you up—I gif you up!"

"Don't—yet," protested Stanwell from the divan.

It was winter again, and though the janitor had not forgotten the fire, the studio gave no other evidence of its master's increasing prosperity. If Stanwell spent his money it was not on himself.

He leaned back against the wall, his hands in his pockets, a cigarette between his lips, while Shepson paced the dirty floor or halted impatiently before an untouched canvas on the easel.

"I tell you vat it is, Mr. Sdanwell, I can't make you out!" he lamented. "Last vinter you got a sdart that vould have kept most men going for years. After making dat hit with Mrs. Millington's picture you could have bainted half the town. And here you are sitting on your difan and saying you can't make up your mind to take another order. Vell, I can only say that if you dake much longer to make it up, you'll find some other chap has cut in and got your job. Mrs. Van Orley has been waiting since last August, and she dells me you haven't even answered her letter."

"How could I? I didn't know if I wanted to paint her."

"My goodness! Don't you know if you vant three thousand tollars?"

Stanwell surveyed his cigarette. "I'm not sure I do," he said.

Shepson flung out his hands. "Ask more den—but do it quick!"

Left to himself, Stanwell stood contemplating the canvas on which the dealer had riveted his reproachful gaze. It had been destined to reflect the opulent image of Mrs. Alpheus Van Orley, but some secret reluctance of Stanwell's had stayed the execution of the task. He had painted two of Mrs. Millington's friends in the spring, had been much praised and liberally paid for his work, and then, declining several orders to be executed at Newport, had surprised his friends by remaining quietly in town. It was not till August that he hired a little cottage on the New Jersey coast and invited the Arrans to visit him. They accepted the invitation, and the three had spent together six weeks of seashore idleness, during which Stanwell's modest rafters shook with Caspar's denunciations of his host's venality, and the brightness of Kate's gratitude was tempered by a tinge of reproach. But her grief over Stanwell's apostasy could not efface the fact that he had offered her brother the means of escape from town, and Stanwell himself was consoled by the reflection that but for Mrs. Millington's portrait he could not have performed even this trifling service for his friends.

When the Arrans left him in September he went to pay a few visits in the country, and on his return, a month later, to the studio building, he found that things had not gone well with Caspar. The little sculptor had caught cold, and the labor and expense of converting his gigantic off-spring into marble seemed to hang heavily upon him. He and Kate were living in a damp company of amorphous clay monsters, unfinished witnesses to the creative frenzy which had seized him after the sale of his group; and the doctor had urged that his patient should be removed to warmer and drier lodgings. But to uproot Caspar was impossible, and his sister could only feed the stove, and swaddle him in mufflers and felt slippers.

Stanwell found that during his absence Mungold had reappeared, fresh and rosy from a summer in Europe, and as prodigal as ever of the only form of attention which Kate could be counted on not to resent. The game and champagne reappeared with him, and he seemed as ready as Stanwell to lend a patient ear to Caspar's homilies. But Stanwell could see that, even now, Kate had not forgiven him for the Cupids. Stanwell himself had spent the early winter months in idleness. The sight of his tools filled him with a strange repugnance, and he absented himself as much as possible from the studio. But Shepson's visit roused him to the fact that he must decide on some definite course of action. If he wished to follow up his success of the previous spring he must refuse no more orders: he must not let Mrs. Van Orley slip away from him. He knew there were competitors enough ready to profit by his hesitations, and since his success was the result of a whim, a whim might undo it. With a gesture of decision he caught up his hat and left the studio.

On the landing he met Kate Arran. She too was going out, drawn forth by the sudden radiance of the January afternoon. She met him with a smile which seemed the answer to his uncertainties, and he asked if she had time to take a walk with him.

Yes; for once she had time, for Mr. Mungold was sitting with Caspar, and had promised to remain till she came in. It mattered little to Stanwell that Mungold was with Caspar as long as he himself was with Kate; and he instantly soared to the suggestion that they should prolong the painter's vigil by taking the "elevated" to the Park. In this too his companion acquiesced after a moment of surprise: she seemed in a consenting mood, and Stanwell augured well from the fact.

The Park was clothed in the double glitter of snow and sunshine. They roamed the hard white alleys to a continuous tinkle of sleigh-bells, and Kate brightened with the exhilaration of the scene. It was not often that she permitted herself such an escape from routine, and in this new environment, which seemed to detach her from her daily setting, Stanwell had his first complete vision of her. To the girl also their unwonted isolation seemed to create a sense of fuller communion, for she began presently, as they reached the leafless solitude of the Ramble, to speak with sudden freedom of her brother. It appeared that the orders against which Caspar had so heroically steeled himself were slow in coming: he had received no commission since the sale of his group, and he was beginning to suffer from a reaction of discouragement. Oh, it was not the craving for popularity—Stanwell knew how far above that he stood. But it had been exquisite, yes, exquisite to him to find himself believed in, understood. He had fancied that the purchase of the group was the dawn of a tardy recognition— and now the darkness of indifference had closed in again, no one spoke of him, no one wrote of him, no one cared.

"If he were in good health it wouldn't matter—he would throw off such weakness, he'd live only for the joy of his work; but he's losing ground, his strength is failing, and he's so afraid there will not be time enough left—time enough for full recognition," she explained.

The quiver in her voice silenced Stanwell: he was afraid of echoing it with his own. At length he said: "Oh, more orders will come. Success is a gradual growth."

"Yes, *real* success," she said, with a solemn note in which he caught—and forgave—a reflection on his own facile triumphs.

"But when the orders do come," she continued, "will he have strength to carry them out? Last winter the doctor thought he only needed work to set him up; now he talks of rest instead! He says we ought to go to a warm climate—but how can Caspar leave the group?"

"Oh, hang the group—let him chuck the order!"

She looked at him tragically. "The money is spent," she said.

Stanwell colored to the roots of his hair. "But ill-health—ill-health excuses everything. If he goes away now he'll come back good for twice the amount of work in the spring. A sculptor's not expected to deliver a statue on a given day, like a package of groceries! You must do as the doctor says—you must make him chuck everything and go."

They had reached a windless nook above the lake, and, pausing in the stress of their talk, she let herself sink on a bench beside the path. The movement encouraged him, and he seated himself at her side.

"You must take him away at once," he repeated urgently. "He must be made comfortable—you must both be free from worry. And I want you to let me manage it for you—"

He broke off, silenced by her rising blush, her protesting murmur.

"Oh, stop, please; let me explain," he went on. "I'm not talking of lending you money; I'm talking of giving you—myself. The offer may be just as unacceptable, but it's of a kind to which it's customary to accord a hearing. I should have made it a year ago—the first day I saw you, I believe!—but that, then, it wasn't in my power to make things easier for you. Now, you know, I've had a little luck. Since I painted Mrs. Millington things have changed. I believe I can get as many orders as I choose—there are two or three people waiting now. What's the use of it all, if it doesn't bring me a little happiness? And the only happiness I know is the kind you can give me."

He paused, suddenly losing the courage to look at her, so that her pained murmur was framed for him in a glittering vision of the frozen lake. He turned with a start and met the refusal in her eyes.

"No—really no?" he repeated.

She shook her head silently.

"I could have helped you—I could have helped you!" he sighed.

She flushed distressfully, but kept her eyes on his.

"It's just that—don't you see?" she reproached him.

"Just that—the fact that I could be of use to you?"

"The fact that, as you say, things have changed since you painted Mrs. Millington. I haven't seen the later portraits, but they tell me—"

"Oh, they're just as bad!" Stanwell jeered.

"You've sold your talent, and you know it: that's the dreadful part. You did it deliberately," she cried with passion.

"Oh, deliberately," he grimly assented.

"And you're not ashamed—you talk of going on!"

"I'm not ashamed; I talk of going on."

She received this with a long shuddering sigh, and turned her eyes away from him.

"Oh, why—why—why?" she lamented.

It was on the tip of Stanwell's tongue to answer: "That I might say to you what I'm saying now—" but he replied instead: "A man may paint bad pictures and be a decent fellow. Look at Mungold, after all!"

The adjuration had an unexpected effect. Kate's color faded suddenly, and she sat motionless, with a stricken face.

"There's a difference—" she began at length abruptly; "the difference you've always insisted on. Mr. Mungold paints as well as he can. He has no idea that his pictures are—less good than they might be."

"Well—?"

"So he can't be accused of doing what he does for money—of sacrificing anything better." She turned on him with troubled eyes. "It was you who made me understand that, when Caspar used to make fun of him."

Stanwell smiled. "I'm glad you still think me a better painter than Mungold. But isn't it hard that for that very reason I should starve in a hole? If I painted badly enough you'd see no objection to my living at the Waldorf!"

"Ah, don't joke about it," she murmured. "Don't triumph in it."

"I see no reason to at present," said Stanwell drily. "But I won't pretend to be ashamed when I'm not. I think there are occasions when a man is justified in doing what I've done."

She looked at him solemnly. "What occasions?"

"Why, when he wants money, hang it!"

She drew a deep breath. "Money—money? Has Caspar's example been nothing to you, then?"

"It hasn't proved to me that I must starve while Mungold lives on truffles!"

Again her face changed and she stirred uneasily, and then rose to her feet.

"There's no occasion which can justify an artist's sacrificing his convictions!" she exclaimed.

Stanwell rose too, facing her with a mounting urgency which sent a flush to his cheek.

"Can't you conceive such an occasion in my case? The wish, I mean, to make things easier for Caspar—to help you in any way you might let me?"

Her face reflected his blush, and she stood gazing at him with a wounded wonder.

"Caspar and I—you imagine we could live on money earned in *that* way?"

Stanwell made an impatient gesture. "You've got to live on something—or he has, even if you don't include yourself!"

Her blush deepened miserably, but she held her head high.

"That's just it—that's what I came here to say to you." She stood a moment gazing away from him at the lake.

He looked at her in surprise. "You came here to say something to me?"

"Yes. That we've got to live on something, Caspar and I, as you say; and since an artist cannot sacrifice his convictions, the sacrifice must—I mean—I wanted you to know that I have promised to marry Mr. Mungold."

"Mungold!" Stanwell cried with a sharp note of irony; but her white look checked it on his lips.

"I know all you are going to say," she murmured, with a kind of nobility which moved him even through his sense of its grotesqueness. "But you must see the distinction, because you first made it clear to me. I can take money earned in good faith—I can let Caspar live on it. I can marry Mr. Mungold because, though his pictures are bad, he does not prostitute his art."

She began to move away from him, and he followed her in silence along the frozen path.

When Stanwell re-entered his studio the dusk had fallen. He lit his lamp and rummaged out some writing-materials. Having found them, he wrote to Shepson to say that he could not paint Mrs. Van Orley, and did not care to accept any more orders for the present. He sealed and stamped the letter and flung it over the banisters for the janitor to post; then he dragged out his unfinished head of Kate Arran, replaced it on the easel, and sat down before it with a grim smile.

HIS FATHER'S SON

AFTER his wife's death Mason Grew took the momentous step of selling out his business and moving from Wingfield, Connecticut, to Brooklyn.

For years he had secretly nursed the hope of such a change, but had never dared to suggest it to Mrs. Grew, a woman of immutable habits. Mr. Grew himself was attached to Wingfield, where he had grown up, prospered, and become what the local press described as "prominent." He was attached to his brick house with sandstone trimmings and a cast-iron area-railing neatly sanded to match; to the similar row of houses across the street, with "trolley" wires forming a kind of aerial pathway between, and to the vista closed by the sandstone steeple of the church which he and his wife had always attended, and where their only child had been baptised.

It was hard to snap all these threads of association, yet still harder, now that he was alone, to live so far from his boy. Ronald Grew was practicing law in New York, and there was no more chance of his returning to live at Wingfield than of a river's flowing inland from the sea. Therefore to be near him his father must move; and it was characteristic of Mr. Grew, and of the situation generally, that the translation, when it took place, was to Brooklyn, and not to New York.

"Why you bury yourself in that hole I can't think," had been Ronald's comment; and Mr. Grew simply replied that rents were lower in Brooklyn, and that he had heard of a house there that would suit him. In reality he had said to himself—being the only recipient of his own confidences—that if he went to New York he might be on the boy's mind; whereas, if he lived in Brooklyn, Ronald would always have a good excuse for not popping over to see him every other day. The sociological isolation of Brooklyn, combined with its geographical nearness, presented in fact the precise conditions that Mr. Grew sought. He wanted to be near enough to New York to go there often, to feel under his feet the same pavement that Ronald trod, to sit now and then in the same theaters, and find on his breakfast-table the journals which, with increasing frequency, inserted Ronald's name in the sacred bounds of the society column. It had always been a trial to Mr. Grew to have to wait twenty-four hours to read that "among those present was Mr. Ronald Grew." Now he had it with his coffee, and left it on the breakfast-table to the perusal of a "hired girl" cosmopolitan enough to do it justice. In such ways Brooklyn attested the advantages of its nearness to New York, while remaining, as regards Ronald's duty to his father, as remote and inaccessible as Wingfield.

It was not that Ronald shirked his filial obligations, but rather because of his heavy sense of them, that Mr. Grew so persistently sought to minimize and lighten them. It was he who insisted, to Ronald, on the immense difficulty of getting from New York to Brooklyn.

"Any way you look at it, it makes a big hole in the day; and there's not much use in the ragged rim left. You say you're dining out next Sunday? Then I forbid you to come over here to lunch. Do you understand me, sir? You disobey at the risk of your father's malediction! Where did you say you were dining? With the Waltham Bankshires again? Why, that's the second time in three weeks, ain't it? Big blow-out, I suppose? Gold plate and orchids—opera singers in afterward? Well, you'd be in a nice box if there was a fog on the river, and you got hung up half-way over. That'd be a handsome return for the attention Mrs. Bankshire has shown you—singling out a whipper-snapper like you twice in three weeks! (What's the daughter's name—Daisy?) No, *sir*—don't you come fooling round here next Sunday, or I'll set the dogs on you. And you wouldn't find me in anyhow, come to think of it. I'm lunching out myself, as it happens—yes, sir, *lunching out*. Is there anything especially comic in my lunching out? I don't often do it, you say? Well, that's no reason why I never should. Who with? Why, with —with old Dr. Bleaker: Dr. Eliphalet Bleaker. No, you wouldn't know about him—he's only an old friend of your mother's and mine."

Gradually Ronald's insistence became less difficult to overcome. With his customary sweetness and tact (as Mr. Grew put it) he began to "take the hint," to give in to "the old gentleman's" growing desire for solitude.

"I'm set in my ways, Ronny, that's about the size of it; I like to go tick-ticking along like a clock. I always did. And when you come bouncing in I never feel sure there's enough for dinner—or that I haven't sent Maria out for the evening. And I don't want the neighbors to see me opening my own door to my son. That's the kind of cringing snob I am. Don't give me away, will you? I want 'em to think I keep four or five powdered flunkeys in the hall day and night—same as the lobby of one of those Fifth Avenue hotels. And if you pop over when you're not expected, how am I going to keep up the bluff?"

Ronald yielded after the proper amount of resistance—his intuitive sense, in every social transaction, of the proper amount of force to be expended, was one of the qualities his father most admired in him. Mr. Grew's perceptions in this line were probably more acute than his son suspected. The souls of short thick-set men, with chubby features, mutton-chop whiskers, and pale eyes peering between folds of fat like almond kernels in half-split shells—souls thus encased do not reveal themselves to the casual scrutiny as delicate emotional instruments. But in spite of the disguise in which he walked Mr. Grew vibrated exquisitely in response to every imaginative appeal; and his son Ronald was always stimulating and feeding his imagination.

Ronald in fact constituted Mr. Grew's one escape from the element of mediocrity which had always hemmed him in. To a

man so enamored of beauty, and so little qualified to add to its
sum total, it was a wonderful privilege to have bestowed on the
world such a being. Ronald's resemblance to Mr. Grew's early conception of what he himself would have liked to look might have
put new life into the discredited theory of pre-natal influences. At
any rate, if the young man owed his beauty, his distinction and his
winning manner to the dreams of one of his parents, it was certainly to those of Mr. Grew, who, while outwardly devoting his
life to the manufacture and dissemination of Grew's Secure Suspender Buckle, moved in an enchanted inward world peopled
with all the figures of romance. In this company Mr. Grew cut as
brilliant a figure as any of its noble phantoms; and to see his vision
of himself projected on the outer world in the shape of a brilliant
popular conquering son, seemed, in retrospect, to give to it a be-
lated reality. There were even moments when, forgetting his face,
Mr. Grew said to himself that if he'd had "half a chance" he might
have done as well as Ronald; but this only fortified his resolve that
Ronald should do infinitely better.

Ronald's ability to do well almost equaled his gift of looking
well. Mr. Grew constantly affirmed to himself that the boy was
"not a genius"; but, barring this slight deficiency, he had almost
every gift that a parent could wish. Even at Harvard he had managed to be several desirable things at once—writing poetry in the
college magazine, playing delightfully "by ear," acquitting himself
creditably of his studies, and yet holding his own in the sporting
set that formed, as it were, the gateway of the temple of Society.
Mr. Grew's idealism did not preclude the frank desire that his son
should pass through that gateway; but the wish was not prompted
by material considerations. It was Mr. Grew's notion that, in the
rough and hurrying current of a new civilization, the little pools
of leisure and enjoyment must nurture delicate growths, material
graces as well as moral refinements, likely to be uprooted and
swept away by the rush of the main torrent. He based his theory
on the fact that he had liked the few "society" people he had met—
had found their manners simpler, their voices more agreeable,

their views more consonant with his own, than those of the leading citizens of Wingfield. But then he had met very few.

Ronald's sympathies needed no urging in the same direction. He took naturally, dauntlessly, to all the high and exceptional things about which his father's imagination had so long ineffectually hovered—from the start he *was* what Mr. Grew had dreamed of being. And so precise, so detailed, was Mr. Grew's vision of his own imaginary career, that as Ronald grew up, and began to travel in a widening orbit, his father had an almost uncanny sense of the extent to which that career was enacting itself before him. At Harvard, Ronald had done exactly what the hypothetical Mason Grew would have done, had not his actual self, at the same age, been working his way up in old Slagden's button factory—the institution which was later to acquire fame, and even notoriety, as the birthplace of Grew's Secure Suspender Buckle. Afterward, at a period when the actual Grew had passed from the factory to the bookkeeper's desk, his invisible double had been reading law at Columbia—precisely again what Ronald did! But it was when the young man left the paths laid out for him by the parental hand, and cast himself boldly on the world, that his adventures began to bear the most astonishing resemblance to those of the unrealized Mason Grew. It was in New York that the scene of this hypothetical being's first exploits had always been laid; and it was in New York that Ronald was to achieve his first triumph. There was nothing small or timid about Mr. Grew's imagination; it had never stopped at anything between Wingfield and the metropolis. And the real Ronald had the same cosmic vision as his parent. He brushed aside with a contemptuous laugh his mother's entreaty that he should stay at Wingfield and continue the dynasty of the Grew Suspender Buckle. Mr. Grew knew that in reality Ronald winced at the Buckle, loathed it, blushed for his connection with it. Yet it was the Buckle that had seen him through Groton, Harvard and the Law School, and had permitted him to enter the office of a distinguished corporation lawyer, instead of being enslaved to some sordid business with quick returns. The Buckle had been Ronald's fairy godmother—yet his father did not blame him for abhorring and disowning it. Mr. Grew himself often bitterly regretted having attached his own name to the instrument of his material success, though, at the time, his doing so had been the natural expression of his romanticism. When he invented the Buckle, and took out his patent, he and his wife both felt that to bestow their name on it was like naming a battle-ship or a peak of the Andes.

Mrs. Grew had never learned to know better; but Mr. Grew had discovered his error before Ronald was out of school. He read it first in a black eye of his boy's. Ronald's symmetry had been marred by the insolent fist of a fourth former whom he had chastised for alluding to his father as "Old Buckles"; and when Mr. Grew heard the epithet he understood in a flash that the Buckle was a thing to blush for. It was too late then to dissociate his name from it, or to efface from the hoardings of the entire continent the picture of two gentlemen, one contorting himself in the abject effort to repair a broken brace, while the careless ease of the other's attitude proclaimed his trust in the Secure Suspender Buckle. These records were indelible, but Ronald could at least be spared all direct connection with them; and that day Mr. Grew decided that the boy should not return to Wingfield.

"You'll see," he had said to Mrs. Grew, "he'll take right hold in New York. Ronald's got my knack for taking hold," he added, throwing out his chest.

"But the way you took hold was in business," objected Mrs. Grew, who was large and literal.

Mr. Grew's chest collapsed, and he became suddenly conscious of his comic face in its rim of sandy whisker. "That's not the only way," he said, with a touch of wistfulness which escaped his wife's analysis.

"Well, of course you could have written beautifully," she rejoined with admiring eyes.

"*Written*? Me!" Mr. Grew became sardonic.

"Why, those letters—weren't *they* beautiful, I'd like to know?"

The couple exchanged a glance, innocently allusive and amused on the wife's part, and charged with a sudden tragic significance on the husband's.

"Well, I've got to be going along to the office now," he merely said, dragging himself out of his chair.

This had happened while Ronald was still at school; and now Mrs. Grew slept in the Wingfield cemetery, under a life-size theological virtue of her own choosing, and Mr. Grew's prognostications as to Ronald's ability to "take right hold" in New York were being more and more brilliantly fulfilled.

II

Ronald obeyed his father's injunction not to come to luncheon on the day of the Bankshires' dinner; but in the middle of the following week Mr. Grew was surprised by a telegram from his son.

"Want to see you important matter. Expect me tomorrow afternoon."

Mr. Grew received the telegram after breakfast. To peruse it he had lifted his eye from a paragraph of the morning paper describing a fancy-dress dinner which the Hamilton Gliddens' had given the night before for the house-warming of their new Fifth Avenue palace.

"Among the couples who afterward danced in the Poets' Quadrille were Miss Daisy Bankshire, looking more than usually lovely as Laura, and Mr. Ronald Grew as the young Petrarch."

Petrarch and Laura! Well—if *anything* meant anything, Mr. Grew supposed he knew what that meant. For weeks past he had noticed how constantly the names of the young people were coupled in the society notes he so insatiably devoured. Even the soulless reporter was getting into the habit of uniting them in his lists. And this Laura and Petrarch business was almost an announcement...

Mr. Grew dropped the telegram, wiped his eye-glasses, and

re-read the paragraph. "Miss Daisy Bankshire... more than usually lovely..." Yes; she *was* lovely. He had often seen her photograph in the papers—seen her represented in every attitude of the mundane game: fondling her prize bulldog, taking a fence on her thoroughbred, dancing a *gavotte*, all patches and plumes, or fingering a guitar, all tulle and lilies; and once he had caught a glimpse of her at the theater. Hearing that Ronald was going to a fashionable first-night with the Bankshires, Mr. Grew had for once overcome his repugnance to following his son's movements, and had secured for himself, under the shadow of the balcony, a stall whence he could observe the Bankshire box without fear of detection. Ronald had never known of his father's presence; and for three blessed hours Mr. Grew had watched his boy's handsome dark head bent above the fair hair and averted shoulder that were all he could catch of Miss Bankshire's beauties.

He recalled the vision now; and with it came, as usual, its ghostly double: the vision of his young self bending above such a shoulder and such shining hair. Needless to say that the real Mason Grew had never found himself in so enviable a situation. The late Mrs. Grew had no more resembled Miss Daisy Bankshire than he had looked like the happy victorious Ronald. And the mystery was that from their dull faces, their dull endearments, the miracle of Ronald should have sprung. It was almost—fantastically—as if the boy had been a changeling, child of a Latmian night, whom the divine companion of Mr. Grew's early reveries had secretly laid in the cradle of the Wingfield bedroom while Mr. and Mrs. Grew slept the sleep of conjugal indifference.

The young Mason Grew had not at first accepted this astral episode as the complete canceling of his claims on romance. He too had grasped at the high-hung glory; and, with his tendency to reach too far when he reached at all, had singled out the prettiest girl in Wingfield. When he recalled his stammered confession of love his face still tingled under her cool bright stare. His audacity had struck her dumb; and when she recovered her voice it was to fling a taunt at him.

"Don't be too discouraged, you know—have you ever thought of trying Addie Wicks?"

All Wingfield would have understood the gibe: Addie Wicks was the dullest girl in town. And a year later he had married Addie Wicks...

He looked up from the perusal of Ronald's telegram with this memory in his mind. Now at last his dream was coming true! His boy would taste of the joys that had mocked his thwarted youth and his dull middle-age. And it was fitting that they should be realized in Ronald's destiny. Ronald was made to take happiness boldly by the hand and lead it home like a bride. He had the carriage, the confidence, the high faith in his fortune, that compel the willful stars. And, thanks to the Buckle, he would also have the background of material elegance that became his conquering person. Since Mr. Grew had retired from business his investments had prospered, and he had been saving up his income for just such a purpose. His own wants were few: he had brought the Wingfield furniture to Brooklyn, and his sitting-room was a replica of that in which the long years of his married life had been spent. Even the florid carpet on which Ronald's first footsteps had been taken was carefully matched when it became too threadbare. And on the marble center-table, with its beaded cover and bunch of dyed pampas grass, lay the illustrated Longfellow and the copy of Ingersoll's lectures which represented literature to Mr. Grew when he had led home his bride. In the light of Ronald's romance, Mr. Grew found himself re-living, with mingled pain and tenderness, all the poor prosaic incidents of his own personal history. Curiously enough, with this new splendor on them they began to emit a faint ray of their own. His wife's armchair, in its usual place by the fire, recalled her placid unperceiving presence, seated opposite to him during the long drowsy years; and he felt her kindness, her equanimity, where formerly he had only ached at her obtuseness. And from the chair he glanced up at the discolored photograph on the wall above, with a withered laurel wreath suspended on a corner of the frame. The photograph represented a young man with a poetic necktie and untrammeled hair, leaning against a Gothic chair-back, a roll of music in his hand; and beneath was scrawled a bar of Chopin, with the words: "*Adieu, Adèle.*"

The portrait was that of the great pianist, Fortuné Dolbrowski; and its presence on the wall of Mr. Grew's sitting-room commemorated the only exquisite hour of his life save that of Ronald's birth. It was some time before the latter event, a few months only after Mr. Grew's marriage, that he had taken his wife to New York to hear the great Dolbrowski. Their evening had been magically beautiful, and even Addie, roused from her usual inexpressiveness, had waked into a momentary semblance of life. "I never—I never—" she gasped out when they had regained their hotel bedroom, and sat staring back entranced at the evening's vision. Her large face was pink and tremulous, and she sat with her hands on her knees, forgetting to roll up her bonnet strings and prepare her curl-papers.

"I'd like to *write* him just how I felt—I wisht I knew how!" she burst out in a final effervescence of emotion.

Her husband lifted his head and looked at her.

"Would you? I feel that way too," he said with a sheepish laugh. And they continued to stare at each other through a transfiguring mist of sound.

The scene rose before Mr. Grew as he gazed up at the pianist's photograph. "Well, I owe her that anyhow—poor Addie!" he said, with a smile at the inconsequences of fate. With Ronald's telegram in his hand he was in a mood to count his mercies.

III

"A clear twenty-five thousand a year: that's what you can tell 'em with my compliments," said Mr. Grew, glancing complacently across the center-table at his boy.

It struck him that Ronald's gift for looking his part in life had never so completely expressed itself. Other young men, at such a moment, would have been red, damp, tight about the collar; but Ronald's cheek was a shade paler, and the contrast made his dark eyes more expressive.

"A clear twenty-five thousand; yes, sir—that's what I always meant you to have."

Mr. Grew leaned carelessly back, his hands thrust in his pockets, as though to divert attention from the agitation of his features. He had often pictured himself rolling out that phrase to Ronald, and now that it was on his lips he could not control their tremor.

Ronald listened in silence, lifting a hand to his slight mustache, as though he, too, wished to hide some involuntary betrayal of emotion. At first Mr. Grew took his silence for an expression of gratified surprise; but as it prolonged itself it became less easy to interpret.

"I—see here, my boy; did you expect more? Isn't it enough?" Mr. Grew cleared his throat. "Do *they* expect more?" he asked nervously. He was hardly able to face the pain of inflicting a disappointment on Ronald at the very moment when he had counted on putting the final touch to his bliss.

Ronald moved uneasily in his chair and his eyes wandered upward to the laurel-wreathed photograph of the pianist.

"*Is* it the money, Ronald? Speak out, my boy. We'll see, we'll look round—I'll manage somehow."

"No, no," the young man interrupted, abruptly raising his hand as though to check his father.

Mr. Grew recovered his cheerfulness. "Well, what's the trouble then, if *she's* willing?"

Ronald shifted his position again and finally rose from his seat and wandered across the room.

"Father," he said, coming back, "there's something I've got to tell you. I can't take your money."

Mr. Grew sat speechless a moment, staring blankly at his son; then he emitted a laugh. "My money? What are you talking about? What's this about my money? Why, it ain't *mine*, Ronny; it's all yours—every cent of it!"

The young man met his tender look with a gesture of tragic refusal.

"No, no, it's not mine—not even in the sense you mean. Not in any sense. Can't you understand my feeling so?"

"Feeling so? I don't know how you're feeling. I don't know what you're talking about. Are you too proud to touch any money you haven't earned? Is that what you're trying to tell me?"

"No. It's not that. You must know—"

Mr. Grew flushed to the rim of his bristling whiskers. "Know? Know *what*? Can't you speak out?"

Ronald hesitated, and the two faced each other for a long strained moment, during which Mr. Grew's congested countenance grew gradually pale again.

"What's the meaning of this? Is it because you've done something...something you're ashamed of...ashamed to tell me?" he gasped; and walking around the table he laid his hand gently on his son's shoulder. "There's nothing you can't tell me, my boy."

"It's not that. Why do you make it so hard for me?" Ronald broke out with passion. "You must have known this was sure to happen sooner or later."

"Happen? What was sure to hap—?" Mr. Grew's question wavered on his lip and passed into a tremulous laugh. "Is it something *I've* done that you don't approve of? Is it—is it *the Buckle* you're ashamed of, Ronald Grew?"

Ronald laughed too, impatiently. "The Buckle? No, I'm not ashamed of the Buckle; not any more than you are," he returned with a flush. "But I'm ashamed of all I owe to it—all I owe to you—when—when—" He broke off and took a few distracted steps across the room. "You might make this easier for me," he protested, turning back to his father.

"Make what easier? I know less and less what you're driving at," Mr. Grew groaned.

Ronald's walk had once more brought him beneath the

photograph on the wall. He lifted his head for a moment and looked at it; then he looked again at Mr. Grew.

"Do you suppose I haven't always known?"

"Known—?"

"Even before you gave me those letters at the time of my mother's death—even before that, I suspected. I don't know how it began...perhaps from little things you let drop...you and she...and resemblances that I couldn't help seeing...in myself...How on earth could you suppose I *shouldn't guess*? I always thought you gave me the letters as a way of telling me—"

Mr. Grew rose slowly from his chair. "The letters? Do you mean Dolbrowski's letters?"

Ronald nodded with white lips. "You must remember giving them to me the day after the funeral."

Mr. Grew nodded back. "Of course. I wanted you to have everything your mother valued."

"Well—how could I help knowing after that?"

"Knowing *what*?" Mr. Grew stood staring helplessly at his son. Suddenly his look caught at a clue that seemed to confront it with a deeper difficulty. "You thought—you thought those letters... Dolbrowski's letters...you thought they meant..."

"Oh, it wasn't only the letters. There were so many other signs. My love of music—my—all my feelings about life...and art... And when you gave me the letters I thought you must mean me to know."

Mr. Grew had grown quiet. His lips were firm, and his small eyes looked out steadily from their creased lids.

"To know that you were Fortuné Dolbrowski's son?"

Ronald made a mute sign of assent.

"I see. And what did you intend to do?"

"I meant to wait till I could earn my living, and then repay you...as far as I can ever repay you...for what you'd spent on me...But now that there's a chance of my marrying...and that your generosity overwhelms me...I'm obliged to speak."

"I see," said Mr. Grew again. He let himself down into his

chair, looking steadily and not unkindly at the young man. "Sit down too, Ronald. Let's talk."

Ronald made a protesting movement. "Is anything to be gained by it? You can't change me—change what I feel. The reading of those letters transformed my whole life—I was a boy till then: they made a man of me. From that moment I understood myself." He paused, and then looked up at Mr. Grew's face. "Don't imagine that I don't appreciate your kindness—your extraordinary generosity. But I can't go through life in disguise. And I want you to know that I have not won Daisy under false pretenses—"

Mr. Grew started up with the first expletive Ronald had ever heard on his lips.

"You damned young fool, you, you haven't *told* her—?"

Ronald raised his head with pride. "Oh, you don't know her, sir! She thinks no worse of me for knowing my secret. She is above and beyond all such conventional prejudices. She's *proud* of my parentage—" he straightened his slim young shoulders— "as I'm proud of it...yes, sir, proud of it..."

Mr. Grew sank back into his seat with a dry laugh. "Well, you ought to be. You come of good stock. And you're your father's son, every inch of you!" He laughed again, as though the humor of the situation grew on him with its closer contemplation.

"Yes, I've always felt that," Ronald murmured, gravely.

"Your father's son, and no mistake." Mr. Grew leaned forward. "You're the son of as big a fool as yourself. And here he sits, Ronald Grew!"

The young man's color deepened to crimson; but his reply was checked by Mr. Grew's decisive gesture. "Here he sits, with all your young nonsense still alive in him. Don't you begin to see the likeness? If you don't I'll tell you the story of those letters."

Ronald stared. "What do you mean? Don't they tell their own story?"

"I supposed they did when I gave them to you; but you've given it a twist that needs straightening out." Mr. Grew squared his elbows on the table, and looked at the young man across the gift-books and dyed pampas grass. "I wrote all the letters that Dolbrowski answered."

Ronald gave back his look in frowning perplexity. "*You* wrote them? I don't understand. His letters are all addressed to my mother."

"Yes. And he thought he was corresponding with her."

"But my mother—what did she think?"

Mr. Grew hesitated, puckering his thick lids. "Well, I guess she kinder thought it was a joke. Your mother didn't think about things much."

Ronald continued to bend a puzzled frown on the question. "I don't understand," he reiterated.

Mr. Grew cleared his throat with a nervous laugh. "Well, I don't know as you ever will—*quite*. But this is the way it came about. I had a toughish time of it when I was young. Oh, I don't mean so much the fight I had to put up to make my way—there was always plenty of fight in me. But inside of myself it was kinder lonesome. And the outside didn't attract callers." He laughed again, with an apologetic gesture toward his broad blinking face. "When I went round with the other young fellows I was always the forlorn hope—the one that had to eat the drumsticks and dance with the left-overs. As sure as there was a blighter at a picnic I had to swing her, and feed her, and drive her home. And all the time I was mad after all the things you've got—poetry and music and all the joy-forever business. So there were the pair of us—my face and my imagination—chained together, and fighting, and hating each other like poison.

"Then your mother came along and took pity on me. It sets up a gawky fellow to find a girl who ain't ashamed to be seen walking with him Sundays. And I was grateful to your mother, and we got along first-rate. Only I couldn't say things to her—and she couldn't answer. Well—one day, a few months after we were married, Dolbrowski came to New York, and the whole place went wild about him. I'd never heard any good music, but I'd always had an inkling of what it must be like, though I couldn't tell you to this day how I knew. Well, your mother read about him in the papers too, and she thought it'd be the swagger thing to go to New York and hear him play—so we went...I'll never forget that evening. Your mother wasn't easily stirred up—she never seemed to need to let off steam. But that night she seemed to understand the way I felt. And when we got back to the hotel she said to me: 'I'd like to tell him how I feel. I'd like to sit right down and write to him.'

" 'Would you?' I said. 'So would I.'

"There was paper and pens there before us, and I pulled a sheet toward me, and began to write. 'Is this what you'd like to say to him?' I asked her when the letter was done. And she got pink and said: 'I don't understand it, but it's lovely.' And she copied it out and signed her name to it, and sent it."

Mr. Grew paused, and Ronald sat silent, with lowered eyes.

"That's how it began; and that's where I thought it would end. But it didn't, because Dolbrowski answered. His first letter was dated January 10, 1872. I guess you'll find I'm correct. Well, I went back to hear him again, and I wrote him after the performance, and he answered again. And after that we kept it up for six months. Your mother always copied the letters and signed them. She seemed to think it was a kinder joke, and she was proud of his answering my letters. But she never went back to New York to hear him, though I saved up enough to give her the treat again. She was too lazy, and she let me go without her. I heard him three times in New York; and in the spring he came to Wingfield and played once at the Academy. Your mother was sick and couldn't go; so I went alone. After the performance I meant to get one of the directors to take me in to see him; but when the time came, I just went back home and wrote to him instead. And the month after, before he went back to Europe, he sent your mother a last little note, and that picture hanging up there..."

Mr. Grew paused again, and both men lifted their eyes to the photograph.

"Is that all?" Ronald slowly asked.

"That's all—every bit of it," said Mr. Grew.

"And my mother—my mother never even spoke to Dolbrowski?"

"Never. She never even saw him but that once in New York at his concert."

The blood crept again to Ronald's face. "Are you sure of that, sir?" he asked in a trembling voice.

"Sure as I am that I'm sitting here. Why, she was too lazy to look at his letters after the first novelty wore off. She copied the answers just to humor me—but she always said she couldn't understand what we wrote."

"But how could you go on with such a correspondence? It's incredible!"

Mr. Grew looked at his son thoughtfully. "I suppose it is, to you. You've only had to put out your hand and get the things I was starving for—music, and good talk, and ideas. Those letters gave me all that. You've read them, and you know that Dolbrowski was not only a great musician but a great man. There was nothing beautiful he didn't see, nothing fine he didn't feel. For six months I breathed his air, and I've lived on it ever since. Do you begin to understand a little now?"

"Yes—a little. But why write in my mother's name? Why make it appear like a sentimental correspondence?"

Mr. Grew reddened to his bald temples. "Why, I tell you it began that way, as a kinder joke. And when I saw that the first letter pleased and interested him, I was afraid to tell him—*I couldn't* tell him. Do you suppose he'd gone on writing if he'd ever seen me, Ronny?"

Ronald suddenly looked at him with new eyes. "But he must have thought your letters very beautiful—to go on as he did," he broke out.

"Well—I did my best," said Mr. Grew modestly.

Ronald pursued his idea. "Where *are* all your letters, I wonder? Weren't they returned to you at his death?"

Mr. Grew laughed. "Lord, no. I guess he had trunks and trunks full of better ones. I guess Queens and Empresses wrote to him."

"I should have liked to see your letters," the young man insisted.

"Well, they weren't bad," said Mr. Grew drily. "But I'll tell you one thing, Ronny," he added. Ronald raised his head with a quick glance, and Mr. Grew continued: "I'll tell you where the best of those letters is—it's in *you.* If it hadn't been for that one look at life I couldn't have made you what you are. Oh, I know you've done a good deal of your own making—but I've been there behind you all the time. And you'll never know the work I've spared you and the time I've saved you. Fortuné Dolbrowski helped me do that. I never saw things in little again after I'd looked at 'em with him. And I tried to give you the big view from the start . . . So that's what became of my letters."

Mr. Grew paused, and for a long time Ronald sat motionless, his elbows on the table, his face dropped on his hands.

Suddenly Mr. Grew's touch fell on his shoulder.

"Look at here, Ronald Grew—do you want me to tell you how you're feeling at this minute? Just a mite let down, after all, at the idea that you ain't the romantic figure you'd got to think yourself . . . Well, that's natural enough, too; but I'll tell you what it proves. It proves you're my son right enough, if any more proof was needed. For it's just the kind of fool nonsense I used to feel at your age—and if there's anybody here to laugh at it's myself, and not you. And you can laugh at me just as much as you like . . ."

FULL CIRCLE

GEOFFREY Betton woke rather late—so late that the winter sunlight sliding across his bedroom carpet struck his eyes as he turned on the pillow.

Strett, the valet, had been in, drawn the bath in the adjoining dressing-room, placed the crystal and silver cigarette-box at his side, put a match to the fire, and thrown open the windows to the bright morning air. It brought in, on the glitter of sun, all the crisp morning noises—those piercing notes of the American thorough-fare that seem to take a sharper vibration from the clearness of the medium through which they pass.

Betton raised himself languidly. That was the voice of Fifth Avenue below his windows. He remembered that, when he moved into his rooms eighteen months before, the sound had been like music to him: the complex orchestration to which the tune of his new life was set. Now it filled him with disgust and weariness, since it had become the symbol of the hurry and noise of that new life. He had been far less hurried in the old days when he had to be up at seven, and down at the office sharp at nine. Now that he got up when he chose, and his life had no fixed framework of duties, the hours hunted him like a pack of blood-hounds.

He dropped back on his pillow with a groan. Yes—not a year ago there had been a positively sensuous joy in getting out of bed, feeling under his bare feet the softness of the warm red carpet, and entering the shining sanctuary where his great porcelain bath proffered its renovating flood. But then a year ago he could still call up the horror of the communal plunge at his earlier lodgings:

the listening for other bathers, the dodging of shrouded ladies in "crimping"-pins, the cold wait on the landing, the descent into a blotchy tin bath, and the effort to identify one's soap and nail-brush among the promiscuous implements of ablution. That memory had faded now, and Betton saw only the dark hours to which his tiled temple of refreshment formed a kind of glittering antechamber. For after his bath came his breakfast, and on the breakfast tray his letters. His letters!

He remembered—and *that* memory had not faded!—the thrill with which, in the early days of his celebrity, he had opened the first missive in a strange feminine hand: the letter beginning: "I wonder if you'll mind an unknown reader's telling you all that your book has been to her?"

Mind? Ye gods, he minded now! For more than a year after the publication of *Diadems and Faggots* the letters, the inane indiscriminate letters of commendation, of criticism, of interrogation, had poured in on him by every post. Hundreds of unknown readers had told him with unsparing detail all that his book had been to them. And the wonder of it was, when all was said and done, that it had really been so little—that when their thick broth of praise was strained through the author's searching vanity there remained to him so small a sediment of definite specific understanding! No—it was always the same thing, over and over and over again—the same vague gush of adjectives, the same incorrigible tendency to estimate his effort according to each writer's personal preferences, instead of regarding it as a work of art, a thing to be measured by fixed standards!

He smiled to think how little, at first, he had felt the vanity of it all. He had found a savor even in the grosser evidences of popularity: the advertisements of his book, the daily shower of "clippings," the sense that, when he entered a restaurant or a theater, people nudged each other and said "That's Betton." Yes, the publicity had been sweet to him—at first. He had been touched by the sympathy of his fellow-men: had thought indulgently of the world, as a better place than the failures and the dyspeptics would acknowledge. And then his success began to submerge him: he gasped under the thickening shower of letters. His admirers were really unappeasable. And they wanted him to do such ridiculous things—to give lectures, to head movements, to be tendered receptions, to speak at banquets, to address mothers, to plead for orphans, to go up in balloons, to lead the struggle for sterilized milk. They wanted his photograph for literary supplements, his autograph for charity bazaars, his name on committees, literary, educational, and social; above all, they wanted his opinion on everything: on Christianity, Buddhism, tight lacing, the drug habit, democratic government, female suffrage and love. Perhaps the chief benefit of this demand was his incidentally learning from it how few opinions he really had: the only one that remained with him was a rooted horror of all forms of correspondence. He had been unspeakably thankful when the letters began to fall off.

Diadems and Faggots was now two years old, and the moment was at hand when its author might have counted on regaining the blessed shelter of oblivion—if only he had not written another book! For it was the worst part of his plight that the result of his first folly had goaded him to the perpetration of the next—that one of the incentives (hideous thought!) to his new work had been the desire to extend and perpetuate his popularity. And this very week the book was to come out, and the letters, the cursed letters, would begin again!

Wistfully, almost plaintively, he looked at the breakfast-tray with which Strett presently appeared. It bore only two notes and the morning journals, but he knew that within the week it would groan under its epistolary burden. The very newspapers flung the fact at him as he opened them.

READY ON MONDAY.
GEOFFREY BETTON'S NEW NOVEL
ABUNDANCE.
BY THE AUTHOR OF *DIADEMS AND FAGGOTS*.

FIRST EDITION OF ONE HUNDRED AND FIFTY THOUSAND
ALREADY SOLD OUT.
ORDER NOW.

A hundred and fifty thousand volumes! And an average of three readers to each! Half a million of people would be reading him within a week, and every one of them would write to him, and their friends and relations would write too. He laid down the paper with a shudder.

The two notes looked harmless enough, and the caligraphy of one was vaguely familiar. He opened the envelope and looked at the signature: *Duncan Vyse*. He had not seen the name in years —what on earth could Duncan Vyse have to say? He ran over the page and dropped it with a wondering exclamation, which the watchful Strett, re-entering, met by a tentative "Yes, sir?"

"Nothing. Yes—that is—" Betton picked up the note. "There's a gentleman, a Mr. Vyse, coming at ten."

Strett glanced at the clock. "Yes, sir. You'll remember that ten was the hour you appointed for the secretaries to call, sir."

Betton nodded. "I'll see Mr. Vyse first. My clothes, please."

As he got into them, in the state of nervous hurry that had become almost chronic with him, he continued to think about Duncan Vyse. They had seen a great deal of each other for the few years after both had left Harvard: the hard happy years when Betton had been grinding at his business and Vyse—poor devil!— trying to write. The novelist recalled his friend's attempts with a smile; then the memory of one small volume came back to him. It was a novel: *The Lifted Lamp*. There was stuff in that, certainly. He remembered Vyse's tossing it down on his table with a gesture of despair when it came back from the last publisher. Betton, taking it up indifferently, had sat riveted till daylight. When he ended, the impression was so strong that he said to himself: "I'll tell Apthorn about it—I'll go and see him to-morrow." His own secret literary yearnings increased his desire to champion Vyse, to see him triumph over the dullness and timidity of the publishers. Apthorn was the youngest of the guild, still capable of opinions and the courage of them, a personal friend of Betton's, and, as it happened, the man afterward to become known as the privileged publisher of *Diadems and Faggots*. Unluckily the next day something unexpected turned up, and Betton forgot about Vyse and his manuscript. He continued to forget for a month, and then came a note from Vyse, who was ill, and wrote to ask what his friend had done. Betton did not like to say "I've done nothing," so he left the note unanswered, and vowed again: "I'll see Apthorn."

The following day he was called to the West on business, and was away a month. When he came back, there was a third note from Vyse, who was still ill, and desperately hard up. "I'll take anything for the book, if they'll advance me two hundred dollars." Betton, full of compunction, would gladly have advanced the sum himself; but he was hard up too, and could only swear inwardly: "I'll write to Apthorn." Then he glanced again at the manuscript, and reflected: "No—there are things in it that need explaining. I'd better see him."

Once he went so far as to telephone Apthorn, but the publisher was out. Then he finally and completely forgot.

One Sunday he went out of town, and on his return, rummaging among the papers on his desk, he missed *The Lifted Lamp*, which had been gathering dust there for half a year. What the deuce could have become of it? Betton spent a feverish hour in vainly increasing the disorder of his documents, and then bethought himself of calling the maid-servant, who first indignantly denied having touched anything ("I can see that's true from the dust," Betton scathingly remarked), and then mentioned with hauteur that a young lady had called in his absence and asked to be allowed to get a book.

"A lady? Did you let her come up?"

"She said somebody'd sent her."

Vyse, of course—Vyse had sent her for his manuscript! He was always mixed up with some woman, and it was just like him to send the girl of the moment to Betton's lodgings, with instructions to force the door in his absence. Vyse had never been remarkable for delicacy. Betton, furious, glanced over his table to see if any of his own effects were missing—one couldn't tell, with the company Vyse kept!—and then dismissed the matter from his mind, with a vague sense of magnanimity in doing so. He felt himself exonerated by Vyse's conduct.

The sense of magnanimity was still uppermost when the valet opened the door to announce "Mr. Vyse," and Betton, a moment later, crossed the threshold of his pleasant library.

His first thought was that the man facing him from the hearth-rug was the very Duncan Vyse of old: small, starved, bleached-looking, with the same sidelong movements, the same air of anemic truculence. Only he had grown shabbier, and bald.

Betton held out a hospitable hand.

"This is a good surprise! Glad you looked me up, my dear fellow."

Vyse's palm was damp and bony: he had always had a disagreeable hand.

"You got my note? You know what I've come for?"

"About the secretaryship? (Sit down.) Is that really serious?"

Betton lowered himself luxuriously into one of his vast Maple armchairs. He had grown stouter in the last year, and the cushion behind him fitted comfortably into the crease of his nape. As he leaned back he caught sight of his image in the mirror between the windows, and reflected uneasily that Vyse would not find *him* unchanged.

"Serious?" Vyse rejoined. "Why not? Aren't *you?*"

"Oh, perfectly." Betton laughed apologetically. "Only—well, the fact is, you may not understand what rubbish a secretary of mine would have to deal with. In advertising for one I never imagined—I didn't aspire to any one above the ordinary hack."

"I'm the ordinary hack," said Vyse drily.

Betton's affable gesture protested. "My dear fellow—. You see it's not business—what I'm in now," he continued with a laugh.

Vyse's thin lips seemed to form a noiseless "*Isn't* it?" which they instantly transposed into the audible reply: "I judged from your advertisement that you want some one to relieve you in your literary work. Dictation, short-hand—that kind of thing?"

"Well, no: not that either. I type my own things. What I'm looking for is somebody who won't be above tackling my correspondence."

Vyse looked slightly surprised. "I should be glad of the job," he then said.

Betton began to feel a vague embarrassment. He had supposed that such a proposal would be instantly rejected. "It would be only for an hour or two a day—if you're doing any writing of your own?" he threw out interrogatively.

"No. I've given all that up. I'm in an office now—business. But it doesn't take all my time, or pay enough to keep me alive."

"In that case, my dear fellow—if you could come every morning; but it's mostly awful bosh, you know," Betton again broke off, with growing awkwardness.

Vyse glanced at him humorously. "What you want me to write?"

"Well, that depends—" Betton sketched the obligatory smile. "But I was thinking of the letters you'll have to answer. Letters about my books, you know—I've another one appearing next week. And I want to be beforehand now—dam the flood before it swamps me. Have you any idea of the deluge of stuff that people write to a successful novelist?"

As Betton spoke, he saw a tinge of red on Vyse's thin cheek, and his own reflected it in a richer glow of shame. "I mean—I mean—" he stammered helplessly.

"No, I haven't," said Vyse; "but it will be awfully jolly finding out."

There was a pause, groping and desperate on Betton's part, sardonically calm on his visitor's.

"You—you've given up writing altogether?" Betton continued.

"Yes; we've changed places, as it were." Vyse paused. "But about these letters—you dictate the answers?"

"Lord, no! That's the reason why I said I wanted somebody— er—well used to writing. I don't want to have anything to do with them—not a thing! You'll have to answer them as if they were written to *you*—" Betton pulled himself up again, and rising in confusion jerked open one of the drawers of his writing-table.

"Here—this kind of rubbish," he said, tossing a packet of letters onto Vyse's knee.

"Oh—you keep them, do you?" said Vyse simply.

"I—well—some of them; a few of the funniest only."

Vyse slipped off the band and began to open the letters. While he was glancing over them Betton again caught his own reflection in the glass, and asked himself what impression he had made on his visitor. It occurred to him for the first time that his high-colored well-fed person presented the image of commercial rather than of intellectual achievement. He did not look like his own idea of the author of *Diadems and Faggots*—and he wondered why.

Vyse laid the letters aside. "I think I can do it—if you'll give me a notion of the tone I'm to take."

"The tone?"

"Yes—that is, if you expect me to sign your name."

"Oh, of course you're to sign for me. As for the tone, say just what you'd—well, say all you can without encouraging them to answer."

Vyse rose from his seat. "I could submit a few specimens," he suggested.

"Oh, as to that—you always wrote better than I do," said Betton handsomely.

"I've never had this kind of thing to write. When do you wish me to begin?" Vyse inquired, ignoring the tribute.

"The book's out on Monday. The deluge will probably begin about three days after. Will you turn up on Thursday at this hour?" Betton held his hand out with real heartiness. "It was great luck for me, your striking that advertisement. Don't be too harsh with my correspondents—I owe them something for having brought us together."

II

The deluge began punctually on the Thursday, and Vyse, arriving as punctually, had an impressive pile of letters to attack. Betton, on his way to the Park for a ride, came into the library, smoking the cigarette of indolence, to look over his secretary's shoulder.

"How many of 'em? Twenty? Good Lord! It's going to be worse than *Diadems*. I've just had my first quiet breakfast in two years—time to read the papers and loaf. How I used to dread the sight of my letter-box! Now I shan't know that I have one."

He leaned over Vyse's chair, and the secretary handed him a letter.

"Here's rather an exceptional one—lady, evidently. I thought you might want to answer it yourself—"

"Exceptional?" Betton ran over the mauve pages and tossed them down. "Why, my dear man, I get hundreds like that. You'll have to be pretty short with her, or she'll send her photograph."

He clapped Vyse on the shoulder and turned away, humming a tune. "Stay to luncheon," he called back gaily from the threshold.

After luncheon Vyse insisted on showing a few of his answers to the first batch of letters. "If I've struck the note I won't bother you again," he urged; and Betton groaningly consented.

"My dear fellow, they're beautiful—too beautiful. I'll be let in for a correspondence with every one of these people."

Vyse, in reply, mused for a while above a blank sheet. "All right—how's this?" he said, after another interval of rapid writing.

Betton glanced over the page. "By George—by George! Won't she *see* it?" he exulted, between fear and rapture.

"It's wonderful how little people see," said Vyse reassuringly.

The letters continued to pour in for several weeks after the appearance of *Abundance*. For five or six blissful days Betton did not even have his mail brought to him, trusting to Vyse to single out his personal correspondence, and to deal with the rest of the letters according to their agreement. During those days he luxuriated in a sense of wild and lawless freedom; then, gradually, he began to feel the need of fresh restraints to break, and learned that the zest of liberty lies in the escape from specific obligations. At first he was conscious only of a vague hunger, but in time the craving resolved itself into a shame-faced desire to see his letters.

"After all, I hated them only because I had to answer them"; and he told Vyse carelessly that he wished all his letters submitted to him before the secretary answered them.

The first morning he pushed aside those beginning: "I have just laid down *Abundance* after a third reading," or: "Every day for the last month I have been telephoning my bookseller to know when your novel would be out." But little by little the freshness of his interest revived, and even this stereotyped homage began to arrest his eye. At last a day came when he read all the letters, from the first word to the last, as he had done when *Diadems and Faggots* appeared. It was really a pleasure to read them, now that he was relieved of the burden of replying: his new relation to his correspondents had the glow of a love-affair unchilled by the contingency of marriage.

One day it struck him that the letters were coming in more slowly and in smaller numbers. Certainly there had been more of a rush when *Diadems and Faggots* came out. Betton began to wonder if Vyse were exercising an unauthorized discrimination, and keeping back the communications he deemed least important. This conjecture carried the novelist straight to his library, where he found Vyse bending over the writing-table with his usual inscrutable pale smile. But once there, Betton hardly knew how to frame his question, and blundered into an inquiry for a missing invitation.

"There's a note—a personal note—I ought to have had this

morning. Sure you haven't kept it back by mistake among the others?"

Vyse laid down his pen. "The others? But I never keep back any."

Betton had foreseen the answer. "Not even the worst twaddle about my book?" he suggested lightly, pushing the papers about.

"Nothing. I understood you wanted to go over them all first."

"Well, perhaps it's safer," Betton conceded, as if the idea were new to him. With an embarrassed hand he continued to turn over the letters at Vyse's elbow.

"Those are yesterday's," said the secretary; "here are today's," he added, pointing to a meager trio.

"H'm—only these?" Betton took them and looked them over lingeringly. "I don't see what the deuce that chap means about the first part of *Abundance* 'certainly justifying the title'—do you?"

Vyse was silent, and the novelist continued irritably: "Damned cheek, his writing, if he doesn't like the book. Who cares what he thinks about it, anyhow?"

And his morning ride was embittered by the discovery that it was unexpectedly disagreeable to have Vyse read any letters which did not express unqualified praise of his books. He began to fancy that there was a latent rancor, a kind of baffled sneer, under Vyse's manner; and he decided to return to the practice of having his mail brought straight to his room. In that way he could edit the letters before his secretary saw them.

Vyse made no comment on the change, and Betton was reduced to wondering whether his imperturbable composure were the mask of complete indifference or of a watchful jealousy. The latter view being more agreeable to his employer's self-esteem, the next step was to conclude that Vyse had not forgotten the episode of *The Lifted Lamp*, and would naturally take a vindictive joy in any unfavorable judgments passed on his rival's work. This did not simplify the situation, for there was no denying that unfavorable criticisms preponderated in Betton's correspondence. *Abundance* was neither meeting with the unrestricted welcome of

Diadems and Faggots, nor enjoying the alternative of an animated controversy: it was simply found dull, and its readers said so in language not too tactfully tempered by comparisons with its predecessor. To withhold unfavorable comments from Vyse was, therefore, to make it appear that correspondence about the book had died out; and its author, mindful of his unguarded predictions, found this even more embarrassing. The simplest solution would be to get rid of Vyse; and to this end Betton began to address his energies.

One evening, finding himself unexpectedly disengaged, he asked Vyse to dine; it had occurred to him that, in the course of an after-dinner chat, he might hint his feeling that the work he had offered his friend was unworthy so accomplished a hand.

Vyse surprised him by a momentary hesitation. "I may not have time to dress."

Betton brushed the objection aside. "What's the odds? We'll dine here—and as late as you like."

Vyse thanked him, and appeared, punctually at eight, in all the shabbiness of his daily wear. He looked paler and more shyly truculent than usual, and Betton, from the height of his florid stature, said to himself, with the sudden professional instinct for "type": "He might be an agent of something—a chap who carries deadly secrets."

Vyse, it was to appear, did carry a deadly secret; but one less perilous to society than to himself. He was simply poor—unpardonably, irremediably poor. Everything failed him, had always failed him: whatever he put his hand to went to bits.

This was the confession that, reluctantly, yet with a kind of white-lipped bravado, he flung at Betton in answer to the latter's tentative suggestion that, really, the letter-answering job wasn't worth bothering him with—a thing that any type-writer could do.

"If you mean that you're paying me more than it's worth, I'll take less," Vyse rushed out after a pause.

"Oh, my dear fellow—" Betton protested, flushing.

"What *do* you mean, then? Don't I answer the letters as you want them answered?"

Betton anxiously stroked his silken ankle. "You do it beautifully, too beautifully. I mean what I say: the work's not worthy of
you. I'm ashamed to ask you—"

"Oh, hang shame," Vyse interrupted. "Do you know why I said
I shouldn't have time to dress tonight? Because I haven't any
evening clothes. As a matter of fact, I haven't much but the clothes
I stand in. One thing after another's gone against me; all the infernal ingenuities of chance. It's been a slow Chinese torture, the
kind where they keep you alive to have more fun killing you." He
straightened himself with a sudden blush. "Oh, I'm all right now
—getting on capitally. But I'm still walking rather a narrow plank;
and if I do your work well enough—if I take your idea—"

Betton stared into the fire without answering. He knew next to
nothing of Vyse's history, of the mischance or mismanagement
that had brought him, with his brains and his training, to so unlikely a pass. But a pang of compunction shot through him as he
remembered the manuscript of *The Lifted Lamp* gathering dust on
his table for half a year.

"Not that it would have made any earthly difference—since
he's evidently never been able to get the thing published." But this
reflection did not wholly console Betton, and he found it impossible, at the moment, to tell Vyse that his services were not needed.

III

During the ensuing weeks the letters grew fewer and fewer, and
Betton foresaw the approach of the fatal day when his secretary, in
common decency, would have to say: "I can't draw my pay for doing nothing."

What a triumph for Vyse!

The thought was intolerable, and Betton cursed his weakness
in not having dismissed the fellow before such a possibility arose.

"If I tell him I've no use for him now, he'll see straight through
it, of course;—and then, hang it, he looks so poor!"

This consideration came after the other, but Betton, in rearranging them, put it first, because he thought it looked better there, and also because he immediately perceived its value in justifying a plan of action that was beginning to take shape in his mind.

"Poor devil, I'm damned if I don't do it for him!" said Betton, sitting down at his desk.

Three or four days later he sent word to Vyse that he didn't care to go over the letters any longer, and that they would once more be carried directly to the library.

The next time he lounged in, on his way to his morning ride, he found his secretary's pen in active motion.

"A lot to-day," Vyse told him cheerfully.

His tone irritated Betton: it had the inane optimism of the physician reassuring a discouraged patient.

"Oh. Lord—I thought it was almost over," groaned the novelist.

"No: they've just got their second wind. Here's one from a Chicago publisher—never heard the name—offering you thirty percent on your next novel, with an advance royalty of twenty thousand. And here's a chap who wants to syndicate it for a bunch of Sunday papers: big offer, too. That's from Ann Arbor. And this —oh, *this* one's funny!"

He held up a small scented sheet to Betton, who made no movement to receive it.

"Funny? Why's it funny?" he growled.

"Well, it's from a girl—a lady—and she thinks she's the only person who understands *Abundance*—has the clue to it. Says she's never seen a book so misrepresented by the critics—"

"Ha, ha! That *is* good!" Betton agreed with too loud a laugh.

"This one's from a lady, too—married woman. Says she's mis-understood, and would like to correspond."

"Oh, Lord," said Betton.—"What are you looking at?" he added sharply, as Vyse continued to bend his blinking gaze on the letters.

"I was only thinking I'd never seen such short letters from women. Neither one fills the first page."

"Well, what of that?" queried Betton.

Vyse reflected. "I'd like to meet a woman like that," he said wearily; and Betton laughed again.

The letters continued to pour in, and there could be no farther question of dispensing with Vyse's services. But one morning, about three weeks later, the latter asked for a word with his employer, and Betton, on entering the library, found his secretary with half a dozen documents spread out before him.

"What's up?" queried Betton, with a touch of impatience.

Vyse was attentively scanning the outspread letters.

"I don't know: can't make out." His voice had a faint note of embarrassment. "Do you remember a note signed *Hester Macklin* that came three or four weeks ago? Married—misunderstood— Western army post—wanted to correspond?"

Betton seemed to grope among his memories; then he assented vaguely.

"A short note," Vyse went on: "the whole story in half a page. The shortness struck me so much—and the directness—that I wrote her: wrote in my own name, I mean."

"In your own name?" Betton stood amazed; then he broke into a groan.

"Good Lord, Vyse—you're incorrigible!"

The secretary pulled his thin mustache with a nervous laugh. "If you mean I'm an ass, you're right. Look here." He held out an envelope stamped with the words: "Dead Letter Office." "My effusion has come back to me marked 'unknown.' There's no such person at the address she gave you."

Betton seemed for an instant to share his secretary's embarrassment; then he burst into an uproarious laugh.

"Hoax, was it? That's rough on you, old fellow!"

Vyse shrugged his shoulders. "Yes; but the interesting question is—why on earth didn't *your* answer come back, too?"

"My answer?"

"The official one—the one I wrote in your name. If she's unknown, what's become of *that*?"

Betton's eyes were wrinkled by amusement. "Perhaps she hadn't disappeared then."

Vyse disregarded the conjecture. "Look here—I believe *all* these letters are a hoax," he broke out.

Betton stared at him with a face that turned slowly red and angry. "What are you talking about? All what letters?"

"These I've got spread out here: I've been comparing them. And I believe they're all written by one man."

Betton's redness turned to a purple that made his ruddy mustache seem pale. "What the devil are you driving at?" he asked.

"Well, just look at it," Vyse persisted, still bent above the letters. "I've been studying them carefully—those that have come within the last two or three weeks—and there's a queer likeness in the writing of some of them. The *g*'s are all like cork-screws. And the same phrases keep recurring—the Ann Arbor news-agent uses the same expressions as the President of the Girl's College at Euphorbia, Maine."

Betton laughed. "Aren't the critics always groaning over the shrinkage of the national vocabulary? Of course we all use the same expressions."

"Yes," said Vyse obstinately. "But how about using the same *g*'s?"

Betton laughed again, but Vyse continued without heeding him: "Look here, Betton—could Strett have written them?"

"Strett?" Betton roared. "*Strett?*" He threw himself into his armchair to shake out his mirth at greater ease.

"I'll tell you why. Strett always posts all my answers. He comes in for them every day before I leave. He posted the letter to the misunderstood party—the letter from *you* that the Dead Letter Office didn't return. *I* posted my own letter to her; and that came back."

A measurable silence followed the emission of this ingenious conjecture; then Betton observed with gentle irony: "Extremely neat. And of course it's no business of yours to supply any valid motive for this remarkable attention on my valet's part."

Vyse cast on him a slanting glance.

"If you've found that human conduct's generally based on valid motives—!"

"Well, outside of mad-houses it's supposed to be not quite incalculable."

Vyse had an odd smile under his thin mustache. "Every house is a mad-house at some time or another."

Betton rose with a careless shake of the shoulders. "This one will be if I talk to you much longer," he said, moving away with a laugh.

IV

Betton did not for a moment believe that Vyse suspected the valet of having written the letters.

"Why the devil don't he say out what he thinks? He was always a tortuous chap," he grumbled inwardly.

The sense of being held under the lens of Vyse's mute scrutiny became more and more exasperating. Betton, by this time, had squared his shoulders to the fact that *Abundance* was a failure with the public: a confessed and glaring failure. The press told him so openly, and his friends emphasized the fact by their circumlocutions and evasions. Betton minded it a good deal more than he had expected, but not nearly as much as he minded Vyse's knowing it. That remained the central twinge in his diffused discomfort. And the problem of getting rid of his secretary once more engaged him.

He had set aside all sentimental pretexts for retaining Vyse; but a practical argument replaced them. "If I ship him now he'll think it's because I'm ashamed to have him see that I'm not getting any more letters."

For the letters had ceased again, almost abruptly, since Vyse had hazarded the conjecture that they were the product of Strett's devoted pen. Betton had reverted only once to the subject—to ask ironically, a day or two later: "Is Strett writing to me as much as ever?"—and, on Vyse's replying with a neutral headshake, had added, laughing: "If you suspect *him* you'll be thinking next that I write the letters myself!"

"There are very few to-day," said Vyse, with an irritating evasiveness; and Betton rejoined squarely: "Oh, they'll stop soon. The book's a failure."

A few mornings later he felt a rush of shame at his own tergiversations, and stalked into the library with Vyse's sentence on his tongue.

Vyse was sitting at the table making pencil-sketches of a girl's profile. Apparently there was nothing else for him to do.

"Is that your idea of Hester Macklin?" asked Betton jovially, leaning over him.

Vyse started back with one of his anemic blushes. "I was hoping you'd be in. I wanted to speak to you. There've been no letters the last day or two," he explained.

Betton drew a quick breath of relief. The man had some sense of decency, then! He meant to dismiss himself.

"I told you so, my dear fellow; the book's a flat failure," he said, almost gaily.

Vyse made a deprecating gesture. "I don't know that I should regard the absence of letters as the final test. But I wanted to ask you if there isn't something else I can do on the days when there's no writing." He turned his glance toward the book-lined walls. "Don't you want your library catalogued?" he asked insidiously.

"Had it done last year, thanks." Betton glanced away from Vyse's face. It was piteous how he needed the job!

"I see...Of course this is just a temporary lull in the letters. They'll begin again—as they did before. The people who read carefully read slowly—you haven't heard yet what *they* think."

Betton felt a rush of puerile joy at the suggestion. Actually, he hadn't thought of that!

"There *was* a big second crop after *Diadems and Faggots*," he mused aloud.

"Of course. Wait and see," said Vyse confidently.

The letters in fact began again—more gradually and in smaller numbers. But their quality was different, as Vyse had predicted. And in two cases Betton's correspondents, not content to compress into one rapid communication the thoughts inspired by his work, developed their views in a succession of really remarkable letters. One of the writers was a professor in a Western college; the other was a girl in Florida. In their language, their point of view, their reasons for appreciating *Abundance*, they differed almost diametrically; but this only made the unanimity of their approval the more striking. The rush of correspondence evoked by Betton's earlier novel had produced nothing so personal, so exceptional as these communications. He had gulped the praise of *Diadems and Faggots* as undiscriminatingly as it was offered; now he knew for the first time the subtler pleasures of the palate. He tried to feign indifference, even to himself; and to Vyse he made no sign. But gradually he felt a desire to know what his secretary thought of the letters, and, above all, what he was saying in reply to them. And he resented acutely the possibility of Vyse's starting one of his clandestine correspondences with the girl in Florida. Vyse's notorious lack of delicacy had never been more vividly present to Betton's imagination; and he made up his mind to answer the letters himself.

He would keep Vyse on, of course: there were other communications that the secretary could attend to. And, if necessary, Betton would invent an occupation: he cursed his stupidity in having betrayed the fact that his books were already catalogued.

Vyse showed no surprise when Betton announced his intention of dealing personally with the two correspondents who showed so flattering a reluctance to take their leave. But Betton immediately read a criticism in his lack of comment, and put forth, on a note of challenge: "After all, one must be decent!"

Vyse looked at him with an evanescent smile. "You'll have to explain that you didn't write the first answers."

Betton halted. "Well—I—I more or less dictated them, didn't I?"

"Oh, virtually, they're yours, of course."

"You think I can put it that way?"

"Why not?" The secretary absently drew an arabesque on the blotting-pad. "Of course they'll keep it up longer if you write yourself," he suggested.

Betton blushed, but faced the issue. "Hang it all, I shan't be sorry. They interest me. They're remarkable letters." And Vyse, without observation, returned to his writings.

The spring, that year, was delicious to Betton. His college professor continued to address him tersely but cogently at fixed intervals, and twice a week eight serried pages came from Florida. There were other letters, too; he had the solace of feeling that at last *Abundance* was making its way, was reaching the people who, as Vyse said, read slowly because they read intelligently. But welcome as were all these proofs of his restored authority they were but the background of his happiness. His life revolved for the moment about the personality of his two chief correspondents. The professor's letters satisfied his craving for intellectual recognition, and the satisfaction he felt in them proved how completely he had lost faith in himself. He blushed to think that his opinion of his work had been swayed by the shallow judgments of a public whose taste he despised. Was it possible that he had allowed himself to think less well of *Abundance* because it was not to the taste of the average novel-reader? Such false humility was less excusable than the crudest appetite for praise: it was ridiculous to try to do conscientious work if one's self-esteem were at the mercy of popular judgments. All this the professor's letters delicately and indirectly conveyed to Betton, with the result that the author of *Abundance* began to recognize in it the ripest flower of his genius.

But if the professor understood his book, the girl from Florida understood *him*; and Betton was fully alive to the superior qualities of discernment which this implied. For his lovely correspondent his novel was but the starting point, the pretext of her discourse: he himself was her real object, and he had the delicious sense, as their exchange of thoughts proceeded, that she was interested in

Abundance because of its author, rather than in the author because of his book. Of course she laid stress on the fact that his ideas were the object of her contemplation; but Betton's agreeable person had permitted him some insight into the incorrigible subjectiveness of female judgments, and he was pleasantly aware, from the lady's tone, that she guessed him to be neither old nor ridiculous. And suddenly he wrote to ask if he might see her...

The answer was long in coming. Betton fidgeted at the delay, watched, wondered, fumed; then he received the one word "Impossible."

He wrote back more urgently, and awaited the reply with increasing eagerness. A certain shyness had kept him from once more modifying the instructions regarding his mail, and Strett still carried the letters directly to Vyse. The hour when he knew they were passing under the latter's eyes was now becoming intolerable to Betton, and it was a relief when the secretary, suddenly advised of his father's illness, asked permission to absent himself for a fortnight.

Vyse departed just after Betton had dispatched to Florida his second missive of entreaty, and for ten days he tasted the joy of a first perusal of his letters. The answer from Florida was not among them; but Betton said to himself, "She's thinking it over," and delay, in that light, seemed favorable. So charming, in fact, was this phase of sentimental suspense that he felt a start of resentment when a telegram apprised him one morning that Vyse would return to his post that day.

Betton had slept later than usual, and, springing out of bed with the telegram in his hand, he learned from the clock that his secretary was due in half an hour. He reflected that the morning's mail must long since be in; and, too impatient to wait for its appearance with his breakfast-tray, he threw on a dressing-gown and went to the library. There lay the letters, half a dozen of them: but his eyes flew to one envelope, and as he tore it open a warm wave rocked his heart.

The letter was dated a few days after its writer must have received his own: it had all the qualities of grace and insight to which his unknown friend had accustomed him, but it contained no allusion, however indirect, to the special purport of his appeal. Even a vanity less ingenious than Betton's might have read in the lady's silence one of the most familiar motions of consent; but the smile provoked by this inference faded as he turned to his other letters. For the uppermost bore the superscription "Dead Letter Office," and the document that fell from it was his own last letter from Florida.

Betton studied the ironic "Unknown" for an appreciable space of time; then he broke into a laugh. He had suddenly recalled Vyse's similar experience with "Hester Macklin," and the light he was able to throw on that episode was searching enough to penetrate all the dark corners of his own adventure. He felt a rush of heat to the ears; catching sight of himself in the glass, he saw a ridiculous congested countenance, and dropped into a chair to hide it between his fists. He was roused by the opening of the door, and Vyse appeared.

"Oh, I beg pardon—you're ill?" said the secretary.

Betton's only answer was an inarticulate murmur of derision; then he pushed forward the letter with the imprint of the Dead Letter Office.

"Look at that," he jeered.

Vyse peered at the envelope, and turned it over slowly in his hands. Betton's eyes, fixed on him, saw his face decompose like a substance touched by some powerful acid. He clung to the envelope as if to gain time.

"It's from the young lady you've been writing to at Swazee Springs?" he asked at length.

"It's from the young lady I've been writing to at Swazee Springs."

"Well—I suppose she's gone away," continued Vyse, rebuilding his countenance rapidly.

"Yes; and in a community numbering perhaps a hundred and

fifty souls, including the dogs and chickens, the local post-office is so ignorant of her movements that my letter has to be sent to the Dead Letter Office."

Vyse meditated on this; then he laughed in turn. "After all, the same thing happened to me—with 'Hester Macklin,' I mean," he suggested sheepishly.

"Just so," said Betton, bringing down his clenched fist on the table. "*Just so,*" he repeated, in italics.

He caught his secretary's glance, and held it with his own for a moment. Then he dropped it as, in pity, one releases something scared and squirming.

"The very day my letter was returned from Swazee Springs she wrote me this from there," he said, holding up the last Florida missive.

"Ha! That's funny," said Vyse, with a damp forehead.

"Yes, it's funny," said Betton. He leaned back, his hands in his pockets, staring up at the ceiling, and noticing a crack in the cornice. Vyse, at the corner of the writing-table, waited.

"Shall I get to work?" he began, after a silence measurable by minutes. Betton's gaze descended from the cornice.

"I've got your seat, haven't I?" he said politely, rising and moving away from the table.

Vyse, with a quick gleam of relief, slipped into the vacant chair, and began to stir about among the papers.

"How's your father?" Betton asked from the hearth.

"Oh, better—better, thank you. He'll pull out of it."

"But you had a sharp scare for a day or two?"

"Yes—it was touch and go when I got there."

Another pause, while Vyse began to classify the letters.

"And I suppose," Betton continued in a steady tone, "your anxiety made you forget your usual precautions—whatever they were —about this Florida correspondence, and before you'd had time to prevent it the Swazee post-office blundered?"

Vyse lifted his head with a quick movement. "What do you mean?" he asked, pushing back his chair.

"I mean that you saw I couldn't live without flattery, and that you've been ladling it out to me to earn your keep."

Vyse sat motionless and shrunken, digging the blotting-pad with his pen. "What on earth are you driving at?" he repeated.

"Though why the deuce," Betton continued in the same steady tone, "you should need to do this kind of work when you've got such faculties at your service—those letters were wonderful, my dear fellow! Why in the world don't you write novels, instead of writing to other people about them?"

Vyse straightened himself with an effort. "What are you talking about, Betton? Why the devil do you think *I* wrote those letters?"

Betton held back his answer with a brooding face. "Because I wrote 'Hester Macklin's'—to myself!"

Vyse sat stock-still, without the least outcry of wonder. "Well—?" he finally said, in a low tone.

"And because you found me out (you see, you can't even feign surprise!)—because you saw through it at a glance, knew at once that the letters were faked. And when you'd foolishly put me on my guard by pointing out to me that they were a clumsy forgery, and had then suddenly guessed that *I* was the forger, you drew the natural inference that I had to have popular approval, or at least had to make *you* think I had it. You saw that, to me, the worst thing about the failure of the book was having *you* know it was a failure. And so you applied your superior—your immeasurably superior—abilities to carrying on the humbug, and deceiving me as I'd tried to deceive you. And you did it so successfully that I don't see why the devil you haven't made your fortune writing novels!"

Vyse remained silent, his head slightly bent under the mounting tide of Betton's denunciation.

"The way you differentiated your people—characterized them —avoided my stupid mistake of making the women's letters too short and too logical, of letting my different correspondents use the same expressions: the amount of ingenuity and art you wasted on it! I swear, Vyse, I'm sorry that damned post-office went back on you," Betton went on, piling up the waves of his irony.

But at this height they suddenly paused, drew back on themselves, and began to recede before the sight of Vyse's misery. Something warm and emotional in Betton's nature—a lurking kindliness, perhaps, for any one who tried to soothe and smooth his writhing ego—softened his eye as it rested on the figure of his secretary.

"Look here, Vyse—I'm not sorry—not altogether sorry this has happened!" He moved across the room, and laid his hand on Vyse's drooping shoulder. "In a queer illogical way it evens up things, as it were. I did you a shabby turn once, years ago—oh, out of sheer carelessness, of course—about that novel of yours I promised to give to Apthorn. If I *had* given it, it might not have made any difference—I'm not sure it wasn't too good for success —but anyhow, I dare say you thought my personal influence might have helped you, might at least have got you a quicker hearing. Perhaps you thought it was because the thing *was* so good that I kept it back, that I felt some nasty jealousy of your superiority. I swear to you it wasn't that—I clean forgot it. And one day when I came home it was gone: you'd sent and taken it away. And I've always thought since that you might have owed me a grudge —and not unjustly; so this…this business of the letters…the sympathy you've shown…for I suppose it *is* sympathy…?"

Vyse startled and checked him by a queer crackling laugh.

"It's *not* sympathy?" broke in Betton, the moisture drying out of his voice. He withdrew his hand from Vyse's shoulder. "What is it, then? The joy of uncovering my nakedness? An eye for an eye? Is it *that*?"

Vyse rose from his seat, and with a mechanical gesture swept into a heap all the letters he had sorted.

"I'm stone broke, and wanted to keep my job—that's what it is," he said wearily…

AUTRES TEMPS...

MRS. LIDCOTE, as the huge menacing mass of New York defined itself far off across the waters, shrank back into her corner of the deck and sat listening with a kind of unreasoning terror to the steady onward drive of the screws.

She had set out on the voyage quietly enough,—in what she called her "reasonable" mood,—but the week at sea had given her too much time to think of things and had left her too long alone with the past.

When she was alone, it was always the past that occupied her. She couldn't get away from it, and she didn't any longer care to. During her long years of exile she had made her terms with it, had learned to accept the fact that it would always be there, huge, obstructing, encumbering, bigger and more dominant than anything the future could ever conjure up. And, at any rate, she was sure of it, she understood it, knew how to reckon with it; she had learned to screen and manage and protect it as one does an afflicted member of one's family.

There had never been any danger of her being allowed to forget the past. It looked out at her from the face of every acquaintance, it appeared suddenly in the eyes of strangers when a word enlightened them: "Yes, *the* Mrs. Lidcote, don't you know?" It had sprung at her the first day out, when, across the dining-room, from the captain's table, she had seen Mrs. Lorin Boulger's revolving eyeglass pause and the eye behind it grow as blank as a dropped blind. The next day, of course, the captain had asked: "You know your ambassadress, Mrs. Boulger?" and she had replied that, No, she seldom left Florence, and hadn't been to Rome for more than a day since the Boulgers had been sent to Italy. She was so used to these phrases that it cost her no effort to repeat them. And the captain had promptly changed the subject.

No, she didn't, as a rule, mind the past, because she was used to it and understood it. It was a great concrete fact in her path that she had to walk around every time she moved in any direction. But now, in the light of the unhappy event that had summoned her from Italy,—the sudden unanticipated news of her daughter's divorce from Horace Pursh and remarriage with Wilbour Barkley —the past, her own poor miserable past, started up at her with eyes of accusation, became, to her disordered fancy, like the afflicted relative suddenly breaking away from nurses and keepers and publicly parading the horror and misery she had, all the long years, so patiently screened and secluded.

Yes, there it had stood before her through the agitated weeks since the news had come—during her interminable journey from India, where Leila's letter had overtaken her, and the feverish halt in her apartment in Florence, where she had had to stop and gather up her possessions for a fresh start—there it had stood grinning at her with a new balefulness which seemed to say: "Oh, but you've got to look at me *now*, because I'm not only your own past but Leila's present."

Certainly it was a master-stroke of those arch-ironists of the shears and spindle to duplicate her own story in her daughter's. Mrs. Lidcote had always somewhat grimly fancied that, having so signally failed to be of use to Leila in other ways, she would at least serve her as a warning. She had even abstained from defending herself, from making the best of her case, had stoically refused to plead extenuating circumstances, lest Leila's impulsive sympathy should lead to deductions that might react disastrously on her own life. And now that very thing had happened, and Mrs. Lidcote could hear the whole of New York saying with one voice: "Yes, Leila's done just what her mother did. With such an example what could you expect?"

Yet if she had been an example, poor woman, she had been an awful one; she had been, she would have supposed, of more use as a deterrent than a hundred blameless mothers as incentives. For how could any one who had seen anything of her life in the last eighteen years have had the courage to repeat so disastrous an experiment?

Well, logic in such cases didn't count, example didn't count, nothing probably counted but having the same impulses in the blood; and that was the dark inheritance she had bestowed upon her daughter. Leila hadn't consciously copied her; she had simply "taken after" her, had been a projection of her own long-past rebellion.

Mrs. Lidcote had deplored, when she started, that the *Utopia* was a slow steamer, and would take eight full days to bring her to her unhappy daughter; but now, as the moment of reunion approached, she would willingly have turned the boat about and fled back to the high seas. It was not only because she felt still so unprepared to face what New York had in store for her, but because she needed more time to dispose of what the *Utopia* had already given her. The past was bad enough, but the present and future were worse, because they were less comprehensible, and because, as she grew older, surprises and inconsequences troubled her more than the worst certainties.

There was Mrs. Boulger, for instance. In the light, or rather the darkness, of new developments, it might really be that Mrs. Boulger had not meant to cut her, but had simply failed to recognize her. Mrs. Lidcote had arrived at this hypothesis simply by listening to the conversation of the persons sitting next to her on deck—two lively young women with the latest Paris hats on their heads and the latest New York ideas in them. These ladies, as to whom it would have been impossible for a person with Mrs. Lidcote's old-fashioned categories to determine whether they were married or unmarried, "nice" or "horrid," or any one or other of the definite things which young women, in her youth and her society, were conveniently assumed to be, had revealed a familiarity with the world of New York that, again according to Mrs. Lidcote's traditions, should have implied a recognized place in it. But in the present fluid state of manners what did anything imply except what their hats implied—that no one could tell what was coming next?

They seemed, at any rate, to frequent a group of idle and opulent people who executed the same gestures and revolved on the same pivots as Mrs. Lidcote's daughter and her friends: their Coras, Matties and Mabels seemed at any moment likely to reveal familiar patronymics, and once one of the speakers, summing up a discussion of which Mrs. Lidcote had missed the beginning, had affirmed with headlong confidence: "Leila? Oh, *Leila's* all right."

Could it be *her* Leila, the mother had wondered, with a sharp thrill of apprehension? If only they would mention surnames! But their talk leaped elliptically from allusion to allusion, their unfinished sentences dangled over bottomless pits of conjecture, and they gave their bewildered hearer the impression not so much of talking only of their intimates, as of being intimate with every one alive.

Her old friend Franklin Ide could have told her, perhaps; but here was the last day of the voyage, and she hadn't yet found courage to ask him. Great as had been the joy of discovering his name on the passenger-list and seeing his friendly bearded face in the throng against the taffrail at Cherbourg, she had as yet said nothing to him except, when they had met: "Of course I'm going out to Leila."

She had said nothing to Franklin Ide because she had always instinctively shrunk from taking him into her confidence. She was sure he felt sorry for her, sorrier perhaps than any one had ever felt; but he had always paid her the supreme tribute of not showing it. His attitude allowed her to imagine that compassion was not the basis of his feeling for her, and it was part of her joy in his friendship that it was the one relation seemingly unconditioned by her state, the only one in which she could think and feel and behave like any other woman.

Now, however, as the problem of New York loomed nearer, she began to regret that she had not spoken, had not at least questioned him about the hints she had gathered on the way. He did not know the two ladies next to her, he did not even, as it chanced, know Mrs. Lorin Boulger; but he knew New York, and New York was the sphinx whose riddle she must read or perish.

Almost as the thought passed through her mind his stooping shoulders and grizzled head detached themselves against the blaze of light in the west, and he sauntered down the empty deck and dropped into the chair at her side.

"You're expecting the Barkleys to meet you, I suppose?" he asked.

It was the first time she had heard any one pronounce her daughter's new name, and it occurred to her that her friend, who was shy and inarticulate, had been trying to say it all the way over and had at last shot it out at her only because he felt it must be now or never.

"I don't know. I cabled, of course. But I believe she's at—they're at—*his* place somewhere."

"Oh, Barkley's; yes, near Lenox, isn't it? But she's sure to come to town to meet you."

He said it so easily and naturally that her own constraint was relieved, and suddenly, before she knew what she meant to do, she had burst out: "She may dislike the idea of seeing people."

Ide, whose absent short-sighted gaze had been fixed on the slowly gliding water, turned in his seat to stare at his companion.

"Who? Leila?" he said with an incredulous laugh.

Mrs. Lidcote flushed to her faded hair and grew pale again. "It took *me* a long time—to get used to it," she said.

His look grew gently commiserating. "I think you'll find—" he paused for a word—"that things are different now—altogether easier."

"That's what I've been wondering—ever since we started." She was determined now to speak. She moved nearer, so that their arms touched, and she could drop her voice to a murmur. "You see, it all came on me in a flash. My going off to India and Siam on that long trip kept me away from letters for weeks at a time; and she didn't want to tell me beforehand—oh, I understand *that*, poor child! You know how good she's always been to me; how she's tried to spare me. And she knew, of course, what a state of horror I'd be in. She knew I'd rush off to her at once and try to stop it. So she never gave me a hint of anything, and she even managed to muzzle Susy Suffern—you know Susy is the one of the family who keeps me informed about things at home. I don't yet see how she prevented Susy's telling me; but she did. And her first letter, the one I got up at Bangkok, simply said the thing was over—the divorce, I mean—and that the very next day she'd—well, I suppose there was no use waiting; and *he* seems to have behaved as well as possible, to have wanted to marry her as much as—"

"Who? Barkley?" he helped her out. "I should say so! Why what do you suppose—" He interrupted himself. "He'll be devoted to her, I assure you."

"Oh, of course; I'm sure he will. He's written me—really beautifully. But it's a terrible strain on a man's devotion. I'm not sure that Leila realizes—"

Ide sounded again his little reassuring laugh. "I'm not sure that you realize. *They're* all right."

It was the very phrase that the young lady in the next seat had applied to the unknown "Leila," and its recurrence on Ide's lips flushed Mrs. Lidcote with fresh courage.

"I wish I knew just what you mean. The two young women next to me—the ones with the wonderful hats—have been talking in the same way."

"What? About Leila?"

"About *a* Leila; I fancied it might be mine. And about society in general. All their friends seem to be divorced; some of them seem to announce their engagements before they get their decree. One of them—*her* name was Mabel—as far as I could make out, her husband found out that she meant to divorce him by noticing that she wore a new engagement-ring."

"Well, you see Leila did everything 'regularly,' as the French say," Ide rejoined.

"Yes; but are these people in society? The people my neighbors talk about?"

He shrugged his shoulders. "It would take an arbitration commission a good many sittings to define the boundaries of society nowadays. But at any rate they're in New York; and I assure you you're *not*; you're farther and farther from it."

"But I've been back there several times to see Leila." She hesitated and looked away from him. Then she brought out slowly: "And I've never noticed—the least change—in—in my own case—"

"Oh," he sounded deprecatingly, and she trembled with the fear of having gone too far. But the hour was past when such scruples could restrain her. She must know where she was and where Leila was. "Mrs. Boulger still cuts me," she brought out with an embarrassed laugh.

"Are you sure? You've probably cut *her*; if not now, at least in the past. And in a cut if you're not first you're nowhere. That's what keeps up so many quarrels."

The word roused Mrs. Lidcote to a renewed sense of realities. "But the Purshes," she said—"the Purshes are so strong! There are so many of them, and they all back each other up, just as my husband's family did. I know what it means to have a clan against one. They're stronger than any number of separate friends. The Purshes will *never* forgive Leila for leaving Horace. Why, his mother opposed his marrying her because of—of me. She tried to get Leila to promise that she wouldn't see me when they went to Europe on their honeymoon. And now she'll say it was my example."

Her companion, vaguely stroking his beard, mused a moment upon this; then he asked, with seeming irrelevance, "What did Leila say when you wrote that you were coming?"

"She said it wasn't the least necessary, but that I'd better come, because it was the only way to convince me that it wasn't."

"Well, then, that proves she's not afraid of the Purshes."

She breathed a long sigh of remembrance. "Oh, just at first, you know—one never is."

He laid his hand on hers with a gesture of intelligence and pity. "You'll see, you'll see," he said.

A shadow lengthened down the deck before them, and a steward stood there, proffering a Marconigram.

"Oh, now I shall know!" she exclaimed.

She tore the message open, and then let it fall on her knees, dropping her hands on it in silence.

Ide's inquiry roused her: "It's all right?"

"Oh, quite right. Perfectly. She can't come; but she's sending Susy Suffern. She says Susy will explain." After another silence she added, with a sudden gush of bitterness: "As if I needed any explanation!"

She felt Ide's hesitating glance upon her. "She's in the country?"

"Yes. 'Prevented last moment. Longing for you, expecting you. Love from both.' Don't you *see*, the poor darling, that she couldn't face it?"

"No, I don't." He waited. "Do you mean to go to her immediately?"

"It will be too late to catch a train this evening; but I shall take the first to-morrow morning." She considered a moment. "Perhaps it's better. I need a talk with Susy first. She's to meet me at the dock, and I'll take her straight back to the hotel with me."

As she developed this plan, she had the sense that Ide was still thoughtfully, even gravely, considering her. When she ceased, he remained silent a moment; then he said almost ceremoniously: "If your talk with Miss Suffern doesn't last too late, may I come and see you when it's over? I shall be dining at my club, and I'll call you up at about ten, if I may. I'm off to Chicago on business to-morrow morning, and it would be a satisfaction to know, before I start, that your cousin's been able to reassure you, as I know she will."

He spoke with a shy deliberateness that, even to Mrs. Lidcote's troubled perceptions, sounded a long-silenced note of feeling. Perhaps the breaking down of the barrier of reticence between them had released unsuspected emotions in both. The tone of his appeal moved her curiously and loosened the tight strain of her fears.

"Oh, yes, come—do come," she said, rising. The huge threat of New York was imminent now, dwarfing, under long reaches of embattled masonry, the great deck she stood on and all the little specks of life it carried. One of them, drifting nearer, took the shape of her maid, followed by luggage-laden stewards, and signing to her that it was time to go below. As they descended to the main deck, the throng swept her against Mrs. Lorin Boulger's shoulder, and she heard the ambassadress call out to some one, over the vexed sea of hats: "So sorry! I should have been delighted, but I've promised to spend Sunday with some friends at Lenox."

II

Susy Suffern's explanation did not end till after ten o'clock, and she had just gone when Franklin Ide, who, complying with an old New York tradition, had caused himself to be preceded by a long white box of roses, was shown into Mrs. Lidcote's sitting-room.

He came forward with his shy half-humorous smile and, taking her hand, looked at her for a moment without speaking.

"It's all right," he then pronounced.

Mrs. Lidcote returned his smile. "It's extraordinary. Everything's changed. Even Susy has changed; and you know the extent to which Susy used to represent the old New York. There's no old New York left, it seems. She talked in the most amazing way. She snaps her fingers at the Purshes. She told me—*me*, that every woman had a right to happiness and that self-expression was the highest duty. She accused me of misunderstanding Leila; she said my point of view was conventional! She was bursting with pride at having been in the secret, and wearing a brooch that Wilbour Barkley'd given her!"

Franklin Ide had seated himself in the armchair she had pushed forward for him under the electric chandelier. He threw back his head and laughed. "What did I tell you?"

"Yes; but I can't believe that Susy's not mistaken. Poor dear, she has the habit of lost causes; and she may feel that, having stuck to me, she can do no less than stick to Leila."

"But she didn't—did she?—openly defy the world for you? She didn't snap her fingers at the Lidcotes?"

Mrs. Lidcote shook her head, still smiling. "No. It was enough to defy *my* family. It was doubtful at one time if they would tolerate her seeing me, and she almost had to disinfect herself after each visit. I believe that at first my sister-in-law wouldn't let the girls come down when Susy dined with her."

"Well, isn't your cousin's present attitude the best possible proof that times have changed?"

"Yes, yes; I know." She leaned forward from her sofa-corner, fixing her eyes on his thin kindly face, which gleamed on her indistinctly through her tears. "If it's true, it's—it's dazzling. She says Leila's perfectly happy. It's as if an angel had gone about lifting gravestones, and the buried people walked again, and the living didn't shrink from them."

"That's about it," he assented.

She drew a deep breath, and sat looking away from him down the long perspective of lamp-fringed streets over which her windows hung.

"I can understand how happy you must be," he began at length.

She turned to him impetuously. "Yes, yes; I'm happy. But I'm lonely, too—lonelier than ever. I didn't take up much room in the world before; but now—where is there a corner for me? Oh, since I've begun to confess myself, why shouldn't I go on? Telling you this lifts a gravestone from *me*! You see, before this, Leila needed me. She was unhappy, and I knew it, and though we hardly ever talked of it I felt that, in a way, the thought that I'd been through the same thing, and down to the dregs of it, helped her. And her needing me helped *me*. And when the news of her marriage came my first thought was that now she'd need me more than ever, that she'd have no one but me to turn to. Yes, under all my distress there was a fierce joy in that. It was so new and wonderful to feel again that there was one person who wouldn't be able to get on without me! And now what you and Susy tell me seems to have taken my child from me; and just at first that's all I can feel."

"Of course it's all you feel." He looked at her musingly. "Why didn't Leila come to meet you?"

"That was really my fault. You see, I'd cabled that I was not sure of being able to get off on the *Utopia*, and apparently my second cable was delayed, and when she received it she'd already asked some people over Sunday—one or two of her old friends, Susy says. I'm so glad they should have wanted to go to her at once; but naturally I'd rather have been alone with her."

"You still mean to go, then?"

"Oh, I must. Susy wanted to drag me off to Ridgefield with her over Sunday, and Leila sent me word that of course I might go if I wanted to, and that I was not to think of her; but I know how disappointed she would be. Susy said she was afraid I might be upset at her having people to stay, and that, if I minded, she wouldn't urge me to come. But if *they* don't mind, why should I? And of course, if they're willing to go to Leila it must mean—"

"Of course. I'm glad you recognize that," Franklin Ide exclaimed abruptly. He stood up and went over to her, taking her hand with one of his quick gestures. "There's something I want to say to you," he began—

The next morning, in the train, through all the other contending thoughts in Mrs. Lidcote's mind there ran the warm undercurrent of what Franklin Ide had wanted to say to her.

He had wanted, she knew, to say it once before, when, nearly eight years earlier, the hazard of meeting at the end of a rainy autumn in a deserted Swiss hotel had thrown them for a fortnight into unwonted propinquity. They had walked and talked together, borrowed each other's books and newspapers, spent the long chill evenings over the fire in the dim lamplight of her little pitch-pine sitting-room; and she had been wonderfully comforted by his presence, and hard frozen places in her had melted, and she had known that she would be desperately sorry when he went. And then, just at the end, in his odd indirect way, he had let her see that it rested with her to have him stay. She could still relive the sleepless night she had given to that discovery. It was preposterous, of course, to think of repaying his devotion by accepting such a sacrifice; but how find reasons to convince him? She could not bear to let him think her less touched, less inclined to him than she was: the generosity of his love deserved that she should repay it with the truth. Yet how let him see what she felt, and yet refuse what he offered? How confess to him what had been on her lips when he made the offer: "I've seen what it did to one man; and there must never, never be another"? The tacit ignoring of her past had been the element in which their friendship lived, and she could not suddenly, to him of all men, begin to talk of herself like a guilty woman in a play. Somehow, in the end, she had managed it, had averted a direct explanation, had made him understand that her life was over, that she existed only for her daughter, and that a more definite word from him would have been almost a breach of delicacy. She was so used to behaving as if her life were over! And, at any rate, he had taken her hint, and she had been able to spare her sensitiveness and his. The next year, when he came to Florence to see her, they met again in the old friendly way; and that till now had continued to be the tenor of their intimacy.

And now, suddenly and unexpectedly, he had brought up the question again, directly this time, and in such a form that she could not evade it: putting the renewal of his plea, after so long an interval, on the ground that, on her own showing, her chief argument against it no longer existed.

"You tell me Leila's happy. If she's happy, she doesn't need you—need you, that is, in the same way as before. You wanted, I know, to be always in reach, always free and available if she should suddenly call you to her or take refuge with you. I understood that—I respected it. I didn't urge my case because I saw it was useless. You couldn't, I understood well enough, have felt free to take such happiness as life with me might give you while she was un-happy, and, as you imagined, with no hope of release. Even then I didn't feel as you did about it; I understood better the trend of things here. But ten years ago the change hadn't really come; and I had no way of convincing you that it was coming. Still, I always fancied that Leila might not think her case was closed, and so I chose to think that ours wasn't either. Let me go on thinking so, at any rate, till you've seen her, and confirmed with your own eyes what Susy Suffern tells you."

III

All through what Susy Suffern told and retold her during their four-hours' flight to the hills this plea of Ide's kept coming back to Mrs. Lidcote. She did not yet know what she felt as to its bearing on her own fate, but it was something on which her confused thoughts could stay themselves amid the welter of new impres-sions, and she was inexpressibly glad that he had said what he had, and said it at that particular moment. It helped her to hold fast to her identity in the rush of strange names and new categories that her cousin's talk poured out on her.

With the progress of the journey Miss Suffern's communica-tions grew more and more amazing. She was like a cicerone preparing the mind of an inexperienced traveler for the marvels about to burst on it.

"You won't know Leila. She's had her pearls reset. Sargent's to paint her. Oh, and I was to tell you that she hopes you won't mind being the least bit squeezed over Sunday. The house was built by Wilbour's father, you know, and it's rather old-fashioned—only ten spare bedrooms. Of course that's small for what they mean to do, and she'll show you the new plans they've had made. Their idea is to keep the present house as a wing. She told me to explain —she's so dreadfully sorry not to be able to give you a sitting-room just at first. They're thinking of Egypt for next winter, un-less, of course, Wilbour gets his appointment. Oh, didn't she write

you about that? Why, he wants Rome, you know—the second secretaryship. Or, rather, he wanted England; but Leila insisted that
if they went abroad she must be near you. And of course what she
says is law. Oh, they quite hope they'll get it. You see Horace's uncle is in the Cabinet,—one of the assistant secretaries,—and I believe he has a good deal of pull—"

"Horace's uncle? You mean Wilbour's, I suppose," Mrs. Lidcote
interjected, with a gasp of which a fraction was given to Miss
Suffern's flippant use of the language.

"Wilbour's? No, I don't. I mean Horace's. There's no bad feeling between them, I assure you. Since Horace's engagement was
announced—you didn't know Horace was engaged? Why, he's
marrying one of Bishop Thorbury's girls: the red-haired one who
wrote the novel that every one's talking about, *This Flesh of Mine.*
They're to be married in the cathedral. Of course Horace *can*, because it was Leila who—but, as I say, there's not the *least* feeling,
and Horace wrote himself to his uncle about Wilbour."

Mrs. Lidcote's thoughts fled back to what she had said to Ide
the day before on the deck of the *Utopia.* "I didn't take up much
room before, but now where is there a corner for me?" Where indeed in this crowded, topsy-turvy world, with its headlong
changes and helter-skelter readjustments, its new tolerances and
indifferences and accommodations, was there room for a character
fashioned by slower sterner processes and a life broken under their
inexorable pressure? And then, in a flash, she viewed the chaos
from a new angle, and order seemed to move upon the void. If the
old processes were changed, her case was changed with them; she,
too, was a part of the general readjustment, a tiny fragment of the
new pattern worked out in bolder freer harmonies. Since her
daughter had no penalty to pay, was not she herself released by the
same stroke? The rich arrears of youth and joy were gone; but was
there not time enough left to accumulate new stores of happiness?
That, of course, was what Franklin Ide had felt and had meant her
to feel. He had seen at once what the change in her daughter's
situation would make in her view of her own. It was almost—

wondrously enough!—as if Leila's folly had been the means of vindicating hers.

Everything else for the moment faded for Mrs. Lidcote in the glow of her daughter's embrace. It was unnatural, it was almost terrifying, to find herself standing on a strange threshold, under an unknown roof, in a big hall full of pictures, flowers, firelight, and hurrying servants, and in this spacious unfamiliar confusion to discover Leila, bareheaded, laughing, authoritative, with a strange young man jovially echoing her welcome and transmitting her orders; but once Mrs. Lidcote had her child on her breast, and her child's "It's all right, you old darling!" in her ears, every other feeling was lost in the deep sense of well-being that only Leila's hug could give.

The sense was still with her, warming her veins and pleasantly fluttering her heart, as she went up to her room after luncheon. A little constrained by the presence of visitors, and not altogether sorry to defer for a few hours the "long talk" with her daughter for which she somehow felt herself tremulously unready, she had withdrawn, on the plea of fatigue, to the bright luxurious bedroom into which Leila had again and again apologized for having been obliged to squeeze her. The room was bigger and finer than any in her small apartment in Florence; but it was not the standard of affluence implied in her daughter's tone about it that chiefly struck her, nor yet the finish and complexity of its appointments. It was the look it shared with the rest of the house, and with the perspective of the gardens beneath its windows, of being part of an "establishment"—of something solid, avowed, founded on sacraments and precedents and principles. There was nothing about the place, or about Leila and Wilbour, that suggested either passion or peril: their relation seemed as comfortable as their furniture and as respectable as their balance at the bank.

This was, in the whole confusing experience, the thing that confused Mrs. Lidcote most, that gave her at once the deepest feeling of security for Leila and the strongest sense of apprehension for herself. Yes, there was something oppressive in the completeness and compactness of Leila's well-being. Ide had been right: her daughter did not need her. Leila, with her first embrace, had unconsciously attested the fact in the same phrase as Ide himself and as the two young women with the hats. "It's all right, you old darling!" she had said; and her mother sat alone, trying to fit herself into the new scheme of things which such a certainty betokened.

Her first distinct feeling was one of irrational resentment. If such a change was to come, why had it not come sooner? Here was she, a woman not yet old, who had paid with the best years of her life for the theft of the happiness that her daughter's contemporaries were taking as their due. There was no sense, no sequence, in it. She had had what she wanted, but she had had to pay too much for it. She had had to pay the last bitterest price of learning that love has a price: that it is worth so much and no more. She had known the anguish of watching the man she loved discover this first, and of reading the discovery in his eyes. It was a part of her history that she had not trusted herself to think of for a long time past: she always took a big turn about that haunted corner. But now, at the sight of the young man down stairs, so openly and jovially Leila's, she was overwhelmed at the senseless waste of her own adventure, and wrung with the irony of perceiving that the success or failure of the deepest human experiences may hang on a matter of chronology.

Then gradually the thought of Ide returned to her. "I chose to think that our case wasn't closed," he had said. She had been deeply touched by that. To every one else her case had been closed so long! *Finis* was scrawled all over her. But here was one man who had believed and waited, and what if what he believed in and waited for were coming true? If Leila's "all right" should really foreshadow hers?

As yet, of course, it was impossible to tell. She had fancied, indeed, when she entered the drawing-room before luncheon, that a too-sudden hush had fallen on the assembled group of Leila's friends, on the slender vociferous young women and the lounging golf-stockinged young men. They had all received her politely, with the kind of petrified politeness that may be either a tribute to age or a protest at laxity; but to them, of course, she must be an old woman because she was Leila's mother, and in a society so dominated by youth the mere presence of maturity was a constraint.

One of the young girls, however, had presently emerged from the group, and, attaching herself to Mrs. Lidcote, had listened to her with a blue gaze of admiration which gave the older woman a sudden happy consciousness of her long-for-gotten social graces. It was agreeable to find herself attracting this young Charlotte Wynn, whose mother had been among her closest friends, and in whom something of the soberness and softness of the earlier manners had survived. But the little colloquy, broken up by the announcement of luncheon, could of course result in nothing more definite than this reminiscent emotion.

No, she could not yet tell how her own case was to be fitted into the new order of things; but there were more people—"older people" Leila had put it—arriving by the afternoon train, and that evening at dinner she would doubtless be able to judge. She began to wonder nervously who the new-comers might be. Probably she would be spared the embarrassment of finding old acquaintances among them; but it was odd that her daughter had mentioned no names.

Leila had proposed that, later in the afternoon, Wilbour should take her mother for a drive: she said she wanted them to have a "nice, quiet talk." But Mrs. Lidcote wished her talk with Leila to come first, and had, moreover, at luncheon, caught stray allusions to an impending tennis-match in which her son-in-law was engaged. Her fatigue had been a sufficient pretext for declining the drive, and she had begged Leila to think of her as peacefully resting in her room till such time as they could snatch their quiet moment.

"Before tea, then, you duck!" Leila with a last kiss had decided; and presently Mrs. Lidcote, through her open window, had heard the fresh loud voices of her daughter's visitors chiming across the gardens from the tennis-court.

IV

Leila had come and gone, and they had had their talk. It had not lasted as long as Mrs. Lidcote wished, for in the middle of it Leila had been summoned to the telephone to receive an important message from town, and had sent word to her mother that she couldn't come back just then, as one of the young ladies had been called away unexpectedly and arrangements had to be made for her departure. But the mother and daughter had had almost an hour together, and Mrs. Lidcote was happy. She had never seen Leila so tender, so solicitous. The only thing that troubled her was the very excess of this solicitude, the exaggerated expression of her daughter's annoyance that their first moments together should have been marred by the presence of strangers.

"Not strangers to me, darling, since they're friends of yours," her mother had assured her.

"Yes; but I know your feeling, you queer wild mother. I know how you've always hated people." (*Hated people!* Had Leila forgotten why?) "And that's why I told Susy that if you preferred to go with her to Ridgefield on Sunday I should perfectly understand, and patiently wait for our good hug. But you didn't really mind them at luncheon, did you, dearest?"

Mrs. Lidcote, at that, had suddenly thrown a startled look at her daughter. "I don't mind things of that kind any longer," she had simply answered.

"But that doesn't console me for having exposed you to the bother of it, for having let you come here when I ought to have *ordered* you off to Ridgefield with Susy. If Susy hadn't been stupid she'd have made you go there with her. I hate to think of you up here all alone."

Again Mrs. Lidcote tried to read something more than a rather obtuse devotion in her daughter's radiant gaze. "I'm glad to have had a rest this afternoon, dear; and later—"

"Oh, yes, later, when all this fuss is over, we'll more than make up for it, sha'n't we, you precious darling?" And at this point Leila had been summoned to the telephone, leaving Mrs. Lidcote to her conjectures.

These were still floating before her in cloudy uncertainty when Miss Suffern tapped at the door.

"You've come to take me down to tea? I'd forgotten how late it was," Mrs. Lidcote exclaimed.

Miss Suffern, a plump peering little woman, with prim hair and a conciliatory smile, nervously adjusted the pendent bugles of her elaborate black dress. Miss Suffern was always in mourning, and always commemorating the demise of distant relatives by wearing the discarded wardrobe of their next of kin. "It isn't *exactly* mourning," she would say; "but it's the only stitch of black poor Julia had—and of course George was only my mother's step-cousin."

As she came forward Mrs. Lidcote found herself humorously wondering whether she were mourning Horace Pursh's divorce in one of his mother's old black satins.

"Oh, *did* you mean to go down for tea?" Susy Suffern peered at her, a little fluttered. "Leila sent me up to keep you company. She thought it would be cozier for you to stay here. She was afraid you were feeling rather tired."

"I was; but I've had the whole afternoon to rest in. And this wonderful sofa to help me."

"Leila told me to tell you that she'd rush up for a minute before dinner, after everybody had arrived; but the train is always dreadfully late. She's in despair at not giving you a sitting-room; she wanted to know if I thought you really minded."

"Of course I don't mind. It's not like Leila to think I should." Mrs. Lidcote drew aside to make way for the house-maid, who appeared in the doorway bearing a table spread with a bewildering variety of tea-cakes.

"Leila saw to it herself," Miss Suffern murmured as the door closed. "Her one idea is that you should feel happy here."

It struck Mrs. Lidcote as one more mark of the subverted state of things that her daughter's solicitude should find expression in the multiplicity of sandwiches and the piping-hotness of muffins; but then everything that had happened since her arrival seemed to increase her confusion.

The note of a motor-horn down the drive gave another turn to her thoughts. "Are those the new arrivals already?" she asked.

"Oh, dear, no; they won't be here till after seven." Miss Suffern craned her head from the window to catch a glimpse of the motor. "It must be Charlotte leaving."

"Was it the little Wynn girl who was called away in a hurry? I hope it's not on account of illness."

"Oh, no; I believe there was some mistake about dates. Her mother telephoned her that she was expected at the Stepleys, at Fishkill, and she had to be rushed over to Albany to catch a train."

Mrs. Lidcote meditated. "I'm sorry. She's a charming young thing. I hoped I should have another talk with her this evening after dinner."

"Yes; it's too bad." Miss Suffern's gaze grew vague. "You *do* look tired, you know," she continued, seating herself at the tea-table and preparing to dispense its delicacies. "You must go straight back to your sofa and let me wait on you. The excitement has told on you more than you think, and you mustn't fight against it any longer. Just stay quietly up here and let yourself go. You'll have Leila to yourself on Monday."

Mrs. Lidcote received the tea-cup which her cousin proffered, but showed no other disposition to obey her injunctions. For a moment she stirred her tea in silence; then she asked: "Is it your idea that I should stay quietly up here till Monday?"

Miss Suffern set down her cup with a gesture so sudden that it endangered an adjacent plate of scones. When she had assured herself of the safety of the scones she looked up with a fluttered laugh. "Perhaps, dear, by to-morrow you'll be feeling differently. The air here, you know—"

"Yes, I know." Mrs. Lidcote bent forward to help herself to a scone. "Who's arriving this evening?" she asked.

Miss Suffern frowned and peered. "You know my wretched head for names. Leila told me—but there are so many—"

"So many? She didn't tell me she expected a big party."

"Oh, not big: but rather outside of her little group. And of course, as it's the first time, she's a little excited at having the older set."

"The older set? Our contemporaries, you mean?"

"Why—yes." Miss Suffern paused as if to gather herself up for a leap. "The Ashton Gileses," she brought out.

"The Ashton Gileses? Really? I shall be glad to see Mary Giles again. It must be eighteen years," said Mrs. Lidcote steadily.

"Yes," Miss Suffern gasped, precipitately refilling her cup.

"The Ashton Gileses; and who else?"

"Well, the Sam Fresbies. But the most important person, of course, is Mrs. Lorin Boulger."

"Mrs. Boulger? Leila didn't tell me she was coming."

"Didn't she? I suppose she forgot everything when she saw you. But the party was got up for Mrs. Boulger. You see, it's very important that she should—well, take a fancy to Leila and Wilbour; his being appointed to Rome virtually depends on it. And you know Leila insists on Rome in order to be near you. So she asked Mary Giles, who's intimate with the Boulgers, if the visit couldn't possibly be arranged; and Mary's cable caught Mrs. Boulger at Cherbourg. She's to be only a fortnight in America; and getting her to come directly here was rather a triumph."

"Yes; I see it was," said Mrs. Lidcote.

"You know, she's rather—rather fussy; and Mary was a little doubtful if—"

"If she would, on account of Leila?" Mrs. Lidcote murmured.

"Well, yes. In her official position. But luckily she's a friend of the Barkleys. And finding the Gileses and Fresbies here will make it all right. The times have changed!" Susy Suffern indulgently summed up.

Mrs. Lidcote smiled. "Yes; a few years ago it would have

seemed improbable that I should ever again be dining with Mary Giles and Harriet Fresbie and Mrs. Lorin Boulger."

Miss Suffern did not at the moment seem disposed to enlarge upon this theme; and after an interval of silence Mrs. Lidcote suddenly resumed: "Do they know I'm here, by the way?"

The effect of her question was to produce in Miss Suffern an exaggerated access of peering and frowning. She twitched the tea-things about, fingered her bugles, and, looking at the clock, exclaimed amazedly: "Mercy! Is it seven already?"

"Not that it can make any difference, I suppose," Mrs. Lidcote continued. "But did Leila tell them I was coming?"

Miss Suffern looked at her with pain. "Why, you don't suppose, dearest, that Leila would do anything—"

Mrs. Lidcote went on: "For, of course, it's of the first importance, as you say, that Mrs. Lorin Boulger should be favorably impressed, in order that Wilbour may have the best possible chance of getting Rome."

"I *told* Leila you'd feel that, dear. You see, it's actually on *your* account—so that they may get a post near you—that Leila invited Mrs. Boulger."

"Yes, I see that." Mrs. Lidcote, abruptly rising from her seat, turned her eyes to the clock. "But, as you say, it's getting late. Oughtn't we to dress for dinner?"

Miss Suffern, at the suggestion, stood up also, an agitated hand among her bugles. "I do wish I could persuade you to stay up here this evening. I'm sure Leila'd be happier if you would. Really, you're much too tired to come down."

"What nonsense, Susy!" Mrs. Lidcote spoke with a sudden sharpness, her hand stretched to the bell. "When do we dine? At half-past eight? Then I must really send you packing. At my age it takes time to dress."

Miss Suffern, thus projected toward the threshold, lingered there to repeat: "Leila'll never forgive herself if you make an effort you're not up to." But Mrs. Lidcote smiled on her without answering, and the icy light-wave propelled her through the door.

V

Mrs. Lidcote, though she had made the gesture of ringing for her maid, had not done so.

When the door closed, she continued to stand motionless in the middle of her soft spacious room. The fire which had been kindled at twilight danced on the brightness of silver and mirrors and sober gilding; and the sofa toward which she had been urged by Miss Suffern heaped up its cushions in inviting proximity to a table laden with new books and papers. She could not recall having ever been more luxuriously housed, or having ever had so strange a sense of being out alone, under the night, in a wind-beaten plain. She sat down by the fire and thought.

A knock on the door made her lift her head, and she saw her daughter on the threshold. The intricate ordering of Leila's fair hair and the flying folds of her dressing-gown showed that she had interrupted her dressing to hasten to her mother; but once in the room she paused a moment, smiling uncertainly, as though she had forgotten the object of her haste.

Mrs. Lidcote rose to her feet. "Time to dress, dearest? Don't scold! I sha'n't be late."

"To dress?" Leila stood before her with a puzzled look. "Why, I thought, dear—I mean, I hoped you'd decided just to stay here quietly and rest."

Her mother smiled. "But I've been resting all the afternoon!"

"Yes, but—you know you *do* look tired. And when Susy told me just now that you meant to make the effort—"

"You came to stop me?"

"I came to tell you that you needn't feel in the least obliged—"

"Of course. I understand that."

There was a pause during which Leila, vaguely averting herself from her mother's scrutiny, drifted toward the dressing-table and began to disturb the symmetry of the brushes and bottles laid out on it.

"Do your visitors know that I'm here?" Mrs. Lidcote suddenly went on.

"Do they— Of course—why, naturally," Leila rejoined, absorbed in trying to turn the stopper of a salts-bottle.

"Then won't they think it odd if I don't appear?"

"Oh, not in the least, dearest. I assure you they'll *all* understand." Leila laid down the bottle and turned back to her mother, her face alight with reassurance.

Mrs. Lidcote stood motionless, her head erect, her smiling eyes on her daughter's. "Will they think it odd if I *do*?"

Leila stopped short, her lips half parted to reply. As she paused, the color stole over her bare neck, swept up to her throat, and burst into flame in her cheeks. Thence it sent its devastating crimson up to her very temples, to the lobes of her ears, to the edges of her eye-lids, beating all over her in fiery waves, as if fanned by some imperceptible wind.

Mrs. Lidcote silently watched the conflagration; then she turned away her eyes with a slight laugh. "I only meant that I was afraid it might upset the arrangement of your dinner-table if I didn't come down. If you can assure me that it won't, I believe I'll take you at your word and go back to this irresistible sofa." She paused, as if waiting for her daughter to speak; then she held out her arms. "Run off and dress, dearest; and don't have me on your mind." She clasped Leila close, pressing a long kiss on the last afterglow of her subsiding blush. "I do feel the least bit overdone, and if it won't inconvenience you to have me drop out of things, I believe I'll basely take to my bed and stay there till your party scatters. And now run off, or you'll be late; and make my excuses to them all."

VI

The Barkleys' visitors had dispersed, and Mrs. Lidcote, completely restored by her two days' rest, found herself, on the following Monday alone with her children and Miss Suffern.

There was a note of jubilation in the air, for the party had "gone off" so extraordinarily well, and so completely, as it appeared, to the satisfaction of Mrs. Lorin Boulger, that Wilbour's early appointment to Rome was almost to be counted on. So certain did this seem that the prospect of a prompt reunion mitigated the distress with which Leila learned of her mother's decision to return almost immediately to Italy. No one understood this decision; it seemed to Leila absolutely unintelligible that Mrs. Lidcote should not stay on with them till their own fate was fixed, and Wilbour echoed her astonishment.

"Why shouldn't you, as Leila says, wait here till we can all pack up and go together?"

Mrs. Lidcote smiled her gratitude with her refusal. "After all, it's not yet sure that you'll be packing up."

"Oh, you ought to have seen Wilbour with Mrs. Boulger," Leila triumphed.

"No, you ought to have seen Leila with her," Leila's husband exulted.

Miss Suffern enthusiastically appended: "I *do* think inviting Harriet Fresbie was a stroke of genius!"

"Oh, we'll be with you soon," Leila laughed. "So soon that it's really foolish to separate."

But Mrs. Lidcote held out with the quiet firmness which her daughter knew it was useless to oppose. After her long months in India, it was really imperative, she declared, that she should get back to Florence and see what was happening to her little place there; and she had been so comfortable on the *Utopia* that she had a fancy to return by the same ship. There was nothing for it, therefore, but to acquiesce in her decision and keep her with them till the afternoon before the day of the *Utopia*'s sailing. This arrangement fitted in with certain projects which, during her two days' seclusion, Mrs. Lidcote had silently matured. It had become to her of the first importance to get away as soon as she could, and the little place in Florence, which held her past in every fold of its curtains and between every page of its books, seemed now to her the one spot where that past would be endurable to look upon.

She was not unhappy during the intervening days. The sight of

Leila's well-being, the sense of Leila's tenderness, were, after all, what she had come for; and of these she had had full measure. Leila had never been happier or more tender; and the contemplation of her bliss, and the enjoyment of her affection, were an absorbing occupation for her mother. But they were also a sharp strain on certain overtightened chords, and Mrs. Lidcote, when at last she found herself alone in the New York hotel to which she had returned the night before embarking, had the feeling that she had just escaped with her life from the clutch of a giant hand.

She had refused to let her daughter come to town with her; she had even rejected Susy Suffern's company. She wanted no viaticum but that of her own thoughts; and she let these come to her without shrinking from them as she sat in the same high-hung sitting-room in which, just a week before, she and Franklin Ide had had their memorable talk.

She had promised her friend to let him hear from her, but she had not kept her promise. She knew that he had probably come back from Chicago, and that if he learned of her sudden decision to return to Italy it would be impossible for her not to see him before sailing; and as she wished above all things not to see him she had kept silent, intending to send him a letter from the steamer.

There was no reason why she should wait till then to write it. The actual moment was more favorable, and the task, though not agreeable, would at least bridge over an hour of her lonely evening. She went up to the writing-table, drew out a sheet of paper and began to write his name. And as she did so, the door opened and he came in.

The words she met him with were the last she could have imagined herself saying when they had parted. "How in the world did you know that I was here?"

He caught her meaning in a flash. "You didn't want me to, then?" He stood looking at her. "I suppose I ought to have taken your silence as meaning that. But I happened to meet Mrs. Wynn, who is stopping here, and she asked me to dine with her and

Charlotte, and Charlotte's young man. They told me they'd seen you arriving this afternoon, and I couldn't help coming up."

There was a pause between them, which Mrs. Lidcote at last surprisingly broke with the exclamation: "Ah, she *did* recognize me, then!"

"Recognize you?" He stared. "Why—"

"Oh, I saw she did, though she never moved an eye-lid. I saw it by Charlotte's blush. The child has the prettiest blush. I saw that her mother wouldn't let her speak to me."

Ide put down his hat with an impatient laugh. "Hasn't Leila cured you of your delusions?"

She looked at him intently. "Then you don't think Margaret Wynn meant to cut me?"

"I think your ideas are absurd."

She paused for a perceptible moment without taking this up; then she said, at a tangent: "I'm sailing to-morrow early. I meant to write to you—there's the letter I'd begun."

Ide followed her gesture, and then turned his eyes back to her face. "You didn't mean to see me, then, or even to let me know that you were going till you'd left?"

"I felt it would be easier to explain to you in a letter—"

"What in God's name is there to explain?" She made no reply, and he pressed on: "It can't be that you're worried about Leila, for Charlotte Wynn told me she'd been there last week, and there was a big party arriving when she left: Fresbies and Gileses, and Mrs. Lorin Boulger—all the board of examiners! If Leila has passed *that*, she's got her degree."

Mrs. Lidcote had dropped down into a corner of the sofa where she had sat during their talk of the week before. "I was stupid," she began abruptly. "I ought to have gone to Ridgefield with Susy. I didn't see till afterward that I was expected to."

"You were expected to?"

"Yes. Oh, it wasn't Leila's fault. She suffered—poor darling; she was distracted. But she'd asked her party before she knew I was arriving."

"Oh, as to that—" Ide drew a deep breath of relief. "I can understand that it must have been a disappointment not to have you to herself just at first. But, after all, you were among old friends or their children: the Gileses and Fresbies—and little Charlotte Wynn." He paused a moment before the last name, and scrutinized her hesitatingly. "Even if they came at the wrong time, you must have been glad to see them all at Leila's."

She gave him back his look with a faint smile. "I didn't see them."

"You didn't see them?"

"No. That is, excepting little Charlotte Wynn. That child is exquisite. We had a talk before luncheon the day I arrived. But when her mother found out that I was staying in the house she telephoned her to leave immediately, and so I didn't see her again."

The color rushed to Ide's sallow face. "I don't know where you get such ideas!"

She pursued, as if she had not heard him: "Oh, and I saw Mary Giles for a minute too. Susy Suffern brought her up to my room the last evening, after dinner, when all the others were at bridge. She meant it kindly—but it wasn't much use."

"But what were you doing in your room in the evening after dinner?"

"Why, you see, when I found out my mistake in coming,—how embarrassing it was for Leila, I mean—I simply told her I was very tired, and preferred to stay upstairs till the party was over."

Ide, with a groan, struck his hand against the arm of his chair. "I wonder how much of all this you simply imagined!"

"I didn't imagine the fact of Harriet Fresbie's not even asking if she might see me when she knew I was in the house. Nor of Mary Giles's getting Susy, at the eleventh hour, to smuggle her up to my room when the others wouldn't know where she'd gone; nor poor Leila's ghastly fear lest Mrs. Lorin Boulger, for whom the party was given, should guess I was in the house, and prevent her husband's giving Wilbour the second secretaryship because she'd been obliged to spend a night under the same roof with his mother-in-law!"

Ide continued to drum on his chair-arm with exasperated fingers. "You don't *know* that any of the acts you describe are due to the causes you suppose."

Mrs. Lidcote paused before replying, as if honestly trying to measure the weight of this argument. Then she said in a low tone: "I know that Leila was in an agony lest I should come down to dinner the first night. And it was for me she was afraid, not for herself. Leila is never afraid for herself."

"But the conclusions you draw are simply preposterous. There are narrow-minded women everywhere, but the women who were at Leila's knew perfectly well that their going there would give her a sort of social sanction, and if they were willing that she should have it, why on earth should they want to withhold it from you?"

"That's what I told myself a week ago, in this very room, after my first talk with Susy Suffern." She lifted a misty smile to his anxious eyes. "That's why I listened to what you said to me the same evening, and why your arguments half convinced me, and made me think that what had been possible for Leila might not be impossible for me. If the new dispensation had come, why not for me as well as for the others? I can't tell you the flight my imagination took!"

Franklin Ide rose from his seat and crossed the room to a chair near her sofa-corner. "All I cared about was that it seemed—for the moment—to be carrying you toward me," he said.

"I cared about that, too. That's why I meant to go away without seeing you." They gave each other grave look for look. "Because, you see, I was mistaken," she went on. "We were both mistaken. You say it's preposterous that the women who didn't object to accepting Leila's hospitality should have objected to meeting me under her roof. And so it is; but I begin to understand why. It's simply that society is much too busy to revise its own judgments. Probably no one in the house with me stopped to consider that my case and Leila's were identical. They only remembered that I'd done something which, at the time I did it, was condemned by society. My case has been passed on and classified: I'm the woman who has been cut for nearly twenty years. The older people have half forgotten why, and the younger ones have never really known: it's simply become a tradition to cut me. And traditions that have lost their meaning are the hardest of all to destroy."

Ide sat motionless while she spoke. As she ended, he stood up with a short laugh and walked across the room to the window. Outside, the immense black prospect of New York, strung with its myriad lines of light, stretched away into the smoky edges of the night. He showed it to her with a gesture.

"What do you suppose such words as you've been using—'society,' 'tradition,' and the rest—mean to all the life out there?"

She came and stood by him in the window. "Less than nothing, of course. But you and I are not out there. We're shut up in a little tight round of habit and association, just as we're shut up in this room. Remember, I thought I'd got out of it once; but what really happened was that the other people went out, and left me in the same little room. The only difference was that I was there alone. Oh, I've made it habitable now, I'm used to it; but I've lost any illusions I may have had as to an angel's opening the door."

Ide again laughed impatiently. "Well, if the door won't open, why not let another prisoner in? At least it would be less of a solitude—"

She turned from the dark window back into the vividly lighted room.

"It would be more of a prison. You forget that I know all about that. We're all imprisoned, of course—all of us middling people, who don't carry our freedom in our brains. But we've accommodated ourselves to our different cells, and if we're moved suddenly into new ones we're likely to find a stone wall where we thought there was thin air, and to knock ourselves senseless against it. I saw a man do that once."

Ide, leaning with folded arms against the window-frame, watched her in silence as she moved restlessly about the room, gathering together some scattered books and tossing a handful of torn letters into the paper-basket. When she ceased, he rejoined: "All you say is based on preconceived theories. Why didn't you put them to the test by coming down to meet your old friends? Don't you see the inference they would naturally draw from your hiding yourself when they arrived? It looked as though you were afraid of them—or as though you hadn't forgiven them. Either way, you put them in the wrong instead of waiting to let them put you in the right. If Leila had buried herself in a desert do you suppose society would have gone to fetch her out? You say you were afraid for Leila and that she was afraid for you. Don't you see what all these complications of feeling mean? Simply that you were too nervous at the moment to let things happen naturally, just as you're too nervous now to judge them rationally." He paused and turned his eyes to her face. "Don't try to just yet. Give yourself a little more time. Give *me* a little more time. I've always known it would take time."

He moved nearer, and she let him have her hand. With the grave kindness of his face so close above her she felt like a child roused out of frightened dreams and finding a light in the room.

"Perhaps you're right—" she heard herself begin; then something within her clutched her back, and her hand fell away from him.

"I know I'm right: trust me," he urged. "We'll talk of this in Florence soon."

She stood before him, feeling with despair his kindness, his patience and his unreality. Everything he said seemed like a painted gauze let down between herself and the real facts of life; and a sudden desire seized her to tear the gauze into shreds.

She drew back and looked at him with a smile of superficial reassurance. "You *are* right—about not talking any longer now. I'm nervous and tired, and it would do no good. I brood over things too much. As you say, I must try not to shrink from people." She turned away and glanced at the clock. "Why, it's only ten! If I send you off I shall begin to brood again; and if you stay we shall go on talking about the same thing. Why shouldn't we go down and see Margaret Wynn for half an hour?"

She spoke lightly and rapidly, her brilliant eyes on his face. As she watched him, she saw it change, as if her smile had thrown a too vivid light upon it.

"Oh, no—not to-night!" he exclaimed.

"Not to-night? Why, what other night have I, when I'm off at dawn? Besides, I want to show you at once that I mean to be more sensible—that I'm not going to be afraid of people any more. And I should really like another glimpse of little Charlotte." He stood before her, his hand in his beard, with the gesture he had in moments of perplexity. "Come!" she ordered him gaily, turning to the door.

He followed her and laid his hand on her arm. "Don't you think—hadn't you better let me go first and see? They told me they'd had a tiring day at the dress-maker's. I daresay they have gone to bed."

"But you said they'd a young man of Charlotte's dining with them. Surely he wouldn't have left by ten? At any rate, I'll go down with you and see. It takes so long if one sends a servant first." She put him gently aside, and then paused as a new thought struck her. "Or wait; my maid's in the next room. I'll tell her to go and ask if Margaret will receive me. Yes, that's much the best way."

She turned back and went toward the door that led to her bedroom; but before she could open it she felt Ide's quick touch again.

"I believe—I remember now—Charlotte's young man was suggesting that they should all go out—to a music-hall or something of the sort. I'm sure—I'm positively sure that you won't find them."

Her hand dropped from the door, his dropped from her arm, and as they drew back and faced each other she saw the blood rise slowly through his sallow skin, redden his neck and ears, encroach upon the edges of his beard, and settle in dull patches under his kind troubled eyes. She had seen the same blush on another face, and the same impulse of compassion she had then felt made her turn her gaze away again.

A knock on the door broke the silence, and a porter put his head into the room.

"It's only just to know how many pieces there'll be to go down to the steamer in the morning."

With the words she felt that the veil of painted gauze was torn in tatters, and that she was moving again among the grim edges of reality.

"Oh, dear," she exclaimed, "I never *can* remember! Wait a minute; I shall have to ask my maid."

She opened her bedroom door and called out: "Annette!"

THE LONG RUN

The shade of those our days that had no tongue.

IT WAS last winter, after a twelve years' absence from New York, that I saw again, at one of the Jim Cumnors' dinners, my old friend Halston Merrick.

The Cumnors' house is one of the few where, even after such a lapse of time, one can be sure of finding familiar faces and picking up old threads; where for a moment one can abandon one's self to the illusion that New York humanity is a shade less unstable than its bricks and mortar. And that evening in particular I remember feeling that there could be no pleasanter way of re-entering the confused and careless world to which I was returning than through the quiet softly-lit dining-room in which Mrs. Cumnor, with a characteristic sense of my needing to be broken in gradually, had contrived to assemble so many friendly faces.

I was glad to see them all, including the three or four I did not know, or failed to recognize, but had no difficulty in passing as in the tradition and of the group; but I was most of all glad—as I rather wonderingly found—to set eyes again on Halston Merrick.

He and I had been at Harvard together, for one thing, and had shared there curiosities and ardors a little outside the current tendencies: had, on the whole, been more critical than our comrades, and less amenable to the accepted. Then, for the next following years, Merrick had been a vivid and promising figure in young American life. Handsome, careless, and free, he had wandered and tasted and compared. After leaving Harvard he had spent two years at Oxford; then he had accepted a private secretaryship to our Ambassador in England, and had come back from this adventure with a fresh curiosity about public affairs at home, and the conviction that men of his kind should play a larger part in them. This led, first, to his running for a State Senatorship which he failed to get, and ultimately to a few months of intelligent activity in a municipal office. Soon after being deprived of this post by a change of party he had published a small volume of delicate verse, and, a year later, an odd uneven brilliant book on Municipal Government. After that one hardly knew where to look for his next appearance; but chance rather disappointingly solved the problem by killing off his father and placing Halston at the head of the Merrick Iron Foundry at Yonkers.

His friends had gathered that, whenever this regrettable contingency should occur, he meant to dispose of the business and continue his life of free experiment. As often happens in just such cases, however, it was not the moment for a sale, and Merrick had to take over the management of the foundry. Some two years later he had a chance to free himself; but when it came he did not choose to take it. This tame sequel to an inspiriting start was disappointing to some of us, and I was among those disposed to regret Merrick's drop to the level of the prosperous. Then I went away to a big engineering job in China, and from there to Africa, and spent the next twelve years out of sight and sound of New York doings.

During that long interval I heard of no new phase in Merrick's evolution, but this did not surprise me, as I had never expected from him actions resonant enough to cross the globe. All I knew—and this did surprise me—was that he had not married, and that he was still in the iron business. All through those years, however, I never ceased to wish, in certain situations and at certain turns of thought, that Merrick were in reach, that I could tell this or that to Merrick. I had never, in the interval, found any one with just his quickness of perception and just his sureness of response.

After dinner, therefore, we irresistibly drew together. In Mrs.

Cumnor's big easy drawing-room cigars were allowed, and there was no break in the communion of the sexes; and, this being the case, I ought to have sought a seat beside one of the ladies among whom we were allowed to remain. But, as had generally happened of old when Merrick was in sight, I found myself steering straight for him past all minor ports of call.

There had been no time, before dinner, for more than the barest expression of satisfaction at meeting, and our seats had been at opposite ends of the longish table, so that we got our first real look at each other in the secluded corner to which Mrs. Cumnor's vigilance now directed us.

Merrick was still handsome in his stooping tawny way: handsomer perhaps, with thinnish hair and more lines in his face, than in the young excess of his good looks. He was very glad to see me and conveyed his gladness by the same charming smile; but as soon as we began to talk I felt a change. It was not merely the change that years and experience and altered values bring. There was something more fundamental the matter with Merrick, something dreadful, unforeseen, unaccountable: Merrick had grown conventional and dull.

In the glow of his frank pleasure in seeing me I was ashamed to analyze the nature of the change; but presently our talk began to flag—fancy a talk with Merrick flagging!—and self-deception became impossible as I watched myself handing out platitudes with the gesture of the salesman offering something to a purchaser "equally good." The worst of it was that Merrick—Merrick, who had once felt everything!—didn't seem to feel the lack of spontaneity in my remarks, but hung on them with a harrowing faith in the resuscitating power of our past. It was as if he hugged the empty vessel of our friendship without perceiving that the last drop of its essence was dry.

But after all, I am exaggerating. Through my surprise and disappointment I felt a certain sense of well-being in the mere physical presence of my old friend. I liked looking at the way his dark hair waved away from the forehead, at the tautness of his dry brown cheek, the thoughtful backward tilt of his head, the way his brown eyes mused upon the scene through lowered lids. All the past was in his way of looking and sitting, and I wanted to stay near him, and felt that he wanted me to stay; but the devil of it was that neither of us knew what to talk about.

It was this difficulty which caused me, after a while, since I could not follow Merrick's talk, to follow his eyes in their roaming circuit of the room.

At the moment when our glances joined, his had paused on a lady seated at some distance from our corner. Immersed, at first, in the satisfaction of finding myself again with Merrick, I had been only half aware of this lady, as of one of the few persons present whom I did not know, or had failed to remember. There was nothing in her appearance to challenge my attention or to excite my curiosity, and I don't suppose I should have looked at her again if I had not noticed that my friend was doing so.

She was a woman of about forty-seven, with fair faded hair and a young figure. Her gray dress was handsome but ineffective, and her pale and rather serious face wore a small unvarying smile which might have been pinned on with her ornaments. She was one of the women in whom increasing years show rather what they have taken than what they have bestowed, and only on looking closely did one see that what they had taken must have been good of its kind.

Phil Cumnor and another man were talking to her, and the very intensity of the attention she bestowed on them betrayed the straining of rebellious thoughts. She never let her eyes stray or her smile drop; and at the proper moment I saw she was ready with the proper sentiment.

The party, like most of those that Mrs. Cumnor gathered about her, was not composed of exceptional beings. The people of the old vanished New York set were not exceptional: they were mostly cut on the same convenient and unobtrusive pattern; but they were often exceedingly "nice." And this obsolete quality marked every look and gesture of the lady I was scrutinizing.

While these reflections were passing through my mind I was aware that Merrick's eyes rested still on her. I took a cross-section of his look and found in it neither surprise nor absorption, but only a certain sober pleasure just about at the emotional level of the rest of the room. If he continued to look at her, his expression seemed to say, it was only because, all things considered, there were fewer reasons for looking at anybody else.

This made me wonder what were the reasons for looking at *her*; and as a first step toward enlightenment I said:—"I'm sure I've seen the lady over there in gray—"

Merrick detached his eyes and turned them on me with a wondering look.

"Seen her? You know her." He waited. "*Don't* you know her? It's Mrs. Reardon."

I wondered that he should wonder, for I could not remember, in the Cumnor group or elsewhere, having known any one of the name he mentioned.

"But perhaps," he continued, "you hadn't heard of her marriage? You knew her as Mrs. Trant."

I gave him back his stare. "Not Mrs. Philip Trant?"

"Yes; Mrs. Philip Trant."

"Not Paulina?"

"Yes—Paulina," he said, with a just perceptible delay before the name.

In my surprise I continued to stare at him. He averted his eyes from mine after a moment, and I saw that they had strayed back to her. "You find her so changed?" he asked.

Something in his voice acted as a warning signal, and I tried to reduce my astonishment to less unbecoming proportions. "I don't find that she looks much older."

"No. Only different?" he suggested, as if there were nothing new to him in my perplexity.

"Yes—awfully different."

"I suppose we're all awfully different. To you, I mean—coming from so far?"

"I recognized all the rest of you," I said, hesitating. "And she used to be the one who stood out most."

There was a flash, a wave, a stir of something deep down in his eyes. "Yes," he said. "*That's* the difference."

"I see it is. She—she looks worn down. Soft but blurred, like the figures in that tapestry behind her."

He glanced at her again, as if to test the exactness of my analogy.

"Life wears everybody down," he said.

"Yes—except those it makes more distinct. They're the rare ones, of course; but she *was* rare."

He stood up suddenly, looking old and tired. "I believe I'll be off. I wish you'd come down to my place for Sunday.... No, don't shake hands—I want to slide away unawares."

He had backed away to the threshold and was turning the noiseless door-knob. Even Mrs. Cumnor's door-knobs had tact and didn't tell.

"Of course I'll come," I promised warmly. In the last ten minutes he had begun to interest me again.

"All right. Good-bye." Half through the door he paused to add:—"*She* remembers you. You ought to speak to her."

"I'm going to. But tell me a little more." I thought I saw a shade of constraint on his face, and did not add, as I had meant to: "Tell me—because she interests me—what wore her down?" Instead, I asked: "How soon after Trant's death did she re-marry?"

He seemed to make an effort of memory. "It was seven years ago, I think."

"And is Reardon here to-night?"

"Yes; over there, talking to Mrs. Cumnor."

I looked across the broken groupings and saw a large glossy man with straw-colored hair and a red face, whose shirt and shoes and complexion seemed all to have received a coat of the same expensive varnish.

As I looked there was a drop in the talk about us, and I heard Mr. Reardon pronounce in a big booming voice: "What I say is:

what's the good of disturbing things? Thank the Lord, I'm content with what I've got!"

"Is *that* her husband? What's he like?"

"Oh, the best fellow in the world," said Merrick, going.

II

Merrick had a little place at Riverdale, where he went occasionally to be near the Iron Works, and where he hid his week-ends when the world was too much with him.

Here, on the following Saturday afternoon I found him awaiting me in a pleasant setting of books and prints and faded parental furniture.

We dined late, and smoked and talked afterward in his book-walled study till the terrier on the hearth-rug stood up and yawned for bed. When we took the hint and moved toward the staircase I felt, not that I had found the old Merrick again, but that I was on his track, had come across traces of his passage here and there in the thick jungle that had grown up between us. But I had a feeling that when I finally came on the man himself he might be dead. . . .

As we started up stairs he turned back with one of his abrupt shy movements, and walked into the study.

"Wait a bit!" he called to me.

I waited, and he came out in a moment carrying a limp folio.

"It's typewritten. Will you take a look at it? I've been trying to get to work again," he explained, thrusting the manuscript into my hand.

"What? Poetry, I hope?" I exclaimed.

He shook his head with a gleam of derision. "No—just general considerations. The fruit of fifty years of inexperience."

He showed me to my room and said good-night.

The following afternoon we took a long walk inland, across the hills, and I said to Merrick what I could of his book. Unluckily there wasn't much to say. The essays were judicious, polished and cultivated; but they lacked the freshness and audacity of his youthful work. I tried to conceal my opinion behind the usual generalizations, but he broke through these feints with a quick thrust to the heart of my meaning.

"It's worn down—blurred? Like the figures in the Cumnors' tapestry?"

I hesitated. "It's a little too damned resigned," I said.

"Ah," he exclaimed, "so am I. Resigned." He switched the bare brambles by the roadside. "A man can't serve two masters."

"You mean business and literature?"

"No; I mean theory and instinct. The gray tree and the green. You've got to choose which fruit you'll try; and you don't know till afterward which of the two has the dead core."

"How can anybody be sure that only one of them has?"

"I'm sure," said Merrick sharply.

We turned back to the subject of his essays, and I was astonished at the detachment with which he criticized and demolished them. Little by little, as we talked, his old perspective, his old standards came back to him; but with the difference that they no longer seemed like functions of his mind but merely like attitudes assumed or dropped at will. He could still, with an effort, put himself at the angle from which he had formerly seen things; but it was with the effort of a man climbing mountains after a sedentary life in the plain.

I tried to cut the talk short, but he kept coming back to it with nervous insistence, forcing me into the last retrenchments of hypocrisy, and anticipating the verdict I held back. I perceived that a great deal—immensely more than I could see a reason for—had hung for him on my opinion of his book.

Then, as suddenly, his insistence dropped and, as if ashamed of having forced himself so long on my attention, he began to talk rapidly and uninterestingly of other things.

We were alone again that evening, and after dinner, wishing to efface the impression of the afternoon, and above all to show that

I wanted him to talk about himself, I reverted to his work. "You must need an outlet of that sort. When a man's once had it in him, as you have—and when other things begin to dwindle—"

He laughed. "Your theory is that a man ought to be able to return to the Muse as he comes back to his wife after he's ceased to interest other women?"

"No; as he comes back to his wife after the day's work is done." A new thought came to me as I looked at him. "You ought to have had one," I added.

He laughed again. "A wife, you mean? So that there'd have been some one waiting for me even if the Muse decamped?" He went on after a pause: "I've a notion that the kind of woman worth coming back to wouldn't be much more patient than the Muse. But as it happens I never tried—because, for fear they'd chuck me, I put them both out-of-doors together."

He turned his head and looked past me with a queer expression at the low paneled door at my back. "Out of that very door they went—the two of 'em, on a rainy night like this: and one stopped and looked back, to see if I wasn't going to call her—and I didn't —and so they both went. . . ."

III

"The Muse?" (said Merrick refilling my glass and stooping to pat the terrier as he went back to his chair)—"well, you've met the Muse in the little volume of sonnets you used to like; and you've met the woman too, and you used to like *her*; though you didn't know her when you saw her the other evening. . . .

"No, I won't ask you how she struck you when you talked to her: I know. She struck you like that stuff I gave you to read last night. She's conformed—I've conformed—the mills have caught us and ground us: ground us, oh, exceedingly small!

"But you remember what she was; and that's the reason why I'm telling you this now. . . .

"You may recall that after my father's death I tried to sell the

Works. I was impatient to free myself from anything that would keep me tied to New York. I don't dislike my trade, and I've made, in the end, a fairly good thing of it; but industrialism was not, at that time, in the line of my tastes, and I know now that it wasn't what I was meant for. Above all, I wanted to get away, to see new places and rub up against different ideas. I had reached a time of life—the top of the first hill, so to speak—where the distance draws one, and everything in the foreground seems tame and stale. I was sick to death of the particular set of conformities I had grown up among; sick of being a pleasant popular young man with a long line of dinners on my list, and the dead certainty of meeting the same people, or their prototypes, at all of them.

"Well—I failed to sell the Works, and that increased my discontent. I went through moods of cold unsociability, alternating with sudden flushes of curiosity, when I gloated over stray scraps of talk overheard in railway stations and omnibuses, when strange faces that I passed in the street tantalized me with fugitive promises. I wanted to be among things that were unexpected and unknown; and it seemed to me that nobody about me understood in the least what I felt, but that somewhere just out of reach there was some one who *did*, and whom I must find or despair....

"It was just then that, one evening, I saw Mrs. Trant for the first time.

"Yes: I know—you wonder what I mean. I'd known her, of course, as a girl; I'd met her several times after her marriage; and I'd lately been thrown with her, quite intimately and continuously, during a succession of country-house visits. But I had never, as it happened, really *seen* her....

"It was at a dinner at the Cumnors'; and there she was, in front of the very tapestry we saw her against the other evening, with people about her, and her face turned from me, and nothing noticeable or different in her dress or manner; and suddenly she stood out for me against the familiar unimportant background, and for the first time I saw a meaning in the stale phrase of a picture's walking out of its frame. For, after all, most people *are* just that to us: pictures, furniture, the inanimate accessories of our little island-area of sensation. And then sometimes one of these graven images moves and throws out live filaments toward us, and the line they make draws us across the world as the moon-track seems to draw a boat across the water. . . .

"There she stood; and as this queer sensation came over me I felt that she was looking steadily at me, that her eyes were voluntarily, consciously resting on me with the weight of the very question I was asking.

"I went over and joined her, and she turned and walked with me into the music-room. Earlier in the evening some one had been singing, and there were low lights there, and a few couples still sitting in those confidential corners of which Mrs. Cumnor has the art; but we were under no illusion as to the nature of these presences. We knew that they were just painted in, and that the whole of life was in us two, flowing back and forward between us. We talked, of course; we had the attitudes, even the words, of the others: I remember her telling me her plans for the spring and asking me politely about mine! As if there were the least sense in plans, now that this thing had happened!

"When we went back into the drawing-room I had said nothing to her that I might not have said to any other woman of the party; but when we shook hands I knew we should meet the next day—and the next. . . .

"That's the way, I take it, that Nature has arranged the beginning of the great enduring loves; and likewise of the little epidermal flurries. And how is a man to know where he is going?

"From the first my feeling for Paulina Trant seemed to me a grave business; but then the Enemy is given to producing that illusion. Many a man—I'm talking of the kind with imagination— has thought he was seeking a soul when all he wanted was a closer view of its tenement. And I tried—honestly tried—to make myself think I was in the latter case. Because, in the first place, I didn't, just then, want a big disturbing influence in my life; and because I didn't want to be a dupe; and because Paulina Trant was not, according to hearsay, the kind of woman for whom it was worth-while to bring up the big batteries. . . .

"But my resistance was only half-hearted. What I really felt—*all* I really felt—was the flood of joy that comes of heightened emotion. She had given me that, and I wanted her to give it to me again. That's as near as I've ever come to analyzing my state in the beginning.

"I knew her story, as no doubt you know it: the current version, I mean. She had been poor and fond of enjoyment, and she had married that pompous stick Philip Trant because she needed a home, and perhaps also because she wanted a little luxury. Queer how we sneer at women for wanting the thing that gives them half their attraction!

"People shook their heads over the marriage, and divided, prematurely, into Philip's partisans and hers: for no one thought it would work. And they were almost disappointed when, after all, it did. She and her wooden consort seemed to get on well enough. There was a ripple, at one time, over her friendship with young Jim Dalham, who was always with her during a summer at Newport and an autumn in Italy; then the talk died out, and she and Trant were seen together, as before, on terms of apparent good-fellowship.

"This was the more surprising because, from the first, Paulina had never made the least attempt to change her tone or subdue her colors. In the gray Trant atmosphere she flashed with prismatic fires. She smoked, she talked subversively, she did as she liked and went where she chose, and danced over the Trant prejudices and the Trant principles as if they'd been a ball-room floor; and all without apparent offense to her solemn husband and his cloud of cousins. I believe her frankness and directness struck them dumb. She moved like a kind of primitive Una through the virtuous rout, and never got a finger-mark on her freshness.

"One of the finest things about her was the fact that she never, for an instant, used her situation as a means of enhancing her attraction. With a husband like Trant it would have been so easy! He was a man who always saw the small sides of big things. He thought most of life compressible into a set of by-laws and the rest unmentionable; and with his stiff frock-coated and tall-hatted mind, instinctively distrustful of intelligences in another dress, with his arbitrary classification of whatever he didn't understand into 'the kind of thing I don't approve of,' 'the kind of thing that isn't done,' and—deepest depth of all—'the kind of thing I'd rather not discuss,' he lived in bondage to a shadowy moral etiquette of which the complex rites and awful penalties had cast an abiding gloom upon his manner.

"A woman like his wife couldn't have asked a better foil; yet I'm sure she never consciously used his dullness to relieve her brilliancy. She may have felt that the case spoke for itself. But I believe her reserve was rather due to a lively sense of justice, and to the rare habit (you said she was rare) of looking at facts as they are, without any throwing of sentimental lime-lights. She knew Trant could no more help being Trant than she could help being herself—and there was an end of it. I've never known a woman who 'made up' so little mentally....

"Perhaps her very reserve, the fierceness of her implicit rejection of sympathy, exposed her the more to—well, to what happened when we met. She said afterward that it was like having been shut up for months in the hold of a ship, and coming suddenly on deck on a day that was all flying blue and silver....

"I won't try to tell you what she was. It's easier to tell you what her friendship made of me; and I can do that best by adopting her metaphor of the ship. Haven't you, sometimes, at the moment of starting on a journey, some glorious plunge into the unknown, been tripped up by the thought: 'If only one hadn't to come back'? Well, with her one had the sense that one would never have to come back; that the magic ship would always carry one farther. And what an air one breathed on it! And, oh, the wind, and the islands, and the sunsets!

"I said just now 'her friendship'; and I used the word advisedly. Love is deeper than friendship, but friendship is a good deal wider.

The beauty of our relation was that it included both dimensions. Our thoughts met as naturally as our eyes: it was almost as if we loved each other because we liked each other. The quality of a love may be tested by the amount of friendship it contains, and in our case there was no dividing line between loving and liking, no disproportion between them, no barrier against which desire beat in vain or from which thought fell back unsatisfied. Ours was a robust passion that could give an open-eyed account of itself, and not a beautiful madness shrinking away from the proof. . . .

"For the first months friendship sufficed us, or rather gave us so much by the way that we were in no hurry to reach what we knew it was leading to. But we were moving there nevertheless, and one day we found ourselves on the borders. It came about through a sudden decision of Trant's to start on a long tour with his wife. We had never foreseen that: he seemed rooted in his New York habits and convinced that the whole social and financial machinery of the metropolis would cease to function if he did not keep an eye on it through the columns of his morning paper, and pronounce judgment on it in the afternoon at his club. But something new had happened to him: he caught a cold, which was followed by a touch of pleurisy, and instantly he perceived the intense interest and importance which ill-health may add to life. He took the fullest advantage of it. A discerning doctor recommended travel in a warm climate; and suddenly, the morning paper, the afternoon club, Fifth Avenue, Wall Street, all the complex phenomena of the metropolis, faded into insignificance, and the rest of the terrestrial globe, from being a mere geographical hypothesis, useful in enabling one to determine the latitude of New York, acquired reality and magnitude as a factor in the convalescence of Mr. Philip Trant.

"His wife was absorbed in preparations for the journey. To move him was like mobilizing an army, and weeks before the date set for their departure it was almost as if she were already gone.

"This foretaste of separation showed us what we were to each other. Yet I was letting her go—and there was no help for it, no way of preventing it. Resistance was as useless as the vain struggles in a nightmare. She was Trant's and not mine: part of his luggage when he traveled as she was part of his household furniture when he stayed at home. . . .

"The day she told me that their passages were taken—it was on a November afternoon, in her drawing-room in town—I turned away from her and, going to the window, stood looking out at the torrent of traffic interminably pouring down Fifth Avenue. I watched the senseless machinery of life revolving in the rain and mud, and tried to picture myself performing my small function in it after she had gone from me.

" 'It can't be—it can't be!' I exclaimed.

" 'What can't be?'

"I came back into the room and sat down by her. 'This—this—' I hadn't any words. 'Two weeks!' I said. 'What's two weeks?'

"She answered, vaguely, something about their thinking of Spain for the spring—

" 'Two weeks—two weeks!' I repeated. 'And the months we've lost—the days that belonged to us!'

" 'Yes,' she said, 'I'm thankful it's settled.'

"Our words seemed irrelevant, haphazard. It was as if each were answering a secret voice, and not what the other was saying.

" 'Don't you *feel* anything at all?' I remember bursting out at her. As I asked it the tears were streaming down her face. I felt angry with her, and was almost glad to note that her lids were red and that she didn't cry becomingly. I can't express my sensation to you except by saying that she seemed part of life's huge league against me. And suddenly I thought of an afternoon we had spent together in the country, on a ferny hill-side, when we had sat under a beech-tree, and her hand had lain palm upward in the moss, close to mine, and I had watched a little black-and-red beetle creeping over it. . . .

"The bell rang, and we heard the voice of a visitor and the click of an umbrella in the umbrella-stand.

"She rose to go into the inner drawing-room, and I caught her suddenly by the wrist. 'You understand,' I said, 'that we can't go on like this?'

" 'I understand,' she answered, and moved away to meet her visitor. As I went out I heard her saying in the other room: 'Yes, we're really off on the twelfth.'

IV

"I wrote her a long letter that night, and waited two days for a reply.

"On the third day I had a brief line saying that she was going to spend Sunday with some friends who had a place near Riverdale, and that she would arrange to see me while she was there. That was all.

"It was on a Saturday that I received the note and I came out here the same night. The next morning was rainy, and I was in despair, for I had counted on her asking me to take her for a drive or a long walk. It was hopeless to try to say what I had to say to her in the drawing-room of a crowded country-house. And only eleven days were left!

"I stayed indoors all the morning, fearing to go out lest she should telephone me. But no sign came, and I grew more and more restless and anxious. She was too free and frank for coquetry, but her silence and evasiveness made me feel that, for some reason, she did not wish to hear what she knew I meant to say. Could it be that she was, after all, more conventional, less genuine, than I had thought? I went again and again over the whole maddening round of conjecture; but the only conclusion I could rest in was that, if she loved me as I loved her, she would be as determined as I was to let no obstacle come between us during the days that were left.

"The luncheon-hour came and passed, and there was no word from her. I had ordered my trap to be ready, so that I might drive over as soon as she summoned me; but the hours dragged on, the early twilight came, and I sat here in this very chair, or measured up and down, up and down, the length of this very rug—and still there was no message and no letter.

"It had grown quite dark, and I had ordered away, impatiently, the servant who came in with the lamps: I couldn't *bear* any definite sign that the day was over! And I was standing there on the rug, staring at the door, and noticing a bad crack in its panel, when I heard the sound of wheels on the gravel. A word at last, no doubt—a line to explain.... I didn't seem to care much for her reasons, and I stood where I was and continued to stare at the door. And suddenly it opened and she came in.

"The servant followed her with a light, and then went out and closed the door. Her face looked pale in the lamp-light, but her voice was as clear as a bell.

"'Well,' she said, 'you see I've come.'

"I started toward her with hands outstretched. 'You've come—you've come!' I stammered.

"Yes; it was like her to come in that way—without dissimulation or explanation or excuse. It was like her, if she gave at all, to give not furtively or in haste, but openly, deliberately, without stinting the measure or counting the cost. But her quietness and serenity disconcerted me. She did not look like a woman who has yielded impetuously to an uncontrollable impulse. There was something almost solemn in her face.

"The effect of it stole over me as I looked at her, suddenly subduing the huge flush of gratified longing.

"'You're here, here, here!' I kept repeating, like a child singing over a happy word.

"'You said,' she continued, in her grave clear voice, 'that we couldn't go on as we were—'

"'Ah, it's divine of you!' I held out my arms to her.

"She didn't draw back from them, but her faint smile said, 'Wait,' and lifting her hands she took the pins from her hat, and laid the hat on the table.

"As I saw her dear head bare in the lamp-light, with the thick hair waving away from the parting, I forgot everything but the bliss and wonder of her being here—here, in my house, on my hearth—that fourth rose from the corner of the rug is the exact spot where she was standing. . . .

"I drew her to the fire, and made her sit down in the chair you're in, and knelt down by her, and hid my face on her knees. She put her hand on my head, and I was happy to the depths of my soul.

" 'Oh, I forgot—' she exclaimed suddenly. I lifted my head and our eyes met. Hers were smiling.

"She reached out her hand, opened the little bag she had tossed down with her hat, and drew a small object from it. 'I left my trunk at the station. Here's the check. Can you send for it?' she asked.

"Her trunk—she wanted me to send for her trunk! Oh, yes—I see your smile, your 'lucky man!' Only, you see, I didn't love her in that way. I knew she couldn't come to my house without running a big risk of discovery, and my tenderness for her, my impulse to shield her, was stronger, even then, than vanity or desire. Judged from the point of view of those emotions I fell terribly short of my part. I hadn't any of the proper feelings. Such an act of romantic folly was so unlike her that it almost irritated me, and I found myself desperately wondering how I could get her to reconsider her plan without—well, without seeming to want her to.

"It's not the way a novel hero feels; it's probably not the way a man in real life ought to have felt. But it's the way I felt—and she saw it.

"She put her hands on my shoulders and looked at me with deep, deep eyes. 'Then you didn't expect me to stay?' she asked.

"I caught her hands and pressed them to me, stammering out that I hadn't dared to dream. . . .

" 'You thought I'd come—just for an hour?'

" 'How could I dare think more? I adore you, you know, for what you've done! But it would be known if you—if you stayed on. My servants—everybody about here knows you. I've no right to expose you to the risk.' She made no answer, and I went on tenderly: 'Give me, if you will, the next few hours: there's a train that will get you to town by midnight. And then we'll arrange something—in town—where it's safer for you—more easily managed. . . . It's beautiful, it's heavenly of you to have come; but I love you too much—I must take care of you and think for you—'

"I don't suppose it ever took me so long to say so few words, and though they were profoundly sincere they sounded unutterably shallow, irrelevant and grotesque. She made no effort to help me out, but sat silent, listening, with her meditative smile. 'It's my duty, dearest, as a man,' I rambled on. 'The more I love you the more I'm bound—'

" 'Yes; but you don't understand,' she interrupted.

"She rose as she spoke, and I got up also, and we stood and looked at each other.

" 'I haven't come for a night; if you want me I've come for always,' she said.

"Here again, if I give you an honest account of my feelings I shall write myself down as the poor-spirited creature I suppose I am. There wasn't, I swear, at the moment, a grain of selfishness, of personal reluctance, in my feeling. I worshipped every hair of her head—when we were together I was happy, when I was away from her something was gone from every good thing; but I had always looked on our love for each other, our possible relation to each other, as such situations are looked on in what is called society. I had supposed her, for all her freedom and originality, to be just as tacitly subservient to that view as I was: ready to take what she wanted on the terms on which society concedes such taking, and to pay for it by the usual restrictions, concealments and hypocrisies. In short, I supposed that she would 'play the game'— look out for her own safety, and expect me to look out for it. It sounds cheap enough, put that way—but it's the rule we live under, all of us. And the amazement of finding her suddenly outside of it, oblivious of it, unconscious of it, left me, for an awful minute, stammering at her like a graceless dolt. . . . Perhaps it wasn't even a minute; but in it she had gone the whole round of my thoughts.

"'It's raining,' she said, very low. 'I suppose you can telephone for a trap?'

"There was no irony or resentment in her voice. She walked slowly across the room and paused before the Brangwyn etching over there. 'That's a good impression. *Will* you telephone, please?' she repeated.

"I found my voice again, and with it the power of movement. I followed her and dropped at her feet. 'You can't go like this!' I cried.

"She looked down on me from heights and heights. 'I can't stay like this,' she answered.

"I stood up and we faced each other like antagonists. 'You don't know,' I accused her passionately, 'in the least what you're asking me to ask of you!'

"'Yes, I do: *everything*,' she breathed.

"'And it's got to be that or nothing?'

"'Oh, on both sides,' she reminded me.

"'*Not* on both sides. It's not fair. That's why—'

"'Why you won't?'

"'Why I cannot—may not!'

"'Why you'll take a night and not a life?'

"The taunt, for a woman usually so sure of her aim, fell so short of the mark that its only effect was to increase my conviction of her helplessness. The very intensity of my longing for her made me tremble where she was fearless. I had to protect her first, and think of my own attitude afterward.

"She was too discerning not to see this too. Her face softened, grew inexpressibly appealing, and she dropped again into that chair you're in, leaned forward, and looked up with her grave smile.

"'You think I'm beside myself—raving? (You're not thinking of yourself, I know.) I'm not: I never was saner. Since I've known you I've often thought this might happen. This thing between us isn't an ordinary thing. If it had been we shouldn't, all these months, have drifted. We should have wanted to skip to the last page—and then throw down the book. We shouldn't have felt we could *trust* the future as we did. We were in no hurry because we knew we shouldn't get tired; and when two people feel that about each other they must live together—or part. I don't see what else they can do. A little trip along the coast won't answer. It's the high seas—or else being tied up to Lethe wharf. And I'm for the high seas, my dear!'

"Think of sitting here—here, in this room, in this chair—and listening to that, and seeing the light on her hair, and hearing the sound of her voice! I don't suppose there ever was a scene just like it. . . .

"She was astounding—inexhaustible; through all my anguish of resistance I found a kind of fierce joy in following her. It was lucidity at white heat: the last sublimation of passion. She might have been an angel arguing a point in the empyrean if she hadn't been, so completely, a woman pleading for her life. . . .

"Her life: that was the thing at stake! She couldn't do with less of it than she was capable of; and a woman's life is inextricably part of the man's she cares for.

"That was why, she argued, she couldn't accept the usual solution: couldn't enter into the only relation that society tolerates between people situated like ourselves. Yes: she knew all the arguments on *that* side: didn't I suppose she'd been over them and over them? She knew (for hadn't she often said it of others?) what is said of the woman who, by throwing in her lot with her lover's, binds him to a life-long duty which has the irksomeness without the dignity of marriage. Oh, she could talk on that side with the best of them: only she asked me to consider the other—the side of the man and woman who love each other deeply and completely enough to want their lives enlarged, and not diminished, by their love. What, in such a case—she reasoned—must be the inevitable effect of concealing, denying, disowning, the central fact, the motive power of one's existence? She asked me to picture the course of such a love: first working as a fever in the blood, distorting and deflecting everything, making all other interests insipid, all other duties irksome, and then, as the acknowledged claims of life regained their hold, gradually dying—the poor starved passion!— for want of the wholesome necessary food of common living and doing, yet leaving life impoverished by the loss of all it might have been.

" 'I'm not talking, dear—' I see her now, leaning toward me with shining eyes: 'I'm not talking of the people who haven't enough to fill their days, and to whom a little mystery, a little maneuvering, gives an illusion of importance that they can't afford to miss; I'm talking of you and me, with all our tastes and curiosities and activities; and I ask you what our love would become if we had to keep it apart from our lives, like a pretty useless animal that we went to peep at and feed with sweet-meats through its cage?'

"I won't, my dear fellow, go into the other side of our strange duel: the arguments I used were those that most men in my situation would have felt bound to use, and that most women in Paulina's accept instinctively, without even formulating them. The exceptionalness, the significance, of the case lay wholly in the fact that she had formulated them all and then rejected them. . . .

"There was one point I didn't, of course, touch on; and that was the popular conviction (which I confess I shared) that when a man and a woman agree to defy the world together the man really sacrifices much more than the woman. I was not even conscious of thinking of this at the time, though it may have lurked somewhere in the shadow of my scruples for her; but she dragged it out into the daylight and held me face to face with it.

" 'Remember, I'm not attempting to lay down any general rule,' she insisted; 'I'm not theorizing about Man and Woman, I'm talking about you and me. How do I know what's best for the woman in the next house? Very likely she'll bolt when it would have been better for her to stay at home. And it's the same with the man: he'll probably do the wrong thing. It's generally the weak heads that commit follies, when it's the strong ones that ought to: and my point is that you and I are both strong enough to behave like fools if we want to. . . .

" 'Take your own case first—because, in spite of the sentimentalists, it's the man who stands to lose most. You'll have to give up the Iron Works: which you don't much care about—because it won't be particularly agreeable for us to live in New York: which you don't care much about either. But you won't be sacrificing what is called "a career." You made up your mind long ago that your best chance of self-development, and consequently of general usefulness, lay in thinking rather than doing; and, when we first met, you were already planning to sell out your business, and travel and write. Well! Those ambitions are of a kind that won't be harmed by your dropping out of your social setting. On the contrary, such work as you want to do ought to gain by it, because you'll be brought nearer to life-as-it-is, in contrast to life-as-a-visiting-list. . . .'

"She threw back her head with a sudden laugh. 'And the joy of not having any more visits to make! I wonder if you've ever thought of *that*? Just at first, I mean; for society's getting so deplorably lax that, little by little, it will edge up to us—you'll see! I don't want to idealize the situation, dearest, and I won't conceal from you that in time we shall be called on. But, oh, the fun we shall have had in the interval! And then, for the first time we shall be able to dictate our own terms, one of which will be that no bores need apply. Think of being cured of all one's chronic bores! We shall feel as jolly as people do after a successful operation.'

"I don't know why this nonsense sticks in my mind when some of the graver things we said are less distinct. Perhaps it's because of a certain iridescent quality of feeling that made her gaiety seem like sunshine through a shower. . . .

" 'You ask me to think of myself?' she went on. 'But the beauty of our being together will be that, for the first time, I shall dare to! Now I have to think of all the tedious trifles I can pack the days with, because I'm afraid—I'm afraid—to hear the voice of the real me, down below, in the windowless underground hole where I keep her. . . .

"'Remember again, please, it's not Woman, it's Paulina Trant, I'm talking of. The woman in the next house may have all sorts of reasons—honest reasons—for staying there. There may be some one there who needs her badly: for whom the light would go out if she went. Whereas to Philip I've been simply—well, what New York was before he decided to travel: the most important thing in life till he made up his mind to leave it; and now merely the starting-place of several lines of steamers. Oh, I didn't have to love you to know that! I only had to live with *him*. . . . If he lost his eye-glasses he'd think it was the fault of the eye-glasses; he'd really feel that the eye-glasses had been careless. And he'd be convinced that no others would suit him quite as well. But at the optician's he'd probably be told that he needed something a little different, and after that he'd feel that the old eye-glasses had never suited him at all, and that *that* was their fault too. . . .'

"At one moment—but I don't recall when—I remember she stood up with one of her quick movements, and came toward me, holding out her arms. 'Oh, my dear, I'm pleading for my life; do you suppose I shall ever want for arguments?' she cried. . . .

"After that, for a bit, nothing much remains with me except a sense of darkness and of conflict. The one spot of daylight in my whirling brain was the conviction that I couldn't—whatever happened—profit by the sudden impulse she had acted on, and allow her to take, in a moment of passion, a decision that was to shape her whole life. I couldn't so much as lift my little finger to keep her with me then, unless I were prepared to accept for her as well as for myself the full consequences of the future she had planned for us. . . .

"Well—there's the point: I wasn't. I felt in her—poor fatuous idiot that I was!—that lack of objective imagination which had always seemed to me to account, at least in part, for many of the so-called heroic qualities in women. When their feelings are involved they simply can't look ahead. Her unfaltering logic notwithstanding, I felt this about Paulina as I listened. She had a specious air of knowing where she was going, but she didn't. She seemed the genius of logic and understanding, but the demon of illusion spoke through her lips. . . .

"I said just now that I hadn't, at the outset, given my own side of the case a thought. It would have been truer to say that I hadn't given it a *separate* thought. But I couldn't think of her without seeing myself as a factor—the chief factor—in her problem, and without recognizing that whatever the experiment made of me, that it must fatally, in the end, make of her. If I couldn't carry the thing through she must break down with me: we should have to throw our separate selves into the melting-pot of this mad adventure, and be 'one' in a terrible indissoluble completeness of which marriage is only an imperfect counterpart. . . .

"There could be no better proof of her extraordinary power over me, and of the way she had managed to clear the air of sentimental illusion, than the fact that I presently found myself putting this before her with a merciless precision of touch.

" 'If we love each other enough to do a thing like this, we must love each other enough to see just what it is we're going to do.'

"So I invited her to the dissecting-table, and I see now the fearless eye with which she approached the cadaver. 'For that's what it is, you know,' she flashed out at me, at the end of my long demonstration. 'It's a dead body, like all the instances and examples and hypothetical cases that ever were! What do you expect to learn from *that*? The first great anatomist was the man who stuck his knife in a heart that was beating; and the only way to find out what doing a thing will be like is to do it!'

"She looked away from me suddenly, as if she were fixing her eyes on some vision on the outer rim of consciousness. 'No: there's one other way,' she exclaimed; 'and that is, *not* to do it! To abstain and refrain; and then see what we become, or what we don't become, in the long run, and to draw our inferences. That's the game that almost everybody about us is playing, I suppose; there's hardly one of the dull people one meets at dinner who hasn't had, just once, the chance of a berth on a ship that was off for the Happy Isles, and hasn't refused it for fear of sticking on a sand-bank!

" 'I'm doing my best, you know,' she continued, 'to see the sequel as you see it, as you believe it's your duty to me to see it. I know the instances you're thinking of: the listless couples wearing out their lives in shabby watering places, and hanging on the favor of hotel acquaintances; or the proud quarreling wretches shut up alone in a fine house because they're too good for the only society they can get, and trying to cheat their boredom by squabbling with their tradesmen and spying on their servants. No doubt there are such cases; but I don't recognize either of us in those dismal figures. Why, to do it would be to admit that our life, yours and mine, is in the people about us and not in ourselves; that we're parasites and not self-sustaining creatures; and that the lives we're leading now are so brilliant, full and satisfying that what we should have to give up would surpass even the blessedness of being to-gether!'

"At that stage, I confess, the solid ground of my resistance began to give way under me. It was not that my convictions were shaken, but that she had swept me into a world whose laws were different, where one could reach out in directions that the slave of gravity hasn't pictured. But at the same time my opposition hardened from reason into instinct. I knew it was her voice, and not her logic, that was unsettling me. I knew that if she'd written out her thesis and sent it me by post I should have made short work of it; and again the part of me which I called by all the finest names: my chivalry, my unselfishness, my superior masculine experience, cried out with one voice: 'You can't let a woman use her graces to her own undoing—you can't, for her own sake, let her eyes convince you when her reasons don't!'

"And then, abruptly, and for the first time, a doubt entered me: a doubt of her perfect moral honesty. I don't know how else to describe my feeling that she wasn't playing fair, that in coming to my house, in throwing herself at my head (I called things by their names), she had perhaps not so much obeyed an irresistible impulse as deeply, deliberately reckoned on the dissolvent effect of her generosity, her rashness and her beauty. . . .

"From the moment that this mean doubt raised its head in me I was once more the creature of all the conventional scruples: I was repeating, before the looking-glass of my self-consciousness, all the stereotyped gestures of the 'man of honor.' . . . Oh, the sorry figure I must have cut! You'll understand my dropping the curtain on it as quickly as I can. . . .

"Yet I remember, as I made my point, being struck by its impressiveness. I was suffering and enjoying my own suffering. I told her that, whatever step we decided to take, I owed it to her to insist on its being taken soberly, deliberately—

"('No: it's "advisedly," isn't it? Oh, I was thinking of the Marriage Service,' she interposed with a faint laugh.)

"—that if I accepted, there, on the spot, her headlong beautiful gift of herself, I should feel I had taken an unfair advantage of her, an advantage which she would be justified in reproaching me with afterward; that I was not afraid to tell her this because she was intelligent enough to know that my scruples were the surest proof of the quality of my love; that I refused to owe my happiness to an unconsidered impulse; that we must see each other again, in her own house, in less agitating circumstances, when she had had time to reflect on my words, to study her heart and look into the future. . . .

"The factitious exhilaration produced by uttering these beautiful sentiments did not last very long, as you may imagine. It fell, little by little, under her quiet gaze, a gaze in which there was neither contempt nor irony nor wounded pride, but only a tender wistfulness of interrogation; and I think the acutest point in my suffering was reached when she said, as I ended: 'Oh; yes, of course I understand.'

" 'If only you hadn't come to me here!' I blurted out in the torture of my soul.

"She was on the threshold when I said it, and she turned and laid her hand gently on mine. 'There was no other way,' she said; and at the moment it seemed to me like some hackneyed phrase in a novel that she had used without any sense of its meaning.

"I don't remember what I answered or what more we either of us said. At the end a desperate longing to take her in my arms and keep her with me swept aside everything else, and I went up to her, pleading, stammering, urging I don't know what. . . . But she held me back with a quiet look, and went. I had ordered the carriage, as she asked me to; and my last definite recollection is of watching her drive off in the rain. . . .

"I had her promise that she would see me, two days later, at her house in town, and that we should then have what I called 'a decisive talk'; but I don't think that even at the moment I was the dupe of my phrase. I knew, and she knew, that the end had come. . . .

V

"It was about that time (Merrick went on after a long pause) that I definitely decided not to sell the Works, but to stick to my job and conform my life to it.

"I can't describe to you the rage of conformity that possessed me. Poetry, ideas—all the picture-making processes stopped. A kind of dull self-discipline seemed to me the only exercise worthy of a reflecting mind. I *had* to justify my great refusal, and I tried to do it by plunging myself up to the eyes into the very conditions I had been instinctively struggling to get away from. The only possible consolation would have been to find in a life of business routine and social submission such moral compensations as may reward the citizen if they fail the man; but to attain to these I should have had to accept the old delusion that the social and the individual man are two. Now, on the contrary, I found soon enough that I couldn't get one part of my machinery to work effectively while another wanted feeding: and that in rejecting what had seemed to me a negation of action I had made all my action negative.

"The best solution, of course, would have been to fall in love with another woman; but it was long before I could bring myself to wish that this might happen to me.... Then, at length, I suddenly and violently desired it; and as such impulses are seldom without some kind of imperfect issue I contrived, a year or two later, to work myself up into the wished-for state.... She was a woman in society, and with all the awe of that institution that Paulina lacked. Our relation was consequently one of those unavowed affairs in which triviality is the only alternative to tragedy. Luckily we had, on both sides, risked only as much as prudent people stake in a drawing-room game; and when the match was over I take it that we came out fairly even.

"My gain, at all events, was of an unexpected kind. The adventure had served only to make me understand Paulina's abhorrence of such experiments, and at every turn of the slight intrigue I had felt how exasperating and belittling such a relation was bound to be between two people who, had they been free, would have mated openly. And so from a brief phase of imperfect forgetting I was driven back to a deeper and more understanding remembrance....

"This second incarnation of Paulina was one of the strangest episodes of the whole strange experience. Things she had said during our extraordinary talk, things I had hardly heard at the time, came back to me with singular vividness and a fuller meaning. I hadn't any longer the cold consolation of believing in my own perspicacity: I saw that her insight had been deeper and keener than mine.

"I remember, in particular, starting up in bed one sleepless night as there flashed into my head the meaning of her last words: 'There was no other way'; the phrase I had half-smiled at at the time, as a parrot-like echo of the novel-heroine's stock farewell. I had never, up to that moment, wholly understood why Paulina had come to my house that night. I had never been able to make that particular act—which could hardly, in the light of her subsequent conduct, be dismissed as a blind surge of passion—square with my conception of her character. She was at once the most spontaneous and the steadiest-minded woman I had ever known, and the last to wish to owe any advantage to surprise, to unpreparedness, to any play on the spring of sex. The better I came, retrospectively, to know her, the more sure I was of this, and the less intelligible her act appeared. And then, suddenly, after a night of hungry restless thinking, the flash of enlightenment came. She had come to my house, had brought her trunk with her, had thrown herself at my head with all possible violence and publicity, in order to give me a pretext, a loophole, an honorable excuse, for doing and saying—why, precisely what I had said and done!

"As the idea came to me it was as if some ironic hand had touched an electric button, and all my fatuous phrases had leapt out on me in fire.

"Of course she had known all along just the kind of thing I should say if I didn't at once open my arms to her; and to save my pride, my dignity, my conception of the figure I was cutting in her eyes, she had recklessly and magnificently provided me with the decentest pretext a man could have for doing a pusillanimous thing. . . .

"With that discovery the whole case took a different aspect. It hurt less to think of Paulina—and yet it hurt more. The tinge of bitterness, of doubt, in my thoughts of her had had a tonic quality. It was harder to go on persuading myself that I had done right as, bit by bit, my theories crumbled under the test of time. Yet, after all, as she herself had said, one could judge of results only in the long run. . . .

"The Trants stayed away for two years; and about a year after they got back, you may remember, Trant was killed in a railway accident. You know Fate's way of untying a knot after everybody has given up tugging at it!

"Well—there I was, completely justified: all my weaknesses turned into merits! I had 'saved' a weak woman from herself, I had kept her to the path of duty, I had spared her the humiliation of scandal and the misery of self-reproach; and now I had only to put out my hand and take my reward.

"I had avoided Paulina since her return, and she had made no effort to see me. But after Trant's death I wrote her a few lines, to which she sent a friendly answer; and when a decent interval had elapsed, and I asked if I might call on her, she answered at once that she would see me.

"I went to her house with the fixed intention of asking her to marry me—and I left it without having done so. Why? I don't know that I can tell you. Perhaps you would have had to sit there opposite her, knowing what I did and feeling as I did, to understand why. She was kind, she was compassionate—I could see she didn't want to make it hard for me. Perhaps she even wanted to make it easy. But there, between us, was the memory of the gesture I hadn't made, forever parodying the one I was attempting! There wasn't a word I could think of that hadn't an echo in it of words of hers I had been deaf to; there wasn't an appeal I could make that didn't mock the appeal I had rejected. I sat there and talked of her husband's death, of her plans, of my sympathy; and I knew she understood; and knowing that, in a way, made it harder.... The door-bell rang and the footman came in to ask if she would receive other visitors. She looked at me a moment and said 'Yes,' and I got up and shook hands and went away.

"A few days later she sailed for Europe, and the next time we met she had married Reardon...."

VI

It was long past midnight, and the terrier's hints became imperious.

Merrick rose from his chair, pushed back a fallen log and put up the fender. He walked across the room and stared a moment at the Brangwyn etching before which Paulina Trant had paused at a memorable turn of their talk. Then he came back and laid his hand on my shoulder.

"She summed it all up, you know, when she said that one way of finding out whether a risk is worth taking is *not* to take it, and then to see what one becomes in the long run, and draw one's inferences. The long run—well, we've run it, she and I. I know what I've become, but that's nothing to the misery of knowing what she's become. She had to have some kind of life, and she married Reardon. Reardon's a very good fellow in his way; but the worst of it is that it's not her way. . . .

"No: the worst of it is that now she and I meet as friends. We dine at the same houses, we talk about the same people, we play bridge together, and I lend her books. And sometimes Reardon slaps me on the back and says: 'Come in and dine with us, old man! What you want is to be cheered up!' And I go and dine with them, and he tells me how jolly comfortable she makes him, and what an ass I am not to marry; and she presses on me a second helping of *poulet Maryland,* and I smoke one of Reardon's cigars, and at half-past ten I get into my overcoat, and walk back alone to my rooms. . . ."

AFTER HOLBEIN

ANSON WARLEY had had his moments of being a rather re-markable man; but they were only intermittent; they recurred at ever-lengthening intervals; and between times he was a small poor creature, chattering with cold inside, in spite of his agreeable and even distinguished exterior.

He had always been perfectly aware of these two sides of himself (which, even in the privacy of his own mind, he con-temptuously refused to dub a dual personality); and as the rather remarkable man could take fairly good care of himself, most of Warley's attention was devoted to ministering to the poor wretch who took longer and longer turns at bearing his name, and was more and more insistent in accepting the invitations which New York, for over thirty years, had tirelessly poured out on him. It was in the interest of this lonely fidgety unemployed self that Warley, in his younger days, had frequented the gaudiest restaurants and the most glittering Palace Hotels of two hemispheres, subscribed to the most advanced literary and artistic reviews, bought the pic-tures of the young painters who were being the most vehemently discussed, missed few of the showiest first nights in New York, London or Paris, sought the company of the men and women—especially the women—most conspicuous in fashion, scandal, or any other form of social notoriety, and thus tried to warm the shivering soul within him at all the passing bonfires of success.

The original Anson Warley had begun by staying at home in his little flat, with his books and his thoughts, when the other poor creature went forth; but gradually—he hardly knew when or how—he had slipped into the way of going too, till finally he made the bitter discovery that he and the creature had become one, except on the increasingly rare occasions when, detaching himself from all casual contingencies, he mounted to the lofty water-shed which fed the sources of his scorn. The view from there was vast and glorious, the air was icy but exhilarating; but soon he began to find the place too lonely, and too difficult to get to, especially as the lesser Anson not only refused to go up with him but began to sneer, at first ever so faintly, then with increasing insolence, at this affectation of a taste for the heights.

"What's the use of scrambling up there, anyhow? I could understand it if you brought down anything worth-while—a poem or a picture of your own. But just climbing and staring: what does it lead to? Fellows with the creative gift have got to have their occasional Sinaïs; I can see that. But for a mere looker-on like you, isn't that sort of thing rather a pose? You talk awfully well—brilliantly, even (oh, my dear fellow, no false modesty between you and *me*, please!). But who the devil is there to listen to you, up there among the glaciers? And sometimes, when you come down, I notice that you're rather—well, heavy and tongue-tied. Look out, or they'll stop asking us to dine! And sitting at home every evening—brr! Look here, by the way; if you've got nothing better for tonight, come along with me to Chrissy Torrance's—or the Bob Briggses'—or Princess Kate's; anywhere where there's lots of racket and sparkle, places that people go to in Rollses, and that are smart and hot and overcrowded, and you have to pay a lot—in one way or another—to get in."

Once and again, it is true, Warley still dodged his double and slipped off on a tour to remote uncomfortable places, where there were churches or pictures to be seen, or shut himself up at home for a good bout of reading, or just, in sheer disgust at his companion's platitude, spent an evening with people who were doing or thinking real things. This happened seldomer than of old, however, and more clandestinely; so that at last he used to sneak away to spend two or three days with an archaeologically-minded friend, or an evening with a quiet scholar, as furtively as if he were stealing to a lover's tryst; which, as lovers' trysts were now always kept in the lime-light, was after all a fair exchange. But he always felt rather apologetic to the other Warley about these escapades—and, if the truth were known, rather bored and restless before they were over. And in the back of his mind there lurked an increasing dread of missing something hot and noisy and overcrowded when he went off to one of his mountain-tops. "After all, that high-brow business has been awfully overdone—now hasn't it?" the little Warley would insinuate, rummaging for his pearl studs, and consulting his flat evening watch as nervously as if it were a railway time-table. "If only we haven't missed something really jolly by all this backing and filling..."

"Oh, you poor creature, you! Always afraid of being left out, aren't you? Well—just for once, to humor you, and because I happen to be feeling rather stale myself. But only to think of a sane man's wanting to go to places just because they're hot and smart and overcrowded!" And off they would dash together...

II

All that was long ago. It was years now since there had been two distinct Anson Warleys. The lesser one had made away with the other, done him softly to death without shedding of blood; and only a few people suspected (and they no longer cared) that the pale white-haired man, with the small slim figure, the ironic smile and the perfect evening clothes, whom New York still indefatigably invited, was nothing less than a murderer.

Anson Warley—Anson Warley! No party was complete without Anson Warley. He no longer went abroad now; too stiff in the joints; and there had been two or three slight attacks of dizziness...Nothing to speak of, nothing to think of, even; but somehow one dug one's self into one's comfortable quarters, and felt less and less like moving out of them, except to motor down to Long Island for week-ends, or to Newport for a few visits in summer. A trip to the Hot Springs, to get rid of the stiffness, had not helped much, and the ageing Anson Warley (who really, otherwise, felt as young as ever) had developed a growing dislike for the promiscuities of hotel life and the monotony of hotel food.

Yes; he was growing more fastidious as he grew older. A good sign, he thought. Fastidious not only about food and comfort but about people also. It was still a privilege, a distinction, to have him to dine. His old friends were faithful, and the new people fought for him, and often failed to get him; to do so they had to offer very special inducements in the way of *cuisine*, conversation or beauty. Young beauty; yes, that would do it. He did like to sit and watch a lovely face, and call laughter into lovely eyes. But no dull dinners for *him*, not even if they fed you off gold. As to that he was as firm as the other Warley, the distant aloof one with whom he had—er, well, parted company, oh, quite amicably, a good many years ago…

On the whole, since that parting, life had been much easier and pleasanter; and by the time the little Warley was sixty-three he found himself looking forward with equanimity to an eternity of New York dinners.

Oh, but only at the right houses—always at the right houses; that was understood! The right people—the right setting—the right wines…He smiled a little over his perennial enjoyment of them; said "Nonsense, Filmore," to his devoted tiresome manservant, who was beginning to hint that really, every night, sir, and sometimes a dance afterward, was too much, especially when you kept at it for months on end; and Dr.—

"Oh, damn your doctors!" Warley snapped. He was seldom ill-tempered; he knew it was foolish and upsetting to lose one's self-control. But Filmore began to be a nuisance, nagging him, preaching at him. As if he himself wasn't the best judge…

Besides, he chose his company. He'd stay at home any time rather than risk a boring evening. Damned rot, what Filmore had said about his going out every night. Not like poor old Mrs. Jaspar, for instance…He smiled self-approvingly as he evoked her tottering image. "That's the kind of fool Filmore takes me for," he chuckled, his good-humor restored by an analogy that was so much to his advantage.

Poor old Evelina Jaspar! In his youth, and even in his prime, she had been New York's chief entertainer—"leading hostess," the newspapers called her. Her big house in Fifth Avenue had been an entertaining machine. She had lived, breathed, invested and reinvested her millions, to no other end. At first her pretext had been that she had to marry her daughters and amuse her sons; but when sons and daughters had married and left her she had seemed hardly aware of it; she had just gone on entertaining. Hundreds, no, thousands of dinners (on gold plate, of course, and with orchids, and all the delicacies that were out of season), had been served in that vast pompous dining-room, which one had only to close one's eyes to transform into a railway buffet for millionaires, at a big junction, before the invention of restaurant trains...

Warley closed his eyes, and did so picture it. He lost himself in amused computation of the annual number of guests, of saddles of mutton, of legs of lamb, of terrapin, canvas-backs, magnums of champagne and pyramids of hot-house fruit that must have passed through that room in the last forty years.

And even now, he thought—hadn't one of old Evelina's nieces told him the other day, half bantering, half shivering at the avowal, that the poor old lady, who was gently dying of softening of the brain, still imagined herself to be New York's leading hostess, still sent out invitations (which of course were never delivered), still ordered terrapin, champagne and orchids, and still came down every evening to her great shrouded drawing-rooms, with her tiara askew on her purple wig, to receive a stream of imaginary guests?

Rubbish, of course—a macabre pleasantry of the extravagant Nelly Pierce, who had always had her joke at Aunt Evelina's expense... But Warley could not help smiling at the thought that those dull monotonous dinners were still going on in their hostess's clouded imagination. Poor old Evelina, he thought! In a way she was right. There was really no reason why that kind of standardized entertaining should ever cease; a performance so undiscriminating, so undifferentiated, that one could almost imagine, in the hostess's tired brain, all the dinners she had ever given merging into one Gargantuan pyramid of food and drink, with the same faces, perpetually the same faces, gathered stolidly about the same gold plate.

Thank heaven, Anson Warley had never conceived of social values in terms of mass and volume. It was years since he had dined at Mrs. Jaspar's. He even felt that he was not above reproach in that respect. Two or three times, in the past, he had accepted her invitations (always sent out weeks ahead), and then chucked her at the eleventh hour for something more amusing. Finally, to avoid such risks, he had made it a rule always to refuse her dinners. He had even—he remembered—been rather funny about it once, when someone had told him that Mrs. Jaspar couldn't understand...was a little hurt...said it couldn't be true that he always had another engagement the nights she asked him..."*True*? Is the truth what she wants? All right! Then the next time I get a 'Mrs. Jaspar requests the pleasure' I'll answer it with a 'Mr. Warley declines the boredom.' Think she'll understand that, eh?" And the phrase became a catchword in his little set that winter. " 'Mr. Warley declines the boredom'—good, good, *good*!" "Dear Anson, I do hope you won't decline the boredom of coming to lunch next Sunday to meet the new Hindu Yoghi"—or the new saxophone soloist, or that genius of a mulatto boy who plays Negro spirituals on a toothbrush; and so on and so on. He only hoped poor old Evelina never heard of it...

"Certainly I shall *not* stay at home tonight—why, what's wrong with me?" he snapped, swinging round on Filmore.

The valet's long face grew longer. His way of answering such questions was always to pull out his face; it was his only means of putting any expression into it. He turned away into the bedroom, and Warley sat alone by his library fire... Now what did the man see that was wrong with him, he wondered? He had felt a little confusion that morning, when he was doing his daily sprint around the Park (his exercise was reduced to that!); but it had been only a passing flurry, of which Filmore could of course know nothing. And as soon as it was over his mind had seemed more lucid, his eye keener, than ever; as sometimes (he reflected) the electric light in his library lamps would blaze up too brightly after a break in the current, and he would say to himself, wincing a little at the sudden glare on the page he was reading: "That means that it'll go out again in a minute."

Yes; his mind, at that moment, had been quite piercingly clear and perceptive; his eye had passed with a renovating glitter over every detail of the daily scene. He stood still for a minute under the leafless trees of the Mall, and looking about him with the sudden insight of age, understood that he had reached the time of life when Alps and cathedrals become as transient as flowers.

Everything was fleeting, fleeting... yes, that was what had given him the vertigo. The doctors, poor fools, called it the stomach, or high blood-pressure; but it was only the dizzy plunge of the sands in the hour-glass, the everlasting plunge that emptied one of heart and bowels, like the drop of an elevator from the top floor of a sky-scraper.

Certainly, after that moment of revelation, he had felt a little more tired than usual for the rest of the day; the light had flagged in his mind as it sometimes did in his lamps. At Chrissy Torrance's, where he had lunched, they had accused him of being silent, his hostess had said that he looked pale; but he had retorted with a joke, and thrown himself into the talk with a feverish loquacity. It was the only thing to do; for he could not tell all these people at the lunch table that very morning he had arrived at the turn in the path from which mountains look as transient as flowers—and that one after another they would all arrive there too.

He leaned his head back and closed his eyes, but not in sleep. He did not feel sleepy, but keyed up and alert. In the next room he heard Filmore reluctantly, protestingly, laying out his evening clothes...He had no fear about the dinner tonight; a quiet intimate little affair at an old friend's house. Just two or three congenial men, and Elfmann, the pianist (who would probably play), and that lovely Elfrida Flight. The fact that people asked him to dine to meet Elfrida Flight seemed to prove pretty conclusively that he was still in the running! He chuckled softly at Filmore's pessimism, and thought: "Well, after all, I suppose no man seems young to his valet...Time to dress very soon," he thought; and luxuriously postponed getting up out of his chair...

III

"She's worse than usual tonight," said the day nurse, laying down the evening paper as her colleague joined her. "Absolutely determined to have her jewels out."

The night nurse, fresh from a long sleep and an afternoon at the movies with a gentleman friend, threw down her fancy bag, tossed off her hat and rumpled up her hair before old Mrs. Jaspar's tall toilet mirror. "Oh, I'll settle that—don't you worry," she said brightly.

"Don't you fret her, though, Miss Cress," said the other, getting wearily out of her chair. "We're very well off here, take it as a whole, and I don't want her pressure rushed up for nothing."

Miss Cress, still looking at herself in the glass, smiled reassuringly at Miss Dunn's pale reflection behind her. She and Miss Dunn got on very well together, and knew on which side their bread was buttered. But at the end of the day Miss Dunn was always fagged out and fearing the worst. The patient wasn't as hard to handle as all that. Just let her ring for her old maid, old Lavinia, and say: "My sapphire velvet tonight, with the diamond stars"— and Lavinia would know exactly how to manage her.

Miss Dunn had put on her hat and coat, and crammed her knitting, and the newspaper, into her bag, which, unlike Miss Cress's, was capacious and shabby; but she still loitered undecided on the threshold. "I could stay with you till ten as easy as not..."

She looked almost reluctantly about the big high-studded dressing-room (everything in the house was high-studded), with its rich dusky carpet and curtains, and its monumental dressing-table draped with lace and laden with gold-backed brushes and combs, gold-stoppered toilet-bottles, and all the charming paraphernalia of beauty at her glass. Old Lavinia even renewed every morning the roses and carnations in the slim crystal vases between the powder boxes and the nail polishers. Since the family had shut down the hot-houses at the uninhabited country place on the Hudson, Miss Cress suspected that old Lavinia bought these flowers out of her own pocket.

"Cold out tonight?" queried Miss Dunn from the door.

"Fierce... Reg'lar blizzard at the corners. Say, shall I lend you my fur scarf?" Miss Cress, pleased with the memory of her afternoon (they'd be engaged soon, she thought), and with the drowsy prospect of an evening in a deep armchair near the warm gleam of the dressing-room fire, was disposed to kindliness toward that poor thin Dunn girl, who supported her mother, and her brother's idiot twins. And she wanted Miss Dunn to notice her new fur.

"My! Isn't it too lovely? No, not for worlds, thank you..." Her hand on the door-knob, Miss Dunn repeated: "Don't you cross her now," and was gone.

Lavinia's bell rang furiously, twice; then the door between the dressing-room and Mrs. Jaspar's bedroom opened, and Mrs. Jaspar herself emerged.

"Lavinia!" she called, in a high irritated voice; then, seeing the nurse, who had slipped into her print dress and starched cap, she added in a lower tone: "Oh, Miss Lemoine, good evening." Her first nurse, it appeared, had been called Miss Lemoine; and she gave the same name to all the others, quite unaware that there had been any changes in the staff.

"I heard talking, and carriages driving up. Have people begun to arrive?" she asked nervously. "Where is Lavinia? I still have my jewels to put on."

She stood before the nurse, the same petrifying apparition

which always, at this hour, struck Miss Cress to silence. Mrs. Jaspar was tall; she had been broad; and her bones remained impressive though the flesh had withered on them. Lavinia had encased her, as usual, in her low-necked purple velvet dress, nipped in at the waist in the old-fashioned way, expanding in voluminous folds about the hips and flowing in a long train over the darker velvet of the carpet. Mrs. Jaspar's swollen feet could no longer be pushed into the high-heeled satin slippers which went with the dress; but her skirts were so long and spreading that, by taking short steps, she managed (so Lavinia daily assured her) entirely to conceal the broad round tips of her black orthopedic shoes.

"Your jewels, Mrs. Jaspar? Why, you've got them on," said Miss Cress brightly.

Mrs. Jaspar turned her porphyry-tinted face to Miss Cress, and looked at her with a glassy incredulous gaze. Her eyes, Miss Cress thought, were the worst...She lifted one old hand, veined and knobbed as a raised map, to her elaborate purple-black wig, groped among the puffs and curls and undulations (queer, Miss Cress thought, that it never occurred to her to look into the glass), and after an interval affirmed: "You must be mistaken, my dear. Don't you think you ought to have your eyes examined?"

The door opened again, and a very old woman, so old as to make Mrs. Jaspar appear almost young, hobbled in with sidelong steps. "Excuse me, madam. I was downstairs when the bell rang."

Lavinia had probably always been small and slight; now, beside her towering mistress, she looked a mere feather, a straw. Everything about her had dried, contracted, been volatilized into nothingness, except her watchful gray eyes, in which intelligence and comprehension burned like two fixed stars. "Do excuse me, madam," she repeated.

Mrs. Jaspar looked at her despairingly. "I hear carriages driving up. And Miss Lemoine says I have my jewels on; and I know I haven't."

"With that lovely necklace!" Miss Cress ejaculated.

Mrs. Jaspar's twisted hand rose again, this time to her denuded shoulders, which were as stark and barren as the rock from which the hand might have been broken. She felt and felt, and tears rose in her eyes ...

"Why do you lie to me?" she burst out passionately.

Lavinia softly intervened. "Miss Lemoine meant, how lovely you'll be when you get the necklace on, madam."

"Diamonds, diamonds," said Mrs. Jaspar with an awful smile.

"Of course, madam."

Mrs. Jaspar sat down at the dressing-table, and Lavinia, with eager random hands, began to adjust the *point de Venise* about her mistress's shoulders, and to repair the havoc wrought in the purple-black wig by its wearer's gropings for her tiara.

"Now you do look lovely, madam," she sighed.

Mrs. Jaspar was on her feet again, stiff but incredibly active. ("Like a cat she is," Miss Cress used to relate.) "I do hear carriages —or is it an automobile? The Magraws, I know, have one of those new-fangled automobiles. And now I hear the front door opening. Quick, Lavinia! My fan, my gloves, my handkerchief ... how often have I got to tell you? I used to have a *perfect* maid—"

Lavinia's eyes brimmed. "That was me, madam," she said, bending to straighten out the folds of the long purple velvet train. ("To watch the two of 'em," Miss Cress used to tell a circle of appreciative friends, "is a lot better than any circus.")

Mrs. Jaspar paid no attention. She twitched the train out of Lavinia's vacillating hold, swept to the door, and then paused there as if stopped by a jerk of her constricted muscles. "Oh, but my diamonds—you cruel woman, you! You're letting me go down without my diamonds!" Her ruined face puckered up in a grimace like a new-born baby's, and she began to sob despairingly. "Everybody ... Every ... body's ... against me ..." she wept in her powerless misery.

Lavinia helped herself to her feet and tottered across the floor. It was almost more than she could bear to see her mistress in distress. "Madam, madam—if you'll just wait till they're got out of the safe," she entreated.

The woman she saw before her, the woman she was entreating and consoling, was not the old petrified Mrs. Jaspar with porphyry face and wig awry whom Miss Cress stood watching with a smile, but a young proud creature, commanding and splendid in her Paris gown of amber *moiré*, who, years ago, had burst into just such furious sobs because, as she was sweeping down to receive her guests, the doctor had told her that little Grace, with whom she had been playing all the afternoon, had a diphtheritic throat, and no one must be allowed to enter. "Everybody's against me, everybody..." she had sobbed in her fury; and the young Lavinia, stricken by such Olympian anger, had stood speechless, longing to comfort her, and secretly indignant with little Grace and the doctor...

"If you'll just wait, madam, while I go down and ask Munson to open the safe. There's no one come yet, I do assure you..."

Munson was the old butler, the only person who knew the combination of the safe in Mrs. Jaspar's bedroom. Lavinia had once known it too, but now she was no longer able to remember it. The worst of it was that she feared lest Munson, who had been spending the day in the Bronx, might not have returned. Munson was growing old too, and he did sometimes forget about these dinner-parties of Mrs. Jaspar's, and then the stupid footman, George, had to announce the names; and you couldn't be sure that Mrs. Jaspar wouldn't notice Munson's absence, and be excited and angry. These dinner-party nights were killing old Lavinia, and she did so want to keep alive; she wanted to live long enough to wait on Mrs. Jaspar to the last.

She disappeared, and Miss Cress poked up the fire, and persuaded Mrs. Jaspar to sit down in an armchair and "tell her who was coming." It always amused Mrs. Jaspar to say over the long list of her guests' names, and generally she remembered them fairly well, for they were always the same—the last people, Lavinia and Munson said, who had dined at the house, on the very night before her stroke. With recovered complacency she began, counting over one after another on her ring-laden fingers: "The Italian Ambassador, the Bishop, Mr. and Mrs. Torrington Bligh, Mr. and

Mrs. Fred Amesworth, Mr. and Mrs. Mitchell Magraw, Mr. and Mrs. Torrington Bligh..." ("You've said them before," Miss Cress interpolated, getting out her fancy knitting—a necktie for her friend—and beginning to count the stitches.) And Mrs. Jaspar, distressed and bewildered by the interruption, had to repeat over and over: "Torrington Bligh, Torrington Bligh," till the connection was re-established, and she went on again swimmingly with "Mr. and Mrs. Fred Amesworth, Mr. and Mrs. Mitchell Magraw, Miss Laura Ladew, Mr. Harold Ladew, Mr. and Mrs. Benjamin Bronx, Mr. and Mrs. Torrington Bl—no, I mean, Mr. Anson Warley. Yes, Mr. Anson Warley; that's it," she ended complacently.

Miss Cress smiled and interrupted her counting. "No, that's *not* it."

"What do you mean, my dear—not it?"

"Mr. Anson Warley. He's not coming."

Mrs. Jaspar's jaw fell, and she stared at the nurse's coldly smiling face. "Not coming?"

"No. He's not coming. He's not on the list." (That old list! As if Miss Cress didn't know it by heart! Everybody in the house did, except the booby, George, who heard it reeled off every other night by Munson, and who was always stumbling over the names, and having to refer to the written paper.)

"Not on the list?" Mrs. Jaspar gasped.

Miss Cress shook her pretty head.

Signs of uneasiness gathered on Mrs. Jaspar's face and her lip began to tremble. It always amused Miss Cress to give her these little jolts, though she knew Miss Dunn and the doctors didn't approve of her doing so. She knew also that it was against her own interests, and she did try to bear in mind Miss Dunn's oft-repeated admonition about not sending up the patient's blood-pressure; but when she was in high spirits, as she was tonight (they would certainly be engaged), it was irresistible to get a rise out of the old lady. And she thought it funny, this new figure unexpectedly appearing among those time-worn guests. ("I wonder what the rest of 'em 'll say to him," she giggled inwardly.)

"No; he's not on the list." Mrs. Jaspar, after pondering deeply, announced the fact with an air of recovered composure.

"That's what I told you," snapped Miss Cress.

"He's not on the list; but he promised me to come. I saw him yesterday," continued Mrs. Jaspar, mysteriously.

"You *saw* him—where?"

She considered. "Last night, at the Fred Amesworths' dance."

"Ah," said Miss Cress, with a little shiver; for she knew that Mrs. Amesworth was dead, and she was the intimate friend of the trained nurse who was keeping alive, by dint of *piqûres* and high frequency, the inarticulate and inanimate Mr. Amesworth. "It's funny," she remarked to Mrs. Jaspar, "that you'd never invited Mr. Warley before."

"No, I hadn't; not for a long time. I believe he felt I'd neglected him; for he came up to me last night, and said he was so sorry he hadn't been able to call. It seems he's been ill, poor fellow. Not as young as he was! So of course I invited him. He was very much gratified."

Mrs. Jaspar smiled at the remembrance of her little triumph; but Miss Cress's attention had wandered, as it always did when the patient became docile and reasonable. She thought: "Where's old Lavinia? I bet she can't find Munson." And she got up and crossed the floor to look into Mrs. Jaspar's bedroom, where the safe was.

There an astonishing sight met her. Munson, as she had expected, was nowhere visible; but Lavinia, on her knees before the safe, was in the act of opening it herself, her twitching hand slowly moving about the mysterious dial.

"Why, I thought you'd forgotten the combination!" Miss Cress exclaimed.

Lavinia turned a startled face over her shoulder. "So I had, Miss. But I've managed to remember it, thank God. I *had* to, you see, because Munson's forgot to come home."

"Oh," said the nurse incredulously. ("Old fox," she thought, "I wonder why she's always pretended she'd forgotten it.") For Miss Cress did not know that the age of miracles is not yet past.

Joyous, trembling, her cheeks wet with grateful tears, the little old woman was on her feet again, clutching to her breast the diamond stars, the necklace of *solitaires*, the tiara, the earrings. One by one she spread them out on the velvet-lined tray in which they always used to be carried from the safe to the dressing-room; then, with rambling fingers, she managed to lock the safe again, and put the keys in the drawer where they belonged, while Miss Cress continued to stare at her in amazement. "I don't believe the old witch is as shaky as she makes out," was her reflection as Lavinia passed her, bearing the jewels to the dressing-room where Mrs. Jaspar, lost in pleasant memories, was still computing: "The Italian Ambassador, the Bishop, the Torrington Blighs, the Mitchell Magraws, the Fred Amesworths..."

Mrs. Jaspar was allowed to go down to the drawing-room alone on dinner-party evenings because it would have mortified her too much to receive her guests with a maid or a nurse at her elbow; but Miss Cress and Lavinia always leaned over the stair-rail to watch her descent, and make sure it was accomplished in safety.

"She do look lovely yet, when all her diamonds is on," Lavinia sighed, her purblind eyes bedewed with memories, as the bedizened wig and purple velvet disappeared at the last bend of the stairs. Miss Cress, with a shrug, turned back to the fire and picked up her knitting, while Lavinia set about the slow ritual of tidying up her mistress's room. From below they heard the sound of George's stentorian monologue: "Mr. and Mrs. Torrington Bligh, Mr. and Mrs. Mitchell Magraw...Mr. Ladew, Miss Laura Ladew..."

IV

Anson Warley, who had always prided himself on his equable temper, was conscious of being on edge that evening. But it was an irritability which did not frighten him (in spite of what those doctors always said about the importance of keeping calm) because he knew it was due merely to the unusual lucidity of his mind. He was in fact feeling uncommonly well, his brain clear and all his perceptions so alert that he could positively hear the thoughts passing through his man-servant's mind on the other side of the door, as Filmore grudgingly laid out the evening clothes.

Smiling at the man's obstinacy, he thought: "I shall have to tell them tonight that Filmore thinks I'm no longer fit to go into society." It was always pleasant to hear the incredulous laugh with which his younger friends received any allusion to his supposed senility. "What, *you*? Well, that's a good one!" And he thought it was, himself.

And then, the moment he was in his bedroom, dressing, the sight of Filmore made him lose his temper again. "No; *not* those studs, confound it. The black onyx ones—haven't I told you a hundred times? Lost them, I suppose? Sent them to the wash again in a soiled shirt? That it?" He laughed nervously, and sitting down before his dressing-table began to brush back his hair with short angry strokes.

"Above all," he shouted out suddenly, "don't stand there staring at me as if you were watching to see exactly at what minute to telephone for the undertaker!"

"The under—? Oh, sir!" gasped Filmore.

"The—the—damn it, are you *deaf* too? Who said undertaker? I said *taxi*; can't you hear what I say?"

"You want me to call a taxi, sir?"

"No; I don't. I've already told you so. I'm going to walk." Warley straightened his tie, rose and held out his arms toward his dress-coat.

"It's bitter cold, sir; better let me call a taxi all the same."

Warley gave a short laugh. "Out with it, now! What you'd really like to suggest is that I should telephone to say I can't dine out. You'd scramble me some eggs instead, eh?"

"I wish you would stay in, sir. There's eggs in the house."

"My overcoat," snapped Warley.

"Or else let me call a taxi; now do, sir."

Warley slipped his arms into his overcoat, tapped his chest to see if his watch (the thin evening watch) and his note-case were in their proper pockets, turned back to put a dash of lavender on his handkerchief, and walked with stiff quick steps toward the front door of his flat.

Filmore, abashed, preceded him to ring for the lift; and then, as it quivered upward through the long shaft, said again: "It's a bitter cold night, sir; and you've had a good deal of exercise today."

Warley leveled a contemptuous glance at him. "Daresay that's why I'm feeling so fit," he retorted as he entered the lift.

It *was* bitter cold; the icy air hit him in the chest when he stepped out of the overheated building, and he halted on the door-step and took a long breath. "Filmore's missed his vocation; ought to be nurse to a paralytic," he thought. "He'd love to have to wheel me about in a chair."

After the first shock of the biting air he began to find it exhilarating, and walked along at a good pace, dragging one leg ever so little after the other. (The *masseur* had promised him that he'd soon be rid of that stiffness.) Yes—decidedly a fellow like himself ought to have a younger valet; a more cheerful one, anyhow. He felt like a young'un himself this evening; as he turned into Fifth Avenue he rather wished he could meet some one he knew, some man who'd say afterward at his club: "Warley? Why, I saw him sprinting up Fifth Avenue the other night like a two-year-old; that night it was four or five below..." He needed a good counter-irritant for Filmore's gloom. "Always have young people about you," he thought as he walked along; and at the words his mind turned to Elfrida Flight, next to whom he would soon be sitting in a warm pleasantly lit dining-room—*where*?

It came as abruptly as that: the gap in his memory. He pulled up at it as if his advance had been checked by a chasm in the pavement at his feet. Where the dickens was he going to dine? And with whom was he going to dine? God! But things didn't happen in that way; a sound strong man didn't suddenly have to stop in the middle of the street and ask himself where he was going to dine...

"Perfect in mind, body and understanding." The old legal phrase bobbed up inconsequently into his thoughts. Less than two minutes ago he had answered in every particular to that description; what was he now? He put his hand to his forehead, which was bursting; then he lifted his hat and let the cold air blow for a while on his overheated temples. It was queer, how hot he'd got, walking. Fact was, he'd been sprinting along at a damned good pace. In future he must try to remember not to hurry... Hang it—one more thing to remember!... Well, but what was all the fuss about? Of course, as people got older their memories were subject to these momentary lapses; he'd noticed it often enough among his contemporaries. And, brisk and alert though he still was, it wouldn't do to imagine himself totally exempt from human ills...

Where was it he was dining? Why, somewhere farther up Fifth Avenue; he was perfectly sure of that. With that lovely... that lovely... No; better not make any effort for the moment. Just keep calm, and stroll slowly along. When he came to the right street corner of course he'd spot it; and then everything would be perfectly clear again. He walked on, more deliberately, trying to empty his mind of all thoughts. "Above all," he said to himself, "don't worry."

He tried to beguile his nervousness by thinking of amusing things. "Decline the boredom—" He thought he might get off that joke tonight. "Mrs. Jaspar requests the pleasure—Mr. Warley declines the boredom." Not so bad, really; and he had an idea he'd never told it to the people... what in hell *was* their name?... the people he was on his way to dine with... *Mrs. Jaspar requests the pleasure.* Poor old Mrs. Jaspar; again it occurred to him that he hadn't always been very civil to her in old times. When everybody's running after a fellow it's pardonable now and then to chuck a boring dinner at the last minute; but all the same, as one grew older one understood better how an unintentional slight of that sort might cause offense, cause even pain. And he hated to cause people pain... He thought perhaps he'd better call on Mrs.

Jaspar some afternoon. She'd be surprised! Or ring her up, poor old girl, and propose himself, just informally, for dinner. One dull evening wouldn't kill him—and how pleased she'd be! Yes—he thought decidedly... When he got to be her age, he could imagine how much he'd like it if somebody still in the running should ring him up unexpectedly and say—

He stopped, and looked up, slowly, wonderingly, at the wide illuminated façade of the house he was approaching. Queer coincidence—it was the Jaspar house. And all lit up; for a dinner evidently. And that was queerer yet; almost uncanny; for here he was, in front of the door, as the clock struck a quarter past eight; and of course—he remembered it quite clearly now—it was just here, it was with Mrs. Jaspar, that he was dining... Those little lapses of memory never lasted more than a second or two. How right he'd been not to let himself worry. He pressed his hand on the door-bell.

"God," he thought, as the double doors swung open, "but it's good to get in out of the cold."

V

In that hushed sonorous house the sound of the door-bell was as loud to the two women upstairs as if it had been rung in the next room.

Miss Cress raised her head in surprise, and Lavinia dropped Mrs. Jaspar's other false set (the more comfortable one) with a clatter on the marble wash-stand. She stumbled across the dressing-room, and hastened out to the landing. With Munson absent, there was no knowing how George might muddle things...

Miss Cress joined her. "Who is it?" she whispered excitedly. Below, they heard the sound of a hat and a walking stick being laid down on the big marble-topped table in the hall, and then George's stentorian drone: "Mr. Anson Warley."

"It is—it *is*! I can see him—a gentleman in evening clothes," Miss Cress whispered, hanging over the stair-rail.

"Good gracious—mercy me! And Munson not here! Oh, whatever, whatever shall we do?" Lavinia was trembling so violently that she had to clutch the stair-rail to prevent herself from falling. Miss Cress thought, with her cold lucidity: "She's a good deal sicker than the old woman."

"What shall we do, Miss Cress? That fool of a George—he's showing him in! Who could have thought it?" Miss Cress knew the images that were whirling through Lavinia's brain: the vision of Mrs. Jaspar's having another stroke at the sight of this mysterious intruder, of Mr. Anson Warley's seeing her there, in her impotence and her abasement, of the family's being summoned, and rushing in to exclaim, to question, to be horrified and furious—and all because poor old Munson's memory was going, like his mistress's, like Lavinia's, and because he had forgotten that it was one of the *dinner nights.* Oh, misery!... The tears were running down Lavinia's cheeks, and Miss Cress knew she was thinking: "If the daughters send him off—and they will—where's he going to, old and deaf as he is, and all his people dead? Oh, if only he can hold on till she dies, and get his pension..."

Lavinia recovered herself with one of her supreme efforts. "Miss Cress, we must go down at once, at once! Something dreadful's going to happen..." She began to totter toward the little velvet-lined lift in the corner of the landing.

Miss Cress took pity on her. "Come along," she said. "But nothing dreadful's going to happen. You'll see."

"Oh, thank you, Miss Cress. But the shock—the awful shock to her—of seeing that strange gentleman walk in."

"Not a bit of it." Miss Cress laughed as she stepped into the lift. "He's not a stranger. She's expecting him."

"Expecting him? Expecting Mr. Warley?"

"Sure she is. She told me so just now. She says she invited him yesterday."

"But, Miss Cress, what are you thinking of? Invite him—how? When you know she can't write nor telephone?"

"Well, she says she saw him; she saw him last night at a dance."

"Oh, God," murmured Lavinia, covering her eyes with her hands.

"At a dance at the Fred Amesworths'—that's what she said," Miss Cress pursued, feeling the same little shiver run down her back as when Mrs. Jaspar had made the statement to her.

"The Amesworths—oh, not the Amesworths?" Lavinia echoed, shivering too. She dropped her hands from her face, and followed Miss Cress out of the lift. Her expression had become less anguished, and the nurse wondered why. In reality, she was thinking, in a sort of dreary beatitude: "But if she's suddenly got as much worse as this, she'll go before me, after all, my poor lady, and I'll be able to see to it that she's properly laid out and dressed, and nobody but Lavinia's hands'll touch her."

"You'll see—if she was expecting him, as she says, it won't give her a shock, anyhow. Only, how did *he* know?" Miss Cress whispered, with an acuter renewal of her shiver. She followed Lavinia with muffled steps down the passage to the pantry, and from there the two women stole into the dining-room, and placed themselves noiselessly at its farther end, behind the tall Coromandel screen through the cracks of which they could peep into the empty room.

The long table was set, as Mrs. Jaspar always insisted that it should be on these occasions; but old Munson not having returned, the gold plate (which his mistress also insisted on) had not been got out, and all down the table, as Lavinia saw with horror, George had laid the coarse blue and white plates from the servants' hall. The electric wall-lights were on, and the candles lit in the branching Sèvres candelabra—so much at least had been done. But the flowers in the great central dish of Rose Dubarry porcelain, and in the smaller dishes which accompanied it—the flowers, oh shame, had been forgotten! They were no longer real flowers; the family had long since suppressed that expense; and no wonder, for Mrs. Jaspar always insisted on orchids. But Grace, the youngest daughter, who was the kindest, had hit on the clever device of arranging three beautiful clusters of artificial orchids and

maiden-hair, which had only to be lifted from their shelf in the
pantry and set in the dishes—only, of course, that imbecile footman had forgotten, or had not known where to find them. And,
oh, horror, realizing his oversight too late, no doubt, to appeal to
Lavinia, he had taken some old newspapers and bunched them up
into something that he probably thought resembled a bouquet,
and crammed one into each of the priceless Rose Dubarry dishes.

Lavinia clutched at Miss Cress's arm. "Oh, look—look what
he's done; I shall die of the shame of it . . . Oh, Miss, hadn't we better slip around to the drawing-room and try to coax my poor lady
upstairs again, afore she ever notices?"

Miss Cress, peering through the crack of the screen, could
hardly suppress a giggle. For at that moment the double doors of
the dining-room were thrown open, and George, shuffling about in
a baggy livery inherited from a long-departed predecessor of more
commanding build, bawled out in his loud sing-song: "Dinner is
served, madam."

"Oh, it's too late," moaned Lavinia. Miss Cress signed to her to
keep silent, and the two watchers glued their eyes to their respec-
tive cracks of the screen.

What they saw, far off down the vista of empty drawing-rooms,
and after an interval during which (as Lavinia knew) the imaginary guests were supposed to file in and take their seats, was the
entrance, at the end of the ghostly cortège, of a very old woman,
still tall and towering, on the arm of a man somewhat smaller
than herself, with a fixed smile on a darkly pink face, and a slim
erect figure clad in perfect evening clothes, who advanced with
short measured steps, profiting (Miss Cress noticed) by the support of the arm he was supposed to sustain. "Well—I never!" was
the nurse's inward comment.

The couple continued to advance, with rigid smiles and eyes
staring straight ahead. Neither turned to the other, neither spoke.
All their attention was concentrated on the immense, the almost
unachievable effort of reaching that point, half-way down the
long dinner table, opposite the big Dubarry dish, where George

was drawing back a gilt armchair for Mrs. Jaspar. At last they reached it, and Mrs. Jaspar seated herself, and waved a stony hand to Mr. Warley. "On my right." He gave a little bow, like the bend of a jointed doll, and with infinite precaution let himself down into his chair. Beads of perspiration were standing on his forehead, and Miss Cress saw him draw out his handkerchief and wipe them stealthily away. He then turned his head somewhat stiffly toward his hostess.

"Beautiful flowers," he said, with great precision and perfect gravity, waving his hand toward the bunched-up newspaper in the bowl of Sèvres.

Mrs. Jaspar received the tribute with complacency. "So glad... orchids... From High Lawn... every morning," she simpered.

"Mar-velous," Mr. Warley completed.

"I always say to the Bishop..." Mrs. Jaspar continued.

"Ha—of course," Mr. Warley warmly assented.

"Not that I don't think..."

"Ha—rather!"

George had reappeared from the pantry with a blue crockery dish of mashed potatoes. This he handed in turn to one after another of the imaginary guests, and finally presented to Mrs. Jaspar and her right-hand neighbor.

They both helped themselves cautiously, and Mrs. Jaspar addressed an arch smile to Mr. Warley. "'Nother month—no more oysters."

"Ha—no more!"

George, with a bottle of Apollinaris wrapped in a napkin, was saying to each guest in turn: "Perrier-Jouet, 'ninety-five." (He had picked that up, thought Miss Cress, from hearing old Munson repeat it so often.)

"Hang it—well, then just a sip," murmured Mr. Warley.

"Old times," bantered Mrs. Jaspar; and the two turned to each other and bowed their heads and touched glasses.

"I often tell Mrs. Amesworth..." Mrs. Jaspar continued, bending to an imaginary presence across the table.

"Ha—*ha!*" Mr. Warley approved.

George reappeared and slowly encircled the table with a dish of spinach. After the spinach the Apollinaris also went the rounds again, announced successively as Château Lafite, 'seventy-four, and "the old Newbold Madeira." Each time that George approached his glass, Mr. Warley made a feint of lifting a defensive hand, and then smiled and yielded. "Might as well—hanged for a sheep . . ." he remarked gaily; and Mrs. Jaspar giggled.

Finally a dish of Malaga grapes and apples was handed. Mrs. Jaspar, now growing perceptibly languid, and nodding with more and more effort at Mr. Warley's pleasantries, transferred a bunch of grapes to her plate, but nibbled only two or three. "Tired," she said suddenly, in a whimper like a child's; and she rose, lifting herself up by the arms of her chair, and leaning over to catch the eye of an invisible lady, presumably Mrs. Amesworth, seated opposite to her. Mr. Warley was on his feet too, supporting himself by resting one hand on the table in a jaunty attitude. Mrs. Jaspar waved to him to be re-seated. "Join us—after cigars," she smilingly ordained; and with a great and concentrated effort he bowed to her as she passed toward the double doors which George was throwing open. Slowly, majestically, the purple velvet train disappeared down the long enfilade of illuminated rooms, and the last door closed behind her.

"Well, I do believe she's enjoyed it!" chuckled Miss Cress, taking Lavinia by the arm to help her back to the hall. Lavinia, for weeping, could not answer.

VI

Anson Warley found himself in the hall again, getting into his fur-lined overcoat. He remembered suddenly thinking that the rooms had been intensely over-heated, and that all the other guests had talked very loud and laughed inordinately. "Very good talk though, I must say," he had to acknowledge.

In the hall, as he got his arms into his coat (rather a job, too, after that Perrier-Jouet) he remembered saying to somebody (perhaps it was to the old butler): "Slipping off early—going on; 'nother engagement," and thinking to himself the while that when he got out into the fresh air again he would certainly remember where the other engagement was. He smiled a little while the servant, who seemed a clumsy fellow, fumbled with the fastening of the door. "And Filmore, who thought I wasn't even well enough to dine out! Damned ass! What would he say if he knew I was going on?"

The door opened, and with an immense sense of exhilaration Mr. Warley issued forth from the house and drew in a first deep breath of night air. He heard the door closed and bolted behind him, and continued to stand motionless on the step, expanding his chest, and drinking in the icy draft.

"'Spose it's about the last house where they give you 'ninety-five Perrier-Jouet," he thought; and then: "Never heard better talk either…"

He smiled again with satisfaction at the memory of the wine and the wit. Then he took a step forward, to where a moment before the pavement had been—and where now there was nothing.

DIAGNOSIS

"NOTHING to worry about—absolutely nothing. Of course not...just what they all say!" Paul Dorrance walked away from his writing-table to the window of his high-perched flat. The window looked south, over the crowded towering New York below Wall Street which was the visible center and symbol of his life's work. He drew a great breath of relief—for under his surface incredulity a secret reassurance was slowly beginning to unfold. The two eminent physicians he had just seen had told him he would be all right again in a few months; that his dark fears were delusions; that all he needed was to get away from work till he had recovered his balance of body and brain. Dorrance had smiled acquiescence and muttered inwardly: "Infernal humbugs: as if I didn't know how I felt!"; yet hardly a quarter of an hour later their words had woven magic passes about him, and with a timid avidity he had surrendered to the sense of returning life. "By George, I *do* feel better," he muttered, and swung about to this desk, remembering he had not breakfasted. The first time in months that he had remembered that! He touched the bell at his elbow, and with a half-apologetic smile told his servant that...well, yes... the doctors said he ought to eat more....Perhaps he'd have an egg or two with his coffee...yes, with bacon....He chafed with impatience till the tray was brought.

Breakfast over, he glanced through the papers with the leisurely eye of a man before whom the human comedy is likely to go on unrolling itself for many years. "Nothing to be in a hurry about, after all," was his half-conscious thought. That line which had so haunted him lately, about "Time's wingèd chariot," relapsed into the region of pure aesthetics, now that in his case the wings were apparently to be refurled. "No reason whatever why you shouldn't live to be an old man." That was pleasant hearing, at forty-nine. What did they call an old man, nowadays? He had always imagined that he shouldn't care to live to be an old man: now he began by asking himself what he understood by the term "old." Nothing that applied to himself, certainly; even if he were to be mysteriously metamorphosed into an old man at some far distant day— what then? It was too far off to visualize, it did not affect his imagination. Why, old age no longer began short of seventy; almost every day the papers told of hearty old folk celebrating their hundredth birthdays—sometimes by remarriage. Dorrance lost himself in pleasant musings over the increased longevity of the race, evoking visions of contemporaries of his grandparents, infirm and toothless at an age which found their descendants still carnivorous and alert.

The papers read, his mind drifted agreeably among the rich possibilities of travel. A busy man ordered to interrupt his work could not possibly stay in New York. Names suggestive of idleness and summer clothes floated before him: the West Indies, the Canaries, Morocco—why not Morocco, where he had never been? And from there he could work his way up through Spain. He rose to reach for a volume from the shelves where his travel books were ranged—but as he stood fluttering its pages, in a state of almost thoughtless beatitude, something twitched him out of his dream. "I suppose I ought to tell her—" he said aloud.

Certainly he ought to tell her; but the mere thought let loose a landslide of complications, obligations, explanations ... their suffocating descent made him gasp for breath. He leaned against the desk, closing his eyes.

But of course she would understand. The doctors said he was going to be all right—that would be enough for her. She would see the necessity of his going away for some months; a year perhaps. She couldn't go with him; that was certain! So what was there to make a fuss about? Gradually, insidiously, there stole into his mind the thought—at first a mere thread of a suggestion—that this might be the moment to let her see, oh, ever so gently, that things couldn't go on forever—nothing did—and that, at his age, and with this new prospect of restored health, a man might reasonably be supposed to have his own views, his own plans; might think of marriage; marriage with a young girl; children; a place in the country...his mind wandered into that dream as it had into the dream of travel....

Well, meanwhile he must let her know what the diagnosis was. She had been awfully worried about him, he knew, though all along she had kept up so bravely. (Should he, in the independence of his recovered health, confess under his breath that her celebrated "braveness" sometimes got a little on his nerves?) Yes, it had been hard for her; harder than for anyone; he owed it to her to tell her at once that everything was all right; all right as far as *he* was concerned. And in her beautiful unselfishness nothing else would matter to her—at first. Poor child! He could hear her happy voice! "Really—really and truly? They both said so? You're *sure*? Oh, of course I've always known...haven't I always told you?" Bless her, yes; but he'd known all along what she was thinking....He turned to the desk, and took up the telephone.

As he did so, his glance lit on a sheet of paper on the rug at his feet. He had keen eyes: he saw at once that the letterhead bore the name of the eminent consultant whom his own physician had brought in that morning. Perhaps the paper was one of the three or four prescriptions they had left with him; a chance gust from door or window might have snatched it from the table where the others lay. He stooped and picked it up—

That was the truth, then. That paper on the floor held his fate. The two doctors had written out their diagnosis, and forgotten to pocket it when they left. There were their two signatures; and the date. There was no mistake....Paul Dorrance sat for a long time with the paper on the desk before him. He propped his chin on his locked hands, shut his eyes, and tried to grope his way through the illimitable darkness. . . .

Anything, anything but the sights and sounds of the world outside! If he had had the energy to move he would have jumped up, drawn the curtains shut, and cowered in his armchair in absolute blackness till he could come to some sort of terms with this new reality—for him henceforth the sole reality. For what did anything matter now except that he was doomed—was dying? That these two scoundrels had known it, and had lied to him? And that, having lied to him, in their callous professional haste, they had tossed his death sentence down before him, forgotten to carry it away, left it there staring up at him from the floor?

Yes; it would be easier to bear in a pitch-black room, a room from which all sights and sounds, all suggestions of life, were excluded. But the effort of getting up to draw the curtains was too great. It was easier to go on sitting there, in the darkness created by pressing his fists against his lids. "Now, then, my good fellow— this is what it'll be like in the grave. . . ."

Yes; but if he had known the grave was *there*, so close, so all-including, so infinitely more important and real than any of the trash one had tossed the years away for; if somebody had told him . . . he might have done a good many things differently, put matters in a truer perspective, discriminated, selected, weighed. . . . Or, no! A thousand times no! Be beaten like that? Go slinking off to his grave before it was dug for him? His folly had been that he had not packed enough into life; that he had always been sorting, discriminating, trying for a perspective, choosing, weighing—God! When there was barely time to seize life before the cup that held it was cracked, and gulp it down while you had a throat that could swallow!

Ah, well—no use in retrospection. What was done was done: what undone must remain so to all eternity. Eternity—what did the word mean? How could the least fringe of its meaning be grasped by ephemeral creatures groping blindly through a few short years to the grave? Ah, the pity of it—pity, pity! That was the feeling that rose to the surface of his thoughts. Pity for all the millions of blind gropers like himself, the millions and millions who thought themselves alive, as he had, and suddenly found themselves dead: as he had! Poor mortals all, with that seed of annihilation that made them brothers—how he longed to help them, how he winced at the thought that he must so often have hurt them, brushing by in his fatuous vitality! How many other lives had he used up in his short span of living? Not consciously, of course—that was the worst of it! The old nurse who had slaved for him when he was a child, and then vanished from his life, to be found again, years after, poor, neglected, dying—well, for her he had done what he could. And that thin young man in his office, with the irritating cough, who might perhaps have been saved if he had been got away sooner? Stuck on to the end because there was a family to support—of course! And the old bookkeeper whom Dorrance had inherited from his father, who was deaf and half blind, and wouldn't go either till he had to be gently told—? All that had been, as it were, the stuff out of which he, Paul Dorrance, had built up his easy, affluent, successful life. But, no, what nonsense! He had been fair enough, kind enough, whenever he found out what was wrong; only he hadn't really pitied them, had considered his debt discharged when he had drawn a check or rung up a Home for Incurables. Whereas pity, he now saw—oh, curse it, he was talking like a Russian novel! Nonsense . . . nonsense . . . everybody's turn came sooner or later. The only way to reform the world was to reform Death out of it. And instead of that, Death was always there, was there now, at the door, in the room, at his elbow . . . *his* Death, his own private and particular end-of-everything. *Now!* He snatched his hands away from his face. They were wet.

A bell rang hesitatingly and the door opened behind him. He heard the servant say: "Mrs. Welwood." He stood up, blinking at the harsh impact of light and life. "Mrs. Welwood." Everything was going on again, going on again . . . people were behaving exactly as if he were not doomed . . . the door shut.

"Eleanor!"

She came up to him quickly. How close, alive, oppressive everyone seemed! She seldom came to his flat—he wondered dully why she had come today.

She stammered: "What has happened? You promised to telephone at ten. I've been ringing and ringing. They said nobody answered. . . ."

Ah, yes; he remembered now. He looked at the receiver. It lay on the desk, where he had dropped it when his eye had lit on that paper. All that had happened in his other life—before. . . . Well, here she was. How pale she looked, her eyelids a little swollen. And yet how strong, how healthy—how obviously undiseased. Queer! She'd been crying too! Instinctively he turned, and put himself between her and the light.

"What's all the fuss about, dear?" he began jauntily.

She colored a little, hesitating as if he had caught her at fault. "Why, it's nearly one o'clock; and you told me the consultation was to be at nine. And you promised. . . ."

Oh, yes; of course. He had promised. . . . With the hard morning light on her pale face and thin lips, she looked twenty years older. Older than what? After all, she was well over forty, and had never been beautiful. Had he ever thought her beautiful? Poor Eleanor—oh, poor Eleanor!

"Well, yes; it's my fault," he conceded. "I suppose I telephoned to somebody" (this fib to gain time) "and forgot to hang up the receiver. There it lies; I'm convicted!" He took both her hands—how they trembled!—and drew her to him.

This was Eleanor Welwood, for fifteen years past the heaviest burden on his conscience. As he stood there, holding her hands, he tried to recover a glimpse of the beginnings, and of his own state of mind at the time. He had been captivated; but never to the point of wishing she were free to marry him. Her husband was a pleasant enough fellow; they all belonged to the same little social group; it was a delightful relation, just as it was. And Dorrance had the pretext of his old mother, alone and infirm, who lived with him and whom he could not leave. It was tacitly understood that old Mrs. Dorrance's habits must not be disturbed by any change in the household. So love, on his part, imperceptibly cooled (or should he say ripened?) into friendship; and when his mother's death left him free, there still remained the convenient obstacle of Horace Welwood. Horace Welwood did not die; but one day, as the phrase is, he "allowed" his wife to divorce him. The news had cost Dorrance a sleepless night or two. The divorce was obtained by Mrs. Welwood, discreetly, in a distant and accommodating state; but it was really Welwood who had repudiated his wife, and because of Paul Dorrance. Dorrance knew this, and was aware that Mrs. Welwood knew he knew it. But he had kept his head, she had silenced her heart; and life went on as before, except that since the divorce it was easier to see her, and he could telephone to her house whenever he chose. And they continued to be the dearest of friends.

He had often gone over all this in his mind, with an increasing satisfaction in his own shrewdness. He had kept his freedom, kept his old love's devotion—or as much of it as he wanted—and proved to himself that life was not half bad if you knew how to manage it. That was what he used to think—and then, suddenly, two or three hours ago, he had begun to think differently about everything, and what had seemed shrewdness now unmasked itself as a pitiless egotism.

He continued to look at Mrs. Welwood, as if searching her face for something it was essential he should find there. He saw her lips begin to tremble, the tears still on her lashes, her features gradually dissolving in a blur of apprehension and incredulity. "Ah—this is beyond her! She won't be 'brave' now," he thought with an uncontrollable satisfaction. It seemed necessary, at the moment, that someone should feel the shock of his doom as he was feeling it—should *die with him*, at least morally, since he had to die. And the strange insight which had come to him—this queer "behind-the-veil" penetration he was suddenly conscious of—had already told him that most of the people he knew, however sorry they might think they were, would really not be in the least affected by his fate, would remain as inwardly unmoved as he had been when, in the plenitude of his vigor, someone had said before him: "Ah, poor so-and-so—didn't you know? The doctors say it's all up with him."

With Eleanor it was different. As he held her there under his eyes he could almost trace the course of his own agony in her paling dissolving face, could almost see her as she might one day look if she were his widow—*his widow!* Poor thing. At least if she were that she could proclaim her love and her anguish, could abandon herself to open mourning on his grave. Perhaps that was the only comfort it was still in his power to give her...or in hers to give him. For the grave might be less cold if watered by her warm tears. The thought made his own well up, and he pressed her closer. At that moment his first wish was to see how she would look if she were really happy. His friend—his only friend! How he would make up to her now for his past callousness!

"Eleanor—"

"Oh, won't you tell me?" she entreated.

"Yes. Of course. Only I want you to promise me something first—"

"Yes...."

"To do what I want you to—whatever I want you to."

She could not still the trembling of her hands, though he pressed them so close. She could scarcely articulate: "Haven't I, always—?"

Slowly he pronounced: "I want you to marry me."

Her trembling grew more violent, and then subsided. The shadow of her terrible fear seemed to fall from her, as the shadow of living falls from the face of the newly dead. Her face looked young and transparent; he watched the blood rise to her lips and cheeks.

"Oh, Paul, Paul—then the news is *good*?"

He felt a slight shrinking at her obtuseness. After all, she was alive (it wasn't her fault), she was merely alive, like all the rest.... Magnanimously he rejoined: "Never mind about the news now." But to himself he muttered: "*Sancta Simplicitas!*"

She had thought he had asked her to marry him because the news was good!

II

They were married almost immediately, and with as little circumstance as possible. Dorrance's ill-health, already vaguely known of in his immediate group of friends, was a sufficient pretext for hastening and simplifying the ceremony; and the next day the couple sailed for France.

Dorrance had not seen again the two doctors who had pronounced his doom. He had forbidden Mrs. Welwood to speak of the diagnosis, to him or to anyone else. "For God's sake, don't let's dramatize the thing," he commanded her; and she acquiesced.

He had shown her the paper as soon as she had promised to marry him; and had hastened, as she read it, to inform her that of course he had no intention of holding her to her promise. "I only wanted to hear you say 'yes,'" he explained, on a note of emotion so genuine that it deceived himself as completely as it did her. He was sure she would not accept his offer to release her; if he had not been sure he might not have dared to make it. For he understood now that he must marry her; he simply could not live out these last months alone. For a moment his thoughts had played sentimentally with the idea that he was marrying her to acquit an old debt, to make her happy before it was too late; but that delusion had been swept away like a straw on the torrent of his secret fears. A new form of egotism, fiercer and more impatient than the other, was dictating his words and gestures—and he knew it. He was marrying simply to put a sentinel between himself and the presence lurking on his threshold—with the same blind instinct of self-preservation which had made men, in old days, propitiate death by the lavish sacrifice of life. And, confident as he was, he had felt an obscure dread of her failing him till his ring was actually on her finger; and a great ecstasy of reassurance and gratitude as he walked out into the street with that captive hand on his arm. Could it be that together they would be able to cheat death after all?

They landed at Genoa, and traveled by slow stages toward the Austrian Alps. The journey seemed to do Dorrance good; he was bearing the fatigue better than he had expected; and he was conscious that his attentive companion noted the improvement, though she forbore to emphasize it. "Above all, don't be too cheerful," he had warned her, half smilingly, on the day when he had told her of his doom. "Marry me if you think you can stand it; but don't try to make me think I'm going to get well."

She had obeyed him to the letter, watching over his comfort, sparing him all needless fatigue and agitation, carefully serving up to him, on the bright surface of her vigilance, the flowers of travel stripped of their thorns. The very qualities which had made her a perfect mistress—self-effacement, opportuneness, the art of being present and visible only when he required her to be—made her (he had to own it) a perfect wife for a man cut off from everything but the contemplation of his own end.

They were bound for Vienna, where a celebrated specialist was said to have found new ways of relieving the suffering caused by such cases as Dorrance's—sometimes even (though Dorrance and his wife took care not to mention this to each other) of checking the disease, even holding it for years in abeyance. "I owe it to the poor child to give the thing a trial," the invalid speciously argued, disguising his own passionate impatience to put himself in the great man's hands. "If she *wants* to drag out her life with a half-dead man, why should I prevent her?" he thought, trying to sum up all the hopeful possibilities on which the new diagnostician might base his verdict.... "Certainly," Dorrance thought, "I have had less pain lately...."

———

It had been agreed that he should go to the specialist's alone; his wife was to wait for him at their hotel. "But you'll come straight back afterward? You'll take a taxi—you won't walk?" she had pleaded, for the first time betraying her impatience. "She knows the hours are numbered, and she can't bear to lose one," he thought, a choking in his throat; and as he bent to kiss her he had a vision of what it would have been, after the interview that lay ahead of him, the verdict he had already discounted, to walk back to an hotel in which no one awaited him, climb to an empty room and sit down alone with his doom. "Bless you, child, of course I'll take a taxi. . . ."

Now the consultation was over, and he had descended from the specialist's door, and stood alone in the summer twilight, watching the trees darken against the illumination of the street lamps. What a divine thing a summer evening was, even in a crowded city street! He wondered that he had never before felt its peculiar loveliness. Through the trees the sky was deepening from pearl gray to blue as the stars came out. He stood there, unconscious of the hour, gazing at the people hurrying to and fro on the pavement, the traffic flowing by in an unbroken stream, all the ceaseless tides of the city's life which had seemed to him, half an hour ago, forever suspended. . . .

"No, it's too lovely; I'll walk," he said, rousing himself, and took a direction opposite to that in which his hotel lay. "After all," he thought, "there's no hurry. . . . What a charming town Vienna is—I think I should like to live here," he mused as he wandered on under the trees. . . .

When at last he reached his hotel he stopped short on the threshold and asked himself: "How am I going to tell her?" He realized that during his two hours' perambulations since he had left the doctor's office he had thought out nothing, planned nothing, not even let his imagination glance at the future, but simply allowed himself to be absorbed into the softly palpitating life about him, like a tired traveler sinking, at his journey's end, into a warm bath. Only now, at the foot of the stairs, did he see the future facing him, and understand that he knew no more how to prepare for the return to life than he had for the leaving it. . . . "If only she takes it quietly—without too much fuss," he thought, shrinking in advance from any disturbance of those still waters into which it was so beatific to subside.

"That New York diagnosis was a mistake—an utter mistake," he began vehemently, and then paused, arrested, silenced, by something in his wife's face which seemed to oppose an invisible resistance to what he was in the act of saying. He had hoped she would not be too emotional—and now: what was it? Did he really resent the mask of composure she had no doubt struggled to adjust during her long hours of waiting? He stood and stared at her. "I suppose you don't believe it?" he broke off, with an aimless irritated laugh.

She came to him eagerly. "But of course I do, of course!" She seemed to hesitate for a second. "What I never did believe," she said abruptly, "was the other—the New York diagnosis."

He continued to stare, vaguely resentful of this new attitude, and of the hint of secret criticism it conveyed. He felt himself suddenly diminished in her eyes, as though she were retrospectively stripping him of some prerogative. If she had not believed in the New York diagnosis, what must her secret view of him have been all the while? "Oh, you never believed in it? And may I ask why?" He heard the edge of sarcasm in his voice.

She gave a little laugh that sounded almost as aimless as his. "I—I don't know. I suppose I couldn't *bear* to, simply; I couldn't believe fate could be so cruel."

Still with a tinge of sarcasm he rejoined: "I'm glad you had your incredulity to sustain you." Inwardly he was saying: "Not a tear . . . not an outbreak of emotion . . ." and his heart, dilated by the immense inrush of returning life, now contracted as if an invisible plug had been removed from it, and its fullness were slowly ebbing. "It's a queer business, anyhow," he mumbled.

"What is, dear?"

"This being alive again. I'm not sure I know yet what it consists in."

She came up and put her arms about him, almost shyly. "We'll try to find out, love—together."

III

This magnificent gift of life, which the Viennese doctor had restored to him as lightly as his New York colleagues had withdrawn it, lay before Paul Dorrance like something external, outside of himself, an honor, an official rank, unexpectedly thrust on him: he did not discover till then how completely he had dissociated himself from the whole business of living. It was as if life were a growth which the surgeon's knife had already extirpated, leaving him, disembodied, on the pale verge of nonentity. All the while that he had kept saying to himself: "In a few weeks more I shall be dead," had he not really known that he was dead already?

"But what are we to do, then, dearest?" he heard his wife asking. "What do you want? Would you like to go home at once? Do you want me to cable to have the flat got ready?"

He looked at her in astonishment, wounded by such unperceivingness. Go home—to New York? To his old life there? Did she really think of it as something possible, even simple and natural? Why, the small space he had occupied there had closed up already; he felt himself as completely excluded from that other life as if his absence had lasted for years. And what did she mean by "going home"? The old Paul Dorrance who had made his will, wound up his affairs, resigned from his clubs and directorships, pensioned off his old servants and married his old mistress—that Dorrance was as dead as if he had taken that final step for which all those others were but the hasty preparation. He *was* dead; this new man, to whom the doctor had said: "Cancer? Nothing of the sort—not a trace of it. Go home and tell your wife that in a few months you'll be as sound as any man of fifty I ever met—" This new Dorrance, with his new health, his new leisure and his new wife, was an intruder for whom a whole new existence would have to be planned out. And how could anything be decided until one got to know the new Paul Dorrance a little better?

Conscious that his wife was waiting for his answer, he said: "Oh, this fellow here may be all wrong. Anyhow, he wants me to take a cure somewhere first—I've got the name written down. After that we'll see.... But wouldn't you rather travel for a year or so? How about South Africa or India next winter?" he ventured at random, after trying to think of some point of the globe even more remote from New York.

IV

The cure was successful, the Viennese specialist's diagnosis proved to be correct; and the Paul Dorrances celebrated the event by two years of foreign travel. But Dorrance never felt again the unconditioned ecstasy he had tasted as he walked out from the doctor's door into the lamplit summer streets. After that, at the very moment of re-entering his hotel, the effort of readjustment had begun; and ever since it had gone on.

For a few months the wanderers, weary of change, had settled in Florence, captivated by an arcaded villa on a cypress-walled hill, and the new Paul Dorrance, whom it was now the other's incessant task to study and placate, had toyed with the idea of a middle life of cultivated leisure. But he soon grew tired of his opportunities, and found it necessary to move on, and forget in strenuous travel his incapacity for assimilation and reflection. And before the two years were over the old Paul Dorrance, who had constituted himself the other's courier and prime minister, discovered that the old and the new were one, and that the original Paul Dorrance was there, unchanged, unchangeable, and impatient to get back to his old niche because it was too late to adapt himself to any other. So the flat was reopened and the Dorrances returned to New York.

The completeness of his identity with the old Paul Dorrance was indelibly impressed on the new one on the first evening of his return home. There he was, the same man in the same setting as when, two years earlier, he had glanced down from the same armchair and seen the diagnosis of the consulting physicians at his feet. The hour was late, the room profoundly still; no touch of outward reality intervened between him and that hallucinating vision. He almost saw the paper on the floor, and with the same gesture as before he covered his eyes to shut it out. Two years ago—and nothing was changed, after so many changes, except that he should not hear the hesitating ring at the door, should not again see Eleanor Welwood, pale and questioning, on the threshold. Eleanor Welwood did not ring his door-bell now; she had her own latch-key; she was no longer Eleanor Welwood but Eleanor Dorrance, and asleep at this moment in the bedroom which had been Dorrance's, and was now encumbered with feminine properties, while his own were uncomfortably wedged into the cramped guest room of the flat.

Yes—that was the only change in his life; and how aptly the change in the rooms symbolized it! During their travels, even after Dorrance's return to health, his wife's presence had been like a soft accompaniment of music, a painted background to the idle episodes of convalescence; now that he was about to fit himself into the familiar furrow of old habits and relations he felt as if she were already expanding and crowding him into a corner. He did not mind about the room—so he assured himself, though with a twinge of regret for the slant of winter sun which never reached the guest room; what he minded was what he now recognized as the huge practical joke that fate had played on him. He had never meant, he the healthy, vigorous, middle-aged Paul Dorrance, to marry this faded woman for whom he had so long ceased to feel anything but a friendly tenderness. It was the bogey of death, starting out from the warm folds of his closely-curtained life, that had tricked him into the marriage, and then left him to expiate his folly.

Poor Eleanor! It was not her fault if he had imagined, in a

moment of morbid retrospection, that happiness would transform and enlarge her. Under the surface changes she was still the same: a perfect companion while he was ill and lonely, an unwitting encumbrance now that (unchanged also) he was restored to the life from which his instinct of self-preservation had so long excluded her. Why had he not trusted to that instinct, which had warned him she was the woman for a sentimental parenthesis, not for the pitiless continuity of marriage? Why, even her face declared it. A lovely profile, yes; but somehow the full face was inadequate. . . .

Dorrance suddenly remembered another face; that of a girl they had met in Cairo the previous winter. He felt the shock of her young fairness, saw the fruity bloom of her cheeks, the light animal vigor of every movement, he heard her rich beckoning laugh, and met the eyes questioning his under the queer slant of her lids. Someone had said: "She's had an offer from a man who can give her everything a woman wants; but she's refused, and no one can make out why. . . ." Dorrance knew. . . . She had written to him since, and he had not answered her letters. And now here he was, installed once more in the old routine he could not live without, yet from which all the old savor was gone. "I wonder why I was so scared of dying," he thought; then the truth flashed on him. "Why, you fool, you've been dead all the time. That first diagnosis was the true one. Only they put it on the physical plane by mistake. . . ." The next day he began to insert himself painfully into his furrow.

V

One evening some two years later, as Paul Dorrance put his latch-key into his door, he said to himself reluctantly: "Perhaps I really ought to take her away for a change."

There was nothing nowadays that he dreaded as much as change. He had had his fill of the unexpected, and it had not agreed with him. Now that he had fitted himself once more into his furrow all he asked was to stay there. It had even become an effort, when summer came, to put off his New York habits and go with his wife to their little place in the country. And the idea that he might have to go away with her in mid-February was positively disturbing.

For the past ten days she had been fighting a bad bronchitis, following on influenza. But "fighting" was hardly the right word. She, usually so elastic, so indomitable, had not shown her usual resiliency, and Dorrance, from the vantage ground of his recovered health, wondered a little at her lack of spirit. She mustn't let herself go, he warned her gently. "I was in a good deal tighter place myself not so many years ago—and look at me now. Don't you let the doctors scare you." She had promised him again that morning that she wouldn't, and he had gone off to his office without waiting for the physician's visit. But during the day he began in an odd way to feel his wife's nearness. It was as though she needed him, as though there were something she wanted to say; and he concluded that she probably knew she ought to go south, and had been afraid to tell him so. "Poor child—of course I'll take her if the doctor says it's really necessary." Hadn't he always done everything he could for her? It seemed to him that they had been married for years and years, and that as a husband he had behind him a long and irreproachable record. Why, he hadn't even answered that girl's letters. . . .

As he opened the door of the flat a strange woman in a nurse's dress crossed the hall. Instantly Dorrance felt the alien atmosphere of the place, the sense of something absorbing and exclusive which ignores and averts itself from the common doings of men. He had felt that same atmosphere, in all its somber implications, the day he had picked up the cancer diagnosis from the floor.

The nurse stopped to say "Pneumonia," and hurried down the passage to his wife's room. The doctor was coming back at nine o'clock; he had left a note in the library, the butler said. Dorrance knew what was in the note before he opened it. Precipitately, with the vertical drop of a bird of prey, death was descending on his house again. And this time there was no mistake in the diagnosis.

The nurse said he could come in for a minute; but he wasn't to stay long, for she didn't like the way the temperature was rising…and there, between the chalk-white pillows, in the green-shaded light, he saw his wife's face. What struck him first was the way it had shrunk and narrowed after a few hours of fever; then, that though it wore a just-perceptible smile of welcome, there was no sign of the tremor of illumination which usually greeted his appearance. He remembered how once, encountering that light, he had grumbled inwardly: "I wish to God she wouldn't always unroll a red carpet when I come in—" and then been ashamed of his thought. She never embarrassed him by any public show of feeling; that subtle play of light remained invisible to others, and his irritation was caused simply by knowing it was there. "I don't want to be anybody's sun and moon," he concluded. But now she was looking at him with a new, an almost critical equality of expression. His first thought was: "Is it possible she doesn't know me?" But her eyes met his with a glance of recognition, and he understood that the change was simply due to her being enclosed in a world of her own, complete, and independent of his.

"Please, now—" the nurse reminded him; and obediently he stole out of the room.

The next day there was a slight improvement; the doctors were encouraged; the day nurse said: "If only it goes on like this—"; and as Dorrance opened the door of his wife's room he thought: "If only she looks more like her own self—!"

But she did not. She was still in that new and self-contained world which he had immediately identified as the one he had lived in during the months when he had thought he was to die. "After all, I didn't die," he reminded himself; but the reminder brought no solace, for he knew exactly what his wife was feeling, he had tested the impenetrability of the barrier which shut her off from the living. "The truth is, one doesn't only die once," he mused, aware that he had died already; and the memory of the process, now being re-enacted before him, laid a chill on his heart. If only he could have helped her, made her understand! But the barrier was there, the transparent barrier through which everything on the hither side looked so different. And today it was he who was on the hither side.

Then he remembered how, in his loneliness, he had yearned for the beings already so remote, the beings on the living side; and he felt for his wife the same rush of pity as when he had thought himself dying, and known what agony his death would cost her.

That day he was allowed to stay five minutes; the next day ten; she continued to improve, and the doctors would have been perfectly satisfied if her heart had not shown signs of weakness. Hearts, however, medically speaking, are relatively easy to deal with; and to Dorrance she seemed much stronger.

Soon the improvement became so marked that the doctor made no objection to his sitting with her for an hour or two; the nurse was sent for a walk, and Dorrance was allowed to read the morning paper to the invalid. But when he took it up his wife stretched out her hand. "No—I want to talk to you."

He smiled, and met her smile. It was as if she had found a slit in the barrier and were reaching out to him. "Dear—but won't talking tire you?"

"I don't know. Perhaps." She waited. "You see, I'm talking to you all the time, while I lie here. . . ."

He knew—he knew! How her pangs went through him! "But you see, dear, raising your voice. . . ."

She smiled incredulously, that remote behind-the-barrier smile he had felt so often on his own lips. Though she could reach through to him the dividing line was still there, and her eyes met his with a look of weary omniscience.

"But there's no hurry," he argued. "Why not wait a day or two? Try to lie there and not even think."

"Not think!" She raised herself on a weak elbow. "I want to think every minute—every second. I want to relive everything, day by day, to the last atom of time. . . ."

"Time? But there'll be plenty of time!"

She continued to lean on her elbow, fixing her illumined eyes on him. She did not seem to hear what he said; her attention was concentrated on some secret vision of which he felt himself the mere transparent mask.

"Well," she exclaimed, with a sudden passionate energy, "it was worth it! I always knew—"

Dorrance bent toward her. "What was worth—?" But she had sunk back with closed eyes, and lay there reabsorbed into the cleft of the pillows, merged in the inanimate, a mere part of the furniture of the sick room. Dorrance waited for a moment, hardly understanding the change; then he started up, rang, called, and in a few moments the professionals were in possession, the air was full of ether and camphor, the telephone ringing, the disarray of death in the room. Dorrance knew that he would never know what she had found worth it. . . .

VI

He sat in his library, waiting. Waiting for what? Life was over for him now that she was dead. Until after the funeral a sort of factitious excitement had kept him on his feet. Now there was nothing left but to go over and over those last days. Every detail of them stood out before him in unbearable relief; and one of the most salient had been the unexpected appearance in the sick room of Dorrance's former doctor—the very doctor who, with the cancer specialist, had signed the diagnosis of Dorrance's case. Dorrance, since that day, had naturally never consulted him professionally; and it chanced that they had never met. But Eleanor's physician, summoned at the moment of her last heart attack, without even stopping to notify Dorrance, had called in his colleague. The latter had a high standing as a consultant (the idea made Dorrance smile); and besides, what did it matter? By that time they all knew—nurses, doctors, and most of all Dorrance himself—that nothing was possible but to ease the pangs of Eleanor's last hours. And Dorrance had met his former doctor without resentment; hardly even with surprise.

But the doctor had not forgotten that he and his former

patient had been old friends; and the day after the funeral, late in the evening, had thought it proper to ring the widower's doorbell and present his condolences. Dorrance, at his entrance, looked up in surprise, at first resenting the intrusion, then secretly relieved at the momentary release from the fiery wheel of his own thoughts. "The man is a fool—but perhaps," Dorrance reflected, "he'll give me something that will make me sleep...."

The two men sat down, and the doctor began to talk gently of Eleanor. He had known her for many years, though not professionally. He spoke of her goodness, her charity, the many instances he had come across among his poor patients of her discreet and untiring ministrations. Dorrance, who had dreaded hearing her spoken of, and by this man above all others, found himself listening with a curious avidity to these reminiscences. He needed no one to tell him of Eleanor's kindness, her devotion—yet at the moment such praise was sweet to him. And he took up the theme; but not without a secret stir of vindictiveness, a vague desire to make the doctor suffer for the results of his now-distant blunder. "She always gave too much of herself—that was the trouble. No one knows that better than I do. She was never really the same after those months of incessant anxiety about me that you doctors made her undergo." He had not intended to say anything of the sort; but as he spoke the resentment he had thought extinct was fanned into flame by his words. He had forgiven the two doctors for himself, but he suddenly found he could not forgive them for Eleanor, and he had an angry wish to let them know it. "That diagnosis of yours nearly killed her, though it didn't kill *me*," he concluded sardonically.

The doctor had followed this outburst with a look of visible perplexity. In the crowded life of a fashionable physician, what room was there to remember a mistaken diagnosis? The sight of his forgetfulness made Dorrance continue with rising irritation: "The shock of it *did* kill her—I see that now."

"Diagnosis—what diagnosis?" echoed the doctor blankly.

"I see you don't remember," said Dorrance.

"Well, no; I don't, for the moment."

"I'll remind you, then. When you came to see me with that cancer specialist four or five years ago, one of you dropped your diagnosis by mistake in going out...."

"Oh, *that*?" The doctor's face lit up with sudden recollection. "Of course! The diagnosis of the other poor fellow we'd been to see before coming to you. I remember it all now. Your wife—Mrs. Welwood then, wasn't she?—brought the paper back to me a few hours later—before I'd even missed it. I think she said you'd picked it up after we left, and thought it was meant for *you*." The doctor gave an easy retrospective laugh. "Luckily I was able to re-assure her at once." He leaned back comfortably in his armchair and shifted his voice to the pitch of condolence. "A beautiful life, your wife's was. I only wish it had been in our power to prolong it. But these cases of heart failure...you must tell yourself that at least you had a few happy years; and so many of us haven't even that." The doctor stood up and held out his hand.

"Wait a moment, please," Dorrance said hurriedly. "There's something I want to ask you." His brain was whirling so that he could not remember what he had started to say. "I can't sleep...." he began.

"Yes?" said the doctor, assuming a professional look, but with a furtive glance at his wrist watch.

Dorrance's throat felt dry and his head empty. He struggled with the difficulty of ordering his thoughts, and fitting rational words to them.

"Yes—but no matter about my sleeping. What I meant was: do I understand you to say that the diagnosis you dropped in leaving was not intended for me?"

The doctor stared. "Good Lord, no—of course it wasn't. You never had a symptom. Didn't we both tell you so at the time?"

"Yes," Dorrance slowly acquiesced.

"Well, if you didn't believe us, your scare was a short one, any-how," the doctor continued with a mild jocularity; and he put his hand out again.

"Oh, wait," Dorrance repeated. "What I really wanted to ask was what day you said my wife returned the diagnosis to you? But I suppose you don't remember."

The doctor reflected. "Yes, I do; it all comes back to me now. It was the very same day. We called on you in the morning, didn't we?"

"Yes; at nine o'clock," said Dorrance, the dryness returning to his throat.

"Well, Mrs. Welwood brought the diagnosis back to me directly afterward."

"You think it was the very same day?" (Dorrance wondered to himself why he continued to insist on this particular point.)

The doctor took another stolen glance at his watch. "I'm sure it was. I remember now that it was my consultation day, and that she caught me at two o'clock, before I saw my first patient. We had a good laugh over the scare you'd had."

"I see," said Dorrance.

"Your wife had one of the sweetest laughs I ever heard," continued the doctor, with an expression of melancholy reminiscence.

There was a silence, and Dorrance was conscious that his vistor was looking at him with growing perplexity. He too gave a slight laugh. "I thought perhaps it was the day after," he mumbled vaguely. "Anyhow, you did give me a good scare."

"Yes," said the doctor. "But it didn't last long, did it? I asked your wife to make my peace with you. You know such things will happen to hurried doctors. I hope she persuaded you to forgive me?"

"Oh, yes," said Dorrance, as he followed the doctor to the door to let him out.

"Well, now about that sleeping—" the doctor checked himself on the threshold to ask.

"Sleeping?" Dorrance stared. "Oh, I shall sleep all right tonight," he said with sudden decision, as he closed the door on his visitor.

POMEGRANATE SEED

CHARLOTTE Ashby paused on her door-step. Dark had descended on the brilliancy of the March afternoon, and the grinding rasping street life of the city was at its highest. She turned her back on it, standing for a moment in the old-fashioned, marble-flagged vestibule before she inserted her key in the lock. The sash curtains drawn across the panes of the inner door softened the light within to a warm blur through which no details showed. It was the hour when, in the first months of her marriage to Kenneth Ashby, she had most liked to return to that quiet house in a street long since deserted by business and fashion. The contrast between the soulless roar of New York, its devouring blaze of lights, the oppression of its congested traffic, congested houses, lives, minds and this veiled sanctuary she called home, always stirred her profoundly. In the very heart of the hurricane she had found her tiny islet—or thought she had. And now, in the last months, everything was changed, and she always wavered on the door-step and had to force herself to enter.

While she stood there she called up the scene within: the hall hung with old prints, the ladderlike stairs, and on the left her husband's long shabby library, full of books and pipes and worn arm-chairs inviting to meditation. How she had loved that room! Then, up stairs, her own drawing-room, in which, since the death of Kenneth's first wife, neither furniture nor hangings had been changed, because there had never been money enough, but which Charlotte had made her own by moving furniture about and adding more books, another lamp, a table for the new reviews.

Even on the occasion of her only visit to the first Mrs. Ashby—a distant, self-centered woman, whom she had known very slightly—she had looked about her with an innocent envy, feeling it to be exactly the drawing-room she would have liked for herself; and now for more than a year it had been hers to deal with as she chose—the room to which she hastened back at dusk on winter days, where she sat reading by the fire, or answering notes at the pleasant roomy desk, or going over her stepchildren's copy-books, till she heard her husband's step.

Sometimes friends dropped in; sometimes—oftener—she was alone; and she liked that best, since it was another way of being with Kenneth, thinking over what he had said when they parted in the morning, imagining what he would say when he sprang up the stairs, found her by herself and caught her to him.

Now, instead of this, she thought of one thing only—the letter she might or might not find on the hall table. Until she had made sure whether or not it was there, her mind had no room for anything else. The letter was always the same—a square grayish envelope with "Kenneth Ashby, Esquire," written on it in bold but faint characters. From the first it had struck Charlotte as peculiar that anyone who wrote such a firm hand should trace the letters so lightly; the address was always written as though there were not enough ink in the pen, or the writer's wrist were too weak to bear upon it. Another curious thing was that, in spite of its masculine curves, the writing was so visibly feminine. Some hands are sexless, some masculine, at first glance; the writing on the gray envelope, for all its strength and assurance, was without doubt a woman's. The envelope never bore anything but the recipient's name; no stamp, no address. The letter was presumably delivered by hand—but by whose? No doubt it was slipped into the letter-box, whence the parlor-maid, when she closed the shutters and lit the lights, probably extracted it. At any rate, it was always in the evening, after dark, that Charlotte saw it lying there. She thought of the letter in the singular, as "it," because, though there had been several since her marriage—seven, to be exact—they were so alike in appearance that they had become merged in one another in her mind, become one letter, become "it."

The first had come the day after their return from their honeymoon—a journey prolonged to the West Indies, from which they had returned to New York after an absence of more than two months. Re-entering the house with her husband, late on that first evening—they had dined at his mother's—she had seen, alone on the hall table, the gray envelope. Her eye fell on it before Kenneth's, and her first thought was: "Why, I've seen that writing before"; but where she could not recall. The memory was just definite enough for her to identify the script whenever it looked up at her faintly from the same pale envelope; but on that first day she would have thought no more of the letter if, when her husband's glance lit on it, she had not chanced to be looking at him. It all happened in a flash—his seeing the letter, putting out his hand for it, raising it to his short-sighted eyes to decipher the faint writing, and then abruptly withdrawing the arm he had slipped through Charlotte's, and moving away to the hanging light, his back turned to her. She had waited—waited for a sound, an exclamation; waited for him to open the letter; but he had slipped it into his pocket without a word and followed her into the library. And there they had sat down by the fire and lit their cigarettes, and he had remained silent, his head thrown back broodingly against the armchair, his eyes fixed on the hearth, and presently had passed his hand over his forehead and said: "Wasn't it unusually hot at my mother's tonight? I've got a splitting head. Mind if I take myself off to bed?"

That was the first time. Since then Charlotte had never been present when he had received the letter. It usually came before he got home from his office, and she had to go up stairs and leave it lying there. But even if she had not seen it, she would have known it had come by the change in his face when he joined her—which, on those evenings, he seldom did before they met for dinner. Evidently, whatever the letter contained, he wanted to be by himself to deal with it; and when he reappeared he looked years older, looked emptied of life and courage, and hardly conscious of her presence. Sometimes he was silent for the rest of the evening; and if he spoke, it was usually to hint some criticism of her household arrangements, suggest some change in the domestic administration, to ask, a little nervously, if she didn't think Joyce's nursery governess was rather young and flighty, or if she herself always saw to it that Peter—whose throat was delicate—was properly wrapped up when he went to school. At such times Charlotte would remember the friendly warnings she had received when she became engaged to Kenneth Ashby: "Marrying a heartbroken widower! Isn't that rather risky? You know Elsie Ashby absolutely dominated him"; and how she had jokingly replied: "He may be glad of a little liberty for a change." And in this respect she had been right. She had needed no one to tell her, during the first months, that her husband was perfectly happy with her. When they came back from their protracted honeymoon the same friends said: "What have you done to Kenneth? He looks twenty years younger"; and this time she answered with careless joy: "I suppose I've got him out of his groove."

But what she noticed after the gray letters began to come was not so much his nervous tentative faultfinding—which always seemed to be uttered against his will—as the look in his eyes when he joined her after receiving one of the letters. The look was not unloving, not even indifferent; it was the look of a man who had been so far away from ordinary events that when he returns to familiar things they seem strange. She minded that more than the faultfinding.

Though she had been sure from the first that the handwriting on the gray envelope was a woman's, it was long before she associated the mysterious letters with any sentimental secret. She was too sure of her husband's love, too confident of filling his life, for such an idea to occur to her. It seemed far more likely that the letters—which certainly did not appear to cause him any sentimental pleasure—were addressed to the busy lawyer than to the private person. Probably they were from some tiresome client—

women, he had often told her, were nearly always tiresome as clients—who did not want her letters opened by his secretary and therefore had them carried to his house. Yes; but in that case the unknown female must be unusually troublesome, judging from the effect her letters produced. Then again, though his professional discretion was exemplary, it was odd that he had never uttered an impatient comment, never remarked to Charlotte, in a moment of expansion, that there was a nuisance of a woman who kept badgering him about a case that had gone against her. He had made more than one semi-confidence of the kind—of course without giving names or details; but concerning this mysterious correspondent his lips were sealed.

There was another possibility: what is euphemistically called an "old entanglement." Charlotte Ashby was a sophisticated woman. She had few illusions about the intricacies of the human heart; she knew that there were often old entanglements. But when she had married Kenneth Ashby, her friends, instead of hinting at such a possibility, had said: "You've got your work cut out for you. Marrying a Don Juan is a sinecure to it. Kenneth's never looked at another woman since he first saw Elsie Corder. During all the years of their marriage he was more like an unhappy lover than a comfortably contented husband. He'll never let you move an armchair or change the place of a lamp; and whatever you venture to do, he'll mentally compare with what Elsie would have done in your place."

Except for an occasional nervous mistrust as to her ability to manage the children—a mistrust gradually dispelled by her good humor and the children's obvious fondness for her—none of these forebodings had come true. The desolate widower, of whom his nearest friends said that only his absorbing professional interests had kept him from suicide after his first wife's death, had fallen in love, two years later, with Charlotte Gorse, and after an impetuous wooing had married her and carried her off on a tropical honeymoon. And ever since he had been as tender and loverlike as during those first radiant weeks. Before asking her to marry him he had spoken to her frankly of his great love for his first wife and his despair after her sudden death; but even then he had assumed no stricken attitude, or implied that life offered no possibility of renewal. He had been perfectly simple and natural, and had confessed to Charlotte that from the beginning he had hoped the future held new gifts for him. And when, after their marriage, they returned to the house where his twelve years with his first wife had been spent, he had told Charlotte at once that he was sorry he couldn't afford to do the place over for her, but that he knew every woman had her own views about furniture and all sorts of household arrangements a man would never notice, and had begged her to make any changes she saw fit without bothering to consult him. As a result, she made as few as possible; but his way of beginning their new life in the old setting was so frank and unembarrassed that it put her immediately at her ease, and she was almost sorry to find that the portrait of Elsie Ashby, which used to hang over the desk in his library, had been transferred in their absence to the children's nursery. Knowing herself to be the indirect cause of this banishment, she spoke of it to her husband; but he answered: "Oh, I thought they ought to grow up with her looking down on them." The answer moved Charlotte, and satisfied her; and as time went by she had to confess that she felt more at home in her house, more at ease and in confidence with her husband, since that long coldly beautiful face on the library wall no longer followed her with guarded eyes. It was as if Kenneth's love had penetrated to the secret she hardly acknowledged to her own heart—her passionate need to feel herself the sovereign even of his past.

With all this stored-up happiness to sustain her, it was curious that she had lately found herself yielding to a nervous apprehension. But there the apprehension was; and on this particular afternoon—perhaps because she was more tired than usual, or because of the trouble of finding a new cook or, for some other ridiculously trivial reason, moral or physical—she found herself unable to react against the feeling. Latch-key in hand, she looked back down the silent street to the whirl and illumination of the great thoroughfare beyond, and up at the sky already aflare with the

for her husband; a letter from a woman—no doubt another vulgar case of "old entanglement." What a fool she had been ever to doubt it, to rack her brains for less obvious explanations! She took up the envelope with a steady contemptuous hand, looked closely at the faint letters, held it against the light and just discerned the outline of the folded sheet within. She knew that now she would have no peace till she found out what was written on that sheet.

Her husband had not come in; he seldom got back from his office before half-past six or seven, and it was not yet six. She would have time to take the letter up to the drawing-room, hold it over the tea-kettle which at that hour always simmered by the fire in expectation of her return, solve the mystery and replace the letter where she had found it. No one would be the wiser, and her gnawing uncertainty would be over. The alternative, of course, was to question her husband; but to do that seemed even more difficult. She weighed the letter between thumb and finger, looked at it again under the light, started up the stairs with the envelope—and came down again and laid it on the table.

"No, I evidently can't," she said, disappointed.

What should she do, then? She couldn't go up alone to that warm welcoming room, pour out her tea, look over her correspondence, glance at a book or review—not with that letter lying below and the knowledge that in a little while her husband would come in, open it and turn into the library alone, as he always did on the days when the gray envelope came.

Suddenly she decided. She would wait in the library and see for herself; see what happened between him and the letter when they thought themselves unobserved. She wondered the idea had never occurred to her before. By leaving the door ajar, and sitting in the corner behind it, she could watch him unseen . . . Well, then, she would watch him! She drew a chair into the corner, sat down, her eyes on the crack, and waited.

As far as she could remember, it was the first time she had ever tried to surprise another person's secret, but she was conscious of no compunction. She simply felt as if she were fighting her way through a stifling fog that she must at all costs get out of.

At length she heard Kenneth's latch-key and jumped up. The impulse to rush out and meet him had nearly made her forget why she was there; but she remembered in time and sat down again. From her post she covered the whole range of his movements—saw him enter the hall, draw the key from the door and take off his hat and overcoat. Then he turned to throw his gloves on the hall table, and at that moment he saw the envelope. The light was full on his face, and what Charlotte first noted there was a look of surprise. Evidently he had not expected the letter—had not thought of the possibility of its being there that day. But though he had not expected it, now that he saw it he knew well enough what it contained. He did not open it immediately, but stood motionless, the color slowly ebbing from his face. Apparently he could not make up his mind to touch it; but at length he put out his hand, opened the envelope, and moved with it to the light. In doing so he turned his back on Charlotte, and she saw only his bent head and slightly stooping shoulders. Apparently all the writing was on one page, for he did not turn the sheet but continued to stare at it for so long that he must have reread it a dozen times—or so it seemed to the woman breathlessly watching him. At length she saw him move; he raised the letter still closer to his eyes, as though he had not fully deciphered it. Then he lowered his head, and she saw his lips touch the sheet.

"Kenneth!" she exclaimed, and went out into the hall.

The letter clutched in his hand, her husband turned and looked at her. "Where were you?" he said, in a low bewildered voice, like a man waked out of his sleep.

"In the library, waiting for you." She tried to steady her voice: "What's the matter! What's in that letter? You look ghastly."

Her agitation seemed to calm him, and he instantly put the envelope into his pocket with a slight laugh. "Ghastly? I'm sorry. I've had a hard day in the office—one or two complicated cases. I look dog-tired, I suppose."

"You didn't look tired when you came in. It was only when you opened that letter—"

He had followed her into the library, and they stood gazing at each other. Charlotte noticed how quickly he had regained his self-control; his profession had trained him to rapid mastery of face and voice. She saw at once that she would be at a disadvantage in any attempt to surprise his secret, but at the same moment she lost all desire to maneuver, to trick him into betraying anything he wanted to conceal. Her wish was still to penetrate the mystery, but only that she might help him to bear the burden it implied. "Even if it *is* another woman," she thought.

"Kenneth," she said, her heart beating excitedly, "I waited here on purpose to see you come in. I wanted to watch you while you opened that letter."

His face, which had paled, turned to dark red; then it paled again. "That letter? Why especially that letter?"

"Because I've noticed that whenever one of those letters comes it seems to have such a strange effect on you."

A line of anger she had never seen before came out between his eyes, and she said to herself: "The upper part of his face is too narrow; this is the first time I ever noticed it."

She heard him continue, in the cool and faintly ironic tone of the prosecuting lawyer making a point: "Ah; so you're in the habit of watching people open their letters when they don't know you're there?"

"Not in the habit. I never did such a thing before. But I had to find out what she writes to you, at regular intervals, in those gray envelopes."

He weighted this for a moment; then: "The intervals have not been regular," he said.

"Oh, I daresay you've kept a better account of the dates than I have," she retorted, her magnanimity vanishing at his tone. "All I know is that every time that woman writes to you—"

"Why do you assume it's a woman?"

"It's a woman's writing. Do you deny it?"

He smiled. "No, I don't deny it. I asked only because the writing is generally supposed to look more like a man's."

Charlotte passed this over impatiently. "And this woman—what does she write to you about?"

Again he seemed to consider a moment. "About business."

"Legal business?"

"In a way, yes. Business in general."

"You look after her affairs for her?"

"Yes."

"You've looked after them for a long time?"

"Yes. A very long time."

"Kenneth, dearest, won't you tell me who she is?"

"No. I can't." He paused, and brought out, as if with a certain hesitation: "Professional secrecy."

The blood rushed from Charlotte's heart to her temples. "Don't say that—don't!"

"Why not?"

"Because I saw you kiss the letter."

The effect of the words was so disconcerting that she instantly repented having spoken them. Her husband, who had submitted to her cross-questioning with a sort of contemptuous composure, as though he were humoring an unreasonable child, turned on her a face of terror and distress. For a minute he seemed unable to speak; then, collecting himself with an effort, he stammered out: "The writing is very faint; you must have seen me holding the letter close to my eyes to try to decipher it."

"No; I saw you kissing it." He was silent. "Didn't I see you kissing it?"

He sank back into indifference. "Perhaps."

"Kenneth! You stand there and say that—to me?"

"What possible difference can it make to you? The letter is on business, as I told you. Do you suppose I'd lie about it? The writer is a very old friend whom I haven't seen for a long time."

"Men don't kiss business letters, even from women who are very old friends, unless they have been their lovers, and still regret them."

He shrugged his shoulders slightly and turned away, as if he considered the discussion at an end and were faintly disgusted at the turn it had taken.

"Kenneth!" Charlotte moved toward him and caught hold of his arm.

He paused with a look of weariness and laid his hand over hers. "Won't you believe me?" he asked gently.

"How can I? I've watched these letters come to you—for months now they've been coming. Ever since we came back from the West Indies—one of them greeted me the very day we arrived. And after each one of them I see their mysterious effect on you, I see you disturbed, unhappy, as if someone were trying to estrange you from me."

"No, dear; not that. Never!"

She drew back and looked at him with passionate entreaty. "Well, then, prove it to me, darling. It's so easy!"

He forced a smile. "It's not easy to prove anything to a woman who's once taken an idea into her head."

"You've only got to show me the letter."

His hand slipped from hers and he drew back and shook his head.

"You won't?"

"I can't."

"Then the woman who wrote it is your mistress."

"No, dear. No."

"Not now, perhaps. I suppose she's trying to get you back, and you're struggling, out of pity for me. My poor Kenneth!"

"I swear to you she never was my mistress."

Charlotte felt the tears rushing to her eyes. "Ah, that's worse, then—that's hopeless! The prudent ones are the kind that keep their hold on a man. We all know that." She lifted her hands and hid her face in them.

Her husband remained silent; he offered neither consolation nor denial, and at length, wiping away her tears, she raised her eyes almost timidly to his.

"Kenneth, think! We've been married such a short time. Imagine what you're making me suffer. You say you can't show me this letter. You refuse even to explain it."

"I've told you the letter is on business. I will swear to that too."

"A man will swear to anything to screen a woman. If you want me to believe you, at least tell me her name. If you'll do that, I promise you I won't ask to see the letter."

There was a long interval of suspense, during which she felt her heart beating against her ribs in quick admonitory knocks, as if warning her of the danger she was incurring.

"I can't," he said at length.

"Not even her name?"

"No."

"You can't tell me anything more?"

"No."

Again a pause; this time they seemed both to have reached the end of their arguments and to be helplessly facing each other across a baffling waste of incomprehension.

Charlotte stood breathing rapidly, her hands against her breast. She felt as if she had run a hard race and missed the goal. She had meant to move her husband and had succeeded only in irritating him; and this error of reckoning seemed to change him into a stranger, a mysterious incomprehensible being whom no argument or entreaty of hers could reach. The curious thing was that she was aware in him of no hostility or even impatience, but only of a remoteness, an inaccessibility, far more difficult to overcome. She felt herself excluded, ignored, blotted out of his life. But after a moment or two, looking at him more calmly, she saw that he was suffering as much as she was. His distant guarded face was drawn with pain; the coming of the gray envelope, though it always cast a shadow, had never marked him as deeply as this discussion with his wife.

Charlotte took heart; perhaps, after all, she had not spent her last shaft. She drew nearer and once more laid her hand on his arm. "Poor Kenneth! If you knew how sorry I am for you—"

She thought he winced slightly at this expression of sympathy, but he took her hand and pressed it.

"I can think of nothing worse than to be incapable of loving long," she continued; "to feel the beauty of a great love and to be too unstable to bear its burden."

He turned on her a look of wistful reproach. "Oh, don't say that of me. Unstable!"

She felt herself at last on the right tack, and her voice trembled with excitement as she went on: "Then what about me and this other woman? Haven't you already forgotten Elsie twice within a year?"

She seldom pronounced his first wife's name; it did not come naturally to her tongue. She flung it out now as if she were flinging some dangerous explosive into the open space between them, and drew back a step, waiting to hear the mine go off.

Her husband did not move; his expression grew sadder, but showed no resentment. "I have never forgotten Elsie," he said.

Charlotte could not repress a faint laugh. "Then, you poor dear, between the three of us—"

"There are not—" he began; and then broke off and put his hand to his forehead.

"Not what?"

"I'm sorry; I don't believe I know what I'm saying. I've got a blinding headache." He looked wan and furrowed enough for the statement to be true, but she was exasperated by his evasion.

"Ah, yes; the gray-envelope headache!"

She saw the surprise in his eyes. "I'd forgotten how closely I've been watched," he said coldly. "If you'll excuse me, I think I'll go up and try an hour in the dark, to see if I can get rid of this neuralgia."

She wavered; then she said, with desperate resolution: "I'm sorry your head aches. But before you go I want to say that sooner or later this question must be settled between us. Someone is trying to separate us, and I don't care what it costs me to find out who it is." She looked him steadily in the eyes. "If it costs me your love, I don't care! If I can't have your confidence I don't want anything from you."

He still looked at her wistfully. "Give me time."

"Time for what? It's only a word to say."

"Time to show you that you haven't lost my love or my confidence."

"Well, I'm waiting."

He turned toward the door, and then glanced back hesitatingly. "Oh, do wait, my love," he said, and went out of the room.

She heard his tired step on the stairs and the closing of his bedroom door above. Then she dropped into a chair and buried her face in her folded arms. Her first movement was one of compunction; she seemed to herself to have been hard, unhuman, unimaginative. "Think of telling him that I didn't care if my insistence cost me his love! The lying rubbish!" She started up to follow him and unsay the meaningless words. But she was checked by a reflection. He had had his way, after all; he had eluded all attacks on his secret, and now he was shut up alone in his room, reading that other woman's letter.

III

She was still reflecting on this when the surprised parlor-maid came in and found her. No, Charlotte said, she wasn't going to dress for dinner; Mr. Ashby didn't want to dine. He was very tired and had gone up to his room to rest; later she would have something brought on a tray to the drawing-room. She mounted the stairs to her bedroom. Her dinner dress was lying on the bed, and at the sight the quiet routine of her daily life took hold of her and she began to feel as if the strange talk she had just had with her husband must have taken place in another world, between two beings who were not Charlotte Gorse and Kenneth Ashby, but phantoms projected by her fevered imagination. She recalled the year since her marriage—her husband's constant devotion; his persistent, almost too insistent tenderness; the feeling he had given her at times of being too eagerly dependent on her, too searchingly close to her, as if there were not air enough between her soul and his. It seemed preposterous, as she recalled all this, that a few moments ago she should have been accusing him of an intrigue with another woman! But, then, what—

Again she was moved by the impulse to go up to him, beg his pardon and try to laugh away the misunderstanding. But she was restrained by the fear of forcing herself upon his privacy. He was troubled and unhappy, oppressed by some grief or fear; and he had shown her that he wanted to fight out his battle alone. It would be wiser, as well as more generous, to respect his wish. Only, how strange, how unbearable, to be there, in the next room to his, and feel herself at the other end of the world! In her nervous agitation she almost regretted not having had the courage to open the letter and put it back on the hall table before he came in. At least she would have known what his secret was, and the bogey might have been laid. For she was beginning now to think of the mystery as something conscious, malevolent: a secret persecution before which he quailed, yet from which he could not free himself. Once or twice in his evasive eyes she thought she had detected a desire for help, an impulse of confession, instantly restrained and suppressed. It was as if he felt she could have helped him if she had known, and yet had been unable to tell her!

There flashed through her mind the idea of going to his mother. She was very fond of old Mrs. Ashby, a firm-fleshed clear-eyed old lady, with an astringent bluntness of speech which responded to the forthright and simple in Charlotte's own nature. There had been a tacit bond between them ever since the day when Mrs. Ashby senior, coming to lunch for the first time with her new daughter-in-law, had been received by Charlotte downstairs in the library, and glancing up at the empty wall above her son's desk, had remarked laconically: "Elsie gone, eh?" adding, at Charlotte's murmured explanation: "Nonsense. Don't have her back. Two's company." Charlotte, at this reading of her thoughts, could hardly refrain from exchanging a smile of complicity with her mother-in-law; and it seemed to her now that Mrs. Ashby's almost uncanny directness might pierce to the core of this new mystery. But here again she hesitated, for the idea almost suggested a betrayal. What right had she to call in any one, even so close a relation, to surprise a secret which her husband was trying to keep from her? "Perhaps, by and by, he'll talk to his mother of his own accord," she thought, and then ended: "But what does it matter? He and I must settle it between us."

She was still brooding over the problem when there was a knock on the door and her husband came in. He was dressed for dinner and seemed surprised to see her sitting there, with her evening dress lying unheeded on the bed.

"Aren't you coming down?"

"I thought you were not well and had gone to bed," she faltered.

He forced a smile. "I'm not particularly well, but we'd better go down." His face, though still drawn, looked calmer than when he had fled upstairs an hour earlier.

"There it is; he knows what's in the letter and has fought his battle out again, whatever it is," she reflected, "while I'm still in darkness." She rang and gave a hurried order that dinner should be served as soon as possible—just a short meal, whatever could be got ready quickly, as both she and Mr. Ashby were rather tired and not very hungry.

Dinner was announced, and they sat down to it. At first neither seemed able to find a word to say; then Ashby began to make conversation with an assumption of ease that was more oppressive than his silence. "How tired he is! How terribly overtired!" Charlotte said to herself, pursuing her own thoughts while he rambled on about municipal politics, aviation, an exhibition of modern French painting, the health of an old aunt and the installing of the automatic telephone. "Good heavens, how tired he is!"

When they dined alone they usually went into the library after dinner, and Charlotte curled herself up on the divan with her knitting while he settled down in his armchair under the lamp and lit a pipe. But this evening, by tacit agreement, they avoided the room in which their strange talk had taken place, and went up to Charlotte's drawing-room.

They sat down near the fire, and Charlotte said: "Your pipe?" after he had put down his hardly tasted coffee.

He shook his head. "No, not tonight."

"You must go to bed early; you look terribly tired. I'm sure they overwork you at the office."

"I suppose we all overwork at times."

She rose and stood before him with sudden resolution. "Well, I'm not going to have you use up your strength slaving in that way. It's absurd. I can see you're ill." She bent over him and laid her hand on his forehead. "My poor old Kenneth. Prepare to be taken away soon on a long holiday."

He looked up at her, startled. "A holiday?"

"Certainly. Didn't you know I was going to carry you off at Easter? We're going to start in a fortnight on a month's voyage to somewhere or other. On any one of the big cruising steamers." She paused and bent closer, touching his forehead with her lips. "I'm tired, too, Kenneth."

He seemed to pay no heed to her last words, but sat, his hands on his knees, his head drawn back a little from her caress, and looked up at her with a stare of apprehension. "Again? My dear, we can't; I can't possibly go away."

"I don't know why you say 'again,' Kenneth; we haven't taken a real holiday this year."

"At Christmas we spent a week with the children in the country."

"Yes, but this time I mean away from the children, from servants, from the house. From everything that's familiar and fatiguing. Your mother will love to have Joyce and Peter with her."

He frowned and slowly shook his head. "No, dear; I can't leave them with my mother."

"Why, Kenneth, how absurd! She adores them. You didn't hesitate to leave them with her for over two months when we went to the West Indies."

He drew a deep breath and stood up uneasily. "That was different."

"Different? Why?"

"I mean, at that time I didn't realize"— He broke off as if to choose his words and then went on: "My mother adores the children, as you say. But she isn't always very judicious. Grandmothers always spoil children. And she sometimes talks before them without thinking." He turned to his wife with an almost pitiful gesture of entreaty. "Don't ask me to, dear."

Charlotte mused. It was true that the elder Mrs. Ashby had a fearless tongue, but she was the last woman in the world to say or hint anything before her grandchildren at which the most scrupulous parent could take offense. Charlotte looked at her husband in perplexity.

"I don't understand."

He continued to turn on her the same troubled and entreating gaze. "Don't try to," he muttered.

"Not try to?"

"Not now—not yet." He put up his hands and pressed them against his temples. "Can't you see that there's no use in insisting? I can't go away, no matter how much I might want to."

Charlotte still scrutinized him gravely. "The question is, *do* you want to?"

He returned her gaze for a moment; then his lips began to tremble, and he said, hardly above his breath: "I want—anything you want."

"And yet—"

"Don't ask me. I can't leave—I can't!"

"You mean that you can't go away out of reach of those letters!"

Her husband had been standing before her in an uneasy half-hesitating attitude; now he turned abruptly away and walked once or twice up and down the length of the room, his head bent, his eyes fixed on the carpet.

Charlotte felt her resentfulness rising with her fears. "It's that," she persisted. "Why not admit it? You can't live without them."

He continued his troubled pacing of the room; then he stopped short, dropped into a chair and covered his face with his hands. From the shaking of his shoulders, Charlotte saw that he was weeping. She had never seen a man cry, except her father after her mother's death, when she was a little girl; and she remembered still how the sight had frightened her. She was frightened now; she felt that her husband was being dragged away from her into some mysterious bondage, and that she must use up her last atom of strength in the struggle for his freedom, and for hers.

"Kenneth—Kenneth!" she pleaded, kneeling down beside him. "Won't you listen to me? Won't you try to see what I'm suffering? I'm not unreasonable, darling; really not. I don't suppose I should ever have noticed the letters if it hadn't been for their effect on you. It's not my way to pry into other people's affairs; and even if the effect had been different—yes, yes; listen to me—if I'd seen that the letters made you happy, that you were watching eagerly for them, counting the days between their coming, that you wanted them, that they gave you something I haven't known how to give—why, Kenneth, I don't say I shouldn't have suffered from that, too; but it would have been in a different way, and I should have had the courage to hide what I felt, and the hope that some day you'd come to feel about me as you did about the writer of the letters. But what I can't bear is to see how you dread them, how they make you suffer, and yet how you can't live without them and won't go away lest you should miss one during your absence. Or perhaps," she added, her voice breaking into a cry of accusation— "perhaps it's because she's actually forbidden you to leave. Kenneth, you must answer me! Is that the reason? Is it because she's forbidden you that you won't go away with me?"

She continued to kneel at his side, and raising her hands, she drew his gently down. She was ashamed of her persistence, ashamed of uncovering that baffled disordered face, yet resolved that no such scruples should arrest her. His eyes were lowered, the muscles of his face quivered; she was making him suffer even more than she suffered herself. Yet this no longer restrained her.

"Kenneth, is it that? She won't let us go away together?"

Still he did not speak or turn his eyes to her; and a sense of defeat swept over her. After all, she thought, the struggle was a losing one. "You needn't answer. I see I'm right," she said.

Suddenly, as she rose, he turned and drew her down again. His hands caught hers and pressed them so tightly that she felt her rings cutting into her flesh. There was something frightened, convulsive in his hold; it was the clutch of a man who felt himself slipping over a precipice. He was staring up at her now as if salvation lay in the face she bent above him. "Of course we'll go away together. We'll go wherever you want," he said in a low confused voice; and putting his arm about her, he drew her close and pressed his lips on hers.

IV

Charlotte had said to herself: "I shall sleep tonight," but instead she sat before her fire into the small hours, listening for any sound that came from her husband's room. But he, at any rate, seemed to be resting after the tumult of the evening. Once or twice she stole to the door and in the faint light that came in from the street through his open window she saw him stretched out in heavy sleep—the sleep of weakness and exhaustion. "He's ill," she thought—"he's undoubtedly ill. And it's not overwork; it's this mysterious persecution."

She drew a breath of relief. She had fought through the weary fight and the victory was hers—at least for the moment. If only they could have started at once—started for anywhere! She knew it would be useless to ask him to leave before the holidays; and meanwhile the secret influence—as to which she was still so completely in the dark—would continue to work against her, and she would have to renew the struggle day after day till they started on their journey. But after that everything would be different. If once she could get her husband away under other skies, and all to herself, she never doubted her power to release him from the evil spell he was under. Lulled to quiet by the thought, she too slept at last.

When she woke, it was long past her usual hour, and she sat up in bed surprised and vexed at having overslept herself. She always liked to be down to share her husband's breakfast by the library fire; but a glance at the clock made it clear that he must have started long since for his office. To make sure, she jumped out of bed and went into his room; but it was empty. No doubt he had looked in on her before leaving, seen that she still slept, and gone down stairs without disturbing her; and their relations were sufficiently loverlike for her to regret having missed their morning hour.

She rang and asked if Mr. Ashby had already gone. Yes, nearly an hour ago, the maid said. He had given orders that Mrs. Ashby should not be waked and that the children should not come to her till she sent for them . . . Yes, he had gone up to the nursery himself to give the order. All this sounded usual enough; and Charlotte hardly knew why she asked: "And did Mr. Ashby leave no other message?"

Yes, the maid said, he did; she was so sorry she'd forgotten. He'd told her, just as he was leaving, to say to Mrs. Ashby that he was going to see about their passages, and would she please be ready to sail to-morrow?

Charlotte echoed the woman's "To-morrow," and sat staring at her incredulously. "To-morrow—you're sure he said to sail tomorrow?"

"Oh, ever so sure, ma'am. I don't know how I could have forgotten to mention it."

"Well, it doesn't matter. Draw my bath, please." Charlotte sprang up, dashed through her dressing, and caught herself singing at her image in the glass as she sat brushing her hair. It made her feel young again to have scored such a victory. The other woman vanished to a speck on the horizon, as this one, who ruled the foreground, smiled back at the reflection of her lips and eyes. He loved her, then—he loved her as passionately as ever. He had divined what she had suffered, had understood that their happiness depended on their getting away at once, and finding each other again after yesterday's desperate groping in the fog. The nature of the influence that had come between them did not much matter to Charlotte now; she had faced the phantom and dispelled it. "Courage—that's the secret! If only people who are in love weren't always so afraid of risking their happiness by looking it in the eyes." As she brushed back her light abundant hair it waved electrically above her head, like the palms of victory. Ah, well, some women knew how to manage men, and some didn't—and only the fair—she gaily paraphrased—deserve the brave! Certainly she was looking very pretty.

The morning danced along like a cockleshell on a bright sea— such a sea as they would soon be speeding over. She ordered a particularly good dinner, saw the children off to their classes, had her trunks brought down, consulted with the maid about getting out summer clothes—for of course they would be heading for heat and sunshine—and wondered if she oughtn't to take Kenneth's flannel suits out of camphor. "But how absurd," she reflected, "that I don't yet know where we're going!" She looked at the clock, saw that it was close on noon, and decided to call him up at his office. There was a slight delay; then she heard his secretary's voice saying that Mr. Ashby had looked in for a moment early, and left again almost immediately... Oh, very well; Charlotte would ring up later. How soon was he likely to be back? The secretary answered that she couldn't tell; all they knew in the office was that when he left he had said he was in a hurry because he had to go out of town.

Out of town! Charlotte hung up the receiver and sat blankly gazing into new darkness. Why had he gone out of town? And where had he gone? And of all days, why should he have chosen the eve of their suddenly planned departure? She felt a faint shiver of apprehension. Of course he had gone to see that woman—no doubt to get her permission to leave. He was as completely in bondage as that; and Charlotte had been fatuous enough to see the palms of victory on her forehead. She burst into a laugh and, walking across the room, sat down again before her mirror. What a different face she saw! The smile on her pale lips seemed to mock the rosy vision of the other Charlotte. But gradually her color crept back. After all, she had a right to claim the victory, since her husband was doing what she wanted, not what the other woman exacted of him. It was natural enough, in view of his abrupt decision to leave the next day, that he should have arrangements to make, business matters to wind up; it was not even necessary to suppose that his mysterious trip was a visit to the writer of the letters. He might simply have gone to see a client who lived out of town. Of course they would not tell Charlotte at the office; the secretary had hesitated before imparting even such meager information as the fact of Mr. Ashby's absence. Meanwhile she would go on with her joyful preparations, content to learn later in the day to what particular island of the blest she was to be carried.

The hours wore on, or rather were swept forward on a rush of eager preparations. At last the entrance of the maid who came to draw the curtains roused Charlotte from her labors, and she saw to her surprise that the clock marked five. And she did not yet know where they were going the next day! She rang up her husband's office and was told that Mr. Ashby had not been there since the early morning. She asked for his partner, but the partner could add nothing to her information, for he himself, his suburban train having been behind time, had reached the office after Ashby had come and gone. Charlotte stood perplexed; then she decided to telephone to her mother-in-law. Of course Kenneth, on the eve of a month's absence, must have gone to see his mother. The mere fact that the children—in spite of his vague objections—would certainly have to be left with old Mrs. Ashby, made it obvious that he would have all sorts of matters to decide with her. At another time Charlotte might have felt a little hurt at being excluded from their conference, but nothing mattered now but that she had won the day, that her husband was still hers and not another woman's. Gaily she called up Mrs. Ashby, heard her friendly voice, and began: "Well, did Kenneth's news surprise you? What do you think of our elopement?"

Almost instantly, before Mrs. Ashby could answer, Charlotte knew what her reply would be. Mrs. Ashby had not seen her son, she had had no word from him and did not know what her daughter-in-law meant. Charlotte stood silent in the intensity of her surprise. "But then, where *has* he been?" she thought. Then, recovering herself, she explained their sudden decision to Mrs. Ashby, and in doing so, gradually regained her own self-confidence, her conviction that nothing could ever again come between Kenneth and herself. Mrs. Ashby took the news calmly and approvingly. She, too, had thought that Kenneth looked worried and overtired, and she agreed with her daughter-in-law that in such cases change was the surest remedy. "I'm always so glad when he gets away. Elsie hated traveling; she was always finding pretexts to prevent his going anywhere. With you, thank goodness, it's different." Nor was Mrs. Ashby surprised at his not having had time to let her know of his departure. He must have been in a rush from the moment the decision was taken; but no doubt he'd drop in before dinner. Five minutes' talk was really all they needed. "I hope you'll gradually cure Kenneth of his mania for going over and over a question that could be settled in a dozen words. He never used to be like that, and if he carried the habit into his professional work he'd soon lose all his clients . . . Yes, do come in for a minute, dear, if you have time; no doubt he'll turn up while you're here." The tonic ring of Mrs. Ashby's voice echoed on reassuringly in the silent room while Charlotte continued her preparations.

Toward seven the telephone rang, and she darted to it. Now she would know! But it was only from the conscientious secretary, to say that Mr. Ashby hadn't been back, or sent any word, and before the office closed she thought she ought to let Mrs. Ashby know. "Oh, that's all right. Thanks a lot!" Charlotte called out cheerfully, and hung up the receiver with a trembling hand. But perhaps by this time, she reflected, he was at his mother's. She shut her drawers and cupboards, put on her hat and coat and called up to the nursery that she was going out for a minute to see the children's grandmother.

Mrs. Ashby lived near by, and during her brief walk through the cold spring dusk Charlotte imagined that every advancing figure was her husband's. But she did not meet him on the way, and when she entered the house she found her mother-in-law alone. Kenneth had neither telephoned nor come. Old Mrs. Ashby sat by her bright fire, her knitting needles flashing steadily through her active old hands, and her mere bodily presence gave reassurance to Charlotte. Yes, it was certainly odd that Kenneth had gone off for the whole day without letting any of them know; but, after all, it was to be expected. A busy lawyer held so many threads in his hands that any sudden change of plan would oblige him to make all sorts of unforeseen arrangements and adjustments. He might have gone to see some client in the suburbs and been detained there; his mother remembered his telling her that he had charge of the legal business of a queer old recluse somewhere in New Jersey, who was immensely rich but too mean to have a telephone. Very likely Kenneth had been stranded there.

But Charlotte felt her nervousness gaining on her. When Mrs. Ashby asked her at what hour they were sailing the next day and she had to say she didn't know—that Kenneth had simply sent her word he was going to take their passages—the uttering of the words again brought home to her the strangeness of the situation. Even Mrs. Ashby conceded that it was odd; but she immediately added that it only showed what a rush he was in.

"But, mother, it's nearly eight o'clock! He must realize that I've got to know when we're starting to-morrow."

"Oh, the boat probably doesn't sail till evening. Sometimes they have to wait till midnight for the tide. Kenneth's probably counting on that. After all, he has a level head."

Charlotte stood up. "It's not that. Something has happened to him."

Mrs. Ashby took off her spectacles and rolled up her knitting. "If you begin to let yourself imagine things—"

"Aren't you in the least anxious?"

"I never am till I have to be. I wish you'd ring for dinner, my dear. You'll stay and dine? He's sure to drop in here on his way home."

Charlotte called up her own house. No, the maid said, Mr. Ashby hadn't come in and hadn't telephoned. She would tell him as soon as he came that Mrs. Ashby was dining at his mother's. Charlotte followed her mother-in-law into the dining-room and sat with parched throat before her empty plate, while Mrs. Ashby dealt calmly and efficiently with a short but carefully prepared repast. "You'd better eat something, child, or you'll be as bad as Kenneth . . . Yes, a little more asparagus, please, Jane."

She insisted on Charlotte's drinking a glass of sherry and nibbling a bit of toast; then they returned to the drawing-room, where the fire had been made up, and the cushions in Mrs. Ashby's armchair shaken out and smoothed. How safe and familiar it all looked; and out there, somewhere in the uncertainty and mystery of the night, lurked the answer to the two women's conjectures, like an indistinguishable figure prowling on the threshold.

At last Charlotte got up and said: "I'd better go back. At this hour Kenneth will certainly go straight home."

Mrs. Ashby smiled indulgently. "It's not very late, my dear. It doesn't take two sparrows long to dine."

"It's after nine." Charlotte bent down to kiss her. "The fact is, I can't keep still."

Mrs. Ashby pushed aside her work and rested her two hands on the arms of her chair. "I'm going with you," she said, helping herself up.

Charlotte protested that it was too late, that it was not necessary, that she would call up as soon as Kenneth came in, but Mrs. Ashby had already rung for her maid. She was slightly lame, and stood resting on her stick while her wraps were brought. "If Mr. Kenneth turns up, tell him he'll find me at his own house," she instructed the maid as the two women got into the taxi which had been summoned. During the short drive Charlotte gave thanks that she was not returning home alone. There was something warm and substantial in the mere fact of Mrs. Ashby's nearness, something that corresponded with the clearness of her eyes and the texture of her fresh firm complexion. As the taxi drew up she laid her hand encouragingly on Charlotte's. "You'll see; there'll be a message."

The door opened at Charlotte's ring and the two entered. Charlotte's heart beat excitedly; the stimulus of her mother-in-law's confidence was beginning to flow through her veins.

"You'll see—you'll see," Mrs. Ashby repeated.

The maid who opened the door said no, Mr. Ashby had not come in, and there had been no message from him.

"You're sure the telephone's not out of order?" his mother suggested; and the maid said, well, it certainly wasn't half an hour ago; but she'd just go and ring up to make sure. She disappeared, and Charlotte turned to take off her hat and cloak. As she did so her eyes lit on the hall table, and there lay a gray envelope, her husband's name faintly traced on it. "Oh!" she cried out, suddenly aware that for the first time in months she had entered her house without wondering if one of the gray letters would be there.

"What is it, my dear?" Mrs. Ashby asked with a glance of surprise.

Charlotte did not answer. She took up the envelope and stood staring at it as if she could force her gaze to penetrate to what was within. Then an idea occurred to her. She turned and held out the envelope to her mother-in-law.

"Do you know that writing?" she asked.

Mrs. Ashby took the letter. She had to feel with her other hand for her eye-glasses, and when she had adjusted them she lifted the envelope to the light. "Why!" she exclaimed; and then stopped. Charlotte noticed that the letter shook in her usually firm hand. "But this is addressed to Kenneth," Mrs. Ashby said at length, in a low voice. Her tone seemed to imply that she felt her daughter-in-law's question to be slightly indiscreet.

"Yes, but no matter," Charlotte spoke with sudden decision. "I want to know—do you know the writing?"

Mrs. Ashby handed back the letter. "No," she said distinctly.

The two women had turned into the library. Charlotte switched on the electric light and shut the door. She still held the envelope in her hand.

"I'm going to open it," she announced.

She caught her mother-in-law's startled glance. "But, dearest —a letter not addressed to you? My dear, you can't!"

"As if I cared about that—now!" She continued to look intently at Mrs. Ashby. "This letter may tell me where Kenneth is."

Mrs. Ashby's glossy bloom was effaced by a quick pallor; her firm cheeks seemed to shrink and wither. "Why should it? What makes you believe— It can't possibly—"

Charlotte held her eyes steadily on that altered face. "Ah, then you *do* know the writing?" she flashed back.

"Know the writing? How should I? With all my son's correspondents...What I do know is—" Mrs. Ashby broke off and looked at her daughter-in-law entreatingly, almost timidly.

Charlotte caught her by the wrist. "Mother! What do you know? Tell me! You must!"

"That I don't believe any good ever came of a woman's opening her husband's letters behind his back."

The words sounded to Charlotte's irritated ears as flat as a phrase culled from a book of moral axioms. She laughed impatiently and dropped her mother-in-law's wrist. "Is that all? No good can come of this letter, opened or unopened. I know that well enough. But whatever ill comes, I mean to find out what's in it." Her hands had been trembling as they held the envelope, but now they grew firm, and her voice also. She still gazed intently at Mrs. Ashby. "This is the ninth letter addressed in the same hand that has come for Kenneth since we've been married. Always these same gray envelopes. I've kept count of them because after each one he has been like a man who has had some dreadful shock. It takes him hours to shake off their effect. I've told him so. I've told him I must know from whom they come, because I can see they're killing him. He won't answer my questions; he says he can't tell me anything about the letters; but last night he promised to go away with me—to get away from them."

Mrs. Ashby, with shaking steps, had gone to one of the armchairs and sat down in it, her head drooping forward on her breast. "Ah," she murmured.

"So now you understand—"

"Did he tell you it was to get away from them?"

"He said, to get away—to get away. He was sobbing so that he could hardly speak. But I told him I knew that was why."

"And what did he say?"

"He took me in his arms and said he'd go wherever I wanted."

"Ah, thank God!" said Mrs. Ashby. There was a silence, during which she continued to sit with bowed head, and eyes averted from her daughter-in-law. At last she looked up and spoke. "Are you sure there have been as many as nine?"

"Perfectly. This is the ninth. I've kept count."

"And he has absolutely refused to explain?"

"Absolutely."

Mrs. Ashby spoke through pale contracted lips. "When did they begin to come? Do you remember?"

Charlotte laughed again. "Remember? The first one came the night we got back from our honeymoon."

"All that time?" Mrs. Ashby lifted her head and spoke with sudden energy. "Then— Yes, open it."

The words were so unexpected that Charlotte felt the blood in her temples, and her hands began to tremble again. She tried to slip her finger under the flap of the envelope, but it was so tightly stuck that she had to hunt on her husband's writing table for his ivory letter-opener. As she pushed about the familiar objects his own hands had so lately touched, they sent through her the icy chill emanating from the little personal effects of someone newly dead. In the deep silence of the room the tearing of the paper as she slit the envelope sounded like a human cry. She drew out the sheet and carried it to the lamp.

"Well?" Mrs. Ashby asked below her breath.

Charlotte did not move or answer. She was bending over the page with wrinkled brows, holding it nearer and nearer to the light. Her sight must be blurred, or else dazzled by the reflection of the lamplight on the smooth surface of the paper, for, strain her eyes as she would, she could discern only a few faint strokes, so faint and faltering as to be nearly undecipherable.

"I can't make it out," she said.

"What do you mean, dear?"

"The writing's too indistinct...Wait."

She went back to the table and, sitting down close to Kenneth's reading lamp, slipped the letter under a magnifying glass. All this time she was aware that her mother-in-law was watching her intently.

"Well?" Mrs. Ashby breathed.

"Well, it's no clearer. I can't read it."

"You mean the paper is an absolute blank?"

"No, not quite. There is writing on it. I can make out something like 'mine'—oh, and 'come.' It might be 'come.'"

Mrs. Ashby stood up abruptly. Her face was even paler than before. She advanced to the table and, resting her two hands on it, drew a deep breath. "Let me see," she said, as if forcing herself to a hateful effort.

Charlotte felt the contagion of her whiteness. "She knows," she thought. She pushed the letter across the table. Her mother-in-law lowered her head over it in silence, but without touching it with her pale wrinkled hands.

Charlotte stood watching her as she herself, when she had tried to read the letter, had been watched by Mrs. Ashby. The latter fumbled for her glasses, held them to her eyes, and bent still closer to the outspread page, in order, as it seemed, to avoid touching it. The light of the lamp fell directly on her old face, and Charlotte reflected what depths of the unknown may lurk under the clearest and most candid lineaments. She had never seen her mother-in-law's features express any but simple and sound emotions—cordiality, amusement, a kindly sympathy; now and again a flash of wholesome anger. Now they seemed to wear a look of fear and hatred, of incredulous dismay and almost cringing defiance. It was as if the spirits warring within her had distorted her face to their own likeness. At length she raised her head. "I can't—I can't," she said in a voice of childish distress.

"You can't make it out either?"

She shook her head, and Charlotte saw two tears roll down her cheeks.

"Familiar as the writing is to you?" Charlotte insisted with twitching lips.

Mrs. Ashby did not take up the challenge. "I can make out nothing—nothing."

"But you do know the writing?"

Mrs. Ashby lifted her head timidly; her anxious eyes stole with a glance of apprehension around the quiet familiar room. "How can I tell? I was startled at first..."

"Startled by the resemblance?"

"Well, I thought—"

"You'd better say it out, mother! You knew at once it was *her* writing?"

"Oh, wait, my dear—wait."

"Wait for what?"

Mrs. Ashby looked up; her eyes, traveling slowly past Charlotte, were lifted to the blank wall behind her son's writing table.

Charlotte, following the glance, burst into a shrill laugh of accusation. "I needn't wait any longer! You've answered me now! You're looking straight at the wall where her picture used to hang!"

Mrs. Ashby lifted her hand with a murmur of warning. "Sh-h."

"Oh, you needn't imagine that anything can ever frighten me again!" Charlotte cried.

Her mother-in-law still leaned against the table. Her lips moved plaintively. "But we're going mad—we're both going mad. We both know such things are impossible."

Her daughter-in-law looked at her with a pitying stare. "I've known for a long time now that everything was possible."

"Even this?"

"Yes, exactly this."

"But this letter—after all, there's nothing in this letter—"

"Perhaps there would be to him. How can I tell? I remember his saying to me once that if you were used to a handwriting the faintest stroke of it became legible. Now I see what he meant. He *was* used to it."

"But the few strokes that I can make out are so pale. No one could possibly read that letter."

Charlotte laughed again. "I suppose everything's pale about a ghost," she said stridently.

"Oh, my child—my child—don't say it!"

"Why shouldn't I say it, when even the bare walls cry it out? What difference does it make if her letters are illegible to you and me? If even you can see her face on that blank wall, why shouldn't he read her writing on this blank paper? Don't you see that she's everywhere in this house, and the closer to him because to everyone else she's become invisible?" Charlotte dropped into a chair and covered her face with her hands. A turmoil of sobbing shook her from head to foot. At length a touch on her shoulder made her look up, and she saw her mother-in-law bending over her. Mrs. Ashby's face seemed to have grown still smaller and more wasted, but it had resumed its usual quiet look. Through all her tossing anguish, Charlotte felt the impact of that resolute spirit.

"To-morrow—to-morrow. You'll see. There'll be some explanation to-morrow."

Charlotte cut her short. "An explanation? Who's going to give it, I wonder?"

Mrs. Ashby drew back and straightened herself heroically. "Kenneth himself will," she cried out in a strong voice. Charlotte said nothing, and the old woman went on: "But meanwhile we must act; we must notify the police. Now, without a moment's delay. We must do everything—everything."

Charlotte stood up slowly and stiffly; her joints felt as cramped as an old woman's. "Exactly as if we thought it could do any good to do anything?"

Resolutely Mrs. Ashby cried: "Yes!" and Charlotte went up to the telephone and unhooked the receiver.

ROMAN FEVER

From the table at which they had been lunching two American ladies of ripe but well-cared-for middle age moved across the lofty terrace of the Roman restaurant and, leaning on its parapet, looked first at each other, and then down on the outspread glories of the Palatine and the Forum, with the same expression of vague but benevolent approval.

As they leaned there a girlish voice echoed up gaily from the stairs leading to the court below. "Well, come along, then," it cried, not to them but to an invisible companion, "and let's leave the young things to their knitting"; and a voice as fresh laughed back: "Oh, look here, Babs, not actually *knitting*—" "Well, I mean figuratively," rejoined the first. "After all, we haven't left our poor parents much else to do..." and at that point the turn of the stairs engulfed the dialogue.

The two ladies looked at each other again, this time with a tinge of smiling embarrassment, and the smaller and paler one shook her head and colored slightly.

"Barbara!" she murmured, sending an unheard rebuke after the mocking voice in the stairway.

The other lady, who was fuller, and higher in color, with a small determined nose supported by vigorous black eyebrows, gave a good-humored laugh. "That's what our daughters think of us!"

Her companion replied by a deprecating gesture. "Not of us individually. We must remember that. It's just the collective modern idea of Mothers. And you see—" Half guiltily she drew from her handsomely mounted black hand-bag a twist of crimson silk run through by two fine knitting needles. "One never knows," she murmured. "The new system has certainly given us a good deal of time to kill; and sometimes I get tired just looking—even at this." Her gesture was now addressed to the stupendous scene at their feet.

The dark lady laughed again, and they both relapsed upon the view, contemplating it in silence, with a sort of diffused serenity which might have been borrowed from the spring effulgence of the Roman skies. The luncheon-hour was long past, and the two had their end of the vast terrace to themselves. At its opposite extremity a few groups, detained by a lingering look at the outspread city, were gathering up guide-books and fumbling for tips. The last of them scattered, and the two ladies were alone on the air-washed height.

"Well, I don't see why we shouldn't just stay here," said Mrs. Slade, the lady of the high color and energetic brows. Two derelict basket-chairs stood near, and she pushed them into the angle of the parapet, and settled herself in one, her gaze upon the Palatine. "After all, it's still the most beautiful view in the world."

"It always will be, to me," assented her friend Mrs. Ansley, with so slight a stress on the "me" that Mrs. Slade, though she noticed it, wondered if it were not merely accidental, like the random underlinings of old-fashioned letter-writers.

"Grace Ansley was always old-fashioned," she thought; and added aloud, with a retrospective smile: "It's a view we've both been familiar with for a good many years. When we first met here we were younger than our girls are now. You remember?"

"Oh, yes, I remember," murmured Mrs. Ansley, with the same undefinable stress.— "There's that head-waiter wondering," she interpolated. She was evidently far less sure than her companion of herself and of her rights in the world.

"I'll cure him of wondering," said Mrs. Slade, stretching her hand toward a bag as discreetly opulent-looking as Mrs. Ansley's. Signing to the head-waiter, she explained that she and her friend were old lovers of Rome, and would like to spend the end of the afternoon looking down on the view—that is, if it did not disturb the service? The head-waiter, bowing over her gratuity, assured her that the ladies were most welcome, and would be still more so if they would condescend to remain for dinner. A full moon night, they would remember...

Mrs. Slade's black brows drew together, as though references to the moon were out-of-place and even unwelcome. But she smiled away her frown as the head-waiter retreated. "Well, why not? We might do worse. There's no knowing, I suppose, when the girls will be back. Do you even know back from *where*? I don't!"

Mrs. Ansley again colored slightly. "I think those young Italian aviators we met at the Embassy invited them to fly to Tarquinia for tea. I suppose they'll want to wait and fly back by moonlight."

"Moonlight—moonlight! What a part it still plays. Do you suppose they're as sentimental as we were?"

"I've come to the conclusion that I don't in the least know what they are," said Mrs. Ansley. "And perhaps we didn't know much more about each other."

"No; perhaps we didn't."

Her friend gave her a shy glance. "I never should have supposed you were sentimental, Alida."

"Well, perhaps I wasn't." Mrs. Slade drew her lids together in retrospect; and for a few moments the two ladies, who had been intimate since childhood, reflected how little they knew each other. Each one, of course, had a label ready to attach to the other's name; Mrs. Delphin Slade, for instance, would have told herself, or any one who asked her, that Mrs. Horace Ansley, twenty-five years ago, had been exquisitely lovely—no, you wouldn't believe it, would you?... though, of course, still charming, distinguished ...Well, as a girl she had been exquisite; far more beautiful than her daughter Barbara, though certainly Babs, according to the new standards at any rate, was more effective—had more *edge*, as they say. Funny where she got it, with those two nullities as parents. Yes; Horace Ansley was—well, just the duplicate of his wife. Museum specimens of old New York. Good-looking, irreproachable, exemplary. Mrs. Slade and Mrs. Ansley had lived opposite each other—actually as well as figuratively—for years. When the drawing-room curtains in No. 20 East 73rd Street were renewed, No. 23, across the way, was always aware of it. And of all the movings, buyings, travels, anniversaries, illnesses—the tame chronicle of an estimable pair. Little of it escaped Mrs. Slade. But she had grown bored with it by the time her husband made his big *coup* in Wall Street, and when they bought in upper Park Avenue had already begun to think: "I'd rather live opposite a speak-easy for a change; at least one might see it raided." The idea of seeing Grace raided was so amusing that (before the move) she launched it at a woman's lunch. It made a hit, and went the rounds—she sometimes wondered if it had crossed the street, and reached Mrs. Ansley. She hoped not, but didn't much mind. Those were the days when respectability was at a discount, and it did the irreproachable no harm to laugh at them a little.

A few years later, and not many months apart, both ladies lost their husbands. There was an appropriate exchange of wreaths and condolences, and a brief renewal of intimacy in the half-shadow of their mourning; and now, after another interval, they had run across each other in Rome, at the same hotel, each of them the modest appendage of a salient daughter. The similarity of their lot had again drawn them together, lending itself to mild jokes, and the mutual confession that, if in old days it must have been tiring to "keep up" with daughters, it was now, at times, a little dull not to.

No doubt, Mrs. Slade reflected, she felt her unemployment more than poor Grace ever would. It was a big drop from being the wife of Delphin Slade to being his widow. She had always regarded herself (with a certain conjugal pride) as his equal in social gifts, as contributing her full share to the making of the exceptional couple they were; but the difference after his death was irremediable. As the wife of the famous corporation lawyer, always with an international case or two on hand, every day brought its exciting and unexpected obligation: the impromptu entertaining of eminent colleagues from abroad, the hurried dashes on legal business to London, Paris or Rome, where the entertaining was so handsomely reciprocated; the amusement of hearing in her wake: "What, that handsome woman with the good clothes and the eyes is Mrs. Slade—*the* Slade's wife? Really? Generally the wives of celebrities are such frumps."

Yes; being *the* Slade's widow was a dullish business after that. In living up to such a husband all her faculties had been engaged; now she had only her daughter to live up to, for the son who seemed to have inherited his father's gifts had died suddenly in boyhood. She had fought through that agony because her husband was there, to be helped and to help; now, after the father's death, the thought of the boy had become unbearable. There was nothing left but to mother her daughter; and dear Jenny was such a perfect daughter that she needed no excessive mothering. "Now with Babs Ansley I don't know that I *should* be so quiet," Mrs. Slade sometimes half-enviously reflected; but Jenny, who was younger than her brilliant friend, was that rare accident, an extremely pretty girl who somehow made youth and prettiness seem as safe as their absence. It was all perplexing—and to Mrs. Slade a little boring. She wished that Jenny would fall in love—with the wrong man, even; that she might have to be watched, out-maneuvered, rescued. And instead, it was Jenny who watched her mother, kept her out of drafts, made sure that she had taken her tonic...

Mrs. Ansley was much less articulate than her friend, and her mental portrait of Mrs. Slade was slighter, and drawn with fainter touches. "Alida Slade's awfully brilliant; but not as brilliant as she thinks," would have summed it up; though she would have added, for the enlightenment of strangers, that Mrs. Slade had been an extremely dashing girl; much more so than her daughter, who was pretty, of course, and clever in a way, but had none of her mother's —well, "vividness," some one had once called it. Mrs. Ansley would take up current words like this, and cite them in quotation marks, as unheard-of audacities. No; Jenny was not like her mother. Sometimes Mrs. Ansley thought Alida Slade was disappointed; on the whole she had had a sad life. Full of failures and mistakes; Mrs. Ansley had always been rather sorry for her...

So these two ladies visualized each other, each through the wrong end of her little telescope.

II

For a long time they continued to sit side by side without speaking. It seemed as though, to both, there was a relief in laying down their somewhat futile activities in the presence of the vast Memento Mori which faced them. Mrs. Slade sat quite still, her eyes fixed on the golden slope of the Palace of the Caesars, and after a while Mrs. Ansley ceased to fidget with her bag, and she too sank into meditation. Like many intimate friends, the two ladies had never before had occasion to be silent together, and Mrs. Ansley was slightly embarrassed by what seemed, after so many years, a new stage in their intimacy, and one with which she did not yet know how to deal.

Suddenly the air was full of that deep clangor of bells which periodically covers Rome with a roof of silver. Mrs. Slade glanced at her wrist watch. "Five o'clock already," she said, as though surprised.

Mrs. Ansley suggested interrogatively: "There's bridge at the Embassy at five." For a long time Mrs. Slade did not answer. She appeared to be lost in contemplation, and Mrs. Ansley thought the remark had escaped her. But after a while she said, as if speaking out of a dream: "Bridge, did you say? Not unless you want to... But I don't think I will, you know."

"Oh, no," Mrs. Ansley hastened to assure her. "I don't care to at all. It's so lovely here; and so full of old memories, as you say." She settled herself in her chair, and almost furtively drew forth her knitting. Mrs. Slade took sideway note of this activity, but her own beautifully cared-for hands remained motionless on her knee.

"I was just thinking," she said slowly, "what different things Rome stands for to each generation of travelers. To our grand-mothers, Roman fever; to our mothers, sentimental dangers—how we used to be guarded!—to our daughters, no more dangers than the middle of Main Street. They don't know it—but how much they're missing!"

The long golden light was beginning to pale, and Mrs. Ansley lifted her knitting a little closer to her eyes. "Yes; how we were guarded!"

"I always used to think," Mrs. Slade continued, "that our mothers had a much more difficult job than our grandmothers. When Roman fever stalked the streets it must have been compara-tively easy to gather in the girls at the danger hour; but when you and I were young, with such beauty calling us, and the spice of disobedience thrown in, and no worse risk than catching cold during the cool hour after sunset, the mothers used to be put to it to keep us in—didn't they?"

She turned again toward Mrs. Ansley, but the latter had reached a delicate point in her knitting. "One, two, three—slip two; yes, they must have been," she assented, without looking up.

Mrs. Slade's eyes rested on her with a deepened attention. "She can knit—in the face of *this*! How like her..."

Mrs. Slade leaned back, brooding, her eyes ranging from the ruins which faced her to the long green hollow of the Forum, the fading glow of the church fronts beyond it, and the outlying im-mensity of the Colosseum. Suddenly she thought: "It's all very well to say that our girls have done away with sentiment and moonlight. But if Babs Ansley isn't out to catch that young avia-tor—the one who's a Marchese—then I don't know anything. And Jenny has no chance beside her. I know that too. I wonder if that's why Grace Ansley likes the two girls to go everywhere to-gether? My poor Jenny as a foil—!" Mrs Slade gave a hardly audi-ble laugh, and at the sound Mrs. Ansley dropped her knitting.

"Yes—?"

"I—oh, nothing. I was only thinking how your Babs carries

everything before her. That Campolieri boy is one of the best matches in Rome. Don't look so innocent, my dear—you know he is. And I was wondering, ever so respectfully, you understand ...wondering how two such exemplary characters as you and Horace had managed to produce anything quite so dynamic." Mrs. Slade laughed again, with a touch of asperity.

Mrs. Ansley's hands lay inert across her needles. She looked straight out at the great accumulated wreckage of passion and splendor at her feet. But her small profile was almost expressionless. At length she said: "I think you overrate Babs, my dear."

Mrs. Slade's tone grew easier. "No; I don't. I appreciate her. And perhaps envy you. Oh, my girl's perfect; if I were a chronic invalid I'd—well, I think I'd rather be in Jenny's hands. There must be times...but there! I always wanted a brilliant daughter...and never quite understood why I got an angel instead."

Mrs. Ansley echoed her laugh in a faint murmur. "Babs is an angel too."

"Of course—of course! But she's got rainbow wings. Well, they're wandering by the sea with their young men; and here we sit...and it all brings back the past a little too acutely."

Mrs. Ansley had resumed her knitting. One might almost have imagined (if one had known her less well, Mrs. Slade reflected) that, for her also, too many memories rose from the lengthening shadows of those august ruins. But no; she was simply absorbed in her work. What was there for her to worry about? She knew that Babs would almost certainly come back engaged to the extremely eligible Campolieri. "And she'll sell the New York house, and settle down near them in Rome, and never be in their way...she's much too tactful. But she'll have an excellent cook, and just the right people in for bridge and cocktails...and a perfectly peaceful old age among her grandchildren."

Mrs. Slade broke off this prophetic flight with a recoil of self-disgust. There was no one of whom she had less right to think unkindly than of Grace Ansley. Would she never cure herself of envying her? Perhaps she had begun too long ago.

She stood up and leaned against the parapet, filling her troubled eyes with the tranquilizing magic of the hour. But instead of tranquilizing her the sight seemed to increase her exasperation. Her gaze turned toward the Colosseum. Already its golden flank was drowned in purple shadow, and above it the sky curved crystal clear, without light or color. It was the moment when afternoon and evening hang balanced in mid-heaven.

Mrs. Slade turned back and laid her hand on her friend's arm. The gesture was so abrupt that Mrs. Ansley looked up, startled.

"The sun's set. You're not afraid, my dear?"

"Afraid—?"

"Of Roman fever or pneumonia? I remember how ill you were that winter. As a girl you had a very delicate throat, hadn't you?"

"Oh, we're all right up here. Down below, in the Forum, it does get deathly cold, all of a sudden . . . but not here."

"Ah, of course you know because you had to be so careful." Mrs. Slade turned back to the parapet. She thought: "I must make one more effort not to hate her." Aloud she said: "Whenever I look at the Forum from up here, I remember that story about a great-aunt of yours, wasn't she? A dreadfully wicked great-aunt?"

"Oh, yes; Great-aunt Harriet. The one who was supposed to have sent her young sister out to the Forum after sunset to gather a night-blooming flower for her album. All our great-aunts and grandmothers used to have albums of dried flowers."

Mrs. Slade nodded. "But she really sent her because they were in love with the same man—"

"Well, that was the family tradition. They said Aunt Harriet confessed it years afterward. At any rate, the poor little sister caught the fever and died. Mother used to frighten us with the story when we were children."

"And you frightened *me* with it, that winter when you and I were here as girls. The winter I was engaged to Delphin."

Mrs. Ansley gave a faint laugh. "Oh, did I? Really frightened you? I don't believe you're easily frightened."

"Not often; but I was then. I was easily frightened because I was too happy. I wonder if you know what that means?"

"I—yes . . ." Mrs. Ansley faltered.

"Well, I suppose that was why the story of your wicked aunt made such an impression on me. And I thought: 'There's no more Roman fever, but the Forum is deathly cold after sunset—especially after a hot day. And the Colosseum's even colder and damper.'"

"The Colosseum—?"

"Yes. It wasn't easy to get in, after the gates were locked for the night. Far from easy. Still, in those days it could be managed; it *was* managed, often. Lovers met there who couldn't meet elsewhere. You knew that?"

"I—I daresay. I don't remember."

"You don't remember? You don't remember going to visit some ruins or other one evening, just after dark, and catching a bad chill? You were supposed to have gone to see the moon rise. People always said that expedition was what caused your illness."

There was a moment's silence; then Mrs. Ansley rejoined: "Did they? It was all so long ago."

"Yes. And you got well again—so it didn't matter. But I suppose it struck your friends—the reason given for your illness, I mean—because everybody knew you were so prudent on account of your throat, and your mother took such care of you . . . You *had* been out late sight-seeing, hadn't you, that night?"

"Perhaps I had. The most prudent girls aren't always prudent. What made you think of it now?"

Mrs. Slade seemed to have no answer ready. But after a moment she broke out: "Because I simply can't bear it any longer—!"

Mrs. Ansley lifted her head quickly. Her eyes were wide and very pale. "Can't bear what?"

"Why—your not knowing that I've always known why you went."

"Why I went—?"

"Yes. You think I'm bluffing, don't you? Well, you went to meet the man I was engaged to—and I can repeat every word of the letter that took you there."

While Mrs. Slade spoke Mrs. Ansley had risen unsteadily to her feet. Her bag, her knitting and gloves, slid in a panicstricken heap to the ground. She looked at Mrs. Slade as though she were looking at a ghost.

"No, no—don't," she faltered out.

"Why not? Listen, if you don't believe me. 'My one darling, things can't go on like this. I must see you alone. Come to the Colosseum immediately after dark tomorrow. There will be somebody to let you in. No one whom you need fear will suspect'—but perhaps you've forgotten what the letter said?"

Mrs. Ansley met the challenge with an unexpected composure. Steadying herself against the chair she looked at her friend, and replied: "No; I know it by heart too."

"And the signature? 'Only *your* D. S.' Was that it? I'm right, am I? That was the letter that took you out that evening after dark?"

Mrs. Ansley was still looking at her. It seemed to Mrs. Slade that a slow struggle was going on behind the voluntarily controlled mask of her small quiet face. "I shouldn't have thought she had herself so well in hand," Mrs. Slade reflected, almost resentfully. But at this moment Mrs. Ansley spoke. "I don't know how you knew. I burnt that letter at once."

"Yes; you would, naturally—you're so prudent!" The sneer was open now. "And if you burnt the letter you're wondering how on earth I know what was in it. That's it, isn't it?"

Mrs. Slade waited, but Mrs. Ansley did not speak.

"Well, my dear, I know what was in that letter because I wrote it!"

"You wrote it?"

"Yes."

The two women stood for a minute staring at each other in the last golden light. Then Mrs. Ansley dropped back into her chair. "Oh," she murmured, and covered her face with her hands.

Mrs. Slade waited nervously for another word or movement. None came, and at length she broke out: "I horrify you."

Mrs. Ansley's hands dropped to her knee. The face they uncovered was streaked with tears. "I wasn't thinking of you. I was thinking—it was the only letter I ever had from him!"

"And I wrote it. yes; I wrote it! But I was the girl he was engaged to. Did you happen to remember that?"

Mrs. Ansley's head drooped again. "I'm not trying to excuse myself . . . I remembered . . ."

"And still you went?"

"Still I went."

Mrs. Slade stood looking down on the small bowed figure at her side. The flame of her wrath had already sunk, and she wondered why she had ever thought there would be any satisfaction in inflicting so purposeless a wound on her friend. But she had to justify herself.

"You do understand? I'd found out—and I hated you, hated you. I knew you were in love with Delphin—and I was afraid; afraid of you, of your quiet ways, your sweetness . . . your . . . well, I wanted you out of the way, that's all. Just for a few weeks; just till I was sure of him. So in a blind fury I wrote that letter . . . I don't know why I'm telling you now."

"I suppose," said Mrs. Ansley slowly, "it's because you've always gone on hating me."

"Perhaps. Or because I wanted to get the whole thing off my mind." She paused. "I'm glad you destroyed the letter. Of course I never thought you'd die."

Mrs. Ansley relapsed into silence, and Mrs. Slade, leaning above her, was conscious of a strange sense of isolation, of being cut off from the warm current of human communion. "You think me a monster!"

"I don't know . . . It was the only letter I had, and you say he didn't write it?"

"Ah, how you care for him still!"

"I cared for that memory," said Mrs. Ansley.

Mrs. Slade continued to look down on her. She seemed physically reduced by the blow—as if, when she got up, the wind might scatter her like a puff of dust. Mrs. Slade's jealousy suddenly leapt up again at the sight. All these years the woman had been living on that letter. How she must have loved him, to treasure the mere memory of its ashes! The letter of the man her friend was engaged to. Wasn't it she who was the monster?

"You tried your best to get him away from me, didn't you? But you failed; and I kept him. That's all."

"Yes. That's all."

"I wish now I hadn't told you. I'd no idea you'd feel about it as you do; I thought you'd be amused. It all happened so long ago, as you say; and you must do me the justice to remember that I had no reason to think you'd ever taken it seriously. How could I, when you were married to Horace Ansley two months afterward? As soon as you could get out of bed your mother rushed you off to Florence and married you. People were rather surprised—they wondered at its being done so quickly; but I thought I knew. I had an idea you did it out of *pique*—to be able to say you'd got ahead of Delphin and me. Girls have such silly reasons for doing the most serious things. And your marrying so soon convinced me that you'd never really cared."

"Yes. I suppose it would," Mrs. Ansley assented.

The clear heaven overhead was emptied of all its gold. Dusk spread over it, abruptly darkening the Seven Hills. Here and there lights began to twinkle through the foliage at their feet. Steps were coming and going on the deserted terrace—waiters looking out of the doorway at the head of the stairs, then reappearing with trays and napkins and flasks of wine. Tables were moved, chairs straightened. A feeble string of electric lights flickered out. Some vases of faded flowers were carried away, and brought back replenished. A stout lady in a dust-coat suddenly appeared, asking in broken Italian if any one had seen the elastic band which held together her tattered Baedeker. She poked with her stick under the table at which she had lunched, the waiters assisting.

The corner where Mrs. Slade and Mrs. Ansley sat was still shadowy and deserted. For a long time neither of them spoke. At length Mrs. Slade began again: "I suppose I did it as a sort of joke—"

"A joke?"

"Well, girls are ferocious sometimes, you know. Girls in love especially. And I remember laughing to myself all that evening at the idea that you were waiting around there in the dark, dodging out of sight, listening for every sound, trying to get in—. Of course I was upset when I heard you were so ill afterward."

Mrs. Ansley had not moved for a long time. But now she turned slowly toward her companion. "But I didn't wait. He'd arranged everything. He was there. We were let in at once," she said.

Mrs. Slade sprang up from her leaning position. "Delphin there? They let you in?—Ah, now you're lying!" she burst out with violence.

Mrs. Ansley's voice grew clearer, and full of surprise. "But of course he was there. Naturally he came—"

"Came? How did he know he'd find you there? You must be raving!"

Mrs. Ansley hesitated, as though reflecting. "But I answered the letter. I told him I'd be there. So he came."

Mrs. Slade flung her hands up to her face. "Oh, God—you answered! I never thought of your answering..."

"It's odd you never thought of it, if you wrote the letter."

"Yes. I was blind with rage."

Mrs. Ansley rose, and drew her fur scarf about her. "It is cold here. We'd better go...I'm sorry for you," she said, as she clasped the fur about her throat.

The unexpected words sent a pang through Mrs. Slade. "Yes; we'd better go." She gathered up her bag and cloak. "I don't know why you should be sorry for me," she muttered.

Mrs. Ansley stood looking away from her toward the dusky secret mass of the Colosseum. "Well—because I didn't have to wait that night."

Mrs. Slade gave an unquiet laugh. "Yes; I was beaten there. But I oughtn't to begrudge it to you, I suppose. At the end of all these years. After all, I had everything; I had him for twenty-five years. And you had nothing but that one letter that he didn't write."

Mrs. Ansley was again silent. At length she turned toward the door of the terrace. She took a step, and turned back, facing her companion.

"I had Barbara," she said, and began to move ahead of Mrs. Slade toward the stairway.

TITLES IN SERIES